SUN OF ENDLESS DAYS

L. G. JENKINS

BOOK ONE OF THE MERIT-HUNTERS SERIES

Grace & Down
PUBLISHING

This book was originally published as Crowned Worthy
Copyright 2021 Malcolm Down Publishing

First published 2024 by Grace & Down Publishing,
an imprint of Malcolm Down Publishing Ltd
www.malcolmdown.co.uk

28 27 26 25 24   7 6 5 4 3 2 1

This book you're reading is a work of fiction. Characters, places,
events, and names are the product of this author's imagination.
Any resemblance to other events, other locations, or other
persons, living or dead, is coincidental.

British Library Cataloguing in Publication Data
A catalogue record for this book is available from the British Library.

Unless otherwise indicated, Scripture quotations taken from
The ESV® Bible (The Holy Bible, English Standard Version®).
ESV® Text Edition: 2016. Copyright © 2001 by Crossway,
a publishing ministry of Good News Publishers.

ISBN 978-1-915046-89-5

Cover design by Liz Carter
Map Illustration by Sarah Jenkins
Art direction by Sarah Grace

Printed in the UK

Dedication

To you, the reader.

Map of Tulo

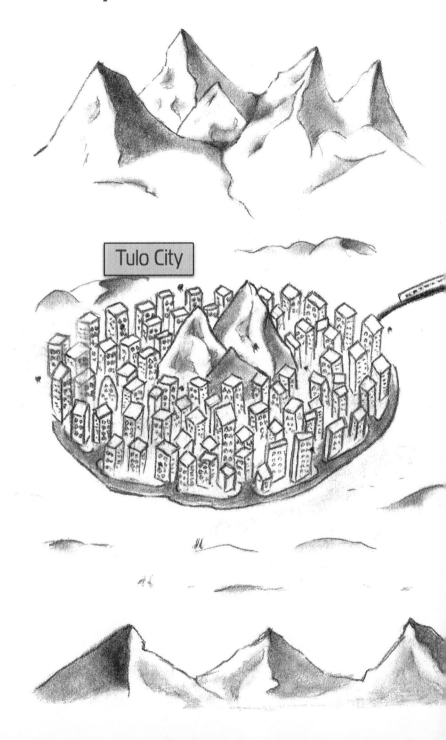

Tulo City

CHAPTER
ONE

It wasn't often that Ajay Ambers felt this alive. He kept telling himself it was a good thing. Healthy. Refreshing. It would give him the edge over his colleagues as he'd be more alert, produce better work and be able to stay later. Yet they'd all been there hours before him, so there was no escaping it.

He was behind.

The thought unnerved him, as it should. He breathed and allowed the stale air to fill his lungs while listening to the subtle hum of the sky train, gliding over the City below.

He'd never been this late, nor had he been so naturally awake. In need of a distraction, he engaged in his favourite pastime and observed the others in his carriage. But he was only reminded of his lateness when he didn't recognise anyone. Of course, living in a city of millions, this shouldn't have surprised him, but if he were there at his usual time, he'd be seeing the same people. There was the girl with a dark complexion who wore some skirt under a brightly coloured anorak, even when storms weren't forecast. She always stood by the doors, never looking up from scrolling through her Watch.

Today, her place was taken by an older lady whose face was also hidden by the black screen projecting from her wrist. Ajay instantly noticed the golden earrings hanging from her limp earlobes. They looked real. He glanced down to make sure his tie was still straight and tucked his shirt deeper into his suit trousers.

Ugly Briefcase Man, as he called him, was missing too. Every day, this guy would sit on one of the few seats with his briefcase on his lap, scowling at the City behind his thick, dark eyebrows and tapping his clown feet until the train arrived at his station. Ajay often considered 'accidentally' stepping on his feet so the annoyance would stop. He never did. That would be rude, and no merit was available for being rude. But had he been tempted to steal the briefcase, just to know what was in it? Yes. Wasn't everything he needed on his Watch? *That's one reason to be late. No incessant foot-tapping. One reason. The only one.*

Ajay did miss the other guy – his train mate. They weren't exactly friends. They didn't even know each other, but Ajay wondered if they might become acquainted one day. It was strange how seeing the same person every day made him believe he knew them somehow. He definitely lived in his neighbourhood on the Outer Inner-Ring, as he and Ajay boarded at the same stop. He also considered the guy to be well-off credit-wise, as he often wore the latest brands of office wear and, without fail, had varying Watch strap designs. They didn't come cheap. Ajay was confident that he must have had Glorified connections or at least worked there, because Ajay's stop was the one before the Quarters and they never departed together. What would it be like to have a permanent job there, instead of only volunteering?

Maybe one day his train mate would tell him.

Genni often told him he was a creep for thinking so much about a guy he didn't know. Over the years, he had exhausted the tactic of passing time by Watch scrolling or clicking on personalised adverts for merit-making bonuses, so what else could he do? Without his usual commute gang with him, he opted to look out the window, the scary unfamiliarity of doing nothing unsettling him, but that didn't stop a strange sense of gratitude from seeping in.

It's all the natural sleep. It's making me too reflective. But it was hard not to marvel over the City he lived in. A thriving metropolis that never stopped sparkling. Skyscraper windows glinted in the white sunlight, driverless cars slid past each other, drones moved peacefully like a flock of birds in flight, and thousands of billboard adverts flickered with colour. It was a masterpiece, and *I'm part of it.*

An advert for a new line of beer swiftly stole his attention. The train pulled into its next stop and Ajay lifted his wrist, so his projected screen was in line with the billboard. He just managed to scan it before the train moved away again with its fast yet silent simplicity. Looking down at his Watch, Ajay ordered a crate of the beers to his apartment after checking it was lower than 0.5 per cent. As he shut down his screen, he saw an email pop through. He didn't fully digest its contents, as it wasn't addressed to him, but it was a ruthless reminder that he wasn't in the office. A pang of anxiety ricocheted across his chest.

He and Genni had overslept this morning. Or rather, they'd absolutely indulged in sleep. Eight straight hours of solid shut-eye. As a result, they'd both been frantic.

'I can't believe this . . .' Genni had been ranting and flapping her arms about, as if she was trying to dance but failing badly. Nothing was attractive to Ajay in that moment. She had tossed her red dress on and begun to throw stuff into her handbag with enough speed and frustration that each item had landed with a sharp clunk. Ajay barely acknowledged her at first, as he'd rushed from the shower with a towel wrapped around his waist.

'Morning, Genni.'

A soft, mechanical female voice sounded from behind the mirrored screen of her dressing table. It had informed her that her facial pores had improved by 14 per cent but recommended increasing her moisturiser routine. Ajay had breathed through the irritating, inconsistent noises of Genni smacking her make-up brushes back into their containers.

'You can't put anything else on your face. If anything, your skin is looking drier,' Ajay had said.

That was the mistake. That comment. After that, Genni had slouched her shoulders and started to mumble words Ajay presumed were profanities. Rightly so. He didn't know why he'd said it. It was a slip of the tongue, or maybe somehow he thought sharing her frustration might make her feel better. She always complained about her pores. He'd obviously got it wrong. Usually, he was very good at keeping his thoughts to himself. He preferred to judge silently without the consequences; yet, this morning, it was as if his filter had fallen down his throat. Then again, he reminded himself, he was gracious enough not to highlight the rip he'd noticed in the armpit of her red dress. He let her go without burdening her with the weight of another imperfection. Ajay felt the train tip slightly, as it took one of its spiral route's sharp curves. He and others around him grabbed quickly at the purple handrails, clammy as the desert air.

After the train whistled into his stop, he didn't hesitate to advance towards the steps down to the lower street level. Marching past the all too familiar line of the station's digital displays, he hesitated slightly as he noticed that one of them had changed. It was once an advert for a line of very provocative female swimsuits, now replaced with a message about safe credit investments. *A huge shift in vibe.* He moved quickly into the hustle and bustle, inhaling sharply as he was engulfed by the crowds and the street sellers. He closed his nostrils from the smell of standard meat and ducked away from those displaying products on floating monitors. He noticed one sweaty man trying to flog a few knock-off necklaces. *Get one for Genni. Will that help? No, you're spiralling. You know she's worth more than that.* Satisfied that he'd corrected himself, he pressed on towards the Prosper building.

'Fella.' Ajay heard a gruff voice scramble after him. *For Tulo's sake, why?* He kept walking. 'Fella, hey. You at Prosper? I got books and movies to help your merit.'

The man was mid-twenties, probably around Ajay's age, and was wearing a tattered, dark-green vest. Small wisps of black chest hair protruded out from its neckline. It was hard not to grimace. The man walked along with him, and Ajay had a fleeting thought of punching him, but as usual, he opted for a deadpan expression and silence. *Why did I ever humour them?* In his early days on the job, he would use words and phrases such as 'sorry' and 'I'll come back later', thinking they deserved his kindness. As a result, he lost precious minutes getting into the office. He now understood that kindness to strangers needed to be strategic and exclusive.

He eventually told the seller to back off and briefly watched him launch himself and his products onto his next victim. *He's fine, see? Forget him.*

Ajay marched quickly up the glass steps, but groaned playfully as he was pulled back by a familiar voice.

'What time do you call this, lover boy?'

Ajay welcomed Ace's sarcastic, beaming smile as he watched him take the steps two at a time, the fabric of his navy suit tightening around his stocky legs. *That's a new suit.* It was nicely complemented by a maroon tie, fastened to perfection beneath broad shoulders and a square jawline. Ajay was quite aware that Ace wasn't only just arriving at work. He was way too merit-hungry, no longer as stupid as Ajay, and he wasn't wearing a hat. Apparently, according to Ace, he was particularly susceptible to sunstroke, and so never spent extended amounts of time outside without his cap.

'Genni and I slept for eight last night.' The words fell from Ajay's mouth. That lost filter again. What was he doing? *Get a grip.*

'Eight? That's rough.' Ace rubbed the smooth skin of his chin.

The two of them walked through the doors into the lobby as Ajay scratched the rough surface of his own chin. *Shave later.*

'I can't remember when I last slept that long. Maybe I'll see you selling on the street soon.' Ace nudged Ajay with his elbow. Ajay wanted to take the joke lightly, so he laughed, but inside, it felt so heavy. He wiggled his tie to loosen it slightly, but not enough to ruin his appearance. They reached the elevator and Ajay completed his usual office greetings to those from other departments, disingenuous, honourable nods and smiles.

Ace turned to the book cover floating above his Watch.

'Just got this new one from outside.' Ajay looked down at Ace's purchase entitled *Spending Credit Right: The Relationship between Credit and Personal Growth*. Ajay couldn't help but grunt.

'What?' Ace asked with another shove. The elevator stopped at floor fifty and a slender woman with blonde hair stepped on board. Her small lips formed a lascivious smile, and her eyes were only looking at Ace, who gifted her with a wink. Ajay subtly shook his head. *Does he ever just talk to women?*

'You don't need to worry about credit. Why waste your time?' Ajay let his words fall bluntly.

Ace's eyes turned almost wild.

'You . . .' Ace breathed through cursing. 'I don't waste time. Honestly, you'll ruin my M-470 reputation.' Ace raised his voice slightly, presumably so his female acquaintance could hear him from the front. Work, exercise, girls. That was Ace's life. Ajay sometimes envied that much simpler way of living. Less complicated, no strings attached. *But what you have is good. Yes, it's good.*

Despite the elevator's state-of-the-art speed technology, Ajay was becoming aware of how slow it felt. His breath was quickening. Ace was still talking, but his voice was lost in the maze of his thoughts. He began to wonder how many others, like Ace, had noticed he was late. He imagined the disapproving glances that awaited him. It felt a little like his first-ever day. The sweating. The apprehension. The unknown. That realisation that for the rest of his days, he'd be battling to have one-up on his equally capable colleagues, just for the next promotion, credit-rise, or merit bonus. He'd let go of his A-game. It was OK. Merely a slip-up he could make up for. Mr Hollday was impressed enough with him as it was. No need to worry. He began to impatiently tap his forefinger against his trouser leg. *No. I'm like Ugly Briefcase Man and his big, unwelcome feet. Don't become that.*

Eventually, the elevator glided to a smooth, noiseless stop and the doors slid seamlessly open to the 156th floor. He and Ace stepped out into the bright, open space encased in repeated diamond glass windows. Not bothering to say goodbye to Ace as they parted ways, Ajay discreetly moved through the office, past the usual whirlwind of people storming between meeting rooms and desks and throwing information from screen to screen. It was going well. No one seemed to notice him. Except for Dana. Ajay usually tolerated her poor attempts to flirt with him, but after this morning's stress, he anticipated he'd need a fresh wave of patience not to shout at her. *Keep it cool.* Not doing so would tamper with his performance metrics.

Dana rose from her desk and skipped over in Ajay's direction, but not without disturbing the determined path of another worker. He watched them with one eye as they both jumped from side to side awkwardly, and politely smiled through their mutual frustration. She spoke with smooth articulation.

'Morning, Ajay.'

Ajay sat down with a forced smile. *Go away.*

'Wow, you look great. New moisturiser or something?'

She faffed with her long hair to get it all sitting nicely over her right shoulder. *It does look better like that.*

Ajay responded curtly. 'Something like that. Sorry, Dana, I've got to get on.' Ajay placed his Watch over the small oval of his desk's activation pad and summoned three transparent monitor screens up from the desk.

'Yes, you are in later. I've been here since 4 a.m.' Dana persisted. *How is she still talking?* 'Anyway, I just wanted to say hello. I'm about to do an order, want anything?'

Ajay shook his head. He never understood that question. If he wanted something, it would be quicker for another drone to come straight to his desk rather than Dana having to trot over to him after her delivery. *Another excuse to flirt?*

'Suit yourself.' Dana lingered for a moment. What did she want from him? She knew Genni. They'd met before. Was she wanting to be friends? Ajay didn't have many friends at work. Ace was an exception. His focus was on impressing Mr Hollday and anyone above him, which Dana wasn't. She was just an account manager, whose main job was to look after customers. Sure, Ajay knew that was important, but it was easily replaceable. He started interacting with his screens, calmly swinging his arms to bring up the algorithm he had started yesterday. Dana finally got the message and bounced back to her desk as Ajay felt his wrist vibrate.

Hi, Ajay, I detect you have begun your working day. Do you give me permission to record your progress?

Ajay selected 'Yes', like every day, allowing his Watch to record his activity.

Have a happy merit-making day, Ajay, the Watch encouraged. Ajay activated the earpiece in his right ear and felt the smooth tickle as it extended slickly over his head, through his black hair, to form a complete set of headphones. Music invaded and the office became a moving blur, his mind focusing on the task before him.

CHAPTER
TWO

The tips of her fingers felt delicate against the nib of the pencil. It danced around the small page stylishly, leaving the path of its beautifully crafted mark. In some places dark as night, in others light and soft, altogether becoming a grayscale picture of someone Genni didn't know.

'Genni, that toxicology report . . .' Genni slapped the cover of her black notebook down fast, staring into her screen as Mafi's patronising tone accompanied the heavy tap of her heels. 'My desk. By the end of the day. To get you the merit you've lost.'

Genni's manager brushed past her desk, without even looking at her. *Ouch. I thought it was OK. Why would I think it was OK? After what she said?*

'I haven't had an employee log that many inactive hours in months. To say it's disappointing would probably be an understatement.' Mafi's small, tight lips had curled into a circle as she raised her strong, pencilled eyebrows. Genni had somehow not reacted appropriately. She knew Mafi probably expected her to cry or beg, but Genni had stayed silent. The confirmation of her manager's disapproval sent her into such a delusional spin that instead of responding quickly, she found herself debating why Mafi had drawn her eyebrows a solid black rather than a light brown. Once she'd pulled herself back to reality and the self-condemnation sank in, she'd been apologetic, explaining to Mafi that it wouldn't happen again. It ended as well as it could, but Mafi was colder with her than ever. Genni was exhausted trying to get that woman to like her, or approve of her, or even just give her a tiny piece of praise that would be nothing to her but everything to Genni. Sometimes, she wanted to give up, but it would never be an option.

'Of course, I'll get it done,' Genni shouted after her, almost jumping off her chair. She gingerly smiled at her neighbouring colleagues; no one seemed to react. Ignoring the nausea stewing in her stomach and slipping her sketchbook into her bag, Genni ruffled her hair back into a small, neat bun. She checked the camera on her screen and padded her cheeks. Ajay was right: her skin was drier. Pulling her skin back, the emails and messages popping up onscreen were fuzzy to her. Her mind moved elsewhere. *The chin.* She thought back to the portrait she'd drawn. *The chin is too thin.* She sat back in her chair. *It's out of proportion with the top of the head. Wrong angle?* Tasks continued to bounce in, but Genni didn't register them. *More definition?* She'd always been better at painting landscapes, ones she'd seen in movies; there were only so many times you could draw the desert and City you grew up in. *Perhaps if* . . . Genni had an unrelenting urge to slap herself; it was only the rules of socially acceptable behaviour which stopped her. She had to stop this daydreaming. *You'll never make it like this.*

Her thoughts turned to her father, making her legs go floppy and tingle with her rising frustration. They were to have lunch today. *Come on, Genni.*

After inputting the report deadline into her Watch, she knew her head needed clearing, so she took to some observational therapy. The office felt quiet to her today. It was almost numb, despite its usual activity: the deafening noise of chatter, the beeps and bleeps of computers and many drones delivering low-fat snacks. Yet the subtle pink walls of the Beauty Dome felt grey, its usual glittering not quite as sharp. Genni craned her neck. She spent a mindless moment watching people walk one way or another on the suspended walkways above, all nipping into a meeting room or office. She could paint a great canvas of the place – all the pinks, purples and blues of the walls cleverly disguising the blandness that existed within. Slowly pulling her cumbersome body up, she ordered an iced water. Maybe she was being ungrateful. Working in the beauty industry did have some advantages – she experienced working long hours with the top scientists in the field, soaking up all their knowledge and the merit that came with it. Not to mention the great fashion advice, beauty tips and complementary products. It was this department change that had knocked her. Mafi said moving from Dressing Tables to Fat Reduction was a promotion. Genni had forced herself not to scoff in her manager's face. A promotion? She didn't call a drop in short-term merit a promotion. As the water arrived by drone, she gulped it down to settle the turning of her stomach while considering her lack of determination for the project.

'I'm not excited about it,' she'd confessed to Ajay one night, as they were walking to the library under the swoop of night drones and motivational adverts. 'I won't add as much value into the business as before. They've taken key responsibility and merit from me. It's not even a sustainable proposition yet.'

'Well, isn't that why they're building a team to test it?' he'd asked sensibly, as he bit into a carrot stick.

'I guess. But will people *really* be better off after it? There aren't even many significant people who are overweight.'

They'd shuffled through the library doors, moving in sync with hundreds of others at two in the morning.

'Not who you know,' he suggested, chewing through more of the carrot before swallowing it lightly. 'Look, your job is to make it work the way you always do. Then the merit will flood in. You watch, you'll be Glorified before the rest of us.'

Ajay swooped down to kiss her cheek as Genni sighed into a laugh.

After three years of cheek-kissing, Genni never knew if it was love or just a custom. Sometimes it bothered her how vague Ajay was in his romanticism, only whispering the words 'I love you' late at night, as if others would judge him if they heard it.

As she walked back to her desk, she tried desperately to remember his reassurance, but when she thought of him more deeply, his rudeness from this morning was the only thing that seemed to sift through.

Their oversleeping had set her mind spinning. One minute, she was thinking about the stranger in her sketch. The next, a beautiful waterfall and then, Ajay.

Before Mafi and the report, or the loss of merit-making time, or how she wasn't invited to that planning meeting when Josia was. Then, finally, she screamed inside her head, which wasn't an unfamiliar feeling and one which usually forced her to give herself some 'help' so she could just focus. She always told herself she didn't need *it* and could get by, just like everyone else, but then that sneaky voice in her head whispered: *you're not good enough.* Battling through her emotions, she felt relieved to see no merit had been deducted for her idle water break. *You're being stupid. No one loses merit for that.* Command was always banging on about the freedom it gave each citizen. *It's a citizen's choice how they use their time, though if no merit is recorded after forty-eight hours, we will do some routine checks and merit may be deducted for time-wasting.* It was the same guff at every annual announcement. She finally began to throw together some statistics, grimacing once more at the painful pang in her belly, before giving her Watch permission to record and she struggled through her report ahead of that lunch date with her father.

Lunch came too soon.

'Angel! It's great to see you.' Her father immediately forced her into a strong, customary embrace before she'd even fully emerged from the spinning of the turnstile door. Feeling the warmth of his large arms around her, she moved in close, trying to dispel a lingering dizziness. Unfortunately, it made her side of the hug clingier and needier than she would have liked. Recognising this, she pulled away, appreciating the smell of fresh garlic and other tantalising spices wafting around the restaurant, also alerting her to her hunger, despite the swirling of nausea still dancing around inside her.

She said hello and as always, was compelled to smile, watching her father lean on the welcome counter, one hand in the pocket of his dark-green tweed trousers and the other holding a glass flute of sparkling water. Genni noticed the amount of silver flicks in his hair had grown and the small wrinkles around his eyes were deeper than she remembered. *If he's getting older, will he become less 'him'?*

'Come on.' He presented her with the familiar soft yet demeaning smile. 'I got us our usual spot.'

Genni obeyed as they brushed past other diners indulging in splendidly crafted gourmet dishes. Genni liked this restaurant with the decadence of a ballroom, though it was let down by a few grubby marks and blemishes across its white walls. Her father pointed that out every time they visited. To be fair to him, this was the most upper-merit venue outside of the Glorified Quarters, so it was slightly downmarket compared with what he, and the child in her, was used to. *Is it fair, though, to comment on that difference? He's Glorified. Hasn't he earned the right?*

In the Quarters, she remembered, there would be real plants whose floral smell would lift the room. There'd be a peaceful, tranquil view of the desert mountains – not the riff-raff of the working-district streets. Genni and her father approached their usual place, a secluded booth away from the window. *It'll be me one day.* She thought more through the calming clatter of dishes from the kitchen; one day, she would claim a M-500 score and she too could demand a non-Glorified establishment to seat her away from the sight of street sellers or scrambling Unworthies. She could bring her children there; her children who were working with every ounce of their being to get back to where she was. Then she could say things like *'You don't get any of this nonsense in the Quarters'* and she'd let them wonder why she'd ever come to lunch with them in the first place, if anything outside the decadent, golden walls was so beneath her. Eventually they'd start to resent her and never visit her at her Glorified, overly pompous mansion, and on the whole, they'd be trapped in a roundabout life between wanting everything she had and longing for something different altogether.

They slid into the booth and, as was their custom, her father spoke first.

'So, tell me. What's new at the Beauty Dome?' He clasped his hands together, the gold ring on his middle finger glinting. 'The drama of the explosive robo-stylists dying down?' he laughed, condescendingly. Genni took a deep breath, listing reasons in her head why she loved her father. It was short: *he's your father.*

'Not quite, but there's been lots of positivity with its development despite the loss of staff,' she said, 'and those with the lost hair got good credit compensation. They're thinking of approaching you about them.'

She nodded at him, creating a smile and almost congratulating herself on trying to drive the conversation from her side. A business opportunity might sway him away from his favourite subjects; her job, her credit situation, or her merit score. Ordinarily, she'd probably add her relationship to that list, but Ajay was the only choice she'd made that her father seemed pleased by. The

Prosper job and the high M-400s score had something to do with it.

'Well, there's a long way to go to be worthy of a Mansald Spa.' He flicked his eyebrows up in casual dismissal and Genni watched his ageing, wise eyes move to his screen. 'I'm having kale.' He quickly dismissed it with an overexaggerated tap. 'Have you decided?'

Decided? She hadn't even looked. Genni quickly flicked up the menu on her Watch, after hurrying to scan the table's activation pad. *Pick something, pick something. He'll get impatient. You have about thirty seconds.* Her head was beginning to sting, meeting nicely with the strange flipping of her stomach. *Just have the kale, too. But the camel looks so good. Camel does real damage to the hips and waist.*

What she wanted was a glass of water. Had a drone not realised they were here? He was Boris Mansald, for Tulo's sake. His privilege and status were another advantage of being his daughter, yet here they clearly hadn't programmed the drones to recognise him. *Wouldn't have this nonsense in the Quarters.* She eventually settled for the kale because there wasn't time for anything else.

'Good choice,' he grunted, pulling down the cuffs of his shirt. 'So, how are the dressing tables? There's something worth talking about. People rave about them in my changing rooms, and I always boast that you're on the team behind them.'

He looked at her as if he was proud, and Genni, despite having eaten nothing all day, thought she was going to re-see everything else she'd consumed in the last few weeks. She'd have to tell him. It would eventually come out, especially if her average daily merit went down; she guessed he checked that. A man of his calibre probably had the connections so he could see everything: her current location, activities, merit count, acquaintances. It wouldn't even surprise her if he knew about the painting and all the sleep she had last night.

Those thoughts made her feel even more unwell. She just had to say it. *Quickly.*

'I've actually been moved to Fat Reduction.' The words tumbled from her mouth with the same pace of her nerves sky-rocketing.

Her father paused for a moment before speaking bluntly, as a laughter brewed cruelly in his tone. 'That computerised fat removal thing? The one with all the bad press?'

Genni curled her tongue within her mouth, holding her father's eyes and nodding her head. She could feel the sweat on her hands, wiping them on the seat by her legs subtly. It was at that moment that her father exploded into laughter. Genni longed to remove herself from the situation, just shuffle out of the booth and never come back, but there was a pull inside of her that kept her chained to him somehow. So, she sat still and looked on. Reaching into his pocket, her father found a handkerchief to dab his increasingly wet eyes and Genni spotted the curly calligraphic 'BM' on its corner. Something twinged within her; the memories of all the tears, or the drops of blood on a graze of skin that handkerchief had once wiped away.

'You're joking?' he asked, letting the laugh stick around longer than necessary.

'Not joking,' Genni managed, feeling calmer, knowing she needed to defend herself, if not for anything but her pride, even though the stabs of that headache were now forcefully making their way across her forehead. *You can do this.*

'What merit will that give you?' Her father was no longer laughing, and his eyes suddenly irritated. 'Credit will be enough, I'm sure, but you're not even at M-450 yet.' His persistent stare told her to be terrified, and the tone of his voice took all the moisture from her mouth. 'I was back in the Glorified Quarters by the time I was your age. Come on, girl.'

Breathe. Remember the list: he's your father.

Genni spoke calmly again.

'Yes, at first I was sad to leave the tables, but that started out small. Remember, everyone thought they'd flop?' Genni thought back to all the bad press around having tech assistance to highlight your imperfections, and how again, her father had been damning. 'If we get this right,' she swallowed, 'people losing weight in a fast but safe way will give them the confidence to become their most effective selves. Their contribution could be higher than ever.' Genni's eyes darted around the restaurant for a drone to deliver their water jug; it was a distraction from her father's unwavering eyes and deliberately patronising silence. 'Plus, it will decrease the sales of weight loss drugs Downtown,' she mumbled, still watching a drone swooping to an older couple's table and retrieving their empty, sauce-painted plates.

Her father finally shrugged his shoulders and straightened his purple tie below his collar. 'It's just a shame you're not home yet, like your brother is.' He coughed through his solemn words and bitterly swiped at his Watch. Genni had been waiting for it.

The Rod drop. Her father never failed to remind her of what a disappointment she was in comparison to her overachieving big brother. A worthless worker next to a merit-making marvel.

'Where is this drone?' The volume of his voice made her jump, her body jolting uncomfortably. Her father sighed as he saw a drone heading in their direction. 'You wouldn't have this nonsense in the Quarters,' he huffed, his irritation amusing Genni as she felt a smirk breed on her lips, and she scratched her face to hide it.

Her father looked at her again, but this time with a strange gaze almost like love. Stretching his arms across the table, he held out his hands. Genni shifted uneasily in her seat and reached her hands over his dry fingers. She considered offering him some moisturiser, but he wouldn't want it. *Too cheap, not enough natural ingredients.*

'Maybe I spoke too harshly. You're still young . . .' He paused, his eyes narrowing towards Genni's right armpit.

Following his eyeline, Genni felt vomit come into her mouth before forcing it back down. *What was that?* Was she nervous? In shock? Anxious about work? That surely wasn't caused by the unfortunate and embarrassing fact her father had noticed a small rip in the armpit of her dress. It had ruined her father's rare attempt at apology. *Didn't you notice that? You should have checked yourself before you left this morning. Has everyone at the office seen too? Oh, kill me.* A drone arrived and set glasses down around their connected arms. Her father let go and smiled without showing his teeth. *He's doing well. It must be painful for him to not pass a negative comment on my appearance.* Genni wanted to go but her brain was now pounding against her skull, and she desperately needed the water that arrived in front of her; she slurped it back and it cut like a knife down her throat.

CHAPTER
THREE

Two hours had passed, but as usual, Ajay barely noticed. In that time, his brain had stretched itself from encryption, to environments, to code, to all those other bugs, until finally came the beautiful moment when the test passed seamlessly. He'd solved the problem, a moment that inspired him to want to punch the air and let a celebratory expletive run loudly from his mouth. Of course, he never did, even though most people in this office would sympathise with the need to channel his little work victory. There was nothing better for a Programmer than finally getting something working. This bug had been affecting the personal banking platform for months. Prosper didn't take client complaints lightly, and this little niggle had caused a whole raft of them. Understandably so, the Watch screen freezing when a client wanted to transfer credit wasn't ideal. It was just a blip and only happened once in 10,000 times, but strangely no one had managed to fix it yet. The job had circled around the team at least twice and Ajay had been disappointed the first time he hadn't managed to crack it. Now that he had, he wondered if he'd be the talk of the office now. Whether it would send him higher in Mr Hollday's estimations. Although, he realised that it might just cancel out his eight hours of inactivity last night. Hollday wasn't upset, only popping up on Ajay's screen, reminding him not to miss merit-making opportunities. There were times when Ajay wondered if it was an invasion of an employee's personal life for management to be alerted after so many meritless hours. But he knew it was necessary for a job that required M-300 and above.

He admired his merit-clock on the right-hand screen. *That must be a personal record.* Maybe he should ask for the niggly bugs no one else wanted more often. Sighing, he leaned forward and pressed the coffee symbol on his middle screen. It was OK to have one today, given he hadn't had a *SkipSleep* boost in the last twelve hours. He inputted the consumption on his Watch to ensure he maintained his diet for the day. The ding of the transaction rang from the drone as it delivered the coffee and Ajay swiped his Watch across it. As he took his first sip and tasted the sweetness of the chocolate sprinkles melting within the froth of milk, Patt rushed up behind him.

'Ajay!' Patt whispered, breathing heavily. Ajay almost dropped his coffee but managed to settle it on his desk before unclipping his headphones and watching Patt stagger to his empty workspace. His hands were shaking as he unloaded the contents of his pockets. As he did so, gadgets and snacks were getting tangled up with torn bits of paper to form one messy mountain on the surface of the pristine glass desk. Ajay grimaced. *That's foul.* He refrained from looking at the mouldy biscuits within the dishevelled mound of Patt's life. Patt frantically cleared away the bits until only his headphones, Watch and crumbs remained.

'Patt . . . where have you been?' Ajay asked, quite surprised to see him. He'd figured he wasn't coming back. Patt hadn't been in the office for days; no one had seen him nor knew where he was. The two of them kept their voices low, neither of them oblivious to the sea of judging eyes tumbling in their direction.

'There's been some stuff going on,' Patt said as he clipped his Watch back onto his wrist. He scrambled to tuck in his unironed shirt and flatten down the flicked-up edges of his hair. The purple around his eyes looked angered and his beard was a forest. *Missing work. No self-care. What's happened, mate?* Ajay watched as Patt lowered his Watch to his activation pad. It was too late for him to stop him.

A warning sound cut through the office, inspiring excited gasps of shock from the other workers. *Damn.* Screens flew from Patt's desk, covered in a red mist and flashing bold words.

GROSS MISCONDUCT.

Neither Ajay or Patt moved. Ajay didn't know why he'd wanted to stop it. He knew Patt couldn't just sit at his desk and not get caught. He'd always have to pay the consequences for not turning up for work. Then, right on cue, Mr Hollday's office door swung open.

Dressed in a cream, tailored suit, Mr Hollday's presence alone earned him everyone's attention. His deep brown eyes and defined cheekbones would surely allow him any modelling contract in Tulo. Well, that's what Dana had told Ajay once in her ramblings. Instead, Hollday had done the sensible thing and used his business intelligence to gain a M-590 score before he was forty. Ajay, forgetting the situation for a moment, was pleased to see that Mr Hollday was wearing a mustard tie. Ajay's wardrobe had told him the right thing: mustard was in fashion. He looked down at his own and felt slightly jealous that it wasn't overlaid with a floral pattern like Mr Hollday's.

'Mr Mull, let's have a chat.' Hollday's hard, grinding voice carried weight across the office floor. Patt gulped as he walked swiftly through the rows of condemning looks. Ajay felt a light grieving settle on his chest as he saw the screen of the girl in front of him. It displayed immediate updates of the recent drama to her social groups. He hoped the conversation became so enthralling that her productivity and point count fell. Ajay didn't make any worry over Patt obvious, simply clipping his headphones back in and getting to work, while remembering the technical conversations he and Patt had in the early days. Ajay had earned significant merit from their friendship, one that he knew would now end. He shouldn't be seen with him, really. It wouldn't be good for his personal brand, and that was important, now more than ever.

As early evening drew in, waves of colleagues returned from afternoon boosts, all of them zinging with a new intensity. *Did they notice I wasn't in the boost room?* Ajay straightened his tie and acted as if he hadn't registered their return. Ajay often wondered where Tulo would be without the invention of *SkipSleep*. Back when people used to sleep more, progress was much slower. Then, after *SkipSleep*, the City just flew. State-of the-art drones certainly wouldn't have existed for every household chore and delivery service; the Robotics industry historically had the highest number of employees going over the legal boost limit. *That was a lot of bad press.* Ajay's fingers still rattled furiously on the surface of his desk and lines of his code reflected horizontally across his retinas, until his flow was interrupted again by a clan of drones, this time not carrying any coffee cups.

They were hovering together outside Hollday's office, increasing in number like a swarm of insects around a sticky beverage left out in the sun. *Why are they here? Me?* Ajay's screen flashed with the simultaneous vibration of his Watch on his wrist. Apparently, his heart rate was rising. Ajay leaned over his desk to Dana, who had a better view from her seat. He hoped that initiating conversation wouldn't make her think he was interested, but with his rising paranoia, that thought dissolved quickly.

'Psst, Dana. What are those drones doing?' Dana took out her earpiece, wide eyes narrowed with initial confusion, before noticing the swarm calibrating at the other side of the office.

'Wow,' Dana responded. 'The only time I've seen drones together like that is when they're from the TPD.' Ajay felt himself go pale, nausea invading his throat at the thought of the Tulo Police Department. *I knew it.* Standard drones were always on the move, delivering a product or service. They didn't tend to hover.

'Are you alright, Ajay? You've gone paler than a Glorified walkway.'

'Yeah . . . I'm fine.'

Ajay retreated slowly back into his seat. *Do I need a toilet break? Yes, I do. But they'd surely still find me. I shouldn't panic.* There was nothing in the situation that meant he should. Nothing at all. They could just be there for an inspection. Nothing to do with him.

Then his heart rate sky-rocketed. The hum of the drones all taking off at speed was thunderous as they headed straight for him. He'd seen this before in his nightmares; a villainous gang of TPD drones hurtling towards him, ready with their red-hot probes and sparking tasers. Ajay's only thought was to move. He jumped up and headed swiftly towards the toilet, not exactly knowing the next part of his plan. As he reached the toilet door, he briefly glanced back to keep track of his hunters.

He stopped. And watched the drones cleaning out Patt's desk from top to bottom. He let out a quiet sigh of relief. *You. Idiot. They're cleaning drones.* He cursed himself.

Vulnerability hit him. His mad flurry hadn't gone unnoticed. Scanning the room, eyes were briefly assessing him before returning to their screens. They were judging him, thinking he was weird. Well, he had just sprinted to the toilet in a blind panic, away from a bunch of drones. It was hardly normal behaviour. *It doesn't matter.* He could hold his head high; he was wearing a mustard tie. Ajay simply scanned his Watch along the wall and advanced into the toilet. He leaned against the sink and swiped one hand over his face, as if to wipe off his embarrassment while ignoring the mirror's suggestion of a product for puffy eyes.

Moments later, he proudly strutted back across the office floor and noted that no one was looking at him. Except for Ace, who seemed to be laughing. He'd boast about his bug fix later, he decided. That would shut up his mocking.

As he arrived back at his desk, he saw how any former presence of Patt had been masked by disinfectant. It had never happened before. Ajay was sure of it. Something about it felt sinister and uncomfortable. A sound chimed from the staff photo board that was projected high above the office floor. Ajay looked at his own photo on the second row daily, taken on a good photo day. His medium-length black hair shone with just the right touch of wax, and his smile was perfect: teeth perfectly straight and glowing against his tanned skin. He couldn't wait for his score to increase. Then that face would be on the top row. It wouldn't matter so much if he embarrassed himself then.

The chime had been an update to Patt's record on the bottom row. His score dropped to M-290 and his picture slowly faded into a blank space. A collective sigh of disapproval filled the air. Ajay felt unnerved. While he knew it was right, he couldn't help but sympathise. Part of him wanted to find out what had been happening at home to facilitate his downfall. He had learned over the years to quench sympathy and its paralysis; it was a distraction, stopping him from moving forward. Not anymore. Patt wasn't strong enough; that was the way it was.

Ajay noticed a torrent of messages from Ace on his middle screen:

Ace: *That was intense. You alright, mate?*

Ajay assumed he was referring to his toilet trip.

Ace: *Where do you think Patt is?*

Ace: *You don't think they've sent him packing to the Side, do you?*

Ace: *Should we try to contact him?*

Ajay looked behind him towards Ace's desk. His middle screen was down so Ajay had a full view of his friend, chatting to a colleague beside him. How that guy managed to get any work done, Ajay would never know. He replied:

Ajay: *Don't be dim. They wouldn't send him to the Side. Don't worry about it.*

Ajay paused.

Ajay: *And I was just desperate.*

Ajay: *For the toilet, I mean.*

Just as Ajay told himself to be more careful, Mr Hollday emerged from his office and all eyes locked on him like flies to syrup. Ajay straightened up and whacked his middle screen down. Hollday scratched his chest through his crisp, white shirt and cleared his throat.

'I'm sure you've noticed that Mr Mull is no longer with us.' Mr Hollday looked up to the staff board, emotionless. 'While this saddens me, I'm sure you understand we have to have the right people to make the contribution that is required of us.' Mr Hollday paused as he swung his arms behind his back and casually walked towards the centre of the office floor. Ajay subtly looked down his own chest to check his tie.

'In better news, I'm happy to announce we can now reveal our plans for Liberation Day and how you can get involved.' Mr Hollday smiled across the room, like a proud parent would look at a well-merited child and clapped his heads together. 'The auditorium, 9 p.m.' He disappeared back into his office, leaving his audience to explode into excitable chatter and Patt to evaporate into nothing but a memory.

Ajay read another message on his screen:

Ace: *Make sure you go to the toilet before the meeting. ;)*

Tapping back at his desk, he buried his head into his work, but not without first throwing a jovial middle finger in the direction of his friend's desk.

CHAPTER
FOUR

'Do you think this will take long?' Ace asked as they all edged forward again, like products on a conveyor belt, down the corridor digitally decorated with the events of Prosper's timeline.

'Dunno. It was about an hour last year.' Ajay absorbed the familiar beeping sound as people scanned their Watches on the door one at a time.

'I'm heading to The Tower after,' Ace said.

'Oh, I was going to ask if you wanted a drink.'

'Where at?'

'Just Skyhouse.'

'I'll meet you after,' Ace said as the line slowed and he leaned against the digital wall behind him, displaying a half-constructed Prosper building. It was then that Ajay noticed a whitening spot on Ace's chin, illuminated by the screen's light.

'What are you working on tonight?' Ajay asked.

'I dunno. Maybe get on the bikes . . .' Ace lifted himself back off the wall as the line moved. 'Unless you fancy tennis?'

Ajay told him he was working overtime before meeting Jaxson and Blake for a drink as they arrived at the entrance to the auditorium. He lifted his Watch to the scanner and felt his wrist vibrate as its screen turned green. Ace did the same after him, and they walked together into the familiar conference space, where thousands of seats descended into a pit towards a central stage.

'Come on. Just ask them to push back an hour. The merit's better with tennis,' Ace encouraged.

That's selfish. Tennis might be better than being on the bikes, but my overtime would be better merit than tennis. There's no way he'll shut up about it, though; it's easier to do what he wants.

'Alright, alright. But you buy me an ale?' In timidity, Ajay regretted such a presumptuous question, but reminded himself, quickly, that he had a right to ask it. Friends owed one another when they sacrificed merit. Ace nodded, no questions asked.

The two of them walked further down the marble steps to find some vacant seats. Ajay never got tired of the atmosphere of these things. He even enjoyed the corporate cheesiness, the soft pounding of motivational techno music, and the swirling spotlights moving and falling over each section of the crowd.

'It gives me an excuse not to go to Mum's as well,' Ace said, as he wiped some imaginary crumbs off the folded seat he was about to sit on. Ajay had never heard much about Ace's family. Maybe it was because he never asked any questions about anyone's family, really. It worked well to avoid being quizzed on his own. He did know that like Genni, Ace was a Glorified kid, now somehow estranged from his parents. Ajay often thought they were both ungrateful; they couldn't have ever been left wanting, growing up in the Quarters, being educated to the absolute top level and having people from the Side waiting on them hand and foot, and yet they both managed to find ways to grumble, which was beyond frustrating. Obviously, he never expressed that frustration out loud. He stayed silent because that was easier, simpler.

The mechanical murmur of a drone came from behind.

Ajay noticed a few heads flinching as it got close. He didn't blame them, he too still had reservations after the infamous malfunction a couple of years ago – termed the 'Drone Dumps'. Some bug in the drone's internal code had thrown their spatial awareness off completely, meaning the Robotics industry had a lot to answer for. His best memory of the whole thing was seeing an Unworthy dumped on by a box of takeaway food. Ajay had managed to avoid such an embarrassment, because he was cleverer than most, and had a more acute sense of focus, so he'd rather enjoyed the whole situation. Disappointingly, it only lasted a day.

In the auditorium, this drone was heading up above the stands and Ajay watched as it produced a projection out into the middle of the room. The Prosper logo, a three-layered flame, spun on its axis against a lilac gradient background.

The music subsided along with talk trickling to a stop as a booming voice filled the room.

'Greetings, treasured colleagues and associates.'

'Oh, here he is, the big man,' Ace smirked.

Ajay smiled, his eyes focused on Bancorp's face, a bulky man he'd never had the honour of meeting in person. This was always the closest he'd ever been to him: Ajay sat in a faraway seat and Bancorp down on the stage below, so distant he was almost a silhouette. He rarely took his eyes off the real him, on stage, rather than the magnified version of him on the overhead screens. It reminded Ajay that they were actually in the same room. Bancorp had become an idol to him. Tall, well-dressed, winner of prestigious business awards, CEO in a top Tulo corporation and, of course, Glorified. Genni always said that Bancorp's handsomeness hadn't diminished despite his age. In fact, she mentioned it every time he was on a news update. He was just *it*. The type that everyone wanted to be like. Accomplished, good-looking and respected, with a solid score on his wrist.

His voice also carried this weight with it. A kind of powerful husk that made people listen.

'As you are all aware, another Liberation Day is fast approaching. Those in HR and senior management have been working diligently to ensure that our celebrations this year reflect the appreciation we have for your hard work and your dedication to our objectives here at Prosper. Before we get started, let's remind ourselves of the importance of this treasured holiday.'

Ajay heard an understandable sigh from Ace. They'd seen this video so many times that they could probably recite the entire thing word perfect if they bothered trying. It began with a bird's-eye view of the old city, an area now known as the Side. Whirring, resonant sounds were repeatedly blasted from the speakers. Grey, boxed homes and miniature skyscrapers were distorted by some strange, brown filter effect. Ajay hated the next part. Actors and actresses dressed in overexaggerated rags walked slowly across the shot, scrounging around on the floor for scraps of food and cowering over empty water buckets. He wondered why Command hadn't bothered paying for better production. Despite not knowing what it was like before, Ajay was convinced this was all some hyperbolic performance. *And here comes the victory story.* The narration began to echo around the audience with its usual gravitas.

Generations ago, Tulo was nothing more than buildings in the desert – defined by poverty. The working citizen was starving, and water was rationed. But only for them.

It then faded into flashes of regally dressed men surrounded by treasured possessions and exuberant food, unwelcomed by sporadic boos from the crowd. The scene always made Ajay think about what to eat later. *Salad?*

The government watched from above, towering over the dying city. They were gluttonous. All the resources that others had worked for, they took for themselves. The commoners, the contributors – people like us – didn't stand a chance.

Triumphant music began to accompany close-up angles of tattered but sturdy boots marching forcefully and flicking sand into the camera.

Our ancestors joined together in defiance against the injustice they were living in. Despite the obstacles and the challenges they faced, they fought valiantly and sacrificed everything for those who came after.

Images of laser bullets, fire and smoke overlaid each other seamlessly. Ajay actually enjoyed this part. It reminded him of Revolution Combat, one of his favourite Watch games. He and Ace used to challenge each other for hours. That was before merit was such a big deal, when they were younger and had the whole 'we've got time' attitude. Then, when promotions, exclusive venues and A-list networks became a potential reality, anything unproductive fell off the agenda. The video continued.

Even though not all joined our new way of life . . . The Side as it was today came back onto the screen. It hadn't changed. *These war heroes gave us our reality. A society based on equality and justice. One where individuals can choose what they contribute, but only reap the benefits of that contribution. Our constitution allows everyone to be fairly rewarded, according to the time they dedicate to moving society forward through technological reform, personal development and community spirit. Merit has become a statement of status: one earned, not simply given.*

Drone footage of the beauty and grandeur of Tulo City reflected brightly across all sides of the conference hall. *We press forward, but never forget their bravery.* The narrator's final line was made even more powerful by Mr Bancorp joining him in chorus. *Progress is Strength. For a greater Tulo.* Ajay mouthed the words too, almost instinctively, as if he wouldn't be welcomed without doing so.

The video ended and, like every year, the auditorium erupted into applause. Ajay and Ace were both on their feet to contribute, that too was like some ingrained, automatic response. Mr Bancorp returned to the podium and the screen, smiling and gesturing for the crowd to calm down.

'Liberation Day is not just about a week or so of partying and holidaying. It's a time to remember.' He held a dramatic pause. 'To remember that we didn't get here alone.' He banged his fist on the podium in time with the rhythm of his speech. 'That in unity, there is progress. In progress, there is strength. Every single one of you has the required skills and capabilities needed here at Prosper to move the Tulo economy forward.' Ajay couldn't help himself. He was mesmerised by the man. He leaned forward in an attempt to get closer.

'To create more efficient personal banking, to design seamless transaction technology, to provide more security for the credit of businesses, and, indirectly, to improve the efficiency and well-being of working individuals in our society. That is what we remember on Liberation Day. Together, at Prosper, we can create more.' The crowd clapped again, the applause shorter and more subtle. Bancorp raised his hands again, clearly keen to continue. Ajay noticed that his Watch clasp was a solid gold colour with what he assumed were engravings of phrases or names. *Note to self: look up what they mean later.* Ajay turned his own wrist over. His strap was the same as the day he got it – black and dull. Bancorp spoke again.

'Of course, like every year, you have the day itself to enjoy with your families and loved ones and to attend the celebrations in the Glorified Quarters. But as a treat for this year, we are giving you the day before Liberation Day as a networking event here at Prosper.' Ajay watched as people's heads flicked rapidly to one another, bursting into excitable conversation. Bancorp paused for a moment, smiling proudly and scratching his round stumbled chin where wrinkles had started to form; Genni said even they were attractive. 'This will be an exceptional merit-making opportunity, one that won't come around often.'

He was right – it was rare to take a whole day out for networking, an easy and effective way to rack up the merit. Ajay once read the entire Command Guide on how to make the most of networking, also known as others helping you learn valuable skills that could improve your contribution. Despite his research, he'd never been very good at it. It wasn't that he had a problem with small talk, it was his little enthusiasm to listen to insignificant others drone on; he'd once almost lost it when a woman hammered on about how to put shoes on more efficiently. The merit also wasn't that good when being educated. Rather, the real bonus was in educating others, or meeting high scorers with Worthy connections. *Where's the benefit in it for me?* If there wasn't a good answer to the question, whatever it was wasn't worth doing.

To finish up, Bancorp stared sternly and deeply into the drone's camera lens, indirectly looking into the eyes of every Prosper employee who felt the chill of his final words, as if spoken just for them.

'Don't waste it.'

CHAPTER
FIVE

Genni's day had picked up. She'd had a lunchtime boost and then she was flying. That toxicology report was handed in three hours early and in her manager's words was 'surprisingly insightful'. Genni decided to not take the 'surprisingly' as a personal insult and regardless, it was extra merit earned very cleanly. Plus, she'd managed to order a needle and thread from a drone, and sew the armpit of her dress back together. It was a bit of a half-job, but she found herself not just worrying about the meritless activity but feeling too vulnerable to sit on the toilet in just her bra and knickers for any longer than she needed to. And it seemed to be paying off; the dress was holding together for now and that's all she needed to get through the day.

As evening drew in, she was desperate for a break, her eyes feeling tired as she stared through her screens rather than absorbing anything on them. Just a quick breather to renew her mind and then she'd be more productive. Only five minutes wouldn't hurt her. Surely, the respite would help. *If they could hear you, Genni. It's all an excuse; what you want to do will never be deemed a productive or meritful practice.* But she couldn't help it, she needed to, and the temptation worsened as she pulled her black, battered, expensive paper notebook from her bag. Flicking over the pages back to her morning sketch, she affirmed to herself that the chin was definitely too thin. Gazing over the face of a stranger she'd crafted in pencil, she began to trace an outline underneath his cheekbones faintly and softly. Time ticked by. Whenever she was drawing or painting, she felt as if she were on a cloud or in another world where time was insignificant, where she could do this all day, every day. It had become her sanctuary. A release. A land where merit didn't exist, and all the staring eyes turned to joyful petals from the pupils of seasonal flowers in the desert.

Then, after an hour had passed, that all too familiar feeling began to line her insides and sit heavily in the base of her gut. Guilt. Shame. Frustration. Genni's screen alerted her to the lack of merit earned and she dropped her pencil. Looking around her, she was relieved that the office was still buzzing, and no one seemed to notice the warning notification looming over her desk. As if they'd take any notice of her anyway. She scraped her fingers through her hair and looked over her drawing once more. *A waste of time. Always a waste of time.* Her brain felt scrambled; she couldn't focus on work, on anything. She needed help. *Downtown. It's time to go.*

Bleeping out of the Dome and walking across the Retail District's fountained plaza, she was graced by the sharp ringing of her Watch: *Pearl & Mila calling.* As Genni accepted the video chat, she was tempted to sit down on a bench, but she determinedly continued towards the station. Two smiling faces sprang up from her wrist.

'Hey, gorgeous,' Pearl shouted in her overly obtrusive voice as Genni observed the shine of her lustrous black locks and skin tone, perfect even through cyberspace. She glanced at her own face: dry, bland and undistinctive. She replied and then greeted Mila, who was leaning over a table in her work lab, dressed in her white coat with a thick elastic headband keeping her hair from her eyes. Her sweet voice travelled through the speakers.

'Good day today?' Mila asked.

Genni huffed as the approaching sky train blew the ends of her own brown hair back. 'Not really, but I did submit a really good report an–'

'Gen, not being rude, but I haven't got a lot of time,' Pearl said proudly, before continuing to tell her that she had a business proposition to run by her. Genni listened more intently after getting over the tone in which Pearl majestically announced her busyness like a badge of honour, despite the fact that everyone was busy. Maybe not as busy as her, but still busy. If Genni was honest with herself, though, she was inspired by Pearl and the impact her job made, most of the time. Her social recommendations of clothing brands, beauty and fitness products had instilled positivity and efficiency into hundreds of thousands of her followers. But Genni justified her grievances towards her friend, because Pearl could suffer from not being a very nice person. Genni watched her flick her long, black hair back to reveal the hooped earrings underneath, accompanied beautifully by her delicately crafted eye make-up. Slightly conscious about the volume of Pearl's voice, Genni made herself small in the corner of the sky train carriage, not taking any notice of the other passengers who flooded the space. She was surrounded, but alone.

'So, it was actually Mila's idea. Why don't you explain it, hun?' Pearl gave Mila permission to speak.

Mila's face was closer to the camera now, her newly coloured eyes blinking quickly. 'Pearl was telling me she was hoping to widen her audience to people of greater merit scores than her current audience, who are . . . average, low M-400ish. I was at work and was thinking, what do many of my bosses in healthcare really care about? Merit and contribution, of course. But credit is also big.' Mila paused as she lightly scratched underneath her eye, being careful to avoid smudging her eyeliner. Genni looked up momentarily from the screen to see the train passing the stop for home. *Should I have got off?* Her journey continued at speed.

'So, I wondered whether Pearl should start to deviate her content from beauty and fashion to different, more pressing concerns, so she's accepted by the big shots. Like credit management, or updates about the latest economic developments. She could interview those who work in the industry. And then I thought, who works for the top company in the Financial District?'

They both announced Ajay's name energetically. Genni was taken aback by the sudden outburst, moving her wrist away. A woman beside her grimaced with polite disgust at the noise from Genni's wrist. Genni turned her back to her and looked out the window as they descended into the Outer-Rings of the City.

'You want Ajay to feature on your channel?' Pearl nodded her head dramatically while making some agreeable murmur. 'You know he's awful in front of a camera? He hates being judged by others. He might act as if he's cool with it, but he doesn–'

'Oh, don't worry. I have producers and stylists to make him look good.' Pearl pursed her lips as Genni watched the Outer-Ring buildings, cream-sided cuboids that held simple bay windows instead of wall-to-ceiling glass. Adverts for cheaper and less exclusive products hung on their walls, tainted with specks of sand and dust. Maintenance and delivery drones following the line of the train started to drop off until only a dozen remained.

She needed to sign off. 'I've got to get off now. I'll mention it to him, but Ace might be the better choice. OK?'

'Sure thing. But push him, Gen, he's a better communicator than Ace,' Pearl said. All three girls blew kisses to their screens, and Genni felt a loose ache in her legs and a sharp pain in her stomach as she staggered out into the night's pressing humidity, not giving much further thought to their conversation.

Genni heard the familiar squelch of the sticky pavements beneath her feet as she walked quickly over the bridge into Downtown. She marched through the row of market stalls selling fresh produce and raw building materials; a Command-worthy disguise for what really went on. It wasn't long until she encountered the usual things she ignored: the indulgence of salty, fatty, highly saturated foods, illegal product trading between stall workers, people who wore sunglasses and covered their Watches with their sleeves. Unworthies were also hunched up asleep in doorways beneath the flicker of cheap, neon lighting. All of it was more harrowing at night, but Genni had learned to blur it all out. She was here for one thing. Always was. She held her bag strap tightly to her shoulder with both hands and, by some miracle, managed to step back and avoid being flattened by two men in some sort of brawl.

She stopped still as a market worker smashed a rugged-looking man into a wall.

'You steal from my stash again, I'll kill you, you disgusting Unworthy.' The market worker had a rough voice that grated against Genni. As he held the throat of the Unworthy tighter, he noticed Genni beside him and loosened his grip. His voice became lighter, but was almost predatory. 'Sorry, darling. We gotta teach them; we only get what we work for, right?' Genni managed to return his smile to hide her apprehension. 'He's in there. See you tomorrow.' He winked at Genni and locked his gaze on her body. *He recognises me?* The nausea she had felt simmering all day threatened to manifest itself, not just on the realisation she was now a regular to this game, but because of the way his eyes traced her like a pet fox licking its lips over a meal. She managed to hold down the vomit and forced herself from the situation. Quickly, and without looking back at the Unworthy who had rolled into a ball by her feet, she walked through the grey door behind them. She saw the familiar face, breathed a sigh of relief, and let the door slide swiftly shut.

CHAPTER
SIX

It was a close call. Ace had never beaten Ajay on the tennis court, and when he was two sets down, he couldn't admit his fatigue. He hadn't had one boost today, so no wonder he was tired. But to admit fatigue would be to admit weakness, so he powered on and brought it back, settling the entire match with a blinding shot that hit Ace powerfully on his right arm.

Ajay felt like he might collapse as they made their way out. He scanned his Watch against the exit screen and felt his wrist vibrate as the exercise merit was added to his score. Ace did the same, and as the sliding door opened, Ajay briefly glanced at the lines of the tennis court disappearing from the glass floor, ready to transform into whatever sport was selected next. His gym bag bounced off the back of his legs as they headed for the changing rooms and passed other exercisers. People cycled, ran, danced and circuit trained. They walked past an old man working on boxing with a personal trainer wearing a branded polo shirt. Ajay saw the wobble of the man's degraded limb fat as he slowly jived to hit and kick the pads on the trainer's hands. Ace was a few steps in front, obviously not as enthralled by what others were doing. Then there was a couple ballroom dancing, rather elegantly, then a bunch of girls in a spin class, then a group of men playing football. Ajay stopped in front of the door, watching the ball pass quickly between the men's feet. It wasn't often he saw football being played; like most people, he opted to play sports that were more merit efficient – more people meant less activity. Though he remembered the one time he did play; it instinctively brought a small smile to his face.

It was Tara's birthday, and she'd been wearing that denim pinafore with the luminous red and yellow T-shirt. She was so excited. Their mother had arranged a street party to celebrate. When they had arrived outside, they saw colourful bunting hanging between buildings above a long wooden table that stretched the length of the street. Their neighbours had all come out to see his little sister, and had greeted her with contagious smiles. Ajay had thought it was all a bit of a show, but he didn't complain; the food looked good, and Callum was there to keep him company. He was his best friend back then, before he met Ace. He didn't think of him much now. It was irrelevant. Yet that day, he played football for the first time.

It was their neighbour, Joye, who brought the ball. It was bright yellow, with a few black marks on it. Ajay remembered it vividly. Neon, almost painful to look at. Joye got them all playing behind the street, across the sand. Many people stopped to watch as the yellow ball flew, bounced and tumbled through goals outlined by piled-up T-shirts and jackets.

'What are you looking at?' Ace asked, pulling Ajay away from the memory.

'Nothing. Just thinking about playing sometime.'

'Football? Really? Come on, I thought you wanted that drink.'

I do. Ajay followed Ace, just as a man with legs like tree trunks smashed the ball into the net.

Ajay frantically straightened his tie and shirt as their conversation jumped from work to Ace enlightening Ajay about his latest M-500 hook-up. It was a long story, it seemed, seeing as it lasted from street level all the way up to the bar at the top of a 500-storey skyscraper. It was the same old thing. Ace met a Glorified girl, spent time with her once, twice if she was pretty, three times if her parents were influential, and then they stopped when they each got bored or realised the other wouldn't better their merit score. It was sleazy, Ajay knew that, and something told him it was probably a part of Ace's personality he should despise. He didn't, though; Ace had gained strong merit from the connections it had given him, so it made perfect sense in the end. He often wondered about ending things with Genni to follow his friend's footsteps. The more Ace talked about it, the more Ajay's thoughts ran away. *If I was single, I would know more people. More people, more of the right opportunities, more merit, more credit, more impact, more purpose. Stop, Ajay. Genni is great.*

To his relief, both his mind and Ace shut up as they walked past the familiar sign that read '*M-400 and above*', beeped in, and a fluttering of instrumental music pleased Ajay's ears. The smell of Tulo Cyder, sweet fruits and moderately salted chips permeated the air as people were waited on by drones around glistening, round tables. Constantly moving spotlights on the small, delicately used dancefloor rivalled the twinkle and glitter of the glorious lights of the City. Tulo at night was breathtaking from any height, but at the 500th floor, it still stunned Ajay into a momentary silence.

The Skyhouse was much classier than the likes of City Tree or The Barbican towards the Inner Outer-Ring. Ajay often felt like its service and standard gave him a taste of life in the Glorified Quarters, giving him the motivation for his score to hit M-500 and get there.

He lifted his wrist and messaged Genni. He needed to see her; they hadn't spoken since their stressful morning and something told him things weren't the best they could be between them right now.

Across the venue, he spotted his friends, the two of them sitting at one of the many tall, rounded tables. Jaxson was dressed smartly, but had removed his stripey red and blue tie, which was curled up like a sleeping snake on the tabletop. He slouched slightly on his stool and flicked his long, combed fringe away from his face. Blake was sitting with him, laughing with his large rectangular glasses falling over his nose; his pink and blue tinted hair tied back slickly and sharply contrasted with his neon green suit. *That's a daring colour combination, even for Blake.*

Sauntering through the bar, Ajay noticed how there were more people shopping than usual. They were all crowded by the windows, lifting their Watches up to the billboards outside, strategically placed within the city's shimmering skeleton. As Ace and Ajay reached the table, Blake jumped up in excitement, displaying the bright purple shirt beneath his suit. Another colour in the mix; Ajay couldn't keep up.

'Greetings.' Blake embraced Ace first and kissed him on both cheeks before Ace pulled away and looked down at Blake's outfit.

'Blimey, Blake, you're matching the billboards!'

Blake thanked Ace while slightly opening both sides of his jacket and twirling round on one foot. Ace reacted with a wide smile and a wolf whistle. Ajay laughed as he too received kisses from Blake, whose cologne was strong; he held his breath to stop himself from coughing.

As he and Blake joined them at the table, he overheard the start of Ace's conversation with Jaxson.

'. . . almost M-460? How are you finding it?' Ace had put an arm around Jaxson. Two drones arrived with Tulo Ales, ordered automatically due to the men's statistical preferences. Ajay watched Jaxson nod considerately and start fiddling with his beer bottle, moving it from side to side.

'I'm not doing badly, work has been full-on so that's a win.' Jaxson smiled down at his beer bottle, scratching off its label. 'I've been trying to help Blake out too. You're struggling with getting the right job, aren't you?' He looked at Blake, who turned suddenly sheepish. Ajay wasn't surprised. Jaxson had made Blake suddenly vulnerable to opening up about his problems. He didn't have a right. Ajay knew Blake had been finding things difficult, and he was there to support him when he needed it – on a one-on-one basis, not within a social setting.

'Yeah . . .' Blake spluttered, before smiling. 'You just can't help talking about me, can you, Jaxs?' His calm, friendly response smoothed over the slight awkwardness that had grated through the atmosphere. Ajay was relieved, sitting down on the vacant bar stool, but its golden legs toppled beneath him. Thankfully he managed to stabilise himself by slamming his hands down to grip the rim of the table, and even more pleasingly, the others didn't seem to notice and therefore didn't ridicule him. He was too exhausted for that. He tried to get comfortable on the rose-gold padded seat, still very aware of the wobble in the chair's legs. *What is this junk?* He looked down at the left-hand legs, which he noticed were slightly bent. This wasn't the standard he was used to, so he would have to submit a complaint later, to make sure they got that sorted out.

A few minutes went by as Ace demanded Ajay order another drink. He had forgotten Ace owed him one. It was a great feeling, like whenever he found slightly more credit in his account than he remembered was there. A drone flew over. He initially opted against his preference ale, feeling a bit fed up with the same bittersweet taste. As he tapped at its menu screen, he was reminded of the gorgeous CodeBite beer that came out the previous year. It was smooth on the tongue; the buttery flavours of cocoa and caramel were a taste sensation, absolute gold dust compared to the blandness of Tulo Ale. An Unworthy could have told him it never would have survived. All Command-owned 'Tulo' brands dominated the market; a little bit of the money went back into the City's fund, so merit was earned for investing in the brands that mattered. Ajay longed for a CodeBite but just settled with the taste of ale, and jumped back into the already flowing conversation.

'He's got it in his head that I'm playing copycat,' Blake said as he shot a wink in Jaxson's direction, who shook his head and sneered.

'What's this?' Ajay asked.

'I'm moving closer to Jaxson's apartment,' Blake beamed.

'Oh,' Ajay stuttered. 'That's news.'

'Alright, you don't have to act so surprised.' Blake puffed some air while throwing a sarcastic glance over to Jaxson and Ace.

'No, I'm sorry, it's just . . . don't you need M-470 for that neighbourhood?' Ajay toned the question in a way that he hoped didn't sound condescending. Jaxson's apartment was just inside the Inner-Inner-Ring, not far from Ajay's own apartment in the Inner-Ring. Blake was only at M-430, so it seemed ambitious.

'Yes, you're right. I know I've got to work hard,' Blake nodded. 'It's just the motivation I need so I don't get left behind while you guys climb the ranks.' He flurried his right hand up an imaginary ladder in the air.

'We could get you some merit now, if you like?' Ace asked, pointing to his Watch.

'What?' Ajay contested impulsively. There it was again. Words flying out his mouth without permission. *Now you look like a selfish tool.* 'Sorry, Blake, it's been a long day.'

Ace looked at him like a mother bitterly disappointed in her child. Ajay felt judged, and then ashamed, and then willing. As always, he relented to the peer pressure.

'Fine. What have you got for us?'

'Well,' Blake said. 'I could teach you samba.' He projected his voice, adjusted his glasses and slipped off his chair onto the dancefloor, shaking his hips seamlessly from side to side. Ajay wondered if Blake realised how little people enjoyed dancing. It had become one of the least merit-worthy forms of exercise anyone could do. *That's part of his problem.* In some ways, Ajay admired Blake for spending so much time doing what he loved, but ultimately, it was foolish. His current marketing job wasn't bad, but he needed to spend his free time doing something more valuable. Yet here he was again, trying to dance.

Ace and Ajay looked at each other and smirked.

'You first,' Ace demanded, as he gave Ajay a light push off his chair towards the dance floor.

'Sorry, Blake,' Ajay ignored Ace and asked Blake to return to the table. 'This isn't really a samba type of place. Maybe in a few nights' time at a Middle-Ring bar?'

Blake nodded his head as if he agreed, but his disappointment was reflected in his frown and the lines it produced across his forehead. Ajay wasn't sympathetic, and rightly so, he decided, as his suggestion would be better for Blake anyway. *Tough love.*

'What can you teach us here, around the table?' Ajay asked.

It didn't take long for Blake to get over his disappointment and arrive at something new with the same vibrancy and enthusiasm. Ajay wondered how exhausting that must be, but at the same time, he could see its advantages in a place where serial knockbacks weren't uncommon.

'I could talk you through my tips for organising your home life. I've been writing about it in my memoirs. You need it, Ajay,' Blake chuckled. Ajay nodded gracefully despite his internal irritation. *Really? He's judging me for my organisational habits?*

Ajay saw the Watch's list of merit activities reflected in Blake's glasses; the list included everything from being at work to educating a child. Ajay always thought there should be an option for 'cooking a five-course dinner for an Unworthy', just to see how many people would actually bring themselves to do it. *For a greater Tulo.* Usually, the Watch would automatically detect an activity through the scanning of an activation pad but for merit-making conversations, it had to be set up manually; a real inconvenience in their world of immediacy. Following his input, Blake's Watch asked: *Who are you teaching today, Blake?* Blake looked to Ajay, who bleeped his own Watch against Blake's.

Excellent. Do you give me permission to record your conversation today? Ajay saw Blake select 'yes', allowing the Watch to do its job.

CHAPTER
SEVEN

It was like she was painting the most beautiful landscape. On a cloud. Floating freely. Drifting dreamfully. She felt free with the extra energy. It didn't always feel like this, but the highs had been getting more intense and more addictive. Genni's excitement hit a peak when she received a message from Ajay that they had gone to The Skyhouse and he wanted her there. *He wants me. He loves me. He needs to see me.* She had let out a gleeful squeal at her Watch and tapped her feet joyfully as she'd boarded the sky train like an annoying, peppy teenager but she didn't care, nor did she realise how over-the-top she was being. The looks from others on the carriage went unnoticed, because it was as if nothing could bring her down from her mental paradise. A few blocks from the bar and slightly dazzled by the intensity of the bright lights, she reminded herself not to stay long. Hours couldn't be wasted after her trips to Downtown. *I was back in the Glorified Quarters by the time I was your age.* Her father's words span inside her head and started to lower the high. *Stop thinking. Just go for one drink, then the library. Maybe another boost? Maybe two drinks? Maybe three? Maybe, maybe.* The lights seemed to get brighter and more painful and part of her felt vulnerable being alone. The other part of her was free and as she briefly looked up to the yellow moon, she felt humbled by its magnificence, and began swinging her arms softly with the motion of a paintbrush stroke.

Then she felt it. A dark presence behind her that was getting closer. She stumbled forward due to the strong force inflicted upon her shoulders. Her legs managed to stop her from falling flat on her face and she spun around in fright to see her attacker, adrenaline pumping through her veins, her mind spinning but ready to fight.

Genni lowered her shoulders and relaxed, yet she was still tense with anger.

'What are you doing?' Genni screamed at her older brother. It would be him who would turn up and knock her out of her utopic high.

'Nice to see you too, Gen,' Rod smiled.

Genni looked at him, his perfectly shaped face tinted red as he stood beneath a soda advert. She always wondered how he managed to get all of their parents' best features; Mum's perfect eyes and teeth, Dad's hair and height. Genni was convinced some overpriced genetic manipulation had gone on and they didn't bother when she came along.

'What did you do that for? And why are you even here?' Surely, he had some prissy venue in the Quarters to go to.

'Well, there's something enlightening about hanging out in the peasant's dwellings sometimes,' Rod winked. Genni stayed silent, not giving him the satisfaction of laughing at his so-called joke. 'I didn't mean to scare you.' He leaned in closer, examining her face with his green, piercing eyes shining through the night. 'Are you alright? You look pale.'

Genni answered quickly. 'Yeah. Fine. You just startled me, that's all.' She gulped through her rising dehydration and the heat that was running across her head. 'I'm just off to meet Ajay at The Skyhouse. You can join us, if you like?' She spoke with composure, but she couldn't believe what she was saying. What was she doing inviting him? *Say no, say no.*

'Yeah, why not?' Rod said.

Genni cursed under her breath.

CHAPTER
EIGHT

Ajay gave an internal sigh of relief as he spotted Genni handing over her coat for the cloakroom. He was already tired beyond belief, and if he had to listen to any more talk about how to colour code his socks, he knew he'd end up having too many drinks.

Blake's words became background noise as he watched Genni move from the other side of the bar. She was subtly hunching her back as if she was squeezing her stomach into herself. Under the ambient lighting, she looked sick; her face was riddled with the pale curse of fatigue but then blushed red with fever. Another make-up disaster? Ajay always told her not to slap so much on or she'd look less like her beautiful self. Those moments when she was just natural were the ones that softened Ajay the most. He thought back to that morning after she'd woken up. The morning sun had crept through the window and fallen over the soft dotted freckles on her cheeks. The rich blue of her eyes, not burdened by the heavy weight of mascara or eyeliner, had calmed him in his rush. That was before he had a shower, made that stupid comment about her skin, and she'd left in a justified strop. It was rare that he ever saw her like that.

She just covered everything up, until he could barely see the real her anymore. *Is that our problem at the moment? Not being honest with each other? How could I ever be honest?*

'. . . and if you double-up on your hangers . . . Genni,' Blake's words came back to Ajay as he had spotted Genni's arrival too. He watched Blake skip towards her, and Genni let out an excitable shriek as Blake embraced her in a bear hug and swung her around, off her feet. She looked to the floor, pressing her blue-nailed fingers into her head. Then, there was that smile. Bright. Infectious. She dashed over to greet Ace and Jaxson with hugs and kisses, before eventually coming over to him.

'Hi,' she said. Where was his girlish shriek? He sometimes wondered about the connection between Genni and Blake, and why she wasn't always that excitable and flirtatious towards him, the person who probably should be lifting her up on a dance floor. He didn't worry about it, really. Though, the thought occasionally crossed his mind in a fleeting sort of way, picturing them together, before he reminded himself that Blake's score would never pass the Daddy test, so he wasn't a threat. It was more likely that Ace could whisk her away. That thought was almost unbearable and, by the same token, completely ridiculous. These were his friends, and Genni was faithful – he just had to keep her. *If I had to be honest, how could I ever keep her?*

'Hi.' Ajay told himself to swallow his pride. He grabbed her playfully into a hug and whispered lightly in her ear, 'I'm sorry about this morning.' Genni smiled, scrunched up her face in the endearing way she always did; she placed a hand on Ajay's knee as she sat beside him and a

Tulo Tia arrived by drone. Ajay hated that stuff, basically watered-down juice with a drop of ethanol. He felt a further warmth radiate through him from her touch, and he moved his legs closer to hers.

Someone else sat next to Genni. *What is he doing here?* As soon as Rod sat down and the two of them exchanged small smiles of tolerance, Jaxson immediately wanted to shake Rod's hand. Ajay had noticed that Jaxson had always been enthralled and fascinated by Rod's boastful explanations of what it was like working closely with Tulo Command, especially on the frontline of Liberation Day. He watched Jaxson's conscious movements as he scooped his tie up from the table and proceeded to put it back on. For about five minutes that followed, unfortunately, Rod's life was the topic of discussion.

'. . . and they cook up some fantastic food,' Rod said as he placed a *SkipSleep Pro* into his mouth, a relief to the others and a space for them to talk. Ajay was obviously jealous of the *SkipSleep Pro;* he was in serious need of some energy. However, only M-500s or above could purchase the small e-devices that allowed someone to top up on *SkipSleep* on the go.

'How's the dancing, Blake?' Genni asked, with quite a hefty cough following her words.

'Oh, it's great,' Blake said. 'I can't imagine not doing it. I've been utilising my boosts to do it even more. Did I tell you I'm hoping to move to an Inner-Ring place? By Jaxson's?' He tapped at his Watch to order a drone.

Genni had opened her mouth, but Rod jumped in there first. 'You'll have to do more than dancing to meet that standard,' Rod said, very matter of fact.

Rod often said exactly what Ajay was thinking, which meant they had a strange relationship. Ajay understood Rod's principles, but the way he voiced them out loud just made him a Glorified idiot. And Genni disliked him, so Ajay, of course, was on her side.

Silence fell over the group, until Genni bluntly responded, 'Well, not everything has to be about technological progress; some merit can be about making people happy and more motivated.'

Ajay felt the tension rise like a mounting inferno. *It's awkward. It's so awkward. Stop it, Genni. Don't give him the satisfaction.* He looked at them both; she was staring hard into his eyes.

Rod laughed as he placed his *SkipSleep Pro* back into the pocket of his smart, lightweight jacket.

'No one makes it to M-500 by dancing,' Rod said. Ajay saw Blake was embarrassed; his shoulders slumped, his eyes looked down and his smile slowly flattened like the painful deflating of a lively helium balloon. Jaxson patted Blake's back as some sort of brotherly gesture, though it did little to lift Blake's head.

No one said anything, and just the muffled vibration of classical music disturbed the silence. People sipped at drinks and avoided eye contact with Rod. Except for Genni. Was this it? The moment when she'd actually have it out with him? Ajay hoped not. It wouldn't end well for her. He sympathised that she'd always been expected to follow in his golden footsteps, but his status meant he deserved her respect. *Move on, Genni, move on.* Ajay's hands felt clammy and fidgety. How could he distract her? *Talk about something, anything.*

'How was lunch today?' He cursed himself. *Great one, another conversation about her family. Nice work, Ajay.*

Genni sighed and, understandably, rolled her eyes in Rod's direction, who was Watch scrolling. Ajay then remembered that she didn't talk about her problems with her dad in front of Rod, because to him, to put it in Genni's words, their dad was 'some ethereal power that could do no wrong'.

'You saw Dad today?' Rod jumped in, reminding Ajay he was always listening. 'Did he tell you about Number Two?'

Genni's mouth was full of drink, but she widened her eyes, puffed out her cheeks, nodded her head and placed a hand on Rod's laughing shoulder. Suddenly, any anger she previously had for him disappeared and the two of them morphed into two giggling siblings, amused by some mischievous act they'd just committed.

'What's going on?' Ajay asked.

Rod snarled. 'Just one of Mum and Dad's Side servants asked for a reference for their Purification, a few months early, I might add.'

Genni finally managed to swallow, and her subtle laughter could be heard out loud. Despite the joy in her face, Ajay noticed a dullness in her eyes. She also kept touching her stomach. *Has she eaten something dodgy? Why does she keep doing that?*

'You're joking?' Ace joined the conversation. He had both an interested and amused look on his face.

'She said she was ready to make her contribution to society. You can imagine my father's reaction; apparently, she's too good at folding sheets.'

Genni ordered a drone to stop in the air next to her. 'Another drink, anyone?'

Rod ordered another ale but the others refused, having already been in the bar too long. Ajay wondered whether she should be having another one. Clearly, she wasn't feeling good. He wouldn't ask, though. The others could think he was stifling her.

'I've heard that folding sheets is a one-way ticket to the Quarters,' Ace mocked. There were grunts of amusement around the table.

'Dad said he wasn't giving her the reference; he can't lose her, as the others are completely useless.' Rod ordered the drone to wipe the apparently unclean tabletop. 'It's not surprising. I don't know why they–'

'Right, lads, our half an hour is up,' Ajay said quickly. He couldn't help but have a sudden urge to leave and wanted to remind the others that they'd been inactive for thirty minutes too long. He rose from his golden stool, which wobbled slightly on his departure. He noticed Rod's expression; he clearly didn't care much for being interrupted. Ajay felt anxious. An apology almost fell from his lips, but they were close to breaking the suggested rest regulations, and he didn't want to have to make it up, so his sudden departure was justified.

He moved around the table and tapped Ace on the back, the contact of his hand on the suit jacket making a clapping sound.

'Fair enough. Let's go,' Ace waved goodbye to the table, where Blake and Jaxson were also preparing to leave.

Ajay embraced Genni. He wouldn't ask if she was OK. She'd tell him if she needed him. Instead, he opted for the obvious question. 'What are you doing tonight?'

'Just going back to mine. I have work to do,' Genni said.

Strong answer. Ajay nodded.

'Oh, I've been thinking I want a new Watch strap,' she suddenly said. 'Will you come with me in the morning?'

Bad question. Do I have time? I should be there for her. I can make it, I'll have an extra boost and she'll repay me in some way, I'm sure.

Ajay agreed, before landing a peck on her cheek. She seemed fine, so she probably was fine.

'Bye, everyone.' Ajay waved to the others. He quickly joined Ace at the exit, but not without noticing Rod's eyes, which had been holding him with a subtle disgust since Ajay had interrupted him. *Or, is that look suspicion? It can't be. Walk away. Everything is normal. It must be.* Yet, Ajay couldn't help but feel the strength of those eyes piercing through his skin and electrifying his entire body with unease as he walked away.

CHAPTER
NINE

Ajay swiped into his apartment building after his short walk from the sky train. It was hot. Claustrophobically hot. He loosened the knot of his tie and as the smooth, glass door slid behind him, shutting out the chaotic streets, he bounced his eyes over his Watch – 01.33 a.m. *Score isn't high enough yet. Why does this seem to happen every day?* He staggered into the elevator, untucking his shirt and feeling a cool breeze making its way up his torso as the air-conditioning kicked in. Once over the pleasure of it, he briefly glanced down the rim of his left trouser leg to see the small scruff of dirt a stupid woman's fox had gifted him with. Ajay didn't normally notice anyone in the streets at night, as he was often mindless, desperate for a boost. People only tended to filter past him like ghosts. On tonight's walk, however, this woman, who was probably lower than M-300, easily, what with her cheap, polka-dot shorts, muddied trainers and muffin-topped waist, she allowed her young fox to snap and growl at his feet, tugging on his trouser leg like a predator. His first instinct had been to kick it square in the jaw, but in the end, a scolding look at the owner sufficed. *When did you become so entitled? When it's late at night and I haven't had a boost all day.*

She'd apologised, the dirt on the trousers would come out and the prowling thing hadn't torn them, so they parted ways graciously. It was a shame she looked so ridiculous – her pet seemed to be walking her rather than the other way around; it bounded down the pavement while she was dragged behind by the lead. He imagined that's how Genni would look walking a fox; its strength would definitely master her petite frame. That could be another one for the list of why they weren't getting one when they moved in together. A lynx would be much more manageable. Not that they had an actual plan to live together. It was something they'd talked about, and Ajay had decided he wouldn't be the one to initiate it into a reality. The longer they could go on concentrating on their own merit and careers before any of the other 'stuff', the better. He did miss her when she wasn't around, though. Just her company made him feel more at peace, even when they were working or watching some educational movie neither of them wanted to watch.

The lights faded on as he scanned himself into his apartment; an open-plan studio with high ceilings, grey walls and with an unruly tendency to get messy.

Ajay went about his evening routine. Walk around the bed, pick up dirty clothes, put them on top of the wash basket; walk around the bathroom, pick up dirty clothes, put them on the wash basket; look at the wash basket, tell himself he'd do the washing tomorrow; collect the dirty glasses scattered around the living room, put them in the dishwasher; tell himself to get a cleaning drone, remind himself he didn't want drones in his home and all the reasons why; finally, drop himself down on the sofa.

Tonight, though, all of that was overlaid with his whirring thoughts about Rod. *Why was he looking at me like that? Does he know? Or was his pride just wounded when I interrupted him? Would he bad-mouth me to other Glorified people? If only I knew what he was thinking.* Ajay had decided a long time ago that if he could ever be given a supernatural power, he'd choose to read minds. An ability he could turn on and off whenever he felt like it. So that if he heard old Mrs Kollideman in the apartment across from him humming some health advertisement tune, he'd turn that right off. Then, when he needed to know what someone was thinking about him, he could be enlightened and, most likely, relieved. Like that woman with the fox. When he read her mind, he'd hope to hear her feeling ashamed and embarrassed. He could know whether or not Mr Hollday was considering him for the next promotion, or he could know how Ace really felt about women, or why Genni was looking so wiped out tonight, and if she really did love him like she said she did. And he would know if Rod looked at him in that distasteful way for a reason, and what that reason was, or it would release Ajay from his anxiety because he was making a thing out of nothing. That would be ideal, and then he could concentrate on merit-making and not getting distracted by the agonising spinning of his own stupid mind.

He also knew he was tired. His eyes felt like they were going to fall from their sockets. With that sensation, he sat up with motivation. *Come on.* He tucked his hair behind his ears, wondering when he last washed it, and swiped the activation pad embedded within the glass coffee table in front of him. The *SkipSleep* System elevated itself from underneath the table. It was an elegantly designed cuboid, about thirty centimetres in height and fifteen in width, crafted together with strong, silver Tuloian steel. Its mechanical voice soothed Ajay, almost like a free kick before his imminent refreshment.

Ajay, how many hours' worth of SkipSleep would you like this evening?

He was given the options from one to four hours. He probably didn't need as much as usual, given his dangerous slumber the night before. Then again, if the system allowed him the maximum dose, then he'd be an idiot not to take it. Ajay selected four on his Watch and placed his forearm comfortably onto the black cushion inside the box. Above his arm hung the syringe needle, which glinted slightly in the reflection of the City's panorama of lights outside. The system detected his arm was in position, and released its metal straps around his wrist and the top of his forearm to tie him down. The coolness of its metal was always a welcome touch in the desert's heat. Ajay could feel the tingle of technology running up his arms as the moderation scan began; it creeped across his chest and into his brain to determine whether his body's chemical levels were stable. *Moderation Scan Complete. Dosage level accepted.* The needle began its work, lowering itself smoothly towards Ajay's arm, like a snake would hang from a tree and inspect its dinner: **SkipSleep in progress**. Ajay didn't even wince as the injection went deep through his skin and he watched the red progress bar creep closer to 100 per cent. Proteins, iron, multivitamins, creatine,

Fo Doktrin and other natural herbs were being slowly absorbed by his body. Fo Doktrin was a plant that grew wildly in Tulo Country and infected most of the Side. It brutally destroyed most other plant populations in the desert, but when cut, boiled and prepared, its vitamins and health benefits were anything but brutal. Their effects would be obvious within an hour or so, and Ajay looked forward to it. That fresh wave of energy without the need for sleep.

The progress bar continued forward. Ajay thought back to today's promo video, the shots of the old city, which was now the Side. His grandmother used to tell him stories about people who lived out there. It was in these moments, when it was quiet, and he was waiting, that he missed the concept of bedtime. Waking up, watching the day pan out, and returning to the same springy mattress, ready for his grandma and her bedtime story. She would sit on the small stool by his bed, probably wearing some plain coloured floor-length dress, and would look at him fondly over her bent, narrowly framed glasses. Having her there was comforting. It meant every day always ended on a high, and he never had a bad night's sleep. It was different to this life, where the days didn't really end at all. In the rare, quiet moments, he felt her absence strongly, or just the absence of anyone at all.

Ajay sat up as he heard the satisfying ping. He lifted his arm out from the cushion, ignoring the message that it was his last boost for eight hours. He turned to his wrist as the system lowered itself silently back into the table. Mindlessly, he started scrolling through *Personi*, to find anything to take his mind away from her and his childhood. Ajay repeatedly swiped his finger past people's updates: Davi had bought his own driverless car; some girl he'd met at networking posed in front of the Glorified Gate; Pearl had started a new campaign with a nutrition brand; and his colleague, Matu, had written some boring, political monologue about Command's Clean Streets plan. A picture made him stop.

It was one of Genni's family friends and her husband. He looked good. She looked awful. Pale, red eyes sat heavy beneath a flock of sweaty, tied-back blonde hair, though her smile almost erased all of that. It was astronomical. Ajay wondered if her jaw was hurting afterwards. It was one of those wide, teeth-revealing and completely contagious grins. The baby in her arms was wrapped delicately in a white, cotton blanket, and despite its face being shrivelled up into the resemblance of a prune, Ajay could understand that it was cute. He read the caption: *It's been a long night. We would like to introduce you all to Tiel Ruana, born 7lb 4 ounces at 3.20 this morning. She came out alive and kicking, already ready to earn some merit we think [laughing emoji]. We want to say a special thank you to our midwife. Gyna . . . Darn.* He was supposed to be getting her out of his head. Here Grandma was again, sitting on that stool, telling him a story of Marlena, or was it Marlina? A midwife who worked on the Side.

Ajay flicked away at his Watch. *Stop thinking about it.* The guilt sat on him, heavily. He still went to see her every month, if time allowed it, but she was ill. The pain in his chest urged him to go and see her more, while he still could.

Ajay shuffled on the sofa and willed himself to dismiss his thoughts. *What movie should I watch?* He whizzed through the streaming menu on his floating Watch screen, but nothing grabbed him. In the end, he settled for *The Financial History of Tulo*. Despite having seen it a few times, the merit was still adequate. Apparently finding out about the great developments of the past should inspire citizens to become their most effective selves, and the fact he worked in the Financial District was just an added bonus. He flicked with his fingers and synced his Watch with the projection port on the table. A much larger screen appeared, running the opening sequence to the movie. Ajay lay his head on the back of the black sofa, his hair camouflaging into the material. His eyes felt fresh again, and he reckoned he'd stay awake all night; he even considered going to the office after the film to squeeze in some overtime. If he got there before Hollday, he'd then see him at his desk as he walked to his office. *That's good.* He had told Genni he'd help her shopping, but he could bail on that if he was on a roll.

'She must have got lots of merit for that.' His eight-year-old voice popped back into his head. Ajay closed his eyes slowly in frustration as he thought over the stupid midwife story again.

'Stop it,' he whispered to himself. His mind was racing back to Marlena, Marlina, or was it Madelia? She had been caught in a wildfire drift following a storm, and had helped people evacuate their houses, assisted the medical service, and delivered a baby, all in one night. Yet when Ajay had suggested about her large merit count, his grandma had said words along the lines of, 'It doesn't quite work like that.' Ajay remembered being bewildered. It was the only night that his grandma's story had disturbed his sleep. He soon discovered that people who choose to live like those on the Side, following what they called The Guiding Light, would only ever reach M-200, unless they then applied for Command's Purification process. Ajay thought back to the conversation in the bar; he wasn't so attuned to the humour the others found in Genni's father's servant requesting a reference early. He still didn't really understand why City folk *hated* the Side so much. He suspected the discrimination was so deep-rooted that they themselves didn't even know.

CHAPTER

TEN

Genni felt worse in the morning. A few hours after her shopping date with Ajay, she sat on a bench outside the library, turning her wrist back and forth to admire her new Watch strap.

Get back inside. She knew she needed to. Though the outside air was hot and clammy, it was just fresh enough to ease the headache. She hoped Ajay wasn't thinking about her. In-between their joking and pleasantries, he'd spent the entire time in *Watch, by Command* asking if she was OK. He knew something was up, but she couldn't let on. She could handle it. Heading towards the door, she held her head in her hands to at least try to lessen the pounding. The library was always rammed on a Saturday, even when the sun was setting. She hated the place for everything but the immediate merit. Exhaling deeply, she looked up and noticed a woman from across the square. She was beautiful. Genni couldn't make out all her features as different people wandered across the line between them, but she noticed the way her long brown hair flowed gorgeously down her back. She wasn't doing anything special. Just standing in the sun, looking at her screen, in a loose red dress that was drifting in the slight breeze. Genni closed her eyes and placed the girl next to a waterfall.

The brightness of her dress contrasted with the greens and blues of nature. She considered going home to paint or beginning a sketch in her notebook. Yet when she opened her eyes again, her model was gone, disbanded into the life of the City. *Get. Back. Inside.*

Genni rose from the bench, her mind still partially fixated on the girl and the ideas she could inspire, when she felt the deep soak of sweat on her back. Feeling around her, she realised she had drenched her blouse before grabbing her head as the ache began to stab itself deep over her cheeks and her jaw. Making it to the library bathroom, she stared into the mirror. A red circle appeared, accompanied by the voice of technology. *Your skin is presenting only a 30 per cent moistu* – Genni slammed her hand at the mirror's controls to silence it. She tried to conceal the redness around her eyes, noting that her skin was almost as bright as that girl's dress. Was she just tired? Stressed? What was happening to her? *I was M-500 by the time I was your age.* Her father's words were back. She threw off her blouse and put it in her bag. After adjusting her bra straps beneath her vest, she breathed deeply and staggered back out into the library, breathing through the pain in her head.

She walked back through the building, but all she could detect were blurred figures and strange shapes as her vision began to suffer. Genni wandered past many desks, screens and distracted eyes, all learning more contributory skills. As she struggled to walk in a straight line, drones dodged her as they served people with requested files, drinks, food, or anything else they fancied. She'd spent too much of her life in this place, she decided, as a dull ache crept into her chest. It was depressing how many nights she'd worked through on *SkipSleep*, either here, at home, or at the office. Sometimes in her slippers, just so she was comfortable in some way because there was no other way she could be.

Genni's vision was suffering more, and as she arrived back at her desk, she willed herself to shake off the distortion, turning a page on the screen and downloading information about the Cleaner Tulo Initiative for some awareness merit. Reading but not absorbing, her eyes went from sentence to paragraph as the dull ache in her chest began to sting. Her legs and arms were shaking, her vest was absorbing her sweat, her face got hot, and she quietly yelped as her left foot began to spasm. She scrambled back to the bathroom, whacked open the cubicle door, braced herself against it, and realised she couldn't properly breathe.

CHAPTER
ELEVEN

Ajay was pleased he'd got another hour of work in before volunteering, despite being wound up. His trip to the shopping centre with Genni had left a sour taste in his mouth. Not only had she taken an hour longer than she said, but the Command assistant who gave Genni the Watch strap had totally patronised him.

'Can I help you with anything? I can see you haven't yet opted for personalisation.' She pursed her sickeningly red lips at him from behind the pristine, white counter.

After he refused, she encouraged him that they could 'sort him out'. He had been tempted to put her in her place, seeing as he knew more about the Watch than her, and all her bland Command buddies put together. But that would do him no favours. Nor would Genni have enjoyed it. Not that she seemed to be enjoying anything at the minute. What was wrong with her? She looked worse than yesterday, like her hair hadn't been washed for weeks, and she kept clutching her stomach. He was tempted to ask if she was taking her anti-menstrual tablets, but he was sure that wouldn't be it. However, he felt totally put out by what happened when they were talking about cake.

'It's hard to imagine a life where merit deductions for chocolate wouldn't matter,' Genni had said as a sadness crept into her eyes. 'I guess I would get used to it, if it happened.'

'Why do you always talk in hypotheticals?' he'd asked flippantly, swallowing more of his green smoothie.

'What?'

'Whenever you talk about being Glorified,' Ajay had noticed an alarm in Genni's body language, so stepped more sensitively in highlighting a detail he'd always noticed but never addressed. 'You always talk like it's not going to happen.'

'I mean, it might not,' Genni had mumbled.

'Of course it will, what are you talking about?'

'Not everyone makes Glorified, Ajay.'

'People like *you* do.' Ajay still felt shocked by her sudden lack of confidence. He'd asked if she was OK, and she merely told him she was having a 'low day'. *What does that mean? Is her merit falling? What does it mean for 'us' if it does?*

Ajay turned his mind to more trivial matters, not able to stomach anything else.

The sky train was always busier on a Saturday afternoon; weekends tended to be when people moved about the most: from offices, to the Sports Tower, to volunteering and community services, networking events, and – if there was time – social gatherings. After he'd left Genni, the carriage was so full that Ajay ended up being pressed against the window, in the lovely resting place of an older man's armpit. The upgrade to the sky train's schedule couldn't come quickly enough; Ajay assumed extra services would reduce the congested and hairy travelling conditions.

As the train whizzed closer to the Glorified Gate, more Tuloians disembarked, allowing the remaining passengers to breathe again. Ajay managed to grab a seat and he briefly looked at his Watch strap. He stroked a finger over the Command sign; five dashed circles, all different sizes, all dropping inside each other with small specks of a royal purple colour layered through it. A bird's-eye view of the City; the Outer-Rings to the Inner-Rings, each separated by a river, all of it running towards the bullseye of the walled Glorified Quarters. The corporate design reminded him how much he wanted to change it. Everyone else could. But it wasn't worth the risk for him. He saw it today; they took the Watches away and tampered with them, there was too much at stake for them to get their hands on his. He sat back and flicked a screen up straight, giving himself the reassurance that no one could see his face. He wasn't in the mood to be watched. Words blurred to him as he scrolled through several articles celebrating new business ventures, one about rising stormy weather, and some about population decreases and the formation of anti-Command groups. Then, a live news programme appeared at the bottom of the screen. Ajay tapped to listen while simultaneously reaching for his earphones from his suit trouser pocket.

A news reporter's voice filled his ears.

'. . . will meet tomorrow to begin the debate. It is an unprecedented question, and this is the first time Purification has been reviewed since the merit system was first introduced.' A man in his mid-thirties, with a shaven head and a dimpled chin, spoke with clarity. He was standing on the high street of the Side, as indicated by the text that ran beneath his name. *Stevin Jenk.* Behind him was a huge sand hill, towering over rows of grey-boxed houses and pothole-heavy roads, where the desert sand was resurfacing.

It was sometimes so easy for Ajay to forget he was living in the desert. The City was so chaotic and marvellous in its development that the only real reminders were the heat and the view from the tallest buildings. Though it wasn't easy for anyone to forget the Side. It always came back on the news or in conversation and as he concentrated again on the reporter's words, a familiar compassion sat on his chest.

'It is expected that the clause to have the acceptance age lowered to twenty years old rather than twenty-five will be rejected. However, an alternative has been proposed. Command officials are now also to discuss the possibility that members of the Side community will only have to undergo one year of Glorified service, instead of two following a valid reference.' Stevin Jenk paused, clearly listening to the person in his ear. 'The Hevas family have yet to make a comment, but we do have a few City citizens online to offer their view. First, let's go to Jessa from the Inner-Ring.'

The camera switched to a young girl with a slim jawline. Ajay thought her small, finger-size hoop earrings were a nice touch to her already attractive face.

'I personally don't think anything should change. I don't see how we can be confident that their indoctrination has been fully reversed after just one year in the City. Command is always saying that we need to protect the merit system as it's got us where we are, and I think this could become detrimental to that protection.' Ajay continued to listen as he was presented with Vick from the Inner-Outer-Ring.

'Hi. Thanks ... erm ...' Vick clearly wasn't as prepared to make his argument as Jessa. He was dressed nicely in a light blue shirt, but one side of his collar was pointing up. 'I wonder whether at the age of twenty, you know, with them being younger and that they might be more, you know, easily released from the brainwashing that the Side has done. Then again, Jessi is right.'

Jessa. Ajay shook his head. *He's got his collar turned up, used the wrong name, and clearly has no experience of public speaking. Where did they get this guy?* Ajay briefly wondered whether Vick could be a Purified citizen, blown over from the Side, but soon realised that he was too young to have made it through the programme yet.

Vick continued to stutter through his words so Ajay cut him off by swiping further down his screen to find some more drivel about the illegal administration of *SkipSleep* to people who wanted extra. Ajay dismissed his screen back into his wrist. *Didn't people know what too many boosts do to the body? There are warning adverts everywhere and they limit them for a reason.* He sighed over people's stupidity.

Everyone left on the train was dressed beautifully and held their heads high. Ajay was suddenly conscious he might have been the only non-Glorified left. He sat up, his thoughts turning back to the debate. He never really spoke about constitution politics, mostly just keeping quiet whenever the topic came up which, with the likes of Genni and Ace, was a lot. He occasionally laughed at Ace's mocking of the Unworthies, but he mostly found it cheap. He sympathised with them. Why couldn't they have the chance to make their contribution like everyone else? It seemed inordinately harsh for them to be limited to M-200, just because of the family they were born into. And Genni? She was always saying how she wanted to be cut off from her parents, from their ruthless pressure to get her back in the Quarters. So, Ajay often questioned, why didn't she see that those from the Side merely wanted the same? They were just escaping from a different kind of prison. Ajay knew this view was controversial, so he stayed quiet. It was easier that way.

We are now approaching the Glorified Gate.

His journey's end distracted him and as the train smoothly stopped, he stood by the door, impatient for them to open. Once they did, Ajay bounced off the carriage and walked determinedly towards the Gate. He hadn't noticed his complete disregard for his surroundings until he collided with her: the small woman wore a large beige hat with a tasteful brown ribbon around its centre, and a golden necklace sat simply on her chest. She was clearly Glorified, and he'd knocked her to the ground. *OK, keep calm. Be polite.*

'Ma'am, I'm so sorry,' Ajay cried out, offering his hands to her for support. She didn't take them but lifted her head slowly; not enough so that Ajay could see her features, but enough for him to notice a poorly concealed mark that fell over her slender neck. It was a sort of maroon colour, though it was clearly distorted by a level of make-up above it. Something was familiar about it. Something Ajay couldn't quite capture. He bent lower to see more of her, but she got up too quickly and sprinted on her heels towards the station's exit. Ajay caught a whiff of cheap camel meat. It smelled like the

Outer-Ring streets but it must have been from someone else. It couldn't have been her. *Did she look at me? I don't think she did. That's good.*

Then she wouldn't remember the face of the man who knocked her down, and she wouldn't tell all her Glorified friends about him.

Ajay's Watch vibrated. He was late. Dashing down the steps from the station, he felt relief as he saw the Glorified patrol guards weren't there. There'd be no interrogation today. Ajay wiped the sweat drips from his forehead, leaving a greased shine to his tanned skin tone. His manager was waiting for him outside the Gate.

'Hi,' he said, and climbed into the car. She welcomed him before telling the car to go, and rambling on about some new recruits.

The car glided on and Ajay looked up through its panoramic roof to see 'Progress is Strength' engraved in gold and displayed proudly across the Gate's decadent archway. He never got tired of the Glorified Quarters. It was like being transported to another world engineered by the same craftsman. It still had the usual sights of drones flocking to different jobs, and flurries of people, but rather than walking through the streets, most were carried by hover vehicles encased in black-tinted windows. The rows of neon advertisements had been replaced by immaculate walkways, tastefully planted trees, and flamboyant flowers that shrouded the entrances to pavement cafés. The air felt cleaner, the only smell being from the flowers or freshly baked goods. Spidering off from the main streets were numerous gates that opened onto residents' long driveways, leading to their mansions in the mountainside.

The car hovered left and swung past the gates and around The Old Golden's infamous sculptured fountain; a group of older people carved into a golden material, with detailed facial expressions of joy and delight, surrounded by jets of water. Around the fountain's base was a greyed brick wall covered with letters in a curled typography that read 'Caring for the Best'.

Upon getting in and putting on his blue care uniform, Ajay set off on his list of jobs for the morning, with his Watch listening and recording. He spruced up Mr Moren's front garden with some new lavenders and perfected the edges of Mrs Delwenny's high ceilings and covings with a paint called 'Shining Sunrise'. Next, he walked over to the village hall and up the gleaming steps to take Mrs Laptoff her pills. Ajay walked into the hall, ladened with hanging baskets of yellow and golden flowers that gave the room a constantly fresh and floral smell. It was almost overpowering, hitting him instantly as he made his way over to a group of older women, sitting in exuberantly patterned armchairs. He always felt jealous of these people, coming in here to sit, chat, sip on drinks and look over the splendour of The Old Golden's garden, its greenery so pleasant in the white natural light.

'Another one's here,' Mrs Laptoff snarled to her friends as Ajay approached. 'Why don't they just use drones for these things?'

Ajay widened his eyes as he opened a bottle of water and greeted the group. Mrs Laptoff didn't look at him but gazed out of the wall-to-ceiling windows at an old couple sitting on one of the many garden benches. Ajay wondered what he had done to offend her, and how he might rectify it.

'She doesn't mean that. She's lost the plot in her old age.' Miss Genard was sitting across from Mrs Laptoff, wearing a mint-green golfing outfit.

'No problem,' he said in response. 'You're looking lovely today, it's nice to see you.'

'Oh, stop it,' Miss Genard flapped her hand at him before looking back at Mrs Laptoff. 'You know, back when Julie was working, she was a big advocate for gaining merit through community work. Do you remember, girls?' She looked around at her fellow loungers. 'Even set up protests against using drones for simple jobs.' Miss Genard jumped up triumphantly in impersonation, her arms high. 'Long live volunteers,' she roared, before lowering herself back into her seat as the other ladies found the nostalgia amusing.

Ajay gave his best fake smile while darting a quick glance at the drained gin glass sat poised on the table by Miss Genard, and he wondered how many she'd had. Not engaging any further, he reminded himself to just do his job. He gave Mrs Laptoff her first pill, which was quickly swiped from his hand. She looked disgusted as he held her chin to guide the water from the bottle into her mouth. *What is this snotty woman's problem? I'm helping her.*

'Those were the good old days,' another woman said. Ajay didn't look at her, but continued to eavesdrop. 'I don't know why these young people think they have it so hard. We didn't have the technology they have now. No *SkipSleep* or talking wardrobes.' Ajay felt as if he should defend himself as one of 'these young people', but he didn't have much to say.

'It has come a long way in the last twenty years, because of our lot's contribution.' Miss Genard tried to salvage any last drops of gin from her glass before turning to the other lady beside her. 'Hey, Dess. How's Mindy getting on with her little one?'

'Oh, he is just adorable.' The tiny lady rose from her seat. 'Let me show you a video.' She tapped at her Watch. Over the next few minutes, all the women – apart from Mrs Laptoff, who was still glaring suspiciously at Ajay – gathered around the screen, giggling. Ajay found the persistent laughter annoying, but he kept his eyes sharp and looked out the window in between shoving pills down the old woman's throat.

'Just splendid,' Miss Genard said. 'You've got another, haven't you? I've forgotten his name. David?'

'Daved . . . yes . . . ' The woman shakily closed her screen and tucked her Watch away underneath the sleeve of her pink silk blouse. 'He's doing OK, thank you. Still low on merit, but OK.'

'Oh, I'm sorry to hear that.' Miss Genard ordered a drink from a passing drone. 'Well, maybe he can get you a bit of indirect merit yet.' She took a sip of her bubbly that had arrived on the table beside her. *From the gin to the champers. It's the afternoon, for Tulo's sake.* Ajay was thankful that the conversation seemed to be ending, and that he only had one more pill to go.

He gently placed the remaining pill in the old lady's hand, but Mrs Laptoff flippantly twisted her head to look Ajay straight in the eyes. Ajay felt the sting as she slapped his hand away, spitting at him in anger.

'You know, it's disgusting they let you in here,' she said, her tanned skin reddening with rage. Ajay froze.

She was insane. *Completely lost it.* He wasn't sure what to do so he just stood his ground, water bottle still in hand.

'Julie, calm down,' Miss Genard said, jumping up, and slightly staggering to hold Mrs Laptoff's hand. 'This young man is just here from outside the walls to help, and to raise his merit. For a greater Tulo, remember?' Miss Genard was gently stroking the hand of her friend, who seemed to be falling into a frenzy.

'No!' She flailed her arms out, trying to push Ajay away and knocking over the drinks and furniture around her. *Blimey. I must have delivered the pills too late.* As more care assistants were rushing towards them, Ajay decided as he had completed his task, he better leave. He quickly walked away without wanting to look back, until a sudden crash seemed to shake even the walls out of their skin.

Mrs Laptoff was on the floor, having taken Miss Genard and more glasses down with her. *What a show.* Mrs Laptoff soon had scurrying care workers lifting her from the ground, but her burning eyes were only looking at Ajay.

She screamed at him.

'They'll find you.'

CHAPTER
TWELVE

A few hours later, Ajay was still thinking about Mrs Laptoff when his door chime rang loudly, causing him to jump up and spill his coffee across the desk. He swore as the chime rang again.

'I'm coming,' he shouted, as if whoever was at the building's entrance could hear him. If it was Genni or Ace, he'd have to let them in. They couldn't see *this*, he concluded, as he looked down at his desk and across his computer screens. The chime sounded again. He quickly yanked the electrical cable out from his Watch and held the device above his wrist, letting its strap dance around his skin. He dismissed the screens and swooped into the kitchen for a cloth. Back at his desk, he hurried to wipe up the coffee. The ringing of the chime yet again filled the apartment.

He stood back. Everything looked normal, until he noticed a tiny bit of the cable peeping out from its hiding place underneath his desk. As the chime sounded once more, Ajay dashed forward to ensure the cable couldn't be seen. Satisfied that nothing looked suspicious, he ran over to the intercom by the apartment door and spoke clearly into it.

'Hello.' There was no response so he tried again. Nothing. Ajay assumed it was some stuck-up kids, messing about and wasting themselves. Shrugging it off, Ajay turned away, but then the intercom erupted into a deafening continuous noise as they held their finger down on the button. Frustrated then, Ajay was back at its mouthpiece, shouting for any kind of response. Nothing. His wrist dinged at the elevation of his heart rate. *I'll go tell them to do one*, Ajay decided, swiping himself out of the apartment and heading for the elevator.

As he walked down the nicely lit corridor, the lights tastefully cased in light-blue shades, Ajay couldn't help but think about Mrs Laptoff again. He'd headed straight home after her outburst. He was constantly convincing himself that he had nothing to worry about. She was a deteriorating old woman with a crazy-talking tongue. No one would believe anything she said. There was one question Ajay couldn't dismiss just yet though – how did she know him, and his secret? The elevator arrived at the ground floor, its doors gilding open. Even if she did know, it didn't look like she'd done anything more than give him a bad report, meaning he'd earned a little less merit for today's shift than usual. That ticked him off. He'd done his usual trick to make up the difference, which he had tried to stop doing altogether, but sometimes, like today, he needed to. Before he turned the corner to reach his apartment building's entrance, another thought occurred to him. He could be walking straight into a trap. It could be an Unworthy wanting to take everything he owned, or a Command official there ready to finally arrest him, or the button could just be broken, or someone rang his place by mistake, or this was where he died. Ajay almost laughed. The rate at which his mind raced around sometimes was, even to him, unbelievable. He walked forward confidently, but still had his fists clenched, just in case.

Arriving at the door, his muscles relaxed and he sighed. It was Genni. He could see the top of her head, through the door's glass window, from where she sat on the front step. Ajay waved his wrist to open the door, bidding it to slide away.

'Why didn't you just ring me?' Ajay spoke with a jovial tone, but as he stepped closer to her, he had no more jokes. 'Genni?'

She was hunched up, leaning against the wall, barely moving.

Ajay stood, stunned, still expecting her to move or speak. Nothing happened. He couldn't even see the rise and fall of her chest. Realising what that meant, he promptly crouched towards her and pulled up her head. He felt instantly nauseous. Blue-green veins were angrily pulsating across her face and around her eyes. Ajay's insides suddenly felt severed, like there was something snapping him in two. *How can she be sitting here motionless? This shouldn't be happening. What is happening?* He began to shake her violently, but nothing.

His hands were unsteady, but Ajay managed to sweep her up in his arms and set off upstairs.

The smell of vomit from her clothes was sharp. Ajay moved faster. A loud, fast beeping proceeded from Genni's Watch. Ajay looked down – *an increased heart rate and lowered oxygen levels*. Ajay experienced a desperate relief knowing she was even still breathing. He moved quicker, scanning his wrist to the wall and flying through the gliding door. He lay her down gently on his bed, the veins on her face looking more irritated and her skin feeling volcanic on the back of his hands. He rushed to the windows, opening each one. Then, flinging open a kitchen cupboard, he found the first-aid box and ripped open the packet that contained the at-home cannula kit. Running back to Genni's side, he was thankful for the merit-making first-aid course he'd never thought he'd have to use. Ajay exhaled loudly to steady his nerves. Despite his hands shaking wildly, he managed to get the needle into a vein in Genni's right arm to restore some deficient fluid. He stroked her forehead as a tear fell from his eye onto her face and became stagnant on her skin.

He synced Genni's Watch to the screen port by the bed so he could monitor her stats. She seemed to be stabilising. Stumbling onto his feet, Ajay looked over her veins again and knew they weren't normal. Suspecting what it might be, he spoke into his Watch.

'Show me the side effects of *SkipSleep* overdose.'

His stomach churned. Sick and distorted faces that resembled Genni's flickered across his screen. He felt numb with guilt. *How did I not notice? I did notice. I knew there was something wrong, and I did nothing.* She could look after herself, but he'd failed to protect her. Ajay sat himself down on the trunk at the end of the makeshift hospital bed, looked out of his windows and saw a few humid clouds gathering in the twilight. He put his head in his hands, in an attempt to stop the pounding.

He looked back at Genni and whispered, 'What have you done?'

CHAPTER
THIRTEEN

Sitting on the trunk at the end of the bed, Ajay's hands were clasped together, arms braced on his thighs. He watched Ace as he threw his top layer T-shirt over the sofa and stood panting in a white vest, his muscles bulging. Ajay assumed that he'd run to the apartment after Ajay's call. Despite the trauma, Ajay still managed to feel jealous; he glanced over his own biceps, pathetic in comparison.

'I need her to wake up,' he said.

'Of course, you do, mate.' Ace caught his breath, walking over to Genni and placing the back of his hand on her forehead. He then looked to the screen monitoring her heart and fluid levels. 'When is the medical service getting here?'

Ajay fell silent, staring down at his black ankle boots.

'Jay? They've been notified, haven't they?'

'I stopped her Watch from sending the alert,' Ajay mumbled. He knew Ace would kick off about this. He didn't care. She was *his* girlfriend. He needed to be in control, though he hoped Ace would understand and not judge him for it. Before Ace could vent his anger, Ajay spoke loudly. 'She's the daughter of the biggest businessman in the City, her face would be plastered on every news headline. People would see her differently.' He shook his head. 'I can't let that happen. It's not what she'd want.'

'Are you completely mad? She could die.' Ace immediately sprang towards Ajay who could smell the remnants of kale chips on his breath. 'I'm calling them,' Ace said, lifting his wrist.

Ajay stood, grabbed Ace quickly and said calmly, 'Don't. Please. You can see her stats are good, just give her a few more hours and,' Ajay paused, 'if she's still not awake, we'll call them. OK?' Ajay looked at Ace with pleading eyes. He knew he looked weak, and it hurt.

'OK,' Ace sighed. 'OK.' Ajay, relieved, collapsed back onto the trunk. Ace came with him, patting his shoulder reassuringly.

Ace sighed and stroked the top of his recently shaved head. Ajay's mirror had suggested that trend was growing yesterday; there was a limit to how much he listened to technology. He instinctively tucked his own longer hair behind his ears and watched as Ace chewed his tongue. He did that when he was thinking.

Then he stopped and turned to Ajay with narrowed eyes. 'How did you stop her alert? She must have been past the optional limit.'

Ajay didn't panic. He'd expected the question. It had taken him minutes to get inside Genni's Watch using his hacking equipment, normalise her vital signs to reverse the alert and call the medical service off. 'I selected *no* just before she went over.'

Ace seemed to accept this, as Ajay looked at his friend with tired eyes before tapping at his wrist. 'When she wakes up, she'll be pretty exhausted, and I imagine she will need some time to recover. Would you mind helping me care for her? I can't miss any more work.'

At this request, Ace puffed out some air as Ajay assumed he considered the potential merit sacrifice of this agreement. After a few seconds, Ace agreed.

'Thank you. I'll keep her here, so here's access.' Ajay lifted his Watch to meet Ace's. A dinging sound vibrated in the momentary silence as the access key to his apartment was copied and transferred.

As Ace confirmed everything on his own Watch, he looked over at Ajay empathetically. 'You look dead, mate. Have you had any boosts at all?'

Ajay laughed solemnly and shook his head. He couldn't bear the thought of touching *SkipSleep*; he'd just settle for whatever natural sleep he'd get that night.

'I just can't stop thinking . . . She did that . . . I didn't stop it . . . and . . .' Ajay paused. His words fell over one another and he stood, yelling with a volume that bounced around the white-walled room. 'Command, as well. How can they even let it happen? With everything they have to stop it!' Ajay's veins were pumping as he finally expressed his frustrations out loud. They'd been simmering underneath all the adrenaline ever since Genni had turned up on his doorstep.

Ace twirled his lip in consideration, before jumping to Command's defence like a puppet.

'But they are trying to crack down on it. I heard they caught two admins just last week.' Ace's words grinded on Ajay. He felt angry at him. At everything. He closed his eyes as Ace continued to speak. 'Look, Genni made a bad decision and now she'll lose at least two days when she could have been making merit. It was stupid, but you love her.'

He was right. She was stupid. And he did love her. Though there were moments where he wished he didn't. It would be easier. Simpler. That's the problem with relationships: sacrificing precious time to invest in somebody else's problems. Maybe that wasn't fair. He didn't really know.

'You're lucky you've found her, and she's *right* for you,' Ace mumbled. Ajay sat back down, knowing there was something more behind Ace's comment and it was unlike him to say anything so cliché or romantic. The guy didn't have it in him. So, he meant something else. Wanting a distraction from his own depression about Genni, Ajay decided to push.

'What do you mean?'

'Can I have a boost?'

Ajay wasn't surprised by Ace's dismissal of the question. He calmly raised his arm towards the activation pad on the coffee table to welcome Ace to his *SkipSleep*. Ace swiped in. As the beeps and bleeps of the analysis sounded, Ajay looked over at the bed where he could detect Genni's light delicate breathing beneath the very thin white sheet. He then turned back to Ace, who was staring forward blankly as the progress bar reached 60 per cent.

'Ace? What's going on?' There was a gravity in Ace's eyes that Ajay had rarely seen, so he pushed further. 'You can tell me.'

Sighing and deflating his shoulders, Ace removed his arm from the system and fell backwards on the sofa, groaning. Ajay watched as his friend shifted his body uncomfortably, his head in his hands. He was mumbling to himself words like 'embarrassing' and 'pathetic'. Ajay had never seen Ace like this. It actually disturbed him. He felt too uncomfortable to let this linger, so he clenched his fist and whacked Ace on the arm. Ace moaned at the slight discomfort.

Ace puffed out more air. 'OK. So, I haven't mentioned this to anyone, and I swear, mate, if you do, I'll kill you.' Ace smirked, but his sincerity did not go unnoticed, so Ajay agreed. 'So, there's this girl. I met her on the sky train a few months back. She's gorgeous.' He laughed. 'I was amazed she was even vaguely attracted to me. We've been on dates, you know, but the thing is, this isn't like with a girl from work. You know, a short fling and that's it. I think this is the real deal. I've seriously fallen for her.'

'Ace, that's awesome. What's the problem?' Ajay was confused, and almost happy for him that he'd finally found someone he could actually commit to. Ace's body language changed; he shuffled on the sofa, the leather making a sucking sound beneath his legs.

'She's M-290.' Ace forced the words out quickly.

They were both silent then. Did Ace think Ajay would judge him? Well, he did. A little. M-290 was low. Embarrassingly so. Deep down, Ajay knew it shouldn't matter, but the relationships they had were crucial; they were fundamental to individual status, how people respected each other, and the merit opportunities offered. It was much more respectable to be single than go out with someone below your ranks. Ajay didn't know what to say. His throat felt dry. So, in the end, he said next to nothing.

'That's tough, mate.'

Placing his hand on Ace's shoulder, he could feel the hard surface of refined muscles beneath his fingers. He felt new respect for Ace; he never knew he could be vulnerable like this. In fact, vulnerability was not something he ever saw in anyone.

'Why don't you help her increase her merit?' Ajay suggested, knowing it was futile.

Ace shook his head. 'I think I'm coming to terms with the fact that our relationship would be too much of a risk. It's been killing me, though.' Ace stood up and walked over to the kitchen, probably to avoid Ajay seeing any emotion in his expression, but it was all in his voice.

'I'm sorry, mate,' Ajay called out in consolation.

Ace shrugged his shoulders as he started tapping at his Watch. 'It's OK. It's just a girl, right?'

Yeah, I guess it is. He looked out the window as a drone flew past. *Is Genni just a girl?* There was a low, hoarse moan as she started to wake up behind them.

CHAPTER
FOURTEEN

Opening her eyes, everything felt fuzzy. Strange images; memories of market stalls, drones and flickering light bulbs. A feeling of floating or being carried. More peculiar colours and shifting shapes. Her mind felt like the canvas of a cryptic painting, splattered and chaotic. A fast, black box hurtling towards her.

Genni moved her neck, her muscles sore and protesting. She willed her eyes to open further, but they kept drooping closed again, as if a magnet on her bottom eyelids was forcing them shut. Squinting, she could make out the white walls and a screen covered in coloured lines. She could hear a faint, consistent beeping. Not highly pitched, but soft and non-bothersome. Where was she? The hospital? Was this a dream? She heard herself groan as she tried to stretch her body out. It felt numb. She couldn't move. Her arms felt flaccid at her sides. The thought came that maybe they'd been tied to the bed she was lying in, that she'd been abducted, but as her fingers twitched and she started to regain feeling, she realised it was just a dead-cold weakness in her limbs. What had happened to her? Everything felt bleak. Her eyes started to release, and finally graced her with sight.

His face was there. Ajay. She relaxed, instantly knowing she was safe.

'How are you feeling?' Ajay wiped around her eyes with a wet cloth. The cool touch of the water refreshed her senses and brightened her clouded vision further. She saw the bed, the lines in her arms, Ajay, Ace and the brightness of the sun through the windows.

She responded with a dark croak in her voice. 'Not great.'

'Not surprised. You scared us silly, mate.' Ace stood behind Ajay, wearing a vest and training shorts. All his hair had been cut off. Genni noted how it made him look older. She felt something cool crawling around her fingers then. She knew it was Ajay's hand. Ignoring Ace, she looked at Ajay as he perched on the side of the bed. He looked exhausted. His wavy hair was uncombed and only tucked behind his left ear rather than both. The purple marks around his eyes intensified their confused stare, both sympathetic yet disappointed.

'What . . . what happened?' Genni asked.

'You'll have to tell us that, Gen,' Ajay said, monotonically.

'What do you mean?' She remembered feeling awful at the library, and that she went back Downtown to get help, but everything else was blank.

'You turned up here last night, half-dead on the doorstep.'

'What?' Genni questioned. *How had she got here from Downtown?* Her body then alerted her to a deeply dry throat, as if she was a plant out in the desert, holding out for the rainfall of a storm. 'Can I have some water?' Ace disappeared to the kitchen.

'So you don't remember anything?' Ajay asked, still gripping tightly to her hand.

'No . . . I . . .' Genni wondered if Ajay knew about the *SkipSleep*. He must have figured it out. *Please no.*

'I was at the library, and I went to the bathroom . . .' She paused, looking forwards rather than at Ajay. 'I got . . . a bit breathless . . . then, maybe I fainted?' She scrunched up her face like she was trying to remember something; it added to her performance of this half-truth. Her face relaxed. 'And I can't remember anything after that. I was just at the doorstep?'

That question was real. She really didn't know how she'd got here. Ace returned with a glass of water and offered it to her. So thirsty, she let go of Ajay's hand and raised up her right arm without hesitation.

Pain – sudden and agonising ricocheted along the entirety of her right shoulder. Genni hissed aggressively, feeling the little saliva left in her mouth dribble onto her chin.

'What's wrong?' Ajay quickly said, stroking her right arm tenderly. He took the water from Ace, setting it on the side. Genni could hardly speak, the throbbing crippling her ability to even think. She loosely pointed to her shoulder with her left hand. Tears trickled down her cheeks and snot fell from her nose. She was a mess. She knew that. Ajay got closer to her shoulder. Genni bit her lip in anticipation of more suffering. He was gentle though, and lightly lifted the top of her T-shirt away from her skin.

'Wow, Gen. That's broken.'

She managed to control her breathing and bend her chin so she could see her shoulder. There was a giant lump there, a bruised rainbow of colour: yellows, browns and purples. It resembled the miserable tones of some of her more sinister paintings. They were stashed in a cupboard in this apartment, unbeknown to Ajay.

She didn't understand. When or how had she been in a situation to break a bone? She went Downtown as soon as she caught her breath in the bathroom. That's what they'd said to do if she had any side effects from the enhanced *SkipSleep* they'd given her, to go back to them. She'd assumed they could help her, give her something else to settle things down. Though, when she'd got there, she remembered, her usual administrator wasn't there. It occurred to her then that she didn't even know his name.

The first time she'd gone, she was nervous and so didn't want to make conversation. She was terrified that anyone might see her, and she felt ashamed that she couldn't make enough merit with the normal, Command-accredited doses. After a while, the shame subsided and she didn't feel anything towards it at all, other than she needed it. She went in, got the injection and got out. Ultimately, this meant his name was never important, but this time, he wasn't there. There was another guy. Attractive, young, and . . . that was it. That was all she could remember.

'It's definitely broken. We need help.' Ajay lazily swiped on his Watch to call the medical service, Genni assumed. *He knows.* There was no doubt. He knew what she'd been doing. That's the only reason he wouldn't have already sent her to hospital. To protect her, so the media couldn't latch on to the fact that Boris Mansald's daughter was a failure. An addict who broke the rules. She almost opened her mouth to thank him when she stopped. Ajay held her gaze for a moment, a ring of bitter agitation crawling its way across his eyes, nose and lips. He threw his arms up in the air with exasperation and placed them tightly around the back of his head. He looked at Genni again. Not with love, compassion or even with anger, but as if he had nothing to say to her at all. He turned away, walking solemnly across the room and falling out of sight. Ace said nothing either, but looked down at the floor, following Ajay and leaving Genni alone. The pain in her shoulder was nothing compared to that. Tears began to stream down her face, which she didn't know was completely bruised, and she felt utterly and completely Unworthy.

CHAPTER
FIFTEEN

Developments in Tulo medicine allow a broken clavicle to be restored quickly and non-invasively. Microscopic, wormlike robots burrow their way, by programmed direction, under the skin either side of the broken bone. Using light, their telescopic capabilities and suction, they slither around and dissipate blood clots, and then delicately weave together cloths of artificial cartilage – tightly and comfortably, like a baby in its swaddle. Their work done, they return to the surface, leaving not even a hint of a scar in their wake.

Sat on his sofa, Ajay returned the medical explanation document to his Watch. 'The innovation is incredible,' he said to Mila as he walked over to the bed. Genni had been sleeping incessantly.

'It's not been without its setbacks, from what I've read.' Mila smiled at Ajay; she was wearing brown eyes but Ajay had preferred the blue, they worked better with the black make-up she'd laden around them. Petite and with a soft demeanour, Ajay always thought Mila had a simplistic beauty. He couldn't understand why she was changing that.

'Why didn't we see it, Ajay?' Her voice pierced through his thoughts with its sincerity as it carried over Genni's bare, partially healed face.

'I don't know,' he said honestly, a silence falling like a fog. *Is she blaming me?* Mila wasn't around much. He was with Genni all the time. So really, her question was: *why didn't you see it?* Though, every time he felt guilty, he came back to Genni and how it was her choice to overdose. Her choice to miss her medical check-ups, although Ajay did wonder why Command never picked up on that. It was a requirement. Maybe they didn't notice. Command oversights were no bad thing for him, usually. Now they've left him with a problem – the potential end to his relationship.

'So, how's work?' Ajay asked, needing to distract himself from Genni, his thoughts, everything.

'A bit tough recently. If I'm being honest . . .' Mila paused. 'I want to see patients, not screens. There's this other job going, where the merit and credit aren't as good, but it's on the trauma wards. Androids aren't sophisticated enough for the spontaneity of emergencies.' Mila struggled to stop herself. She couldn't take that job. Ajay knew it. He knew she knew it.

Ajay glanced out the window and saw a man stretching in the apartment building opposite. A screen floated above him, merit-tracking and displaying workout instructions.

'You think I should stay where I am?' Mila interpreted Ajay's non-response correctly as she looked at Genni's newly polished fingernails. Apparently, according to Pearl, she should still look good even when she was sick.

'Is it worth the merit loss?' Ajay responded, honestly again.

'I suppose. I do need to get higher, and I'm currently closer to the ones whose opinions matter than I would be on the wards. It's just that . . .' Mila didn't look up from Genni's hand, twisting her lip, holding back emotion. 'No, you're right. I've got to keep looking up,' she declared, slumping backwards in her seat.

Without his permission, Ajay felt a heaviness fall over him, like a blanket that would never keep him warm. He looked at Genni, the sweet freckles on her face deeper in colour than they had been for days. Their relationship was more than the system, wasn't it? Originally, no. To be vaguely attracted to each other, they had to have met a certain standard. What Ace had done with that M-290 was rare and, quite frankly, out of character. Ajay couldn't afford to be so rash, he'd risked too much for the life he had. But Genni was Genni, *his* Genni and he was *her* Ajay. There was worth in that, somewhere, but surely, he had to ask himself: was it worth the merit?

'OK. I'll get out of your way. I've already wasted ten minutes.' Mila rose and gave Genni a kiss on the forehead; Ajay stood with her, unsteady.

'You're doing a great job looking after her, Ajay.' Mila answered someone on her wrist. 'A really great job.' She glanced up and touched his arm before wandering towards the apartment door. 'By the way, where's your house drone? I've never known anyone above M-400 without one.'

Ajay grunted with laughter. She had to be so observant. 'Maybe I'm more of a simple soul than you thought.' Mila responded with a small nod and a charming smile as she walked away, the door sliding shut behind her.

About a week later, Ajay stood with his hands nestled in the pocket of his hoodie, observing the City on an unusually cool night. He watched a flock of drones fly over the continuous lights to the Outer-Rings and tried to ignore the others on the roof in his desperate attempt to be alone. There were oohs and aahs as they watched the billboards, but Ajay had found nothing in the shopping deals tonight. He looked up higher, hoping to see the shimmer of the night stars, but still they were overshadowed by the sparkles of the artificial. The largest billboard was not surprisingly the biggest disruption. Ajay scoffed at its headline – *Help you and your future family be their most effective selves* – but what captivated him was the image. A young Tuloian couple were in a lush apartment, full of green plants and expensive-looking furniture. They were laughing and holding onto one another while cradling a delightful giggling child between them. The girl was wearing bright-coloured tights, and her hair was tied up in pigtails. It hit Ajay right in the chest. Tara, his sister, used to wear tights like that. He missed her, like he missed his grandma. They were a family, a family like this one, a family like the one he could create with Genni. The one he wanted to create with Genni. He raised his arm to scan the button – *Book Couples Counselling Session* – but he hesitated. No, it's just marketing. That's not his future, that family didn't exist. It wasn't as simple as cuddling in front of the sofa. For one thing, he probably wouldn't have it with Genni. Not with the way things were going.

The two of them had spent the time since her operation in a painful roundabout of disappointment, short-lived reconciliations, falling merit and unspoken misery. Occasionally, they rowed about Genni's bad choices. Other times, they spoke practically and rationally about how Genni's merit had continued to decline. She was struggling at work; her energy was sapped, so volunteering or personal merit-making were tough too. She needed to pull herself together, as Ajay had repeatedly told her. There'd been this invisible fence between them that was slowly growing higher. For Ajay, the distance would make it easier when her merit fell so low that it could affect his own.

As Ajay looked over the picture of the sparkling family, that distance felt even greater. He couldn't see Genni's face in place of this blonde woman with fantastical teeth. He was starting to feel the pain Ace felt after ditching his M-290 lover. Surely this would be worse. It wasn't just a fling. It was three years down the line and was supposed to be *it. What do you do when the one you love is no longer Worthy of you?*

As he could feel his emotions building, he turned away from the perfect, pretend couple and felt numb with confusion. He hated himself for getting so attached. It was never his intention when he created this life. He needed to walk, clear his head.

Down and out on the street, he turned left towards the Inner-Inner-Ring, strolling along at pace. It was around eight in the evening, the main commuter time; thousands of people scurried along under the rays of the televised ball from the Social Sphere. Ajay spotted a few school kids marching earnestly towards their destination, gripping cautiously to books. Others stared zombie-like up at the adverts while passers-by scrolled through websites or *Personi* profiles on floating screens. He never cared much for social merit. Never needed it. Though Genni had got into it since her accident; she was on the phone to Pearl every other minute for hints and tips.

It was exhausting listening to them and having to take part in it. He thought back to the week before.

'Just a quick picture.' Genni had been sitting on the bed, holding her Watch in front of her after demanding Ajay put his head on her shoulder.

They both smiled and the camera snapped. Genni had typed at her Watch while asking, 'Have you spoken to Pearl yet?

Ajay, who had walked away, shook his head and groaned at the question he'd heard four times that week.

'Please just call her? She won't stop asking, you know what she's like.' Genni had been wearing green sweatpants and a baggy top, almost giving the illusion that she was relaxed and comfortable. She had now surrounded herself with a large screen, displaying volunteering opportunities and an article titled 'Top ten tips for gaining merit through Personal Development'.

'What makes her think her channel will improve with me on it?'

'That's a question you can ask Pearl. She just wants to chat about how you can help each other. If for nothing at all, do it for me.' Genni had continued to scroll her finger down the screen while reading.

She'd crunched him up like a tin can. Did she not realise how much he'd already done? He'd lost merit with how much time he'd dedicated to her recovery. He had breathed slowly to prevent himself from erupting, resulting in an unheard mumble from his mouth, 'Yeah, that and saving your life.'

'What was that?' Genni had asked, vulnerably. Ajay was silent. He had opened the fridge and hidden his face behind its silver, mirrored door. As he had looked over the lack of produce inside it, he'd heard the swooshing of the sliding door. With a bottle of water in hand and the fridge closed, he stood static and gazed over the empty space on the bed where Genni had just been sitting. A notification had pinged from Ajay's Watch. There he was. His beaming, smiling face resting on Genni's shoulder. The caption read: 'I've got myself a man who supports me no matter what. Don't stop trying to find yours.'

Now walking towards the Quarters and throwing his hood over his head, he knew he was still mad about the photo. She hadn't even shown him for his approval. It was awful. He looked scruffy in an unironed, stained T-shirt, his hair uncombed and wild. She should have checked with him. Tulo was able to see him, sloppy and unprofessional. *Is that how they'll see me if I stay with her? Will I reach the Quarters quicker with or without her?*

There was suddenly no space for that question, for as he approached a sky train bridge down an unlit alley, he was forced to a stop.

Something was moving beneath it.

He was standing twenty metres away. Whatever it was looked like a large, overfilled bin bag, shuffling slowly towards him and weakly dragging itself along the ground. The black was impenetrable. Ajay couldn't see anything further. What was he thinking, walking down a dark alley at night? The only places that hid from the City's sometimes insufferable light. He considered running, but something willed him to stay. It could be a wild animal that had migrated from the Country, ready for a meal, but curiosity had its teeth into him already. As the creature moved closer, a sky train roared over the bridge above. Its flickering lights revealed that the beast was really a man.

'Please . . .' His voice was dry and coarse with a hint of desperation. 'Help.'

Ajay was close but the train was gone and so was the light. The image of the man had flashed momentarily to the point where Ajay questioned if it was real. He lifted his wrist, enabled the torch from his Watch so he could see the man in full colour. Part of him was relieved he wasn't going to be attacked, the other disgusted by what he saw.

The man's dirty nostrils flared above a sweaty, overgrown beard. His face sagged and was decorated with colonies of bruises over his ballooned cheeks. His black T-shirt was ripped around the neckline, revealing a tuft of presumably unwashed hair. Unworthy. Ajay was sure of it. No one else in the City looked like this. Ajay didn't blame them. *Why self-care when you have no merit to live for?* Following the man's shaky body, Ajay saw a small tattoo on the underside of his right wrist; an imprint of the three-layered flame he knew well. It was only then, under the limited light of his Watch's torchlight, did Ajay see the real problem.

CHAPTER
SIXTEEN

Just below the man's right knee and trailing down his leg was an open gash, pressed on by the man's blood-covered jacket. *He might already be a goner, or his leg will be, especially if it gets infected. What am I supposed to do?* There was no benefit to Ajay in helping him. In fact, there was more to lose than gain. If anyone were to see him assisting an Unworthy, he'd be condemned. Plus, this Unworthy didn't deserve his help. *They don't contribute; they're lazy, mostly, and selfish, in a way, and just look at this guy.* He was drenched in every imaginable detestable substance: blood, sweat, saliva. Not to mention the hole in his leg meant that Ajay would likely have to carry him. Ajay started to feel queasier the more he stared. It wasn't his problem. He put his right foot forward, ready to cross the road, but something dragged him back. A sort of compassion was resurfacing that he hadn't felt for a long time. He groaned internally. *Is this Genni's fault?* Her issues had turned him soft and more susceptible to helping other people without the merit reward. It was a curse that he was born into and had managed to repress in recent years. He knew he shouldn't give into it – he couldn't sacrifice too much, he had worked too hard – but the guy could die. No one was around. It wouldn't be seen. He turned his body round before his mind could stop him.

As he got closer, the man began to wail. 'Oh, thank you, thank you,' he said. Ajay wanted him to be quiet, but he didn't have to tell him. The man fell silent and stumbled in exhaustion into Ajay's arms.

'It's OK,' Ajay said as he held him up, trying to ignore the stench. He needed to cough, or heave, he wasn't sure which. 'How long have you been here like this?'

The man took a big breath and Ajay heard the whistle in his chest. 'About twenty minutes. Two other Unworthies saw me lying here. Neither helped.' He lifted a bruised hand to wipe his battered face, which reminded Ajay of Genni's shoulder; her olive skin disguised by the colours of purple and yellow to paint a dull pattern along her collarbone.

'Do you mind?' Ajay pointed to his leg and the man shook his head. Ajay gently lifted the limb closer to the flashlight on his Watch, listening to the man's hisses of pain. 'It doesn't look critical, nothing a few Stitch Bots won't fix. I can pay for a hover cab to the hospital for – '

'No. No hospital.' He yelped again as his panicked movement agitated his leg.

'Why not? You need stitches,' Ajay said, desperate to get away, or at least cover his nose with his hand.

'Why can't you do them manually?' the man asked, almost confidently. Ajay was silent for a moment. He gazed over the discoloured man's face, his eyes speaking of some vulnerable defiance. He'd never met an Unworthy who would expect such a request to be granted. The audacity of it. *This was a mistake.* He slowly shook his head, standing over the man who appeared frightened by Ajay's sudden lack of empathy, but something pulled Ajay's thoughts back again. He needed his help. Everything within him wanted to walk away, but he just couldn't. Upon the realisation that the stinking idiot would have to come to his apartment, Ajay closed his eyes and took a steady, deep breath.

He sighed. 'OK. I'll do them manually.' The man started to spit out his thanks, but Ajay interrupted and raised his hand. 'Only if you answer two questions.' The man deflated again.

'Why no hospital?' Ajay repeated.

The man turned his face away and Ajay could hear him whispering to himself. *And I'm about to take this psycho to my apartment?*

'I'm . . . in trouble with Command.' The man spoke quietly, and Ajay raised his eyebrows. *Brilliant. A criminal. An Unworthy – filthy, injured, crazy criminal.* He knew how to pick them.

'I dunno why they're bothering me. I'm just a street seller. I guess my stash isn't exactly acquired in the most legal way, I nick it sometimes, but surely there's much bigger players for them to be worrying about.' He hissed again. 'No hospital because the TPD will find me.'

OK, not a criminal. A petty criminal. Do I believe him?

'That's how I bust my leg, you should probably know. I was running from a swarm and managed to lose them by jumping over a wall. It was covered in that historical bird wiring and I caught my leg. Ripped right through me.' The man shrugged his shoulders at the misfortune.

Ajay considered this particularly unlucky, given how little of it was around since birds had been frightened away by drones years ago. *Do I believe him? Do I have an option? The man's desperate.*

He gently rested a hand on the man's shoulder, reassuring himself that he could clean it later.

'If they really wanted you, they'd have overridden the VPG settings.' The man peered up at Ajay with a building smile that brought colour back to his cheeks. It was a look Ajay wasn't sure what to do with; it was almost comforting but sent sinister shivers down his back. Does he suspect something? Know something? *No, Ajay. Stop with the paranoia.* It wasn't uncommon for someone to know about the Virtual Positioning Guide settings. And despite the man's position and status and general repulsiveness, there was something genuine buried beneath all the dirt. Ajay could feel it.

'You had a second question?' the man asked.

'Yes, what's your name?'

'Saman,' he said. 'But please, call me Sam.'

Back at his apartment, Ajay sighed heavily at Sam's bristly voice barking in his ears.

'Steady, man . . . steady.'

Lowering him onto his bed, Ajay strained through the sweat; the guy was heavier than he looked, presumably through consuming too much stolen and fatty food. He didn't have a nutritious diet; the skin of his face was cracked, and his belly ballooned over his waistline. The walk back had been anything but pleasant. Ajay had needed to support Sam all the way, while he hopped about pathetically on one leg. It probably didn't help that Ajay insisted they go the long way round away from the crowds, and he'd pulled them into side alleys each time someone appeared on the street. Ajay had taken the opportunity every time Sam yelped in pain to threaten taking away his aid; it kept him quiet. At least, until they got back, and Sam started shrieking like a traumatised fox and Ajay fancied pressing on his wound as a discipline method. Or he could leave him out on the street where he came from. Of course, he opted for neither.

'I've got to get some supplies for the stitches. I'll give you some fluids and painkillers now, so that will see you through until I get back.'

He went about preparing things, all the while feeling Sam watching him with sceptical eyes. *What is he looking at? Doesn't matter.* Without another word, Ajay turned on his heels and headed out into the night again.

Dashing into the light moving crowd, Ajay felt like running away. What was he doing? It was crazy. Completely and utterly imbecilic. An Unworthy was in his bed, on drugs, in dirty, stinking clothes. Ajay picked up his pace, swerving between people and drones, the noise of the City feeling louder than usual.

The social discreditation could be catastrophic. Helping an Unworthy was down there with becoming one. Why waste time on those who have already wasted themselves? If word got out, he could be excluded from his networks, lose the merit opportunities that tidily came with them, and a struggling girlfriend would be the least of his problems. Ajay stopped, causing a woman behind him to collide into him.

'Oi, watch it,' she said as she moved around his body. She was small, her hair tied nicely into two sweet buns, but the scowl she gave him was anything but.

Seriously, what am I doing? Ajay wiped the sweat from his face. He took himself away from the crowd to lean against a wall. *Just breathe.*

His thoughts started to darken. He wondered whether he could just leave Sam there. He could stay at Genni's, or Ace's. Let the guy starve or bleed out. Then when Ajay had been gone long enough, he could just dispose of the body somehow, and no one would ever miss him. It was unlikely he had a family, or even if he did, he probably wasn't any more useful to them alive than dead. Ajay felt his wrist vibrate. He swiped at it and Ace's face appeared.

Ace stumbled over his opening words, narrowing his eyes at the camera. He was at the office, still wearing his tie with the top button done up. *Hollday must still be at work. I should be at work.*

'Where are you?' Ace finally managed.

'Just out. Getting some stuff from the shop. I missed the drone cut-off.' Ajay congratulated himself on his quick thinking; he had to explain why he'd go out during a main working hour.

'Ah, I hate that. When are the suckers going to be 24/7?'

'Who knows.' Ajay told himself to relax; Ace wouldn't pick up on his panicked, heavy breathing.

'Anyway, you coming back in?'

'No. Not tonight.'

'Fancy a drink later on?'

'I've got some work to do at home.'

'OK, just, I know things aren't great with Gen right now. Wondered if you wanted a distraction.'

Has Genni been talking to Ace? Stop it. He couldn't get angry about that; there was already too much going on. Like the Unworthy in his bed, the one he was considering starving to death.

'I'm good. Thanks.'

They wrapped up the conversation by agreeing to a game of tennis the next day, and Ajay breathed a sigh of relief without knowing what he was relieved about. Ace was never going to suspect what was happening. Ajay still had a big problem. He cursed under his breath. Why did he get himself into this situation? He could have just walked away, but no, he went through the trouble of carrying the stench into his apartment, and then went out to get him medical supplies. Maybe he could help him, no one would find out, and he could get back to his life. Then again, how long would that take?

Ajay then realised he had left a thief in his apartment. A thief. Ajay felt like punching the wall behind him. He could return to an empty apartment, all his possessions sold for credit to spend on fatty foods. As his mind moved towards hysteria, Ajay reminded himself that the flesh of Sam's leg was hanging off – he couldn't move enough alone to even steal a glass. However, Ajay needed a plan. So, what was it? Help him, leave him to die, or get rid of him quickly? He hadn't the first clue of how to get rid of a body. On that thought, he felt sick. He was so twisted.

The last time he felt like this was before, when he'd considered cutting off a dead man's finger. That was equally as disturbing as mulling over the disposal of a body. Memories flickered through Ajay's mind. There was also a Command guard there, downstairs, while Ajay scrambled and hurried to warm up the dead man's hands. It was stressful, and a close call. Ajay ended up lying underneath the bed of the dead guy, holding his breath while Command dealt with the body. He'd been successful, though. Ajay smiled; it was quite a moment. He wouldn't be where he was without it. Would he really risk it all for an Unworthy? The question remained: did he need to kill Sam?

CHAPTER
SEVENTEEN

Your skin's moisture levels have improved by 10 per cent since this time last week.

Genni looked at herself in the mirror as it spoke, the screen displaying its analysis. It was suggesting a soft brown, neutral blend for her eyeshadow, after she had told it she was going to work. It would be the first time she'd put on a full face of make-up since the overdose and having surgery. Working from home had been painfully lonely and Genni thought she might be ready to get back, even though in reality she didn't know how she felt. It was as if she had been put through a fire, and she wasn't sure how to soothe the burns. She could hide them. Cover them over, like the foundation and concealer that masked her freckles. Or she could display her trauma openly, and not be ashamed of what she'd gone through. Yet, would anyone listen? Accept it? The only way she'd known people react to *SkipSleep* addicts, or those who overdosed, was with scorn. They were seen as failures or cheaters of the system, meaning she could never be open about her struggle.

No, she'd hide behind the lie about food poisoning her father had told, though the freedom it gave her only trapped her more. The withdrawal made it worse too. She'd had on and off fevers, vomited occasionally, but above all, it was the muscle aches that crippled her. When they came on, it was like her body was a heavy-loaded hover car she had to push up a hill. The lack of energy was depressing, and she'd only coped because of her regimented sleep schedule. Genni had to make peace with that. She couldn't paint. Her active time had to be for merit, without which she would lose everything. She couldn't bear the thought of not having Ajay. She knew in her heart that he wouldn't stay if the merit went low enough. She wouldn't blame him. She'd wish she'd never met him, but she wouldn't blame him. It was moments like that when she wondered what kind of city she lived in. A city where she couldn't do what she loved, or even be with who she loved if she really let her score drop.

Everything reminded Genni of painting. Even as she patted the brush into the brown eyeshadow palette, she thought of a fresh, blank canvas and the potential of what she could create. She'd always painted best when she had feelings to express. The brush tickled her eyelid as she followed the indication line on her mirror. Her thoughts returned to Ajay. Despite the intensity of her recovery, she couldn't help but worry about him. The trauma probably sparked repressed emotions; a reminder of the loss he'd suffered when his parents died. He said that his childhood was better than some, being raised by his grandma, who sounded amazing. Genni had longed to meet her, and Ajay had assured her that she would soon. Maybe she never would. But on those rare occasions when they spoke about his childhood, Genni had always noticed the sadness in his eyes. Perhaps it had all been too much, that he'd almost lost her too over something so superficial, so reckless on her part. She knew she hadn't explained herself well to him. It didn't help that she still couldn't remember what happened. The broken collarbone was still a mystery, though she continued to have the same flashes of memory: the market stalls, Downtown, and the movement of something large coming towards her. She just couldn't distinguish what it was.

She'd accepted by that point that she wouldn't remember, and actually, it didn't matter. She had to move forward. There was no point dwelling on her mistakes. Work hard, control the merit, no *SkipSleep* for a while, and just hope that Ajay would be there to help her.

She blinked a few times and beheld herself again in the mirror, eyelids shimmering with glitter. Her full, blue eyes spoke loudly. *You can do this.*

CHAPTER
EIGHTEEN

Despite trying to convince himself otherwise, Ajay felt that Sam was too young to die. He guessed around the mid-forties. Even though he was pretty sure that the world wouldn't miss the Unworthy, Ajay wasn't the one to make that decision. The decision he *had* made was to bring him back to his apartment to help him. He had to commit to that. Having resisted the darkness within himself, he'd made it home with the supplies.

He was welcomed by a disturbing snore, which was something he didn't often hear. He'd only ever seen people sleeping this deeply at the retirement village. That was fair enough; they'd already experienced the necessary lifetime of sleepless activity. So, to observe a middle-aged man in a tranquil rhythm of snorting and sniffling was slightly disconcerting. Although, knowing he was still there and not having stolen anything was a relief. Ajay walked towards the bed to find Sam's gaping mouth sending trickles of dribble down his T-shirt and onto the bed linen.

Nasty. He closed his nostrils again to the smell and pulled up a chair, also spotting the yellow stains of what might have been sweat or grease seeping into the bed.

Vile. He told himself to get over it. *Sort Sam out, then kick him out.* Ajay reached out his hand slowly and lightly prodded Sam's shoulder. Clenching his jaw at Sam's lack of response, he tried again, but this time he didn't allow himself to be so gentle.

Sam shuffled in bed and groaned, his eyes flickering as they lazily adjusted to the light. As Ajay watched him rub his face, he was reminded of the way Genni looked after she slept naturally. It was rare, but he liked it. She would rub her eyes like Sam, but not in his brutish way, in a more endearing way as if she were relaxed and peaceful. Though that was a façade. She was never relaxed and peaceful. None of them were. Ajay noticed the tattoo on Sam's wrist again. *So interesting.*

Sam spoke. 'You got the stuff, then?' *How outspoken and demanding can you be?* If Ajay were in his position, he certainly wouldn't talk to a M-460 in that way.

'Yeah.'

Noticing Sam's look of anxiety, Ajay wondered if he was afraid of needles. He lowered the anaesthetic needle to the skin of Sam's leg, the bed covers ruffling suddenly as Sam moaned and clenched his fists around the bedframe. After a few insertions, Ajay got to work, fabricating the stitches. Having moved a screen port over to the end of the bed, Ajay ordered the screen to display an outdated instructional video for manual stitches. He muted it. Knowing that Sam was watching him closely, Ajay evaluated the leg.

'You're going to need at least six here.' Turning to the video for guidance, and after checking the anaesthetic was doing its job, Ajay began. He had avoided asking Sam any personal questions. He didn't want to get involved or attached. He'd once had a habit of doing that and had worked hard to wean himself away from people not worthy of him. But he couldn't stop thinking about Sam's tattoo; the small three-layered flame sitting there on the underside of his wrist. Ajay didn't think it would be rude to ask. After all, he was helping him, in *his* apartment, and he was M-460 and Sam was Unworthy. Even if it was rude, could Sam do anything about it?

Ajay posed the question bluntly. 'So, how did you fall out of merit?' Sam instantly raised his eyebrows in amazement as Ajay had clearly guessed right. 'Your tattoo,' Ajay gestured towards Sam's right wrist where the small flame sat black and blue on his skin. 'I've never seen someone born Unworthy sporting the Prosper branding. So, did you work there?'

'Yeah,' Sam said quietly. 'The tattoos were a stupid thing we did one Liberation Day.'

Heartache seemed to paint itself across the canvas of Sam's face. Ajay didn't feel sorry for him. Unworthies in the City weren't there by chance, they'd often committed crimes or missed work deadlines, leading to lost jobs and falling merit. It was a destiny of their own making. Something didn't quite add up about Sam, though. If he contributed enough to get in at Prosper, Ajay couldn't understand why he'd end up a petty thief. *I can't let that happen to me.*

'What happened?' Ajay finished off the first stitch.

'I guess . . . it was my kids really,' Sam said sorely. 'They live with their mother, in the Quarters.'

'You lived in the *Quarters*?' Ajay paused, disbelieving, with the thread held high. A thought passed through his mind that terrified him. Something he had always known, but never let surface. *If a Glorified could fall, surely anyone could.* He'd never heard of it before, though. It wasn't something they ever advertised or talked about in the news, which made him wonder if it happened a lot more than Command cared to let on.

'I was born there,' Sam continued. Ajay felt his eyes widen. He was born there? He had been raised in the Quarters? Ajay couldn't understand it and Sam clearly noticed. 'I know. How could a lad with a top education, Glorified parents, a Financial District job, end up like me?'

Ajay didn't say anything.

'I told too many lies,' Sam mumbled, took a breath, and looked uneasy. *Lies.* The word almost took Ajay's breath away. He was suddenly very uncomfortable with the conversation, almost as if he didn't want to hear any more. If lies ruined Sam, they could ruin him too.

'My wife and I were part of a high network. I was happy. Gaining reputation, merit and credit. And I was good at it,' Sam paused. 'Really good. People respected me.' Sam paused again but this time, his eyes welled as he looked out to the glow of the lights through the window. Ajay was tempted to tell him he didn't have to carry on, but before he could even convince himself not to, Sam spoke again.

'Then I had kids, and priorities shifted slightly. Suddenly our goal in life was to fabricate their lives, to shelter and guide them; just to make sure *they* gained reputation, merit and credit. In everything they did.'

Ajay spotted Sam following the movements of his hands, going up and down with each weave. 'But Cynthia got obsessive about it. She made them stay in the Education Centre after hours, restricted them from seeing friends, doing creative things, leisure activities – all so they could concentrate on personal development or volunteering at every opportunity.' Sam shook his head and adjusted the bedsheet to cover more of his torso. *To be fair to Cynthia, that's not a bad parenting strategy.* It only seemed right to make sure children had the best shot at a merit-filled life. 'She was suffocating them. The relentless focus on merit was making them miserable.'

Ajay stopped for a second. Suffocation. The word suspended in his mind, dancing around his brain cells. Genni had said that yesterday, when she'd shown him her paintings.

'He's suffocating me. Like he has my whole life,' Genni had exclaimed as she was pacing across the black, furred rug in front of Ajay's sofa in bare feet. She had received a message from her father, detailing his disappointment. Apparently, he'd had a lot of press enquiries about his 'poorly' daughter.

Ajay thought she should be grateful. Her father's influence had saved her from discreditation by her colleagues and the media. Saved her from being reported. That would have been a hefty merit fine.

They'd flung a few tight words back and forth as Ajay expressed his frustration. He was sick of her whining, and she still hadn't told him why she did what she did. The overdose. Her trips to Downtown.

'Why did you do it, Gen? Really? It can't just have been for your father's approval.'

In the heat of her temper, Genni had darted quickly towards the closet room at the back of Ajay's apartment.

'What are those?' he'd asked as she'd returned holding three cardboard tubes.

'They're why I did it.' She'd frantically pulled out a large piece of card or paper, laying it out and weighing the edges down with empty glasses. It was a painting. Alive with colour. Blues, pinks, purples, yellows and greens. He'd gazed over the detail; the intricacies of water falling down a rocky hill and splashing beside deep-green leaves and trees. It was a place he'd never seen but would love to exist, like something from a Country film. And it was one of the first images he'd seen in years without the gloss of a screen. It was beautiful. He'd felt love and hatred all at the same time. Love for her undeniable beauty and talent. Hatred for the fact he didn't know. She'd never told him. *Or did I never let her?*

As he continued stitching up Sam's leg, silently, he ran over the outbursts that followed. She'd claimed that she needed extra boosts to subsidise time for her meritless activity and that she so often felt Unworthy under the likes of Pearl, him, her brother and father. *How is that my fault?* She had no idea what it was like to feel Unworthy. Not like the man lying in his bed. He hadn't felt angry. He'd felt done. She was too much. He didn't care at that moment. He didn't care about his feelings for her. He didn't care about the insanely awesome things she could clearly do with a pencil and paintbrush. He didn't care that it gave her joy. That was the moment when he truly realised; if he wasn't careful, she would pull him down with her.

That was the last time they'd spoken. Ajay snapped out of his trance when his wrist vibrated. He looked down, placing the stitching needle on the bed.

Hi, Ajay, just a reminder that no merit points have been added to your merit score in five hours, seventeen minutes and fifty-six seconds. Is it time to do something of worth?

He paused, feeling slightly disorientated. Even though he knew he shouldn't, he dismissed the message and felt a weight of anxiety in his stomach.

'I wouldn't worry about the alert.' Sam appeared more relaxed. 'One time won't kill you. I don't get them anymore. They stop bothering after a while.' Sam waved his Watch at Ajay; it was dusty and covered in a dried yoghurt-like substance. It confirmed Ajay's suspicion. There was nothing about this man that wasn't dirty. Ajay tried to hide his grimace. Despite the clock ticking, and how he wanted this Unworthy out of his place, he couldn't help it. He needed to know more of Sam's story. Would Genni be like him, and could that help him decide about their future?

CHAPTER
NINETEEN

'What did you do with your kids? To make them feel less suffocated?' Ajay gathered himself and continued with the stitching.

'I offered to start picking them up from the Education Centre for my wife. She could then take more time for her own merit-making. Well, that's how I played it. I said I'd take them to extracurriculars, ensure they were learning the Tulo values, everything they needed for "adult life" . . .' He gestured with his sandy hands. '. . . that they didn't cover in the centre. But really, I'd take them for full-fat ice cream and chocolate and let them watch those old movies with no educational merit. Occasionally, I even took them over to the Side. They have playgrounds there with no drone surveillance. They loved it.' Sam smiled as he spoke, shrugging his shoulders. 'I just wanted them to be kids.'

Ajay thought of Genni and her father. Something hit him like a machete slicing through wood. Was she ever a kid, like he was? Did she ever have anything like a grandmother tucking her into bed at night, and telling her a story, or playing stupid games with her friends? Anything?

'So, your wife found out?' he asked as he prepared the final stitch.

'Obviously.' Sam spoke calmly. 'To cut a long story short, she blocked me out. From my kids, our networks, my colleagues. It started with my socials. No one engaged with me or liked my content so naturally my sphere of influence diminished. That wasn't too critical merit-wise.' Sam swallowed and rubbed his chest. 'Losing my kids completely floored me. At first, I saw them on weekends. But as they grew, they didn't want to spend time with me. So, I struggled to get to work on time, meet deadlines, have any physical or mental motivation to do personal development or community work. I lost the job. Then, someone reported me for what I did with my kids.'

'Do you think it was your wife?' Ajay asked.

'I don't know. I hope not. It doesn't matter now. I fell under M-200. And then below M-100.' Sam stopped talking and smiled, which Ajay could tell was forced. 'Just the way it went for me in the end.'

Ajay set down his instruments and struggled to find the words to say next. He felt nervous to feel sympathy for Sam. It was his own fault. He chose his kids' short-term happiness over their long-term success and well-being. It was right he was punished for that, but it didn't sit well with him. Ajay tried to ensure his facial expression didn't change; he didn't want Sam to sense any of his care towards him. It seemed that he failed.

'It is what it is,' Sam said, lifting his head. 'Eh, maybe I'll be the first Unworthy below M-100 to make it back to Glorified.' Ajay didn't bother laughing, knowing that Sam wasn't expecting it; his irrational positivity hung toxic in the air. 'I have wondered about moving out to the Country, like those crazy folk they're talking about Downtown. One woman apparently—'

The ping of the door chime cut through the moment. 'Are you expecting someone?' Sam snapped his head to the door, eyes wide.

Ajay shot up and swiftly made his way to the intercom.

'It's the TPD, isn't it? They found me!' The veins stood out in Sam's chubby neck. Ajay wondered then if he was right. He started to think about the best place to hide an Unworthy. They'd have no time. He hesitantly pressed the intercom.

'Ajay?' The familiar voice travelled through the apartment. Ajay breathed again. It wasn't often that Blake called.

'Blake, you scared me to death,' Ajay said.

'Are you going to let me up, then?'

Sam desperately shook his head, sitting closer to the end of the bed with his leg raised.

Ajay obviously wasn't going to let him up; he'd helped an Unworthy. His reputation was too important. He couldn't risk it.

'I can't at the minute, Blake. Work is mad. Is it urgent?' Ajay lied. It was easy for him.

'Oh, no bother, no bother. I just wanted you to know that I've got a new job.'

'That's great, Blake,' Ajay said, his eyes fixed on Sam, who was rubbing his throat, clearly uncomfortable.

'But obviously, I've had to stop dancing and I've dyed my hair back. I'm a new man.'

'Oh, right.' Ajay suddenly felt a grieving in his chest. *He loved dancing.*

'I've finally listened to you guys; I wasn't getting enough merit. I didn't want to end up on a downward spiral towards Unworthiness. After all, soon life wouldn't be as glittery without being able to hang out with my beautiful friends,' he said, and Ajay could imagine his white teeth beaming.

'We'd still hang out with you,' Ajay said unthinkingly, before being reminded of everything he'd been saying to Genni, Ace's lover . . . and then there was Sam. The thoughts quickly reminded him of how unlikely that was, and how Blake's sarcastic cackle in response was completely appropriate. He continued through the intercom.

'So, I've got an apprenticeship in Transport Engineering. I've been there a week, *and* I'm close to the apartment I wanted because of it. I'm definitely around the *right* people.' Blake then said he needed to go before adding a parting thought. 'I have to say, I'll miss my pink hair, though.'

'I'll miss it too,' Ajay kept his finger steady on the intercom.

'Do you think I could dance sometimes, though? This girl I met online enjoys it, and I don't want to let her down.'

Ajay could feel the grey fog of disappointment drift through his voice. Is that what Genni felt every time she couldn't paint? Every time she enjoyed sketching and then beat herself up for time-wasting? Maybe he'd misjudged her. Maybe he was wrong. It felt painful to even admit that to himself. He decided to never say it out loud.

'Sure, you can go sometimes. It's up to you, Blake,' Ajay managed. He'd never said that to Genni, he realised, but with her, there was more at stake for him.

Blake quickly finished the conversation and bid Ajay 'farewell'. Ajay said goodbye and lingered by the door, not knowing what to think about Blake, Sam or Genni. Why was this all suddenly happening? He'd never seen it like this before. As if their happiness being governed only by a number, people's opinions and unrealistic expectations was a negative thing. Didn't it push them forward? Of course it did. But what about love? Relationships? It was right for their whole lives to be a frantic, endless race; day by day they ran, furiously pressing for progress, for the greater score that their contribution had promised. Genni fell off that wheel and Ajay must be the one to pick her up again, while keeping his score healthy. If anyone could do that, he could. But did he want to?

His moment of reflection was severed by Sam's gruff voice. 'That's a shame, that.'

Ajay walked over to the bed, saying nothing, looking at the shrivelled offcuts of thread that lay side by side on the bed.

'The kid's dancing.' He was getting frustrated with Sam's audacity by this point. He didn't know Blake, who was way above his score, so he wasn't in a position to offer him sympathy, but Ajay decided to take the comment as genuine.

'Yeah, it is. But it will be better for him in the long run.' Like it would be better for Genni to do less painting. And like it would have been better for Sam to have not taken his kids where he did. It was tough love, but good for them.

'It will be. If you can't beat the system, join it. It's my biggest regret.' Sam glanced lifelessly down to his leg, looking tired again, the purple tinge around his eyes even darker than before. Despite his anxiety, Ajay decided to let him rest there until morning.

It wasn't long until morning came, with the white sun sneaking over the horizon. Ajay had spent the night busying himself to make provisions for Sam – who he needed out. This had been a one-off. He needed to get back to his life. The sun was barely shining when Sam awoke and Ajay ushered him to move quicker. He found some crutches in the back closet from when he'd twisted his ankle, and gave Sam some fresh clothes, allowed him to use the shower and packed up some food in an old satchel. He'd also managed to give himself the merit he could have earned during the past twelve hours. *It's only right.*

'OK. That's everything I can give you now,' Ajay said eagerly, as he steadied a clean-smelling Sam to the apartment door.

'Thanks, pal,' Sam said, standing in the open doorway. He turned to depart, but then turned back. 'Why did you help me?'

They stood for a few moments, considering each other. Ajay was still truly repulsed by him. Most of him hoped that he would never see Sam again, while the rest of him felt glad they'd met. Their encounter had somehow helped him and had given him something familiar. At that moment, some words ran around his head in his grandmother's voice; ones he was taught yet would never say out loud.

Ajay shrugged his shoulders. 'Somebody had to.'

'No, they didn't.' Sam didn't say another word, nor did he look back as he hobbled down the corridor.

When Sam was out of sight, and Ajay ensured no one had seen him leave, he ordered his Watch to call Genni. He wanted to make it right. Genni knew she'd made mistakes, and he couldn't let her end up like Sam – asking someone why they had helped them. She was Worthy. He was stronger than Sam. Cleverer. He could have her and the Worthy life; he'd make sure of it.

Genni's face appeared, still looking angry with him. Ajay spoke to her in a caring, regretful voice. 'Hi, I love you. And I'll ring Pearl tomorrow, *for you.*' Genni didn't smile or even say anything, but she did agree to meet him for breakfast.

CHAPTER
TWENTY

It was Saturday. The skies were hot, as usual, but there was a restlessness in the air. The City's streets were packed; Liberation Day shopping in full swing. Ajay didn't know what to get Genni this year; he watched her standing before her wardrobe mirror fastening up the brass buttons of her suit jacket. She had an interview to volunteer for the summer camps. Big merit. Big opportunity.

'What time will you finish at the village today?' Genni asked.

'About midday,' Ajay lied.

Ajay crawled his arms around her belly, resting his head on her shoulder. Things felt semi-good again, despite Genni's occasional setbacks when she'd paint for an hour. They were working on it. He managed to wish her good luck before she hastily headed for the door.

'Let's not work too late tonight. I got a weather alert, there's a storm due,' she said. 'Shall we watch from the roof? The view might finally be good enough to paint.'

Ajay held back a heavy sigh and nodded as she left. He had to hand it to her though; she had learned to multitask, usually sprawling her papers and paints out while watching an educational film. Her Watch saw the film, not the drawings. And who was he to judge? *The guy who's holding this whole thing together.* He couldn't completely take the painting away, that would end the relationship and her motivation. Little by little, she would change. *Right?*

Ajay turned to his wardrobe and selected the ripped, grey denim jacket that he hid behind his suits. His wardrobe mirror turned to a red mist. *Not on trend.* It was always difficult for Ajay to resist the urge to change, but he reminded himself where he was going. It was *that* Saturday. He shut the wardrobe door, grabbed his hat and quickly left the apartment.

Once outside, Ajay welded the hat to his head as a slight breeze attempted to whisk it away; he craned his neck and mused over the small puff of clouds meeting above the concrete trees. After walking down a few quick shortcuts to the border of the Inner-Rings, he jumped into a taxi, the sky train being too risky for this trip. The car drove him around the City as ladies were brunching and couples walked undersized foxes, all of it filtering past the car's windows.

Soon the buildings became smaller; the houses were less developed, and the pavements were untreated by litter-picking drones. The nearing storm was swooping packets and bags up in the air and the car swung round in front of a rusted arch that led onto a dirty and rusting rail platform. Ajay swiped his Watch onto the car's activation pad and made his way out. As the tip of his shoes reached the platform's yellow line, he could see the carriage approaching. It was an agonising wait from the first sighting to its arrival at the terminal. Ajay almost missed the need to brace himself as the sky train usually hurtled towards him. Instead, this train slouched to a stop. Ajay boarded, the only passenger at the station, before the train chugged and jerked slowly away.

As Ajay walked through the familiar streets, deep in the pool of his thoughts, a vibration disturbed him. He looked to his Watch to see Ace cuddling and smiling with a pretty girl who was kissing him lightly on the cheek. Ajay looked closer and recognised her as Mr Bancorp's niece, a Glorified born and bred. How the heck did he meet *her?* Ajay was secretly envious. He glanced over the caption. *'Are you the one I've been looking for?'* Ajay grimaced at the inauthenticity. Yet he was still jealous – it had got a lot of loves. Good for Ace with his biceps and trendy shaved head.

His thoughts then turned to his grandma and how she might be when he arrived. The last time he'd seen her had been months ago. She had been rather chirpy for a dying woman, a fact that Ajay often ignored. To him, she wasn't dying, just going through a tough spell. Soon, she'd bounce back to how she was. Ajay rebuked himself for his optimism. He, more than most, knew that nothing could ever be how it was back then.

He turned the corner onto the main high street; various shades of blue and green bunting hung above the uninspiring rows of shops and terraced houses. A large red flag hung off the outside of the central mail office, warning the residents of the coming storm. Ajay continued walking beneath the flag and the rim of his jacket blew in the strong gale. He scanned his feet, and then quickly moved them away from a Fo Doktrin leaf. It wouldn't hurt him, just stain his white, branded trainers with its permanent orange mark, damning evidence of where he'd been. It was the unwanted weed which scattered itself along these streets where the pace of life was much slower. Ajay spotted a lady he recognised from childhood; she had the same leisurely wobble as she walked, and wore the same bright purple sandals that matched the colour of her reusable shopping bags. People stopped to chat to one another, but Ajay continued walking. He was startled by a playful scream from the far end of the street but relaxed once he saw it was just a child falling from the monkey bars on the playground. With a squint, he could see that adults were running to her aid next to the slanted merry-go-round. He remembered how he had spent hours spinning Tara round and round on that thing.

A crisp packet flew across Ajay's feet and he smelled the sweet aroma of fresh bread wafting over from the bakery. It was soon masked by the stench of the week-full bins standing outside houses. Ajay kept his eyes low under his hat and hurried towards the third cul-de-sac off the main street. He was greeted by the semi-detached house that sat on top of the street's curve, and he approached the musty green door, turned the brass handle and let himself inside.

The halls of the house were still burdened with the faded wallpaper – flowers of the forest in greens, blues and yellows. Ajay watched as his mother walked delicately across the doorway of the kitchen into the dining area. She was still petite and wore the same pink dress she'd had for years. Ajay couldn't remember a time where there wasn't an apron tied around her waist or her hair wasn't tied in a messy ponytail, though now it looked greyer. He smelled bread. They must have done well on the recent ration, as he remembered that flour was popular. *Maybe times have moved on.* He never brought them anything from the City – they shouldn't expect him to – though for some reason this time, he felt guilty. He had enough credit to redecorate this whole place – so uninspiring, like all houses on the Side.

CHAPTER
TWENTY-ONE

Ajay Ambers had created a space in his brain that would home his childhood and it would only ever be thought about when he allowed it. That was his plan. The events that led up to his City life were unknown to everyone but himself and his birth family. He was originally Karle Blythefen; son of Joon and Keli Blythefen, grandson to Karlane Devlop and brother to Tara Blythefen. The five of them lived, all cooped up together, in a small home on the west part of the Side.

Karle was an inquisitive child and growing up on the Side invited a lot of questions. He wanted to know everything: about the Revolution, the drones, the food rations, the old city, merit, and the Watch. 'All in good time,' his grandma would say at bedtime, when she told Karle stories of their past. He would always ask for more. She would often remind him that they were the lucky ones. The development of drones and robotics had led to the redundancy of many in the Side, who had travelled into the City for what they called 'pre-redundant' jobs. There were even cuts on the camel farms; occasionally he and Tara would go down to a neighbouring farm together. Tara went to feed the camels; Karle went to be fascinated by the robotic machines at work. He only ever saw the milking process, but he would have loved to have watched the technology that processed the meat or that pulled a new calf into the world. Fortunately, Karle's father managed to keep his job as a maintenance worker for the railways. This didn't mean Karle wasn't made aware of how many Side families didn't earn enough credit to even eat. 'It's our job to help them,' his mother would say over his apprehension to share *their* crops from *their* garden. It was part of their culture to share. Every Monday, Karle would have to assist his mother in washing and chopping homegrown potatoes and cucumbers to then divide them into separate baskets, ready for Tara and Grandma to deliver them to their neighbours. Karle made sure never to share the 'good' stuff, like candy or tinned goods from the small convenience shops on the high street. All food was rationed, because the City never quite sent enough and the desert's heat meant not all crops survived, so when Karle got his hands on *that* stuff, it was all for him. Eating food with actual flavour was a luxury he wanted to enjoy alone.

Sometimes he would share it with Tara. Other than his grandma, his little sister was the only person he'd ended up caring about. The others all became irrelevant collateral once he'd left. Tara was also the only one who, in his teenage years, managed to get him to come out of his dust-encrusted bedroom. It would be to teach her how to play cards, or they would run across the sanded streets to the playground and he would spin her on the faulty merry-go-round. 'Karle, it's playtime!' she would say as she bounced outside his bedroom door in her rainbow-striped thin tights, her black hair tied up in adorable pigtails. If Karle ever refused by shutting the door in her face, she would weasel her way back into the room and jump on him, squishing the insides of his stomach. That would lead to Karle grabbing her playfully and tickling her until she squealed for mercy. Even as she got older, her little, immature giggle stayed, and it still somehow influenced Karle. More often than not, he would agree to play. Then she'd run rapidly down the stairs with her blue pinafore slightly dishevelled around her waist. She would erratically bounce towards the tall oak cupboard that leaned, with a slight wonkiness, against the back wall of the dining area. She once pulled at the box on the highest shelf, going as high as her tiptoed feet would lift her. Karle walked into the room and watched most of the contents from the top shelf fall and plummet to the ground. It just missed Tara's head, causing her to topple backwards and be caught by a chair behind her.

Karle never thought to stop Tara from doing things too hard for her. It just became something they did, laughing and clearing up after her clumsiness. If it wasn't the cupboard, it was the dropping of a cup, or the bad scraping of her knee by running into something at the playground. She was the type of person that if Karle met her in the City, he would want to throttle her. That type of incompetence would need to be monitored and hidden. Not on the Side. People were much more accepting of imperfections; they didn't seem to bother trying to better themselves. Everything seemed to stay the same which, as he grew, aggravated Karle. The more he learned about the City, the more the Side felt backward to him.

It started when he'd go to the sand hill, a huge mound that overlooks the Side. 'Can I come with you to the hill?' Tara would ask, but her cute eyes and charming laugh never worked for that.

The hill was Karle's place. It was said to have formed by a drone dump of sand over old government buildings. Karle had never really cared how it had got there. He used to sit and dream about the City he could see but never touch. He would watch as, over time, the silhouette of the skyline became even more dense. Skyscrapers would appear as if overnight, and when the white sun hit the City in the right way, it would glitter and sparkle from across the desert. The hill was where he began to imagine the life of a City kid. He reckoned they had everything they could ever need. Their food wouldn't be rationed, their meals would taste divine; their lights wouldn't flicker, their work would be rewarded; their wallpaper wouldn't be mouldy and they'd go into shopping malls, theatres, sports centres and 300-storey buildings. They would have access to all the latest gadgets and games; he'd always wanted to play in the virtual reality of *TuloCombat* or *DroneDefenders*. Karle would read about them whenever he stole his father's Watch. He would get into the news updates and read up on the latest releases.

His father never liked him taking it. 'Karle, have you got my Watch?' the soft yet authoritative tones of Karle's father would echo up off the walls of the staircase. Karle would jump and quickly turn down the screen of the Watch, hiding whatever it was he was reading. 'Karle?' His father would stand in the doorway and immediately point at his Watch, whether it was resting on Karle's desk, bed, or just in his hands. His father always looked disappointed, but never surprised. That's why Karle never bothered hiding it. His father knew that he took it, and in a way, he let him. 'Just because I take it off now and again, it doesn't mean it's easily replaceable. I'd prefer you not to take it,' his father had said one time. Karle had translated his father's word choice to mean, 'I don't want you to take it, but it's OK if you do.' So, Karle took that liberty. His father's Watch became his personal fix to feed a growing City obsession. He delved deep into everything he could: books on initiations, Watch updates and personalisation, the development of energy boosters, and videos of Glorified celebrities. There were materials on fitness, home life, Education Centres, eating out and looking after pets. He would watch the Liberation Day promo on repeat and then indulge in the highlights of their annual celebrations. Life had so many layers out there, while Karle felt pointless in his plain existence.

Then there were the billboards, which in the City were as common as people. He learned that over there, they advertised everything: nutritional drinks, educational movies, beauty products and even dull stuff like insurance. But there, on the Side, they only ever promoted one thing. *Purification.* It was a word that literally hung over their community, on the side of buildings and within the adults' Watches. The adverts often featured a message like '*Become your most effective self*' or '*Don't let your ancestors down*', or sometimes they'd show an interview with a successful 'Purified'. The most prominent one in Karle's memory was the girl with long, red hair from down the road. She would often walk past Tara and him on the playground, and she would always wear a light-blue anorak with its hood up. Karle never took notice of her, other than the fact that she was older and seemed kind of strange. She did it, though. She applied for Purification and, five years later, she was almost M-400. Karle remembers seeing her face on the billboards. *Be like Carole*, they would say. In the shots they used, her hair held more volume and she wore a pretty, yellow summer dress that complemented her dark skin tone. 'It was the best decision I ever made,' she would say. Karle agreed with her. She hadn't looked so strange anymore, she had looked happy. The first time he saw her story was when he was twelve, and he went home to his grandma and asked the question.

'How does Purification work?' Karle had bounded in, sweating in a black T-shirt and shorts. Grandma was sitting at the kitchen table, sewing up the holes in his father's shirts. She paused, looked up at him and smiled sweetly. She pulled out the chair next to her, which squeaked unpleasantly across the concrete floor. She patted its seat, inviting Karle to sit down.

'Why do you ask that, love?'

'I see it everywhere. It's how people like us get to the City, right?'

'Right. It's a process Command introduced alongside the merit system. After the Revolution.'

'You've never told me about it.' With everything Grandma had taught him about Command and other historical matters, it had seemed bizarre to Karle that this had never come up.

Grandma hesitated, sighed and set down her sewing. 'I wanted to wait until you were ready to hear it.' She stood, walked into the open-plan kitchen, and turned on the fan that sat on its worktop. As it began its rotation, her short, greying hair blew and banished the beads of sweat on her forehead. She removed the blue cardigan to reveal more of her floor-length, brown polyester dress before sitting back down.

'You know, Command believes our lifestyle encourages the ideals of the old government—'

Karle interrupted, 'But they didn't teach anything. Wasn't that the point? They just took everything from those who worked hard. We don't do that.'

'No. We don't, but we don't strive for what Command calls "progress" either, which is classed as anti-constitutional. So, when you reach twenty-five, you can go and serve the Glorified. Those above M-500.'

'Really?'

Grandma gave a slow nod. 'You could go there as their butler or chef or cleaner. Whatever they decide. Then, after two years, you can be submitted for Purification. That's where the court decides whether you have been "Purified" from your upbringing under The Guiding Light.'

'And then you can become . . .'

'An accredited City citizen, yes,' Grandma finished.

Karle had thought for a moment, trying to take it all in. He imagined himself walking the City streets that he had only ever seen on video. He would wear a dark, sophisticated suit and expensive, polished business shoes. People would admire him, reaching out to shake his hand. He would tuck his well-brushed hair behind his ears and snap up the latest gadgets from the boards. Until then, Karle hadn't understood that it was possible for him to ever be a City kid.

'When can I apply?' Karle had asked, fleetingly. His grandma had returned to her sewing, but abruptly appeared blindsided.

'Apply for Purification?' she clarified.

Karle had stood from his chair. The same squeak against concrete. 'I want to go.' A short pause.

'OK, well. All in good time, love.' His grandma had stroked his arm. He'd wondered whether she could feel his goosebumps. 'We'll talk about it when you're older.'

Though as he did get *older*, his desire for the City began to fuel a burning resentment for everything about the Side, especially the teachings of The Guiding Light. It was that which held him back from the dream of expensive, polished business shoes. Soon everyone who believed in The Guiding Light became foolish to him. Karle struggled to build a healthy relationship with anyone near him, especially his father.

Karle saw him as a sad excuse for a man. He would grieve at the way his father would bounce into a room with joy, gazing at everyone behind his crooked glasses. Karle wished others saw him for what he really was: a waste. The only similarities Karle saw between himself and his father were: a) that they were both – annoyingly, for Karle – skinny and lanky, and b) they were both inexplicably clever. It was no surprise that Karle had excelled at school and ended up working at Prosper when his father could hold intellectual conversations about how they could improve drones and railways. One time, his father single-handedly repaired a hover bus that came as scrap from the City. He'd even overridden the driverless function so some lowlife could drive it. It was then used to help old people get to the shops, or the kids rode it to school when there was a storm. If anyone in the neighbourhood had a computer or even a Watch problem, they would come to his father for help. So, Karle found it extremely irritating that his father had never once shown a desire to be Purified. He had more ability than most people to make a better life for himself and for them as a family. Instead, Karle actually felt like his father spent more time with other people. Always visiting their houses if someone had died or was having a hard time. It was like he had no time for them, so Karle decided he would have no time for him, either.

He began to steal his Watch even more. Not just for research, but also as a way to anger him. Unfortunately, it didn't upset him quite as much as Karle had hoped, but then Karle learned the one thing that really bothered his father. It was his refusal to go to the meetings. So, naturally, Karle refused a lot.

CHAPTER
TWENTY-TWO

'I'm not going!' Karle shouted as he darted up the wooden staircase. His father was running after him, anger pulsing over his olive face underneath his smeared glasses. Karle always drew his eyebrows closer together at the sight of them; if they were Worthy, his father could invest in digital optical counterparts and so they served as a constant reminder of their Unworthy state.

'You've got to go. People are expecting you.' His father grabbed the underside of his arm before he made it to his lockable bedroom. His grip had been tight, but not so much that it caused pain. Karle struggled before releasing himself. He didn't retreat, but stood breathless, staring up at his father, who sighed and spoke with a calm yet still agitated tone.

'Look, son. You're coming. These meetings are important for your mother and I, and the rest of our community. You need to show your support.'

Supporting something would mean agreeing with it, Karle had thought. As a kid he'd enjoyed the times they'd spent with neighbours, squished around their inadequately sized dining table, listening to The Guiding Light. It told marvellous stories. Karle's particular favourite had been the one about the lost worker in the storm, and he'd always relish the chance of wafting his small fingers through its dancing figure of light. His mother would always pull him back and tut. It was a device that was once beautiful to him, oblong like a fresh loaf of bread and a flat top surface from which the mesmerising hologram would appear, connected through veins of sparkles. It looked like a man or even a woman, but it didn't have a face – only a strong, joyful, storytelling voice. That was when he was a kid.

Later, as he stared at his father, he thought about how the meetings were dull enough to make him want to eat sand. There was nothing glamorous The Guiding Light or those meetings could offer him that the City couldn't surpass. Now sixteen, he'd only ever expressed his Purification dream to his grandma. In that moment, as his father looked into his eyes, Karle decided it was time he knew, and never once had he regretted what he said next.

'I'm not coming because I want no part in this community. You stifle progress. You believe in something you can't fully explain. You get nothing for the hard work you do.' His eyes flicked behind his father's shocked expression to the mould up the wall. 'Well, not me. I won't be like you, Dad. I'm applying for Purification as soon as I turn twenty-five.'

His defiance and aggression had flattened the air and made it toxic; his father couldn't catch his thoughts before he spoke.

'How dare you,' he said with a volume that rarely passed his lips. 'You are kidding yourself if you think they'll ever see you as Worthy.'

Immediately Karle saw his father's eyes soften with regret and remorse, but he himself had been incensed. He'd spun on his heel, slammed the door in his father's face and bolted the lock with such force that it nearly fell off its hold. On his bed, he bundled himself into a ball and groaned loudly into the mattress.

An hour or so passed before Karle heard the pitter-patter of a knock on the rotting wood of the door. He unbolted the fragile lock and was greeted by his father carrying a huge plastic sack. Karle had immediately tried to see its contents, but his father moved it behind his back.

'I'll get to that in a minute. Sit down, son.' Karle sat on his bed, feeling the springs spiking his backside. His father sat beside him and the two of them dipped closer to the floor. They spent a moment in silence. Karle wondered if his father was expecting him to speak first. He absolutely wasn't going to; he had the right to do what he wanted, and he wasn't going to apologise for voicing the truth of that. To his relief, his father spoke.

'I'm sorry for the way I spoke to you. I was wrong to do that, and I didn't mean how it sounded.' His father hadn't kept his eyes off Karle's empty, rotting desk at the back of the room. It seemed as if he didn't have the decency to look Karle in the eyes when he apologised. Karle thought that was typical. 'And I'm sorry we've not always got along. We're very similar in many ways and sometimes that means we clash. It's my fault. I've been believing I should deal with that by resistance, and that was a mistake.' His father took a long, loud, deep breath. At first, Karle had thought he was struggling to breathe, but in the end, his father looked to be processing something. Like the next words he would say had to be chosen carefully. 'I've now come to accept that you don't feel you belong here. You want to be out there.' His father stopped staring at the desk, instead looking out the small, square window by Karle's bed where the outline of the City's skyline could just be seen. 'And I believed in The Guiding Light when he just told me: I have to let you go.' He stroked the bristles on his chin before pulling the plastic sack towards them, opening it slowly. 'This is for you.'

Karle stood up, open-mouthed and amazed. He'd ignored his father's gaze on him and jumped forward to pull the entirety of the black bag away, revealing an outdated computer set. It wasn't much to look at. It had a clunky transparent screen and stand, and the keyboard came as a separate entity, but Karle didn't care. It belonged to him, and he could do what he liked with it. His father's voice was muffled alongside his excitability.

'I figured if you're going to go for it, you better brush up on your tech skills. Now, I know it's not what they have over there, but it's what they were rationing down–' His father's speech had been broken by Karle's rush. He was completely animated, hurrying to snap up the set and place it onto his desk, which wobbled with the new burden.

'OK, well, I'll leave you to it,' his father choked through his words. Karle hadn't turned back to watch his father leave. The sun filtered behind some clouds and the silhouette of the City glistened. Karle looked towards it with a new hope. He'd shifted the computer further back on his desk, knowing this was how he would prepare himself for a top engineering job in the Inner-Ring.

That was the original plan, but things changed not long before Karle turned seventeen. He did something terrible and so he no longer wanted to be Purified.

CHAPTER
TWENTY-THREE

'Karle, we can't be here. We have to leave now.' Callum had run to catch up with Karle as they walked through the shopping mall. His soft brown hair bounced around his baby face, splattered in freckles. Karle had often thought his best friend was too soft, worrying about everything, though he would soon learn that Callum had been right. They shouldn't have been there.

'Don't you feel free by being here?' Karle hadn't been able to help his enthusiasm. They were inside an M-350+ venue. It was a cathedral of luxury and possibility, wealth and popularity. Groups of well-dressed people filtered in and out of digitally operated stores. He was mesmerised. At the time, he saw it as a good decision, slipping onto the train and heading into the City just for a taste of it. In his ignorance, he never anticipated anything bad would happen.

'Come on, let's just try one suit on.' Karle, empowered and negligent, headed into *Deluxe Suits for Men*. Callum, with a worried expression, followed on. Karle whipped open the curtain of one of the many changing pods that filled the entire store and, ignoring Callum's whimpering, he closed himself inside the pod.

Welcome to Deluxe Suits for Men. I'm Carla, your personal stylist, the voice boomed from the full-length digital scene, its camera acting as a mirror. *First, let's find your style. Please select your preferences from the following options.* Karle proceeded to select his favourite colours and styles that appeared onscreen. In a startling transformation, the mirror showed Karle wearing the sharpest suit he'd ever seen. He had never looked like this – rich, smart, prosperous. He imagined himself wearing this suit to a classy bar and setting his charm on a beautiful woman who actually wanted to speak to him. It was dark-green suede and it shimmered as he twisted and turned in a glorious moment of augmented reality.

Are you happy with your new look? I think you look amazing. Would you like to proceed to payment? Karle, of course, didn't have the credit, but in his delusion, he tapped 'proceed'.

OK, fabulous! First, we need to take your delivery address and an ID scan for merit validation. Only the Worthy can look this good. The disappointment was painful. *Idiot,* he cursed himself. What did he expect? Through gritted teeth, he cancelled the transaction. He looked at himself once more in his suit, which then faded back to his grey shirt and brown, speckled trousers. 'Who says I can never have it?' he whispered to himself. On flicking back the curtain, he was welcomed by a sweating Callum.

'Karle, I cannot stay here any longer, we're going to get caught. I should never have sneaked past those guards with you.'

'Calm down, we can do anything we want to do. Let's check out the food court.'

Karle had set off at pace. Callum ran after him, tugging on his arm and begging him to turn round as they narrowly missed barging into other people in the crowd. As they headed past more white-fronted shops, Karle noticed the huge billboard that hung over the central aisle. It was advertising some new energy-boosting product. An alluring lady with flowing brown hair and shining white teeth smiled down at him, with the words, *'Have more time for you and your merit . . .'* sprawled close to her bewitching eyes. It felt almost magical, but he pulled himself away when they arrived at the food court. Even Callum stopped moaning, for a moment.

Never had the boys seen so much food. Life on rations had willed both their mouths to drop open at the spectacle before them. There were beautifully presented delicacies of every description. There were fat iced cakes, fresh cuts of meat; glazed breads, nicely cut vegetables; gluttonously stuffed pies, and fruits crafted into the shapes of flowers and birds. Trying to compose themselves, they walked slowly past the stalls.

Karle grabbed Callum's shoulder and forced him to duck away from a soaring drone carrying two pink milkshakes.

'I didn't even see that,' Callum laughed nervously.

Karle followed the drone as it arrived at a table and served the drinks to young, giggling girls. He noticed them looking at him, obviously finding the near collision amusing. Karle smiled back at them, and they blushed at one another. Karle couldn't believe the reaction; he'd flirted with City girls and they'd liked him? It felt so good. Then, a sharp tugging had started on his sleeve.

'No, no, no . . . We have to go, we're getting noticed.' Callum pulled on Karle's arm once more, whispering into his ear. Karle felt his hot saliva spitting out onto his cheek.

He shoved Callum off his arm.

'Would you cut it out? We're fine. No one knows who we are. Come on, let's try to sneak something.' Karle began an advance forward, a glazed lemon loaf in his sights. Callum grabbed him, the slap of his hand on Karle's forearm making a loud clap.

'Just look!' Callum moaned, his eyes misting over.

Karle followed shaky Callum's finger to see a man in a lightweight dark suit rising from the comfort of his padded seat. He had abandoned his iced coffee on the table and was walking towards them with piercing, angered eyes, and Karle then saw the security drone that was accompanying him. Karle suddenly understood Callum's alarm, but to him, it didn't mean they knew who they were. Yes, their appearance was slightly dishevelled, but that didn't mean they weren't entitled to be there. Their parents could be M-300 and off buying some clothes.

They were fine.

'It's OK. We should just stay calm. We can say our parents are here. OK, Callum? Callum . . . ?' On his friend's silence, Karle turned quickly and saw Callum sprinting towards the mall's exit. Karle's heart rate rocketed, especially when he then heard the revving of the drone's acceleration, and even more so when he saw there was now a whole swarm of security drones in on the hunt.

Karle didn't think there was anything else to do but run and join his friend in escaping. He was faster than Callum and managed to catch up with him while trying to block out gasps and insulting shouts from the crowds.

'This way,' Karle commanded as they dashed down some stairs through a restricted exit door into a new store that was being refurbished. They slammed the door shut but knew that was unlikely to stop an army of drones.

'What do we do? *What do we do?*' Callum was hysterical. Karle took stock and tried to see beyond the white painting sheets on the walls and tubs of open paint left sporadically across the floor. It felt as if there was no way out, but in that moment, he'd heard the calming yet dangerous sound of moving water. He scanned the store again and saw it: a door labelled 'balcony'.

'The river, come on!' he roared.

'The river, are you joking?' shrieked Callum, pale as the white walls around them.

'We just need to get up on the balcony.'

At that moment, the door to the store exploded open and the drones swirled in like a fierce swarm of bees, covering all directions. Karle sprinted forward, beckoning Callum to join him. He approached the balcony door, delighted to see just a low railing between them and the moving current below. The hairs on his neck stood up when he heard Callum's terrified voice call his name.

That's when he witnessed his friend being tasered and restrained by three or four drones, his body bouncing in electrified spasms until it stopped. Callum's right cheek was pressed hard to the ground, his mouth slightly agape and expressing anger, pain and vulnerability, all rolling together to display uncontrollable and paralytic fear. As Karle watched, the quivering mouth spelt out his name once more.

Karle had no other choice but to mount the railing and jump hopelessly into the moving river below.

Deafened by the roar of the water that was rushing around him furiously, he couldn't move against the strength of the artificial current. His mind was caught in the depth of the darkness beneath him, home to the whirring machines that gave the river movement. He thought of what it would be like to drown or get caught in their spinning blades. His family would be devastated; he knew they wouldn't stop looking for him. A painful lump in his throat had brought a sudden calm. He managed to stretch out and battle the weight of his waterlogged clothes to force his body to desperately splash above the surface for air. The drones were still flying above him as the river moved between two long blocks of buildings and Karle, acting only on instinct, dived low into the water. He resented his parents for many things, but as he ducked lower, he was thankful for his father's swimming lessons, despite the griminess of the Side's badly maintained swimming pool. He resurfaced by a wall not far from where he'd disappeared beneath the current. He kept his head low in the water and watched in relief as the drones flew straight past him and advanced further down the river.

Karle scrambled up the nearest ladder and came out on a residential street, just down from the shopping mall.

It looked no different than any other street, covered in advertisements and excitingly busy. Before he was able to gather his thoughts, he heard a soft but stern voice from behind him.

'Psst, boy.'

Karle turned.

'Psssst, get in here.' A small woman was leaning out of her front door. 'Quickly, they'll be coming back in no time.'

He hesitated. How did he know she wasn't turning him in for a hefty chunk of credit? But he didn't have any other choice, so ran through the steel door and let it slide shut behind him.

Karle had never been into someone's house in the City. He suddenly felt self-conscious as his soaking clothes dripped onto the floor, though as he looked around, he decided not to be so bothered about his appearance. The house was nothing like the glamorous life he'd expected. It was big, without doubt, and the open-plan style and high ceilings had real potential. Unfortunately, that could only be seen if he imagined the piles of clothing, empty food carriers, overloaded worktops and slightly musty smell weren't there. The colour scheme of a dark maroon and cream also didn't complement any other feature in the room. It only made it feel smaller. Karle had stared for a minute, standing still, trying to take it all in.

'Alright, boy. I know it's a mess, but it's a busy life. Don't go judging me.' Her voice was deep and rough.

How did she know what he was thinking? Karle became aware of his facial expressions. She shuffled past him into the kitchen with a certain bullish grace. Her long, patterned tunic was painted in vibrant colours – a big contrast to the current black and white trend Karle had read about. Looking at her from the back, Karle wouldn't have been surprised if she was Unworthy. Her mousy brown hair was unkempt, straggly and sprawling down the length of her back. Karle moved himself towards a sofa and noticed a wall in front of it, littered with children's paintings and sketches of locations in the City – the river, the Glorified Gate, the Quarters, the

Command building, and the Retail and Financial Districts – all places Karle had only ever dreamed of visiting.

He was quickly taken away from the art gallery by a growl and sudden force on his body. A strawberry-red fox had playfully jumped up to lick his face. Karle, slightly surprised and hesitant, stroked the fox as it fussed over him with adoration.

'Alpha, get down,' the woman shouted from the kitchen as she marched over to control her pet and stood squarely in front of Karle. That was the moment when he had seen her face clearly for the first time. Her skin was almost impossibly pale for Tulo's climate, and if put against Karle's skin would resemble the complexion of camel's milk. But that wasn't her distinctive feature. She had some sort of sore on the right side of her neck and chin. Was it a rash or a skin deformity? Karle had never seen anything like it. It was like a stark red, rough textured pond that lay stagnant across her face.

Karle pulled his eyes away from it quickly and spoke timidly. 'Thank you. For letting me in.'

The lady flapped her hand as if to say 'no problem'. 'So what are you doing so far from home?'

Karle gulped with fear over the implication that she knew. 'I just came to explore.'

'A risky thing. Just explore outside, don't be going to venues where you're not accepted. Getting caught for trespassing can lead to complications.' Back in the kitchen and with the fox sniffing at her feet, she swiped the only empty black worktop to activate the electric hobs. 'You're blessed you don't have your Watch yet, they'd be on your VPG, no problem.'

'You can disable that,' Karle spoke too quickly. He was tempted to throw his wet hands over his flippant mouth. She was a City woman. He shouldn't sound so arrogant.

'Well, yes. But there's not always time for that.' She started cooking, steam evaporating instantly into the air.

'Are your children home?' Karle looked up the steel staircase.

'Children?' she asked, still preparing food. Karle felt her eyes on him as he nodded at her drawings. 'You're nosy, aren't you?' She gave Karle a stern look, forcing him to glance down at his squelching shoes, vulnerably. 'If you must know, I'm a teacher in the walled part of the City.' Karle was surprised and he didn't contain himself in showing it.

'You work for a Glorified school?'

'Yes, that's a shock, isn't it?' Her voice was condescending, but then she shrugged her shoulders and spoke softly as if it was a perfectly reasonable question for Karle to ask. 'I teach language and communications.'

Karle wondered then if she was a little unwired. She plunged a knife into an onion with such force, it made Karle jump. She started to fry camel burgers in a pan. The aroma tantalised Karle's tastebuds, a sudden hunger manifesting itself as a growling goblin in his stomach ready to devour some meat.

'So . . . what's your name?' Karle asked.

'Come on, boy.' She slammed a plate down from the cupboard. 'Just mind your own business.'

'Sorry.' Karle smiled in a plea for her to like him until he questioned himself. She'd let him into her house, how was it rude to ask for her name? She simply smiled back with an eyeroll, tied up her straggly long hair, and pushed the juicy burger, plated up, across the worktop in Karle's direction.

'You like onions on top, yes?' she asked as she hovered a spoon of onions over the top of the burger.

Karle hesitantly took the plate, thanked her, and nervously sat on a torn sofa, feeling his wet clothes press into his skin. How would she know he liked onions? He avoided eye contact with her and angled himself away as he took a tentative bite.

'Now, eat that up. And go home. They'll have lost you by now.' Karle didn't respond, both through his distrust and his consumption of the burger. He had never before tasted meat of this quality. 'What about the boy you were with, then?' the lady asked, coming out of nowhere and taking Karle's plate the instant he took his last bite.

Shocked by both this flippancy and her question, Karle found it difficult to swallow. 'Callum? But how did you–?'

She interrupted him. 'It doesn't matter. What matters is, how do you plan on helping him?'

'What do you mean? I'm just a kid. A kid from the Side. There's nothing I can do. They'll just send him back, right?'

'Not automatically. You need to go home and tell his parents what happened. They'll be able to apply for his release.'

'But won't they come after me?' Karle tried to hide his fear.

'I doubt it. The TPD don't tend to waste time on Side kids if they don't catch them the first time. I guess it's the assumption that once you're eighteen, your Watch will do the job for them. And if it doesn't, they have means of dealing with you.' She walked towards Karle then and placed her greasy hands on his shoulders. Karle felt a pinch as she ever so slightly gripped his skin. Was this where she killed him? He supposed it would be fitting. Karle had never realised how people like him were treated in the City. The discrimination and the shame. He was utterly confused and had never felt so lost. Would he experience this feeling even after he'd been Purified? These thoughts all ran through his mind as he stared at the unfortunate monstrosity on the woman's face, which he realised was probably a birthmark. She spoke again with fire in her eyes.

'You've done a bad thing. And there will be consequences. The way you're going, you're set for an unpleasant end. Now, leave my home.' She lifted her grip from his shoulders and paused. 'Please.'

Timidly, Karle turned away from her and her strange house, giving one last look at the drawings on the wall. The door opened and his host had the last word.

'Boy! Don't go right at the end of the road. You'll end up Downtown, it's a place for shady stuff. Go the long way back.'

So Karle did. He went home, the long way back, without Callum and with a full stomach.

CHAPTER
TWENTY-FOUR

That day had ended with Karle sitting on the hill, staring down into the abrasive sand at his brown, tattered sandals. Tears had rolled down his teenage cheeks in a new way; uncontrollably with repeated, coughing sobs. The sun was setting over the City, giving space for the beams of the televised news sphere to shine brighter into the lilac sky. Soon his grandma joined him, panting as she reached the top.

'You had to choose the tallest hill, didn't you?' His grandma put her hands to her knees and let out a few sharp breaths. Karle said nothing, his eyes bloodshot and hair greasy with sweat. They sat in silence for a few minutes until Karle finally spluttered out words.

'Why did that have to happen? Why didn't Callum run faster?' His fists were full of sand and he beat them onto the ground, the sand escaping through the edges of his fingers. He felt the tight squeeze of Grandma's arms around him.

'You were told you should never go to the City; you're not accepted everywhere there.'

'But the City kids have no Watch or merit until they're eighteen, either. Yet they get to go to the shopping malls, the best games arcades and buy the best stuff.'

By this point, Karle had learned so much about the City that he realised he probably knew more than those who lived there.

Yet some questions remained unanswered. Why did he have to wait? Why was Callum taken? Why were they so shut out? Of course, he had read through the political reasons. The lifestyle The Guiding Light taught was based on rest and taking things slower than Command required; that sort of idleness and selfishness had led to Tulo's poverty-stricken past. Command couldn't risk that infecting their City and reversing everything they had all worked hard for. But Karle never understood the injustice that those born here, those who had never been given the choice, were also shut out. Marginalised. As his grandma started to speak, Karle could feel the irritable itch in his mouth intensifying, and he felt as if his limbs were about to start shaking.

'That's not how we live, Karle. It's not what the Guide says is—'

'I don't care what the Guide says.' He shrugged off her arms and bared his teeth. 'I hate it. It's ruined my life.' He wildly threw sand into the humid air; it fell to the ground in the absence of any breeze.

Karle told himself the next time he saw the Guide's shimmering hardware or talking figure of light, he'd throw it into the nearest wall. Its name may have originated from when construction workers were stuck in dark tunnels and used the shine of its hologram to guide their way to safety, but it could never offer him sanctuary. It must be some sort of hypnosis, he decided, convincing people that they couldn't live without it. Yet they made their lives harder; the City would accept them if they were Purified. He didn't understand it, but he knew that he wanted nothing more to do with it. His grandma had then given him some version of the usual guff.

'The City isn't built on a sure foundation. It's as unstable as the moving sand beneath our feet. People are taught to strive for more. They're kept awake endlessly and become selfishly vain in the name of something greater. But eventually they crack. They drive themselves into oblivion for a futile and ungrounded "Worthiness" determined by other people. Yet those who build their life like the Guide teaches, they have a rock-solid foundation. It allows you to rest and take the time to become the person you're destined to be. You're defined by that and not a number on your wrist.' Karle felt his grandma's arm move around him again. 'That's why we stay here and contribute what we believe we should be contributing. We don't always get it right, but we live by a different standard to the City's.'

Karle said nothing in response. He'd heard it all before.

His grandma didn't move, only sighed as they both looked towards floating scaffolding surrounding a newly constructed Prosper building. With tears rolling down his cheeks again, Karle asked his grandma a final question.

'Do you think I'll see Callum again?'

'I don't know, love,' she said, stroking his arm. 'Let's just have faith he'll come home.'

Faith in what? Karle asked himself as his heart hopelessly dropped in his chest. He looked down to see his grandma holding his hand, and that was the moment when Karle Blythefen decided he wouldn't wait for Purification. He didn't want the stigma of his Side upbringing hanging over him for his whole life. He'd have to find a way to become someone other than himself.

CHAPTER
TWENTY-FIVE

His opportunity came on a restless and stormy evening when Theo Badds died. For months, Karle had spent sleepless nights analysing the software of his father's Watch using the old computer, but he'd hit a dead end. To test the concept of changing a Watch's identity would mean turning his father into someone else. He couldn't imagine his father being impressed, or not the least bit suspicious, if his Watch started telling him he was Didi Traves. That was the lady who worked in the shop, whom Karle thought was mind-numbingly boring. She wore the same grey dress under the same grey apron, splattered with the same greasy stain. He'd never noticed it as a kid, but as he got older, he'd spotted more of his neighbours' disgusting appearances. So whenever Karle thought about changing his father's name, Didi always came to mind, because as a seventeen-year-old that was the height of humour. Unfortunately, though, being serious about his plan, his father's Watch wasn't an option. Then, just when Karle thought his luck was out, his father's friend died.

Theo Badds was a mentor to his father and a close companion. When he finally breathed his last, the entire family was invited round to their house to bless his passing.

The five of them shuffled down the narrow, enclosing walls of the Badds' hallway. Their house had a familiar smell. It wasn't unpleasant but like dying flowers, not quite fresh, not quite rotten. Karle had realised that this was the smell of Theo himself; it used to walk around with him and would remain in their house for at least a couple of hours after he'd gone. They made their way through a left-hand doorway, which opened up into the living room. It was similar to their own; slightly dated with chipped paint covering the walls. Admittedly, though, Karle didn't notice this much on that particular day due to the presence of Theo's corpse displayed across a table in the middle of the room. He had been given a bunch of bedraggled flowers to hold.

Karle had never seen one before. A dead body was no way near as gruesome as he'd imagined. Theo could have been sleeping; the only difference was that his tanned skin looked lighter. Karle's thoughts were interrupted by the touch of his little sister's hand slipping into his as they gathered around the table. He held it tightly.

'Thank you so much for coming,' Glenda said, as she immediately gave Karle's father a hug. The poor woman looked as if she could be on the table herself. Her eyes were puffy, her grey hair dishevelled and the skin under her neck sagged like the fat you cut off a camel. Karle avoided looking at her. Instead, he saw *it*.

Just behind his father, to his right, stood a small, raised table. Lying on top of it was Theo's redundant Watch. Karle's pupils widened and his heart skipped as he contemplated the opportunity. If he could use that Watch, he could see deeper inside. Stupidly, he had wondered whether he could ask to borrow it, but his only real option was to steal it. He had made a promise with himself to never invite questions from anyone.

'Shall we bow our heads?' his father said through his continuing tears. Karle took a chance. Everyone else closed their reddened eyes, but Karle transferred Tara's hand from his own to his grandma's and walked towards his father. He carefully positioned himself in front of the table and, in a false act of comfort, put one arm over his grieving father's shoulder. Once confident everyone had their eyes shut, he used his remaining hand to slip the Watch into the gaping pocket of his tattered trousers. Then he bowed his head as if he always had.

Karle had only had the Watch in his possession for less than twenty-four hours before it had been deactivated.

For the first four hours, he'd tapped at his keyboard, mind and eyes focused.

Initially he had attempted to send random requests to the Watch. Fortunately, Karle had developed a lot of ingenuity over the last few months. He had delved into every device he could get his hands on. The alarm clock had been his first victim, slowly followed by a broken screen projector, Tara's only interactive doll, a malfunctioning drone he found on the street, and even The Guiding Light. Even though Karle had played around with his father's Watch, as he was getting deeper into this one's interface, he realised he had never seen software as advanced as this before.

Karle didn't let the challenge scare him. It pushed him on. He had begun sending messages from his computer to the Watch, to get an idea of what the API looked like. He analysed network calls, searched for unencrypted files, even profiled the hardware performance metrics. He then started to piece together the snippets of information he'd gathered to find the Watch's weak spot. Using the command line, he tried injecting code into its graphical user interface, with the help of some automated scripts he'd written. Then, it happened.

'Yes,' he said, but not too loudly. His rotting bedroom door certainly wasn't soundproof, and given his grumpy behaviour recently, his family would ask questions if they'd heard him sounding happy. But he was happy. He'd found that weak spot: a network request made from a server to the Watch, which he could intercept and manipulate.

Karle's excitement mounted. He bounced his fingers across the keyboard. He began changing the details of Theo Badds, as if to erase his existence altogether. 'Come on, come on . . .' he murmured. The code flicked about on the screen. Until it stopped. The test was successful. 'No way,' Karle said beneath his breath. He had been fidgeting in his chair like a fox preparing for a walk. He handled Theo's Watch, staring at it almost in disbelief, to see his own name displayed on it. Karle Blythefen, M-310.

Karle had then spent the next hour back at Theo and Glenda's house. His return there was necessary. Theo's Watch had become inactive. At first, Karle didn't understand and was worried that Command had deactivated it sooner than he had expected. He realised then he was being stupid. Of course, it wouldn't work after a few hours of Theo not touching it. Karle had read all about its security features, and there'd been many times his father's Watch had stopped working after he'd 'borrowed' it.

To test the legitimacy of Theo's identity change, Karle needed to wake the Watch up. To do that, he needed Theo's finger. So, after stealing his father's keys, he ended up on the Badds' front step in the hot, post-storm air. Gasping but not relenting, Karle fumbled into his pocket and rattled through the bunch of keys to find one that fitted the lock. Failed. He tried another. Failed. He tried once more and scrunched his eyes with hopeful anticipation. Success. The key turned a full 360 degrees. Karle was thankful his father was so good with people. Trustworthy enough to have a key for most homes in the neighbourhood. Karle slowly opened the door and sneaked inside.

He stood once again in the incredibly narrow hallway.

Frozen. He hadn't considered this far into his plan. What would he say to Glenda? How was he going to get Theo's fingerprint? All sorts of sickening plans of action had come to Karle at that point. He couldn't quite believe he was considering carrying a dead man's severed finger in his pocket, though he had been more disgusted when he found Glenda sleeping inelegantly over a mouldy floral armchair, mouth wide open and saliva dripping down her wobbly chin. He had also been disappointed to see that Theo's body had gone. No longer on the table but replaced with an empty vase. At that point, Karle's instinct was to give up, but as he got back to the front door, something forced him to go upstairs. Before long, he found himself in a bedroom, staring down at Theo's body.

Karle thought again of how peaceful Theo looked. So at rest. He smiled but felt suddenly uncomfortable. It felt wrong and sinister, smiling over the dead. What did he expect? He went there for a dead man's fingerprint, not to sit and have a chocolate biscuit with his feet up. There was a job to be done. No matter how sick and twisted it might be.

He'd grabbed Theo's Watch from his pocket so quickly he'd almost dropped it. Kneeling by the bed and throwing back the floral duvet to expose Theo's right hand, he nervously grabbed Theo's forefinger and swiped it across the screen. *Access denied.* After a few failed attempts, Karle had thrown Theo's hand back down in frustration and had rubbed his own hands together after feeling the icy touch of death. *Too cold.* Back at work, Karle had rubbed Theo's fingers between his own as if he was spinning a stick to start a fire. He added a few sharp blows from his warm breath into the mix and repeated these two motions intensely. He paused. The unexpected slam of the front door. The voice of a man. Beeps of a drone downstairs.

'Oi! Wake up,' the man said loudly.

Karle was still. He couldn't move. He'd then faintly heard Glenda greeting the man before he dismissed her brutishly. 'Where's the body?'

With adrenaline pumping, Karle had recklessly continued his warming routine over Theo's fingers. He'd tried his luck and swiped the screen once more. *Access denied.* Karle had screamed inside and heard Glenda sending the man upstairs, along with the vibrations of footsteps on the staircase. Karle was red in the face, his hands clamming up as he gave everything he had. One last chance. Karle frantically dived down under the bed as the door behind him had swung open. The room filled with Glenda's sniffles as she blew her nose into a tissue. Karle had seen his black boots walk clockwise around the bed. Despite the fragility of the situation, and all it would take was one noise for him to get caught, he couldn't stop himself from smiling cheek to cheek at the active Watch he held in his hand.

The next two hours Karle had spent in the City. On the journey there, after having sneaked onto the train, he breathed heavily, trying to recover from the stress of the previous hour. Not only was he slightly nauseous remembering the cold feeling of the dead man's hands between his own, but his hands were still shaking after hiding from Command. Karle told himself it didn't matter. Yes, it was a close one, but he had succeeded. The Watch was active and it was time to test it.

Karle had looked out the window to the open stretch of desert between the City and the Side. For miles to the east and west, the orange sand didn't seem to end. Its colour was particularly stark against the reflection of the yellow post-storm horizon. The Side was the only surviving area of the old city, left out on the edge when the new Tulo moved further south. Demolished buildings were left to be buried, but this didn't mean all things were hidden. For years to come, even after becoming Ajay, Karle would ponder over the huge slabs of stone sprouting out from the sand like unwanted weeds. There were also torn pieces of old curtains or sheets, shattered glass panes, broken doors and concrete bricks; all left to the elements. He would wonder why Command left them there. As a reminder of what went before? It was the same for the old Resources Railway line that ran out to the west; it was never used after hover planes replaced the trains. But that only invited another question. Where do they go? Karle had always imagined there were more people out there. A world apart from his own little one. He would miss the wild liberty of his childhood brain. He'd still seen it in Tara; the freedom of imagination. He would always miss her too.

Once the train squeaked to a deafening halt, Karle had jumped off it quickly. He knew he didn't need to go far; he just needed a shop that sold an *M-300 or above* product to test the M-310 version of himself on Theo's Watch. Street after street, Karle found more slightly rundown apartments, but no shops or bars. After the fifth or sixth turn, Karle could see the onset of the next ring of the City, the balcony to its river, and the construction of a new sky train line becoming clearer to him with each step. He had considered turning back when a flash of colour caught his eye.

There was a small convenience store emblazoned in bright purple. It displayed a dozen digital news headlines across its front window. Karle skipped across the road, barely missing a parked hover car with his right leg. Outside the shop, Karle clipped Theo's watch around his wrist. Straightening his jacket and brushing down his sweat-ridden trousers, he went inside.

He was startled slightly by the loud twinkle chime that greeted him as the door automatically slid open. Despite being a small, probably insignificant store, it was a spectacle to Karle. It was a myriad of glistening colours as each aisle presented itself with a floating digital sign aglow with the words of its respective product lines. Rows of indulgence were replicated brilliantly across the store. News headlines circled on an LED display in blue letters, and Karle spun around keenly to follow them on their axis. Not that he was reading them, there was too much information to process all around him. So much stuff. He felt the same elation from when he and Callum salivated over the food court. His mind turned back to Callum. Lost. Never returned. It was painful to think about, so Karle would eventually repress it completely. He dismissed his thoughts and scanned the shelves for something to buy. The twinkling sign over one aisle instantly caught his eye. *Candy.*

He'd made his way over to the aisle and found an unbelievable array of Tulo chocolates, sweets, pop drinks, and basically any other merit-deducting confectionary product that existed. Ignoring the Chocos, Drone Drops and Tulo Caramels, Karle selected what he was looking for: *Merit Millions.* Karle read the small-print description. They were small roundel-shaped chocolates, made with the highest-quality ingredients and low-fat dairy, and excluded any artificial sugars. Then Karle read the red messaging encased in a call-out bubble on its shimmering, silver packaging. *M-300 or Above. Less Merit Deducted.* Perfect.

Without wasting more time, Karle paced over to the checkout. There, a man stood in a bold green suit, clearly expensive and clearly tailored. He was shouting something at the checkout assistant.

'. . . much longer. They'll have you replaced by a drone in no time, Side scum.'

Karle felt like walking around the shop again to avoid any interaction with him.

'That's 22.95 credits please,' the checkout girl said, without looking up.

'More than you'll ever get,' the man snarled, scanned his Watch to pay and promptly left the store. Karle slowly took his place and put the *Merit Millions* down at the till. The man was right. Karle knew it. She wouldn't keep that job. He'd read about drone developments and how they planned to shut down even these Outer-Ring stores. Karle struggled to know if the girl was OK because her fringe covered her eyes. She scanned the candy and mumbled, 'Two credits, please.'

Karle had been so distracted by her and the man in the green suit that he had forgotten that this was it. The moment that would define his future. He'd paused considerably longer than he should have done. The girl even had the nerve to cough impatiently. He lifted Theo's Watch up to the scanner. The connection was made and his stomach flipped. A rejection sound.

The girl didn't look up but spoke quietly. 'I'm sorry, but it's rejecting your identification.'

It was only then that she looked up and her slender fingers moved her hair from her face. Karle winced inside as he saw the recognition in her green eyes. They were surprisingly beautiful, and he knew them. They often passed each other on the high street; she always gave him a sweet smile and he ignored her. She was usually leading big groups of children, either taking them to school in the morning or for after-school activities on the sands, so he assumed she was involved with child caring services. She always had her hair tied back and looked annoyingly happy. But right then, there was no smile on her face.

Seconds ticked by in silence. Karle wondered whether she was battling with herself over what to do: report him or let him go. They stood staring at each other in a sort of stand-off moment as the system repeated the rejection sound.

'Oi, what's the problem? We've all got places to be.' A woman with a wide face in sunglasses stood to the right of Karle with milk and bread in her hands. Karle quickly looked back to his accomplice for guidance and started to edge away. He saw her hand drift towards the screen on the desk, ready to betray one of her own. His heart was racing. Brain throbbing.

Then he saw her mouth a word at him. He made it out to be '*go*'.

After that, Theo's Watch had died. Cut from the system. Karle, though, was both ecstatic and frustrated. Ecstatic because he knew what he had overlooked. Frustrated because he didn't know if he could change it. It was simple, really. Karle had cursed himself for not realising sooner. He had given Theo's Watch the identity of himself. Of course, the transaction couldn't be authenticated. The data sent from the Watch mismatched with Theo's identity that Command stored within its database. It was so obvious that Karle felt like smacking himself between the eyes, not just because he'd been so wrapped up in it that he'd overlooked the most important detail, but also, if he were to start a City life, he would need to get into Command. Surely, that was impossible, wasn't it?

Karle was determined to try, and he soon had an inkling about where he could start.

CHAPTER
TWENTY-SIX

For the week that followed, Karle didn't stop thinking about 'Downtown'. The mysterious place he had never heard about. Yet it was where that strange woman, with the stain on her face and drawings on her wall, had warned him about. *It's a place for shady stuff. Don't go right.* Those were her words. He'd concluded that hacking and identity fraud probably fell into the 'shady' category, so he took a chance.

Karle stood breathless across from her house. It was unchanged since the day he lost Callum. It had come out earlier that week that Command had released Callum a day or so after he was arrested, but he never came home. His parents feared the worst and had frantically tried to appeal for missing person alerts to be issued. Karle heard his own parents talking about it. It seemed Command wouldn't approve it. Of course they wouldn't. It was totally unconstitutional to have Worthy people spending their valuable time looking for an Unworthy. What progress would that give them? By that point, Karle had decided it would do him no good to bother about Callum. Surely, he'd want him to move forward? So, Karle forgot him and continued walking down the street.

It was much like any other street with the hustle and bustle of evening commuters and low-swooping drones. There were more of them than the last time he was there.

Karle was wearing a tight T-shirt with black trousers. He'd tucked one side of his T-shirt in to cover up a gaping rip at its bottom. Slipping through the crowds unnoticed, he crossed a bridge. Looking down to the flowing river, he imagined himself beneath it, swimming away from Callum. *Stop.*

Karle blew on his sweaty fingers as he walked into the unknown. He needed to act casual and give people no reason to become suspicious. He slipped his hands into his pockets; cool and relaxed. A girl with a glowing face strode past him carrying designer shopping bags. Why was someone like her in that part of the City? He stared at her, maybe too intensely, so he glanced away, until he realised how she was smiling at him. Not with disdain, but sweetly. Softly. He returned the gesture and his eyes followed her as she disappeared out of view. Was she flirting with him? She'd feel embarrassed if she knew where he was from. That was the first time Karle fully realised the power of deception and how it could work. He could control how people saw him and so he would.

The evening darkness set in and Karle noted the reflection of the yellow moon on the river, and soon he wandered upon a line of market stalls in a large alley between two buildings. Neon coloured lights flickered, and electronic lanterns glittered. He slowed down. There was loud, intrusive music, accompanied by the shouts of salesmen. Karle had read about night markets. They had a miniature version in the Side occasionally, when the ration had been kind and people made homemade cakes to sell, but this felt different. Karle edged past a group at the top of the market. They were Worthy.

All well-dressed, clean and presentable but smoking nicotine. Karle had never smelled it before. He inhaled the smoke as he walked by. It tickled his throat, so he forced his mouth shut to avoid coughing. Why would they smoke? The e-books clearly stated that merit would be deducted for stuff like that, including what another man was eating. Karle watched as the man indulged noisily and impolitely into a sauce-slathered hot dog. The sauce dripped and oozed down the man's sweat-blanched white vest. He could be Unworthy, but Karle corrected himself when he saw the man's shoes, which were clearly authentic camel skin.

Karle slipped himself down between the stalls and overheard some of the exchanges. His attention was caught by a woman wearing orange-tinted sunglasses, who was trading what looked like an expensive blender for a bag of Tulo Caramels. Looking around him, Karle saw this behaviour mirrored down the entire strip of street; a high-end TV for a bottle of stronger ethanol, a silent hairdryer for a pack of cigarettes, and a ton of fresh, quality meat for litres of fizzy pop. Every Worthy-looking customer wore either a low hat or sunglasses, and other than the group at the front, they never stuck long enough to chat.

'What you want, son?' A man with a vest stretching over his balloon belly appeared in Karle's path. He was holding three bottles of clear liquid in each hand. 'I've got 35 per cent, 50 per cent . . .' He leaned closer and whispered, 'Even 75 per cent, but keep that one between us, huh?' He winked and stood back, waiting for Karle's response.

Karle hesitated. He didn't even know 75 per cent ethanol existed. The thought of being offered it was obscene. He'd never tried it, nor would he want to.

'I don't...I can't...not...erm...' Karle looked behind him, seeing how people had flooded the road between the stalls, blocking his exit.

'Look, if you ain't got anything to trade, I'm happy to take an *I owe you*. I got your face, I'll let the merit police know you got the ethanol if you don't come back.' He was still waving the bottles in his face, and Karle could smell the strength of the drink and the man's sweat, much of which was dripping down his large forehead.

'I don't want it, thank you,' Karle managed.

The man stood back and shrugged his shoulders. 'I don't get why you young lads won't take the drink when there's no merit lost.' The man began to saunter off in pursuit of a willing punter.

'Wait,' Karle touched the back of his shoulder and felt the coarseness of the man's skin. The man turned back, the small amount of red hair he had left mirroring the orange lantern above him.

'I didn't come for a drink. I'm looking for someone who could help me with something.' Karle wasn't sure how to play it. Was he being reckless?

'What kind of "something"?' The man raised a bushy eyebrow.

'Identity fraud,' Karle said quietly, while trying to ignore the jellylike feeling in his legs.

'Yeah, I know someone that can help with that,' the man replied casually, not a tiny bit fazed. 'But you gotta give me something. What you got?'

Karle reached into his pocket and pulled out a round silver object. He willingly handed it over and the man snatched the device from him swiftly with his free hand.

'This is one of those Guiding Light junks,' the man said curiously. 'How did you get it?' Karle opened his mouth to answer, but the sweaty man stopped him. 'It don't matter. It'll do. The scrap materials will go for a credit or two. This way.' He flicked his bottles in the direction he began to walk. As they got deeper into the market, Karle started to smell more cheap meat; he spotted burgers grilling to his right, the grease dripping into a tray beneath. He salivated.

'Oi, you think I got all day?' The man had moved quickly. Karle hurried over to him, where he stood in front of a group of smokers under a flickering maroon light. The man tapped the shoulder of a lady in a cream trench coat.

'I've got some business for ya,' he said. The woman snarled over her shoulder and stepped lightly in Karle's direction. The man grunted at Karle as he brushed past him out of sight.

'What you want, kid?'

Her friends disbanded and she stood before Karle with a cigarette smoking in her left hand. Her brown hair was tied in a braid that fell over her right shoulder; she wore a cap on her head and her coat was secured with a few buttons over what he assumed was her bare chest. She was stylish, on-trend, and beautifully mysterious. Karle had lost his words at first, not getting much out.

'Struggling to get those words out?' She tilted her slim head. 'Here.' She offered her cigarette, caught between two of her pencil-like fingers.

Karle refused and gathered himself.

'I'm looking for a new identity,' he said, rubbing his neck.

She took a drag. Karle suddenly twitched as she threw the cigarette down to the floor and crushed it under her ankle boot, all the while squinting at him.

His heart was pumping, and he covered his wrist as she looked down at it, clearly noticing the absence of a Watch. He didn't know what to do or say. He'd looked at this incredibly mystifying woman, waiting for her to give him hope.

'Come with me,' she said.

Karle felt strangely relieved they were going somewhere. It didn't at that moment occur to him that it probably wasn't the wisest idea to go into a room with a stranger. They walked through a tattered pink curtain, entering a small room. Karle felt the grease on it as he drew the curtain back behind her.

The light was dim, only provided by an industrial cage lamp that sat on the wall. The room housed an off-colour plastic table Karle guessed used to be white, and two matching chairs. As they walked further into the room, she promptly demanded a cup of coffee from a machine on the table.

'Want one?' she asked as she slumped into the chair furthest from the door.

He shook his head, stroking his arms. The unbearable mugginess outside was intensified in such a small space. It had then occurred to him how odd it was that she was wearing a coat. It was a lightweight one, but no storms were forecast, and it was insufferably hot. That was the moment when it first occurred to Karle that this woman could be mad. He had willingly found himself alone, in a strange place, with a mad woman.

'Well, have a seat.' She pointed to the vacant chair.

Karle hesitated as he glanced back at the closed pink curtain – the only thing between them and prying ears.

'No one is listening, kid. Go ahead. How can I help ya?'

Karle sat and, to both his and his listener's surprise, his previous hesitation evaporated to join the humidity. Words began pouring out of him like a violent waterfall. He relayed almost everything about his quest for a new him; from his Side upbringing to what happened with Callum and how Purification wasn't enough, to explaining his failed efforts with Theo's Watch so far.

'Sure it didn't work,' she interrupted him and smiled sardonically. Karle stopped talking, almost panting at the speed of his dialogue and desperate for some water. 'That's pretty obvious, kid. You need someone on the inside, but first you need to chill out.'

Karle wiped his hands on his knees, nodding with his eyes fixed hard on hers in hope and anticipation. She sat back on her chair, the plastic creaking as she did so. She threw her feet up on the table. She casually lit another cigarette, gave a few short puffs, and smirked at him. It wasn't a friendly smile, but cunning and mischievous. It made Karle imagine that she would soon order two brutish men to rip through the curtain and take him away to a Command torture chamber, if they even existed.

But instead, she just spoke.

'I can do it. I work in Command Security. It would be a simple operation.' She lobbed the cigarette onto the table, its black ash flicking across its surface. Karle's muscles turned rigid. She could do it? As easy as that?

He didn't know how to respond. It was clear she wasn't the kind of woman who would enjoy him drowning her in his gratitude.

'So, what you offering me?' She roughly grabbed her coffee and slurped it down in one.

Darn. Not as easy as that. He looked down at his clammy fingers that protruded from his Watchless wrist.

'Nothing.'

'What's that now?' She flung her feet down to the ground. 'You want me to do this for nothing?'

'I have no credit or anything worth having,' Karle said quietly. He looked up so she could see the sincerity in his eyes. She laughed then, a dark and unnerving sound. Yep, he'd thought. She surely believed he was a City-kissing, Side-born imbecile, and she would probably kill him. Karle wanted to shut off his erratic mind.

When she'd stopped laughing, her body language changed, and Karle watched her as she began pacing the small width of the room. Back and forth, back and forth. Some time passed. Maybe she was deciding *how* she would kill him, or whether it would be easier to report him for some credit or merit. Perhaps his grandma, or The Guiding Light, was right. The path of the City really did lead to destruction; he'd hardly started walking it and he already felt the pang of vulnerability as this peculiar and potentially malicious stranger, who wore a coat at the hottest time of year and knew everything about him, was mulling over his fate. How could he have been so stupid?

Finally, she stopped pacing and leaned over the table, the cigarette ash scattering across her fingers. 'You said you were from the Side, right?'

Karle jumped at her sudden movement and was confused by why his origin mattered.

'Right?' she snapped again.

'Yeah,' he cleared his throat. 'The west side.'

Karle recoiled in his seat, not enjoying the uncertainty of what was coming next.

'Alright. I'll do it for you,' she said with another smirk. She sat down and put her legs up on the table once more and returned the cigarette to her mouth. 'This is what you do for me.' She looked at him sternly. 'You know the plant, Fo Doktrin? The one with the lethal leaves?'

'Yeah, I know it,' Karle said.

'That stuff goes for quite a lot of credit round here. Some lads want it for some off-the-market *SkipSleep.*' Karle was reminded of the advert he'd seen at the shopping centre.

Throwing her cap off and pointing to the space between Karle's eyes, she demanded, 'You bring me five kilos of that each week until your Watch day, and you've got a deal.'

She sat back again.

At first, Karle had questions. Why didn't she just go and get it herself? But he'd reminded himself of what he already knew. City citizens had merit deducted for travelling back to the Side without a legitimate contributory reason, which was non-existent because the Side was deemed fundamentally unproductive towards society. And he knew it would be easy enough to collect a good amount of Fo Doktrin to satisfy his new accomplice.

Karle agreed and stood, ready to leave the insufferable cave of heat. She rose too and stuck out her hand, which held a small, rusting key. He hadn't thought anyone used keys in the City anymore.

'Just leave it in the hatch there.'

Karle followed her pointing finger. In the corner of the room, behind where she'd been sitting, lay a bolted wooden hatch over the concrete floor. He was instantly thankful that he hadn't seen it before. That would have sent him into a frenzy believing she was a murderer and that's where she'd keep his body. He'd immediately placed the key in his trouser pocket.

'But kid, don't get caught. They'll shoot us both.'

Karle thought he saw fear pass her eyes. Only for a moment, before her face lifted again.

'We got a deal?'

Karle hesitated, the blatant suggestion of a death sentence from Command temporarily paralysing him. He'd be brave. He'd come too far. They wouldn't catch him if he was careful.

He asked when she'd give him the details of his new identity.

'Your Watch day. I'll be by the Glorified Gate. Leave the details to me. M-350 a good starting point?' She lifted her still-burning cigarette from the table to her mouth, squinting her eyes again.

'That works,' Karle nodded as the rolled tube of nicotine hung between her lips, and they settled things with a sweaty handshake.

CHAPTER
TWENTY-SEVEN

Every morning for the following month, Karle rose early.

'Why are you up at this hour?' his grandma had asked the first time, as she quickly chopped shoots off old potatoes.

'Starting a new fitness cycle,' Karle had lied. There were no questions asked, only praise from his grandma when he returned all sweaty and worn out. Of course, this was from all the exhilaration of being out in the desert, under the beating sun, chopping up Fo Doktrin and then hiding it in bags. He'd got away with it every time. Even when he'd offered to help his mother in the garden, which he rarely did willingly. He would help prune the vegetable patches and pocket any Doktrin that had weeded its way in. Their total lack of suspicion made Karle realise they were even more naïve than he'd originally thought. Although, it was surprising that his grandma didn't wince at his change in behaviour, as she was usually fairly inquisitive. Maybe she knew and was keeping quiet. It didn't matter to Karle if she did or not. He just got on with it: wake early, get the Doktrin; avoid its leaves staining his shorts, pack it up; hide the bag, go to the City; drop it in the hatch and repeat. It was, in some ways, a little *too* easy. He'd even hoped that something would go wrong, just to prove it all wasn't too good to be true. That one day he might whip back that pink curtain, and some Command Guards or TPD drones would be there to arrest him.

Yet there was never anyone there. It was all unbelievably straightforward. Though there was one day that stood out from the others.

Karle's fingers were clamming up, the day's heat scorching his skin. He'd exhaled deeply to combat his increasing dehydration. He flipped his cap around so that the pointed edge protected his neck from the white demon in the sky. Beginning to feel numb, he stood, the electronic scissors still in his right hand. He watched as his six-foot shadow blanketed itself over the Fo Doktrin plant he was disturbing. The orange-dusted leaves were wide with a surface area similar to an ordinary dining plate and its millimetre-thin grey stems just sprouted up from the sand, almost as if there were no roots beneath. But evidence showed that this plant spawned many children, burying its foundations deep under the Tulo sand. Karle stretched his neck back and could make out the huge central tree of the forest within the heat wave. He used to imagine Country folk gathered there around campfires, dancing or telling one another stories. Its branches spread far across the horizon, as if it had arms open wide to embrace another tree in a hug.

Karle had exhaled and squatted again. He placed the scissors under the stems and turned them on. They set to work, chopping away at the stems without Karle having to do anything but direct and hold its end. He gathered the offcuts in bundles and shoved them into his black holdall.

Looking at his analogue watch, he decided he should head out to the City to drop off the cargo for the day.

When he gathered his things, something to the east had caught his eye. Through the floating heat waves and sporadic wafts of orange-red sand in the air, Karle had squinted at some moving black figures. They were shifting slowly in a group, not far from the hugging tree. They were definitely human; their silhouettes plodded across the desert land. It wasn't mindless plodding. They almost marched. Soon they disappeared, fading between the spindles of the trees to leave only a confused teenager wondering who they were and where they were going.

These mysterious forest figures ran across Karle's mind a few weeks afterwards as he stood impatiently on the platform. Despite being thankful for the distraction of the memory, he grew anxious. How would Command react to his hand-me-down suit? Its cuffs were frayed and trousers too short, like scrap material compared to the heights of City fashion. If only there was something more distinguished he could have worn for arguably the most important day of his life.

His eighteenth birthday, the day of his initiation, the day he would get his Watch.

The start of a new era, one where his suits would be tailored. He looked down at the empty platform, pleased that he was the first one there, which wasn't surprising as he'd arrived two hours early, much to the confusion of his family.

'You're going now?' his grandma had cried out, as she put down a cup of tea to tighten the belt of her dressing gown.

'You'll get too hot just waiting at the platform,' his mother had said as she and Tara trotted down the stairs, both still wearing their pyjamas.

'That's OK.' Karle had opened the door and sprinted through it before any family member could even say 'Happy Birthday'. He hadn't noticed the splendidly coloured, handmade card that Tara held in her hands.

Soon, along with six other Side kids, Karle arrived at the Glorified Quarters on a hover bus. Lucie, the City official who had ushered the group from the train, stood up as the vehicle came to a smooth, gliding halt.

'We'll be walking from this point.'

Karle was already bored of her robotic voice, and looking at her, he couldn't believe that someone who worked for Command was so plain and simple. She wore no make-up and appeared disinterested half the time. Her plain white vest and trousers clearly weren't uniform, because Karle noticed no Command logo on her breast. He couldn't help but feel slightly disappointed. Surely Command should advise officials to make a big deal out of initiation day, the day when citizens could start making their contribution, but Karle had reminded himself then: he and the other kids there weren't considered 'citizens'.

Regardless of that, though, Karle felt his breathing quicken as they walked down the gleaming white walkways of the Quarters. He had been looking forward to it for so long. Just to get a glimpse of how the Glorified lived. There were many fancy gates, some gold and some black, but they all guarded a winding driveway that disappeared into the mountains. He'd wanted to stop and overanalyse what the houses up there must be like.

Secluded and paradisal. All those families could surely never want for anything. It did surprise Karle how small the crowds were. He'd almost expected the Glorified to be constantly out and about in their glad rags nattering to one another about their latest accomplishments, but there was no one around, other than the occasional hover car with blacked-out windows. *Perhaps that's what luxury is like*, he'd thought. It wasn't long until the group was at Command.

His heart rate accelerated as he goggled at the rectangular building, encased wall to wall with transparent glass and boasting three white pillars at its front. The walkway was dressed in purple flags on lampposts, all featuring Command's circular logo.

Karle felt terrified by his own insignificance as he walked through the gigantic pillars and then the glass doors. Inside was almost blindingly bright. Everything was white, with small, tasteful purple details such as the cushions on seats and linings on Command workers' suits. They walked around regally, greeting one another as they disappeared and appeared through doors. Karle was transfixed mostly by what stood in the open foyer. Straight in front of him were big three-dimensional blocks of letters, arranged centrally across the floor to read: PROGRESS IS STRENGTH.

Karle's curiosity controlled him. He moved closer to the letters, blazoned white yet with tiny multicoloured specks across their surface. Karle could then see that these specks were, in fact, handwriting. Peoples of all ages and abilities had all scrawled the same thing in varying colours of ink: *For a greater Tulo*. Karle felt himself soften. There was such sweetness in a community, from the young to the old, standing together for something better.

'Blythefen!'

The sharp, coarse voice had startled Karle. He'd turned around to find Lucie standing with one hand on her hip at an open doorway. He was pleased that her voice suddenly had some character to it.

Karle moved quickly, conscious that the rest of the group had disappeared. He followed Lucie through the doorway, down some concrete steps and into a basement room.

'Take a seat,' Lucie said. They entered a box room littered with small wooden desks, not far removed from Karle's desk at home. He chose a seat at the back of the room and grimaced at the screech the chair made across the concrete floor. He felt so claustrophobic, like he was in a tin can. What kind of reception was this? He was pretty sure that City kids weren't thrown down in the basement at their initiation. They were probably pampered and treated to a five-course dinner. He felt himself getting agitated, but he told himself he wouldn't have to deal with this for much longer.

'Welcome everyone to Tulo Command – the centre of governmental operations for Tulo.' Lucie had turned robotic again. Karle dropped his shoulders. 'To begin your initiation, please turn your attention to the screen. We will show you an introductory video before then taking you through for Watch Administration.' She gestured to the screen that ever so slightly wobbled with the floating motion of the powering drone behind it.

A narrated, subtitled video sprang into life and bounced off the four white walls, reflected in the skin and clothing of its bright-eyed young audience. Karle read along with the subtitles, but not without appreciating the authoritative, booming voice emanating from the speakers.

Welcome to Tulo Command.

Before the Revolution, Tulo was run by selfish and greedy dictators who contributed little to the progress of society, leaving most citizens enslaved and insignificant.

But now Tulo is different. Tulo is greater. We are now a society based on the equal contribution of its skilful and ambitious citizens. And to ensure that those who contribute to our positive growth are rewarded with a life they deserve, we instigated the merit system.

Karle stopped himself from audibly sighing. The other kids there looked much more engaged, all eyes staring at the screen and watching words and images fly over each other.

Merit Scores indicate the extent to which an individual has used their time and skills to contribute towards the welfare of all of Tulo. Merit can be earned directly under three main categories: Technological and Societal Advancement, Personal Development and Community Spirit. Merit can also be earned indirectly if an individual keeps themselves healthy enough to contribute and encourages others in their contributions.

Did they not all already know this stuff? Karle almost grunted out loud at the girl sitting next to him. He'd thought he'd heard her gasp at this apparently new information.

Deduction in merit occurs under the following circumstances: when an individual attends a venue or area of Tulo that is deemed unproductive or anti-constitutional; an individual's Watch detects they haven't earned merit for a week; when an individual purchases foods containing high sugars, high saturated fats or high levels of ethanol; or when another citizen reports the individual for proved unproductive behaviour or discouragement of others to contribute. For more specific details about merit gains and deduction, please refer to the constitutional handbook which can be found from your Watch's user interface.

From her baby-faced complexion and fox-pup eyes, Karle could have sworn the girl was about twelve, not eighteen.

We are glad to welcome you from the Side to Tulo Command on this occasion. We hope you will have been made aware of your position. While we never want any citizen to be restricted in their contributory ability, past events mean we have had to put the necessary measures in place to avoid any anti-constitutional ideology infiltrating the values of Tulo City. We hope to welcome you into the City following your Purification in seven years' time. Enjoy your initiation and remember that Progress is Strength.

The light and backing music subsided. Everyone but Karle shuffled restlessly in their seats. Had any of them read up on this? Did they just live with their family and accept that's all there was? Of course, this was all conjecture. Karle knew he was being obnoxious, but with every moment he had got closer to City life, the more he'd stopped caring. Soon these people would be nothing to him but a fading, Unworthy memory.

Lucie appeared again through a door on the left-hand side of the room. 'This way.'

Karle grimaced again at the simultaneous screeches of the chairs as they all stood to leave the room. He was relieved when he saw the next room was much more spacious. The walls were white again, with beautifully blooming plants dotted around in corners. A long, white desk stretched the entirety of the room, forming a barrier between the group and the other side.

Several Command officials dressed in remarkably white suits and dresses sat behind the desk, each one wearing a beaming smile. Karle smiled back.

'Tantley!' shouted the official at the far left of the room. The group simultaneously turned their heads to see the official gesturing towards the empty white chair that sat in front of him. A young girl with a quaint blue bow in her hair tapped on people's shoulders to let her through.

'Slinson,' the next official called, and the boy standing next to Karle made his way across the room, but not before turning to him and whispering, 'The Guiding Light bless you.' Karle held his tongue despite wanting to tell him to get a grip.

'Blythefen!' The name echoed and bounced off the walls, hanging in the air. This was it. He tightened his tie and stood in front of the seat belonging to a blond man with unbelievably smooth skin and shining teeth.

'Please have a seat, Karle.' He pointed to the chair, and Karle appreciated that this one made no sound when he moved it.

'My name's Quain and I'll be your Watch Administrator. Any questions you have along the way, just let me know.' Quain spoke with a confusing tone, both patronising and welcoming. He tapped in a furious motion onto the desk that had become a giant keypad. Karle looked around to see clones of Quain's movement in the other Command officials. 'First things first, we need to do your fingerprint scans. Please place both hands down as indicated,' Quain instructed.

Karle looked down at his side of the desk, where two hand outlines appeared. He'd placed them down and was surprised by the coolness of the desk at his touch. There was a slight tickle and vibration as the scan was completed. Quain swiped his hand across the desk. 'The fingerprint is how you gain access to your Watch and there are also intermittent scans whenever you're using it. Just a security protocol.' Karle nodded, even though he already understood. He probably knew more about Watches than anyone else in that room.

'OK, any second now . . .' Quain said as a drone swooped down beside him. 'Perfect.'

The side of the drone opened and he pulled the contents out. Karle started to fidget. There it was. *His* Watch. 'Are you left-handed?' Quain asked.

'Right, actually,' Karle responded.

'Unusual,' Quain commented as he lowered the Watch over Karle's left wrist. Immediately metal crawled from either side of the Watch and scurried across his wrist in a tickle until the two sides found each other with a satisfying click. Karle looked over it closely, moving his wrist back and forth. Its model was sleek and slimline; it had a black casing with a rectangular screen that covered the width of his wrist.

'Beautiful,' Karle said to himself, before Quain rudely interrupted.

'So, let me just run through the basics. It's waterproof, obviously. The controls are pretty simple, and the majority of commands are produced in a pop-out screen. Oh, there you go.' Quain sounded surprised as Karle had fashioned a screen displaying his health stats. He started flicking through different screens at speed, his eyes dancing as they followed the content. He had yet to find any user differences from this model to the one Mr Badds had, which had been reassuring. Karle then almost tipped off his chair as a hand flew through his screen and almost touched his face.

'OK. You're obviously a natural, but there's still a few things to run through.' Quain was frustrated. Karle found it amusing but made sure not to show it. He turned the screen off. 'So, on a privacy level, no one other than those directly in front of your screen can see its contents. Additionally, the Watch does not record your every move. Tulo Command takes their citizens' privacy very seriously. For merit-making, there is the option for conversation and activity recording, but your Watch will . . .'

'Always ask for your permission?' Karle finished for him.

'Yes . . . exactly.' Quain was surprised again. Hadn't he learned by now? Karle knew what he was doing. Quain then fumbled around on his desk to find his next topic to tick off the list. 'Yes, so . . . just to reassure you, you can absolutely take the Watch off. But it is needed as identification when necessary,' Quain said. 'I personally never take mine off, you never know when your next merit opportunity will come along.' Quain smiled and sat back slightly in his seat. 'I think that's everything, Karle. Do you have any questions?'

Karle didn't hesitate. 'No, I've got everything I need.'

Where was she?

She'd said she'd come. She said she'd be in the Quarters on his Watch day. That was their arrangement. The deal.

Yet as Karle desperately willed her to appear from around a corner, she was nowhere to be seen. Karle could feel his rage and frustration rising the closer they came to boarding the hover bus for the return to the Side. He no longer gazed at the opulent gates or cared much for the tantalising smells coming down from the mountains. Before he even began to wonder what was being cooked up there, he'd felt sick enough for his rations to reappear. For a whole month he had laboured and risked everything to lug that Fo Doktrin around. And for what? So she could break their deal? In some ways, Karle wasn't surprised. He was stupid enough to trust someone he didn't know.

He could see the black bus ready for the group to board. *No, no. Come on. Where are you?* Karle was beside himself, and struggled not to voice or show his desperation.

Then, he saw her. Though he still felt nauseous, she was there, leaning against a lamppost not far from the Glorified Gate. Her head was down and her brown hair was tied in that same braid that fell over her right shoulder. She wore baggy trousers and that cream coat. She became stark and obvious as Karle got closer, standing out in front of the golden walls. She looked up, and their eyes met. Those menacing, evil eyes and that sardonic smile. She started walking towards the group, but no longer looked at Karle, as if to act like a passer-by. Karle's wrist vibrated. He heard the notification sound of a raised heart rate for the first time. She got closer, until she was right there. Next to him and whispering in his ear.

'You did good, kid.'

Karle felt the soft tickle of her fingers drop something into his trouser pocket. They both continued walking, not stopping to look at each other again. He'd told himself that would be the last time he saw her. She would become part of the life he would forget. The life of Karle Blythefen from the Side.

Only when he settled on the bus did he pull the note from his pocket. It was a dirty, torn piece of lined parchment folded two ways. Inside, he found the identification details for Ajay Ambers.

CHAPTER
TWENTY-EIGHT

Ajay, of course, had never let anything slip. Genni, Ace, nor anyone else had even a suspicion about who he really was. When he first arrived in the City, he'd slipped in unnoticed, renting a M-300 apartment and getting an assistant computing job. No one ever questioned him. Why would they? He was a well-presented keen socialite with a healthy score of M-350. It had all worked flawlessly, and never once had he regretted it. Of course, there were sticky moments. He'd have heart palpitations every time he heard rumours over new Watch models or security features, which would be inevitable. But Ajay had learned to have confidence in himself. He would find a way. Karle Blythefen was dead, and Ajay Ambers lived on.

Except *she* kept him hanging on to the past he longed to forget.

Grandma was the person he'd trusted more than anyone. On the day he left, he'd cried only because he couldn't take her with him. He'd even suggested it, but he knew he could never persuade her. 'I am who I was made to be,' she had said on his last night as they'd sipped their hot drinks before bed.

Nowadays, every other month or so, he'd come back to see her because he'd promised. It wasn't for anyone else. Not for his mother, who hadn't noticed him standing by the front door. She walked past through the kitchen again, clunking pots and cutlery together as she was setting the dinner table. It baffled Ajay how everything could be so unchanged. The walls, the carpets, and they still hadn't painted over the childhood graffiti that travelled up the walls. Coming back was the only time he allowed himself to think too much about those memories. He had to stay grounded. *Perhaps I should slip upstairs without saying hello this time.* That would be nice and discreet, and would completely avoid any awkwardness, and he'd probably escape quicker.

Rustles and bangs came from the front room, and its door swung open. Ajay's father stood before him, with a faint smile on his face.

They looked at each other in silence. Ajay laughed internally. It wasn't just the house that never changed. His father's checked shirt pocket had lost its stitching and his dusty glasses were still bent across his face. His hair was slightly thinner than the last time he saw him. Ajay thought he looked even more dishevelled with that bald patch extending across his head.

'Nice to see you, son,' he said.

'Hi.'

'Are you OK?'

'Yeah, doing good.'

'Good.'

This is awkward. He never understood why his father bothered with the small talk. The day before he'd left, they had shaken hands in the kitchen, sort of like a parting gesture. Why couldn't he leave it at that and ignore him when he turned up? It wasn't like Ajay ever stuck around long enough to warrant any actual conversation.

'Fancy a drink?' his father asked. 'Your mother's through here.'

Really? Ajay couldn't be bothered to refuse. With everything that had happened the last few months with Genni, he'd used up all his confrontational energy. He hesitantly followed his father into the kitchen, with one eye on the time. He'll get the drink then dart upstairs.

Quick in and out.

His mother was slicing into a loaf of bread. Ajay met her eyes and she beamed, instantly setting down the knife and rushing towards him.

'It's lovely to see you.' The squeeze on his arms felt compassionate, followed by the firmness of a motherly kiss on his cheek. He hated the way it made him feel warm. He hated any feeling of attachment he had towards her. She'd always looked after him, doing everything a mother should do, but they'd never had much of a connection. It was as if they'd been necessities in each other's lives and that was all. 'A drink? There's also bread. The ration was generous today.' She grabbed the bread knife again and started sawing into the loaf, the wisps of crumbs flaking onto the breadboard.

'Just some water's fine.' Ajay paused. 'Thanks.'

His mother placed the knife down again and moved towards a cupboard above her. Ajay watched as his father graciously stopped her.

'I'll get it, love,' he said over the creaking of the cupboard door. Ajay noticed that they'd never replaced the glasses as his father chose the one with the small chip on its rim and slowly headed to the sink. *Take your sweet time. It's not like my time is worth something.*

As the sound of running water filled the silence between them, Ajay fleetingly scanned the dining room. The table had changed; no longer the wobbly wooden one he'd sat round for many dinners, countless board games, to write innumerable answers to homework questions and for unproductive hours listening to The Guiding Light. He actually thought the one they'd replaced it with was in a worse condition. It was a white, hard plastic, covered in black scratches, and its wooden legs had chunks missing. Strange choice for an upgrade. Tara wasn't sitting there again. For the first few years when Ajay visited, she would sit at the table, just reading or writing while their mother cooked. She didn't speak to him much, but it had been months, maybe even more than a year since she'd last been here. Ajay assumed she was out at a neighbour's or working at the school. His grandma had told him she'd been training as a teacher. She never said anything more and Ajay didn't ask. It had been six years too long for him to start getting too invested in their lives again.

'She's been a bit hit and miss lately. So don't worry if she's not her usual self.' His father placed the chipped glass, full, down onto the cruddy table. Ajay picked it up immediately, expecting it to cool down his sweaty palms. He'd forgotten. The water wasn't chilled from the tap out here. These little reminders of their chosen poverty were welcome to him. It was nice to know how right he'd been. He sipped and swallowed the lukewarm water silently.

His father peered at him as if he expected Ajay to say something else. What did he want from him? He'd left. To him, he wasn't even his son anymore. Maybe he needed to make it clearer to him. *I could shout in his dull face?* Ajay wanted nothing from him, but as always, he opted to say nothing, brushing past his father and heading towards the stairs. He needed to get on with keeping his promise to Grandma; come now and again for a catch-up, and then he could get out.

He took the stairs two at a time and darted straight towards his grandma's closed bedroom door. He hesitated. *Stop it.* He couldn't help himself, he always had to investigate his bedroom. He peeked through the ajar door, which welcomed visitors with red peeling stickers that spelt 'Karle' on its outer side. Seriously? They still hadn't changed it? It was as if they expected Karle, that lanky, skinny kid, to walk through the front door and just slip back into his old life. His bed still wore the same bedclothes since the day he'd left. The posters of City video games hung creased on the wall, and his old computer was practically grey now, cuddled up in its dust blanket. Every time it was the same. Ajay didn't know why he expected anything different. Maybe he thought they might have some sense and use the room for something useful. With that idea, he let out a small, sarcastic laugh; he was kidding himself. This room would be as it was for the rest of their lives, and maybe even the rest of his life. He decided to let them stew in their false hope and closed the door. His grandma had heard him.

'Ajay, is that you?'

Her voice was deep but faint. Ajay was surprised he heard her through the woodwork. He reached for the door, the brass doorknob feeling cool on his skin. He twisted it and pushed open the door to find his grandma sat up in bed. No matter how much he tried to convince himself otherwise, this was his best friend. His energetic, spritely elder who raced him up hills, taught him how to treat a wound, and played hours of cards until he was good enough to beat her. The lady who plaited Tara's hair, who told him all those marvellous stories, who supported him unconditionally. This wasn't her. Or, it was her, imprisoned in some worn, deteriorating shell of a body. He'd seen her just a month ago and she hadn't looked this bad. She looked years older; her wrinkles resembled the deep gorges of a canyon, the skin under her eyes had yellowed and thinned, the moisture of her lips was non-existent, and the deep, strained croak of her voice had no similarity to the vibrancy it carried before. Ajay gulped hard and tried to remain dry-eyed. *Don't get attached. Make it quick and get back home.*

'How are you, Grandma?'

As Ajay walked towards her, he noticed the window was slightly open and there was an orange splatter of sand on the windowsill. The wind was rising outside with the coming storm and wafting sand in. He reached over and pulled the rotten wooden frame towards him.

'Oh, you know.' Grandma coughed as if her insides were ready to project from her mouth. 'Dying,' she laughed muskily.

She looked at Ajay with tired yet intent eyes, smiling sweetly like she used to. Ajay went soft. That smile. Why was it always so good at comforting him? Even with the dryness of her mouth and the wobbly skin surrounding it, that smile was still his weakness. He sat on the wicker stool by the bed.

'What's been happening around here, then?' Ajay knew this question would please her, even if his interest in the neighbourhood was a lie.

'Well,' Grandma had a solemn look on her face and said bluntly, 'Doreena from down the lane has disappeared.'

'Which one was Doreena?'

'You know, Doreena Laptoff? The one with all the foxes?'

'I'm not sure I remember her.'

'Oh, come on, love,' Grandma wheezed. It sounded painful, yet still she was able to talk. 'Her sister was the one who went for Purification?'

Ajay remembered. He knew exactly who she meant. She used to walk her foxes at least five times a day and would let Tara and himself pet them on the street. *Laptoff. Doreena Laptoff.* As in, related to Mrs Laptoff from the village?

'Do you know if her sister did well in the City?' Ajay questioned.

Grandma nodded. 'Oh yes, she was Glorified.'

Ajay shuffled uncomfortably on the stool, his bum already going numb. So, that's how she knew about him. He recalled her face against the ground and the words that she spoke: 'They'll find you.' Ajay felt his fingers tingle and a small pain travelled across his chest. He breathed hard and, of course, Grandma noticed. She was looking at him with a stare of interrogation, like she was telepathic. How did she do that? Looking so deep into him, he knew the question she was asking.

'I met her. She's in the retirement village I work at.'

'Oh, well maybe you could ask about Doreena.'

'Yeah. She's a bit past conversation.'

'She recognised you, didn't she?' Grandma was always able to read his face. It was annoying. Ajay kind of wished that in her deterioration the ability might have subsided.

'Yeah, but she's seen as a bit deranged. I'll be fine.'

'Not forever you won't be.'

Ajay decided to ignore the comment. 'So, when did Doreena disappear?'

'A couple of weeks back. Her neighbour said he'd seen her walking towards the allotments on a morning, as she always does. Then, she never came back. Now the whole community has become a bit engrossed in finding good homes for the hundreds of foxes. Fortunately, with my condition, your parents got out of that extra responsibility.' They laughed briefly together. It was familiar and Ajay enjoyed it.

'So where did she go?' Ajay then asked, as he took a sip of water. Warm and gross.

'Well, apparently her VPG confirmed the City.' Grandma heaved herself upwards to sit straighter.

'Well, there you go. She's followed her sister and is serving the Glorified,' Ajay said.

'That, or *your* thing,' she coughed through her words and spluttered some green-looking substance into a tissue. Ajay couldn't help but wince.

'Here,' he said, swapping her tissue for a new one from the box on the bedside table.

'No offence to Doreena, but she never looked like someone who could hack her way in.' Ajay threw the dirty tissue into the wastebasket beside his feet.

'No, that's true. She'd get caught immediately. But she's like the third one this month who's gone. The others I suppose I can believe, but Doreena was just as committed to The Guiding Light as I am. And why would she go now, in her old age? I just don't believe it.' The saggy skin beneath his grandma's neck wobbled as she shook her head.

'Well,' Ajay paused. He was about to say something about people coming to their senses, but he decided against it. He knew that comments like that upset her. It wasn't worth it. If she was well and active, it'd be different. He'd defend a City-goer to the end.

'So, how's that girlfriend of yours? Will you let me meet her before I die?'

She spoke about death so matter of fact, as if it was as simple and ordinary as having dinner. She wasn't afraid, though Ajay remembered she never was. Even when he left, with all the danger he was putting himself in, his grandma never once looked worried for him. He sometimes wondered if it was because she knew he'd pull it off, but that didn't quite sit right. It was most likely her unfounded expectation that The Guiding Light would protect him. Her faith in it was strong, to Ajay's despair. He let it go, letting her continue believing a fallacy. It made her happy, that was something at least.

'She's fine. And probably not, Grandma.' He was honest. Genni would never go there.

'That's a real shame.' Grandma yawned, opening her mouth so Ajay could see the blackened crevasses of her back teeth. When did she get so old? He stopped himself from thinking about it. If he started down that road, he'd start to regret missing more of her life. *Change the subject.* Or maybe it was time to go. He let out his own yawn.

'Sorry, love. They're so contagious.' She smiled as her breathing grew heavier. She slowly wiped the small blots of sweat off the brow of her greyed hair. 'Could you rearrange my pillows for me?'

Ajay rose instantly from the stool, took his arms behind her and straightened the pillows so they were more supportive of her back.

'It's OK if you need to rest, Grandma.' Ajay lightly tapped her wrinkled fingers, feeling the scrape of her slim rings on his hand. 'I need to go anyway.'

'No, love. Stay a while longer.'

'OK.' Ajay couldn't resist the eyes that told of unrelenting love. It was almost desperate, like she *needed* him to stay. He kept hold of her hand, enjoying her warmth despite the increased humidity that accompanied a Tulo storm. Gazing out the window, Ajay saw how the skyline looked like a child's drawing they weren't happy with, scribbled over and barely recognisable as the sand was carried higher and faster. Bits of trees, plants and rubbish were joining the picture, floating erratically in the angered wind. It was getting darker too, as the rare troops of clouds marched over the defence of the white sun. *I should go.* He didn't want to be caught in the storm, but Grandma was still staring at him in that way. He decided to wait until she was asleep and would slip out then.

'I've been having lots of dreams.' Grandma spoke as if she was drunk, slurring her words as her eyes started to close.

'Yeah?'

'Yeah.'

'What about?'

'Last night I got stuck in the loft.'

Ajay laughed. She was so random. 'What were you doing in the loft?'

'Just going up there. I got locked in.'

'That's traumatic.'

'Not really. Some people would think I was trapped . . .' She yawned again. 'But I was nice and warm.'

There was something so peaceful about watching her fall asleep. But Ajay's heart broke at that moment, because she reminded him of Theo Badds. Content and restful, yet she was alive. Very much alive. Still telling him stories, even if her material was now the crazy dreams of a dying woman.

He rested his eyes then, trying to change his thought pattern.

Ajay needed to stop thinking about losing her, despite the fact he'd already lost her when he left. That was the decision he'd made. He listened to the moving rhythm of his grandma's breathing and the inconsistent tap of flying branches hitting the window.

His eyes must thank him for this. They rarely closed. *SkipSleep* changed people's lives; the ability to stay awake and make merit almost twenty-four hours a day was revolutionary. Yet there was nothing like natural sleep. It was a lust everyone carried but no one spoke about. Only dipping in and out of it, never over-indulging. He needed to open his eyes. Sleep was dangerous. He needed to go. *Ajay, don't.* He lazily lifted his eyes and gazed over the desk beside him. He could rest his head there, just for a minute. Next to that small picture. It was of Tara with her black pigtails and rainbow tights. He assumed, anyway. She was hard to make out as his vision went fuzzy and he placed his head on his arms. *Stop. Get up.* Then his brain went black, and he drifted off into a deep sleep.

CHAPTER
TWENTY-NINE

Genni was sitting on a high stool upholstered in royal-blue fabric with light oak legs. Pearl was pacing around the thirteenth-floor meeting room, tastefully illuminated by stylish, low-hanging ceiling lights. She was barking demands at the walls. Genni felt sorry for the willing soul at the other end of Pearl's headset. She watched as Pearl stopped at the refreshment station and started to inspect each individual apple from a bowl, continuing to talk loudly. Genni slipped off her stool and stood by the window to mindlessly watch the weekend crowds.

The interview for the summer camp had gone well, better than she ever expected. She'd almost sobbed all over the interview table when the organiser had said, 'We'd love to have you on board.' It was a profound moment for her. A realisation that her recovery might not actually be a recovery anymore, that she had, perhaps, recovered? She'd been tempted to ring her father and boast about how she wasn't a complete screw-up. She decided to save her pride. The summer volunteering would give her a merit boost that would speak for itself. She'd have to get fitter, though, and better at teaching. She wasn't sure her body was quite ready for all the activities she'd have to lead. He'd mentioned teaching them military-style circuit training. Genni had nodded along, pretending that she did that often, when the truth was, she'd done it once with Ace and had sworn to herself – never again. So that would be fun, she decided, as she looked down over the Social Sphere.

This place would make a beautiful painting, she considered. It wouldn't quite be her style, but it would have so many layers. Genni mused at the countless buildings that formed a 'social' circle, each one connected to the other via spherical bridges encased in reflectively clean transparent glass. Genni saw people rushing along them, all wearing various colours, not stopping to greet one another on passing. The picture's main feature would be the Content Bank; it was a grey, elliptical building rising high up into the sky and could be seen from most places in the City. There were people streaming in and out of its entrance below; socialites and influencers accessing its trending content library. Genni looked over the televised sphere that sat on its top – the City's sun at night. She recognised the ginger woman on the display. She wore bright-red lipstick and long, fabric earrings that resembled fancy curtains. The text beneath her ran around the sphere's circumference; she'd just been voted off *The Glorified House* and was explaining her experience in the house as 'life-changing'. Genni's upper lip tightened. She despised all that reality TV stuff, despite how it was meant to teach you the best ways to live a merit-efficient life. She'd had enough of her reality, let alone any celebrities' dramas. The colours of the neon social icons travelling around that sphere would pop from a painting's canvas with vibrancy. What a picture.

As Genni followed the rotating purple *Personi* icon, she felt dizzy again. It was fine. Normal. She anticipated what always came next. The vision or the flashback. She wasn't sure what to call it. Maybe she was remembering what happened that night; the visions would flutter in her mind like dark, broken-winged butterflies, fully formed yet distorted. She steadied herself against the window and tried to remember.

It was wet. The rain trickled down in the black night. He was there instead of her usual administrator. He had a gruff voice and wide arms and talked to Genni while his bald head reflected the light of a maroon lantern above him. She was still Downtown. She'd felt numb. She'd felt sick. The image was confused, rattling through her brain. She almost felt the moisture of the water falling on her face as she was carried by . . . someone. Genni scrunched up her face and squeezed hard in a plea for her mind to recall it. The water dropped – tap, tap, tap. She opened her eyes, the sound of Pearl's heels reconnecting her to reality.

'Sorry, Gen.' Pearl's words danced as she strode determinedly across the room, her long legs emphasised in tight black trousers and a flowy grey blouse. 'I was instructing Jove to sign a deal with a property brand, he was being difficult. Anyway, shall we have a look?' Pearl beamed.

She did have the tendencies of a self-involved tyrant, whining and fighting until she got her way, but she was loyal. Genni knew if anyone ever said or did anything to her in front of Pearl, they'd be in trouble. And most of the time, Pearl wanted to help. Even more so if whatever Genni needed presented a merit-making opportunity for her.

Pearl sat at the table and commanded a screen to hover over it. She swiped down with her fingers and found Genni's *Personi* profile.

Pearl, would you like to record this conversation?

They touched Watches as Genni slid onto the stool beside her, feeling both anxious and keen to learn. Genni's filtered face appeared within a small, privately enclosed square at the top of her profile. Pearl scrolled down past Genni's 'About' section, past her merit score, family credentials and relationship network, which had an impressive average. Then, she paused at her latest post – a tasteful shot of a kale smoothie with the City's buildings rising in the background. She'd picked that up on the way to work. She'd felt particularly stressed that day, as she had been engrossed in a new painting and lost track of time. Ajay thought she should give it up, especially after what happened, but Genni was determined to find that balance. As she'd rushed to work, she knew she needed to post something quick for the merit and the smoothie bar was right there. In the caption, she wrote: *'Relaxing with my delicious green friend.'* Genni remembered how it made her heave on the first sip and she was bitterly discouraged when it was all for nothing and the post only got two loves. Pearl was squinting as she browsed through Genni's latest updates, videos and blogs, mainly about what she'd eaten or a picture of her and Ajay. Genni held her breath.

'Oh, honey . . .' Pearl let out a deep sigh.

'I told you I needed help.' Genni swallowed her embarrassment.

'Well,' Pearl leaned back, still narrowing her eyes at the screen. 'This all depends on how much you are committed to gaining significant merit from this. The greater the engagement, the more merit you earn.'

That's a basic start. Everyone knew that correlation, but of course, it wasn't surprising at all, Genni realised: the Watches were listening.

'So if you decide this will be a key personal merit-maker for you, then take the time to provide better content. If you're not going to commit, you're better off not even trying.'

Genni pinched her lips together. Everything within her wanted to tell Pearl that she didn't want to bother. *Personi* was the last thing in Tulo she wanted to do, but she had no choice. She needed all the merit she could get; it was no secret that her and Ajay's relationship was still hanging in the balance. So, with hesitation, she asked Pearl several questions she didn't want the answers to.

'It's got to be stuff that inspires people, encouraging them to be greater than themselves,' Pearl said after making multiple comments about the lighting on Genni's videos. 'They want tips about feeling more confident, or suggestions of brands that offer better personal efficiency. They won't engage otherwise. You'll never go big screens with this stuff.'

Genni rubbed the back of her neck as Pearl continued to scroll through her feed. Did she even want to be on the billboards? Sure, she could see the advantage of her content being up there so millions could connect their Watches as they fluttered and flowed through life. Plus, the merit would be sweet if they hit love or even endorsed it as an effective motivator. And yes, that's what changed Pearl's life. The billboards transformed her merit-making hobby into a credit-making career, but for Genni, it just felt inauthentic. None of that stuff would ever truly be her.

'Just stretch the truth a little,' Pearl flapped her hand after Genni expressed this to her. 'Or you could have a baby. Family stuff is hot right now.'

'Oh, sure. I can't maintain a *Personi* feed, but I could raise a kid.'

'Probably way better than I could,' Pearl said as they shared bemused smiles.

'Could Jove not organise the baby for you?'

'That man can barely organise a lunch.'

'I'm surprised he's still got the job.'

'I haven't time to replace him.'

'Best not have a baby then,' Genni said as she grunted and sat her chin on her hands. 'Seriously, though, what am I going to do about this?'

'Give me a minute to think,' Pearl twisted her plumped lips.

Genni nodded and glanced back towards the windows; drones filtered past, and a billboard swiped between different *Personi* feeds and adverts. It wasn't the first time Genni had thought about being a mother. She'd love her children endlessly, almost enough not to push them into a life like the one she was living. This life had no loopholes or brake pedal and even when you fell, you'd be straight back up, running shoulder to shoulder with everyone else but always pressing to have one foot ahead. It was relentless. Maybe she would teach her child a different way, where the number on your wrist didn't matter. Genni stopped thinking, realising the poison that was invading her mind. The City was the only way she knew or wanted to know. No, a child would not be 'greater' for her. Pearl was still tapping at the desk. Tap, tap, tap – like the water drops on her forehead as she was carried that night, fire in her shoulder.

The moment was broken. The double jingle of a breaking news alert cut through; she and Pearl looked to their wrists.

Weather Update. The coming storm is expected to reach speeds of fifty rings per hour and the electrical activity will likely cause wildfires in the Country. Citizens might experience a slight disturbance when travelling around the City, but this is no cause for concern.

Pearl quickly dismissed her Watch and got back to her growing list of potential Genni content. It was set to be a good storm, which would mean a great view from the roof. Genni loved watching them with Ajay; hopefully tonight she'd get to paint something.

'I'll just ring Ajay. We can probably travel back together. He's in the Quarters.' Genni tapped at her Watch.

'Ask him when he's getting back to me about our collaboration while you're at it. That call we had got us nowhere.'

Genni wanted to scoff out loud. Pearl wouldn't stop nagging her about that. It wouldn't even work – Ajay wouldn't do it, despite him making a bit of an effort for their relationship. She probably should have told Pearl that already, but she'd saved herself the grief. Her Watch started dialling and its noise persisted for more rings than Genni would have liked or expected. He usually took her calls instantly, even when he was volunteering. Pearl widened her eyes as the ringing continued and Genni felt embarrassment tingle in her toes; it rose up her legs in motion with the ring's continuing repetition. Genni fiddled on her Watch to mute the call. She transferred it to her headset to relieve Pearl from the annoyance.

'Sorry,' she said feebly. 'Maybe his Watch is off.'

Pearl shrugged her shoulders. 'Why would his Watch be off? Just find him on the map.'

Genni immediately cowered in a sense of dread; did Pearl find her on the map when she missed her calls? Regardless, she tapped at her wrist and opened the map.

What? She didn't understand, refreshing the map repeatedly. 'I think it might be broken,' she said.

'Why?' Pearl asked.

After the third time refreshing, it still told her the same thing. The same unbelievable thing. 'It says he's in the Side.'

As Pearl raised her eyebrows to mirror Genni's confusion, Ajay's voice boomed through her earphones.

'Genni, hi, hey ...' He sounded alarmed and unbalanced, as if he'd woken up from a dark and twisted dream.

CHAPTER
THIRTY

His head was fuzzy. His vision was blurry. Lights were flashing. Genni's voice was loud and piercing.

'Ajay! What . . . ? Are you?' Genni wasn't speaking sentences, flapping through her words like they were tasering her tongue.

Ajay sought clarity in his surroundings; he saw his grandma sleeping, her peaceful face wrinkled, swollen and dry, but she only came in flashes as lightning cracked outside. He looked to the window, drenched in the clear blood of the sky.

'Ajay . . . The map is saying you're out in–'

Ajay interrupted Genni hurriedly, immediately condemning himself for not turning off his VPG. 'I'm fine, Gen. I'll be back real soon.' He spoke calmly and confidently.

Having no way to explain this one off the cuff, he hung up almost instantly. Panting heavily, still sitting on the wicker stool, he looked over the sweat patch on the desk where his sleeping head had lain. Beside it was the photo of Tara, her pigtails wafting in a rare Side breeze. He knew he had to move. How could he have fallen asleep? What was he thinking? It was time to go. Yet another side of him was glued down by the weight of his grandma's condition. Just looking at her again welcomed tears to sit softly. No. He couldn't let himself do this. Other things were more important. Turning from her, he released his legs from the wicker stool but not before instinctively grabbing the picture of Tara and shoving it in his trouser pocket. He headed for the door, which swung suddenly open.

'Oh, you're still here?' His mother, carrying a tray of food, was startled as Ajay nearly flattened her in his rush. *How long have I been asleep?*

Get. Out.

'Yes. I've got . . .' He paused, noticing his mother's distraction. Her lips parted in a wistful smile as she gazed over at her own mother.

'It's coming soon . . .' she said quietly, before asking, 'Will you still come home after she's gone?'

Ajay didn't answer. Genni and Ace were probably already hunting down clues in his apartment.

Get. Out.

He whipped round his mother and bolted towards the landing. The noise of his quick feet plummeting down the stairs made the whole house shake. He could hear his mother following him.

'Karle . . . Ajay, the storm. You'll get soaked . . .'

But before she could finish, Ajay had battled with the stiffness of the door handle, swung the door open, and set off as fast as his legs would take him.

The air was lava, and the rain was like hot, mushy sweat plummeting against Ajay's head. He ran through the violence of it. Hard drops of water were lashing the ground. A cry of thunder wailed through the clouds. The hot-tempered wind was rough enough to knock Ajay's long legs off course, wafting him into a zigzagging run to the train. On his approach, a zap and crack of lightning beat the dormant telephone wires that hung above the streets. Awestruck, Ajay watched and ran in parallel with the galloping electric sparks as they raced and cantered along the line, hastening towards the ground. Ajay felt the heaviness of vulnerability as the rain whacked his body. He couldn't think of anything else but to get out. If there was a train.

He hurtled himself onto the platform and could barely see through the rainfall, but he heard the sharp blow of a whistle and a howl from a man hanging from the sitting train, ushering Ajay to board. Relief.

He jumped on and planted his feet hard. The door closed behind him and the train pulled away as the rain continued to pour, and the wind threw sand at the window with hard, persistent slaps. Ajay rested his head against it, observing the sheer magnificence of a Tulo storm.

He'd never been out in the thick of it before, though he and Genni often watched from the roof. The lightning didn't relent, and the intense glow of a furnace erupted as the Country forests began to burn wildly behind the Side. Ajay bowed his head, ashamed and guilty over his sudden abandonment of his dying grandmother. It was necessary. Priorities. As he travelled back towards the City, he contemplated the lies he would need to tell. He felt confused by his emotions, ready to defend his identity yet still clutching tightly to the photo of his sister in his pocket.

CHAPTER
THIRTY-ONE

'What were you doing?'

Ajay felt the hard battering against his chest as Genni repeatedly hit him, cursing loudly. Not sure what to do, he pulled her closer to him. It seemed to work as she settled down and sobbed into his chest, not the least bit bothered that Ajay was dripping wet. They stood there for a moment in his open doorway.

'Why did you go there? You could have been killed,' Genni whimpered.

'I'm sorry,' Ajay said. He looked over at Ace for some reassurance. He didn't find it. Ace scowled at him, his arms crossed.

'Well?' he demanded, standing by Ajay's breakfast bar. 'Your VPG confirmed you were in the Side?'

Ajay had mulled it over the entire journey back; how could he have left his VPG on? How could he have been so careless as to fall asleep? What would he say to them? Why was he so selfish, to sprint away from his dying grandma as if he'd just see her again tomorrow? He didn't have a choice, he knew, but everything was so confused.

Genni let him go and wiped her eyes. They both watched him. A weight was pressing down on him, the heaviness of incomprehension and fear crushing his nerves. It was killing all sensation in his feet and legs, driving tingles down his arms and across his chest. His head was burning. He imagined one day that his secret might be threatened, but he never imagined it would feel like this.

'I need a drink,' Ajay breathed strongly as he spoke. Inhale, one, two, three, four . . . Exhale, one, two, three, four. His throat was dry and sore. He thought he was in control.

'No. You're going to sit there and explain to us why you'd do something so stupid.' Genni gestured widely towards a spot on the sofa. 'Ace will get you water,' she said, calmer as they stood in silence, listening to the pop as Ace opened the fridge.

Ajay walked slowly, his wet boots squelching on the concrete floor. As soon as Ace placed the water beside Ajay, he immediately quenched his thirst.

Ace and Genni stood in front of him again, waiting expectantly.

Ajay had conjured up a weak, unbelievable excuse, but there was no other reason a M-460 high-flyer would ever cross the desert. He took a deep breath . . . *Act confident. They won't suspect anything. They won't.*

'OK, so lately I've been having more boosts at night for personal development. Mainly educational documentaries.' Ajay's voice came out assertively, but internally he was shaking his head and whispering 'pathetic' in his own ear. But he reminded himself, he was a master at lying. It had become easy. 'One of which has been . . . what to do in the situation of a wildfire. So, when I was finished with volunteering early, I decided I'd go out there to help shield the fires from the Unworthy houses. You know, for a little merit.' Ajay said nothing more, the wetness of his clothes seeping through to his skin and presumably onto his sofa. He needed to change, but he didn't think walking out on two angered people was the best strategy.

There was silence as both Genni and Ace stared at him, inspiring repeated pangs of anxiety in his stomach as if it were a trampoline being used by an erratic child. Finally, Ace spoke.

'Mate, do you realise how crazy that is?' he said, scratching his shaved head. 'The fire service would have got there quicker. It wouldn't have been worth the merit. Helping the Side earns next to nothing.'

'I know. I just . . .' Ajay sighed, 'had a moment. There's been a lot going on.'

Ajay flicked his eyes on Genni, who immediately seemed to shrivel in the accusation. She turned herself away but Ajay saw her lip wobble. Things weren't bad between them, but both of them knew they might never be the same. He was starting to wish he could reach out, tell them everything and let them into his real world. Like many times before, though, the temptation was axed by the swing of their ancestry. Both Glorified. Both ruthlessly pressured by their parents and undeniably loyal to the system. He could never tell them. In that split second, Ajay spotted Genni's clenched fists, the changing colour of her skin, and the fury rising again in her eyes.

She erupted at him, shouting forcefully and leaving both Ajay and Ace wide-eyed.

'You're unbelievable. You'd risk your life because things haven't been right and blame me for it? Is that it then?' She bared her teeth. 'Everything's my fault, including your death if anything had happened. Liberation Day would have been so joyful without you, so thank you very much for being so considerate.'

Ajay couldn't keep up with her. She was speaking so quickly. He wanted to tell her to calm down and take a breath, but he let her run away with it. 'And the Side? Why would you ever want to help those ineffectual, unproductive nutcases anyway? People are starting to go missing there daily, never mind the wildfires, one of them could have taken you.'

'Those people have just moved to the City, Gen,' Ace said.

'Shut up, Ace. This isn't about them. It's about him.' She pointed violently at Ajay. 'And how . . . how . . . he . . .'

Her speech slurred, her body wobbled, and she lifted her hand weakly to her head. Now what was happening? Ajay thought she might have had a relapse. His heart broke. The colour drained from her face and he grabbed her as she fainted.

CHAPTER
THIRTY-TWO

Genni remembered.

His handsomeness was marred by the way he'd looked at her; a stare that sucked everything good away, making Genni feel like a blank piece of paper – empty and lifeless.

'Where is he?' Genni had asked again, her head rocking on her neck as she felt the nausea spew up inside her. She'd fallen forwards, vomiting over the concrete floor, just missing the tips of his dark, black-booted feet. He jumped from his seat, kicking the plastic chair backwards into the middle of the small, airless room. Dragging her eyes open, she'd lolled her head up towards him – this new, unfamiliar man. He said nothing, but looked down on her with the same evil gaze. She tried to speak again. 'He said . . . my administrator . . . that if I ever had problems with it, to come back and . . .' Genni heaved again, noticing the sick-splattered strands of hair over her face.

'He's not here today. You've got me,' he'd said sinisterly. 'Now, where were we? You were born Glorified, and what Education Centre did you go to?'

'What . . . why?' Genni had looked around the room she'd sat in too many times. There were no needles or vials out ready for administration; the table where they usually sat

had been upturned and was on the other side of the room, like it had been thrown in a rage. And this guy was strange, asking her the most random questions and talking about some club he'd joined who lived out in the Country. It was bizarre and something felt off. She shook her head slowly, trying to shake off the haze. 'I'm going to go ...' She tried, struggling to her feet.

The man looked over, his face gaunt and ghoulish in the clinical strip lighting above them. 'You stay right there.' He'd snapped, striding over and knocking her back down to the floor, his biceps bulging with a strong grip on her shoulders.

'Get ... off ... me ...' she had demanded. He'd tried to restrain her arms as she'd struggled to escape, screaming out for rescue as everything spun around her. As soon as his grip had momentarily loosened, she pulled herself up again and lurched forwards, throwing herself through the door to the street. Genni hadn't looked back, she'd just run. Until there it was, bright and shining in front of her. The lights of a hover vehicle, pressing closer and closer for the inevitable to happen. As it hit her, she was thrown skyward towards the circumference of the yellow moon and gravity pulled her back, smashing her into the ground, bruising her body and snapping her collarbone brutally and swiftly. She lay there, her head pounding and body hurting.

That's when she turned up. At first, Genni thought she was a ghost, but then she spoke to her softly. She'd carried her through the night under the artificial stars and dropped her, blue-veined, on Ajay's doorstep.

Genni felt a sensation on her right arm, a constant tugging. 'Genni, are you alright?' Ajay was pulling persistently at the sleeve of her Tulo-branded T-shirt.

He and Ace were staring at her. They looked concerned. She must have blacked out for a moment. Again. It was probably time to tell them about this.

'I'm having visions, flashbacks of that night,' she said quietly. *The night before everything changed.* She didn't want to explain everything, not when Ajay had sent her into a mad frenzy. She felt embarrassed. A tantrum wasn't how she thought she would react.

Then again, she never expected to find her boyfriend taking a trip to the Side, nor did she think they were still so broken. The memory of that disgusting man grabbing her so violently had left her constantly unsettled. Who was he and what did he want with her? It was all too much to handle.

'I can't talk about it now,' she said, 'but I'm still mad at you. I know I'm overreacting, but I was scared.' She tapped him lightly on the shoulder as he knelt in front of her. She felt the water drip into the skin of her fingers as she ran them through his black hair. She was unbearably in love with him. She couldn't be the one to end things. There was too much at stake. But she also couldn't shake the feeling that he was hiding something. There was no reason to pry further. She knew it was stupid, but if he was lying, she didn't want to know. That would destroy her for good.

CHAPTER
THIRTY-THREE

Ajay felt the movement of the sky train as he rested his head against the glass, staring emptily at the trickles of raindrops that slivered slowly down the window. They resembled the motion of tears he wanted to cry. He felt senseless. Genni was distant. He'd expected more questions from her, but she'd just asked him to give her space. It was a relief but also worrying. That moment when she'd fainted and he thought she'd relapsed, he'd felt as numb as he had when he saw his grandma decrepit. He didn't know if Grandma was dead or alive. For all he knew, she could've died when he ran out on her. She'd looked so feeble. He still had Tara's picture and he wasn't sure why. He wondered whether he could tell Genni. She probably deserved to know, but he wasn't sure how she'd cope. It wasn't a little lie. It was a life-crippling lie.

The train stopped at *Liberty, Outer-Ring*. Ajay felt his legs carry him from his seat and out into the evening chill. Citizens were wearing fleece coats to protect themselves against the sudden drop in temperature that came after a storm. Ajay walked past several people who had borrowed blankets from a bar, locking their bodies in warmth as they marched on. He considered getting one, but it wasn't the air that made him feel cold. Two girls posed in front of a Watch in their new cashmere robes, smiling and cuddling to then turn their backs on one another, stuck in the translucent glow of their wrists. Ajay wondered what those girls were like. Were they only the posey faces that would be seen on *Personi* in a matter of moments, or were there actual personalities there? Were they bubbly or shy? Reckless or sensible? More people filtered past him. More people with stories he'd never know. Yet out on the Side, his parents knew everyone on their street, in their neighbourhood. They knew each other's birthdays, likes, dislikes and habits. Here, Ajay had nothing like that. The City had always been about him. Genni and Ace were exceptions to an unwritten rule; you didn't truly know people.

He looked up at the blinding billboards. Where were these feelings coming from? Everything he saw above him was full of colour, enlightening the darkness in his mind. As he walked, he spotted advertisements for automatic dishwashers, ring jewellers, Liberation Day and motivational courses. Without realising, he soon found himself in a night market. He thought the stalls looked suffocated by their fairy-light coverings. He didn't stop, despite being enticed by the smell of the meat some drones were spinning over hot plates. Even more colour took his attention; the confectionary he'd once longed for so freely available to him. Sweet necklaces, toffee apples, bon-bons, lollipops and candyfloss. All artificial and merit-deducting, yet completely delicious. Karle was tempted but Ajay walked away.

Coming out from the market, Ajay thought again of the photo in his pocket. He didn't even know if it was still there, but he was wearing the same suit trousers. Quickly, he stuck his hand into the loose, gaping pocket and could immediately feel the sharp edges of the curled photographic paper. There was a brisk breeze. He wrapped his suit jacket around himself before seeing him. What was he doing here? He couldn't believe it, he didn't want to tolerate him but, of course, he accepted the handshake offered by Genni's idiot brother.

'Rod. Nice to see you,' Ajay said. He felt the depressed tension in his voice.

'We both got caught in the chill. Fancy a drink to warm up?' Rod's smile curled like a snake slithering down a street.

Ajay hated the suggestion, but he considered how nothing in the whole of Tulo could make him feel any worse, not even Roderick Mansald.

'What are you doing here?' Ajay asked. Once he made Glorified, he certainly wouldn't be coming to the Outer-Ring to get some air.

'Just seeing some friends.' Rod pointed down the street in a generalised fashion. 'Shall we?'

Who are you friends with in the Outer-Ring?

Rod looked towards a bar on their left, The Fox & The Camel, the sign of which was swinging in the temporary icy air. The windows were rife with condensation. Ajay was surprised that Rod would even consider going into such a venue. He followed him through the slow sliding door.

Once they got inside, Ajay wished he'd said no. It was rammed full of giggling, drunken people body bouncing off each other. The music was painfully loud. Ajay joined Rod at the only free table and he could feel the resistance of his shoes as he walked, clinging to the sticky ground beneath him.

'You can tell this is for the M-300s, can't you?' Rod said as he grimaced at the cup rings and crumbs on the table. He ordered a drone to come and sanitise it as another brought them two Tulo Ales. Ajay lifted his arm to pay but Rod intervened and wiped his wrist against the drone's side.

'Thanks,' Ajay shouted over the music as he took a sullen swig.

'So, mate, you've been with my sister three years and I don't know much about you. Whereabouts in the City did you grow up?'

'The west side. Not far from where I live now. Wasn't all bad, but nothing compared to the Quarters from what Genni tells me.'

'Just you wait, mate.' Rod gave a dirty look to a group of men joking with each other a few tables down; they were all poorly dressed and one had a black eye.

'So, does Liberation Day planning make a full-time job?' Ajay asked, changing the subject.

Rod shook his head after filling his mouth with ale. 'I have four months off afterwards. I tend to do community work.'

'Must be intense right now, though,' Ajay said, calculating in his head that it was only two weeks away.

'I'm currently finalising the entertainment side of things, met with The Tulip Twins today to plan their set.'

Ajay smirked, tilting his bottle sideways; he knew Genni would be pleased. Too many times had he asked her to turn that rubbish off when she was getting ready or, more recently, when she painted.

'Don't tell anyone, though, their attendance is on the downlow for now.' Rod sniffed politely. 'So, what about your parents?'

Ajay was momentarily speechless. He'd never had anyone ask such a question so sharply, in a way that suggested they were seeking information. Rod had always been a strange one, but it felt too much of a coincidence for Rod to demand talking about his parents after Genni's outburst about the Side. She must have tipped him off about something. That didn't make much sense, as Rod and Genni hardly spoke. Why would she go to him? It could be a normal question to ask, but it was the way in which he asked it. Flippant. Hard. He felt his fingers clamming. He wiped them on his trousers as he became aware of his thumping heart, and told himself to calm down. There was no way Rod could suspect the truth. They hardly knew each other. It was just his darkened emotions making him paranoid. Ajay had his cover story, and he was reminded that he'd told it too many times for it to suddenly sound disingenuous.

'Dad worked in Genetics, and Mum was a teacher at the school down on Tibble Street.' Ajay paused and took another sip. 'They . . . died, actually. In a hover vehicle accident when they first became driverless. A faulty prototype.'

'Genni never mentioned.' Rod looked at Ajay with his green, piercing eyes. They didn't seem to hold any sympathy and just when Ajay felt even more cross-examined, a news update vibrated on his wrist. *Kole Nuten was captured on the south side of the City, attempting to gain admittance to a health gym. He has been wanted by the TPD following several criminal offences and suspected anti-Command activity. Further investigations are . . .*

'So, how'd you get into Prosper . . . ?' Rod hadn't stopped looking at Ajay.

He noticed how the surface of Rod's skin was tight, tense and smooth around his chiselled jawline. Ajay lifted his head to answer, but then a shrieking volume erupted from the bar's speakers and the disco lights turned to black. Everyone on the tables and on the dance floor ducked and held their ears for protection. The high-pitched vibrations lasted a few seconds but were enough to leave ears ringing. When the lights returned to their former glory, an announcement was made: *We apologise for that minor technical glitch.*

In the sudden moment of darkness, Ajay had been terrorised by uncontrollable fright and agitation. He'd sprung from his stool, which clattered to the ground, ready to fight off invaders or Command guards. But when the lights lifted, in a soothed and easy motion, Ajay felt only embarrassment. Rod and a few other spectators were scowling at him as he stood with his fists up high.

'What are you doing?' Rod asked bluntly.

Ajay sighed, explaining himself through some ramble about loud noises. There was no need to be so uneasy. Ace and Genni may be suspicious, but they weren't sending an army for him. He was being ridiculous. As he wiped the sweat from his brow and gathered himself, fear returned in larger magnitudes. It wrapped around him so tightly he felt like he was being strangled – unable to move or even breathe. Ajay watched as life seemed to move in slow motion, his vision blurry and the music muffled. Rod was reaching for a rectangular piece of paper, probably stuck with grease to the bar floor. Ajay flippantly reached into his pocket. Tara was gone. No longer there, but in the Glorified grasp of Rod's large hands, being examined by the serpent-like eyes.

'Who's this?' Rod asked and Ajay's normal senses returned, the music feeling louder and stronger than before. His mouth was dry and his body felt unsteady, but his mind remained sharp.

'My niece,' he said as he calmly picked up his stool.

'You have a sibling?' Rod asked, still holding on to Tara despite Ajay reaching out his hand in a plea to give her back. He left his hand floating there.

Give. Her. Back.

'A sister. She's a hairdresser in the Outer-Ring, a few circles from here. I don't see them much. Didn't quite walk the merit-line.' Ajay tried to discreetly force his hand closer to Rod, but still he clutched on, peering down and narrowing his eyes with observation. Ajay hoped his explanation would deter Rod's questions about the picture's surroundings and Tara's dishevelled appearance. He felt anger rise in a violent somersault in his belly, a longing to force himself on Rod and get his sister back. It was as if someone had heard him. Rod was thrown slightly forward by a keen socialite colliding with him and throwing some of his ale down his back. Ajay wasn't surprised by Rod's aggressive reaction towards the man, who threw his arms up in surrender with fearful, quivering eyes.

Rod turned back to Ajay and said bluffly, 'I've had enough of this place.' Rod hadn't drunk half of his ale. 'It was nice to see you, Ajay. Let's do it again sometime and you can tell me more about your . . . *niece.'*

Rod gave him a wink, threw Tara thoughtlessly across the table and left the bar. Ajay sat alone and didn't move for a few minutes, letting the pounding music fall over him. He quickly returned Tara to the safe place of his pocket and replayed the last few moments over in his mind. Rod's questions. His huge fingers around the photo. The wink.

Did Rod know? He couldn't. There was no way. Ajay couldn't cope with the paranoia. The fear and the guilt were beginning to cripple him. He needed another drink.

CHAPTER
THIRTY-FOUR

Two weeks later, it was Liberation Day and Ajay was running around his apartment, shirt unbuttoned and only wearing one sock. He frantically pulled the other onto his left foot. He was late. Genni would be here any second. The intercom buzzed. *Darn, she's gonna kill me.* As he scooted over towards the door, he caught a glimpse of himself in the dressing table mirror. His hair was standing on end, natural and uncombed; his skin was dry and the purple markings around his eyes had worsened overnight. Genni had deliberately said to be ready when she arrived so they could get ahead of the crowds. Yet somehow, he'd managed to do the exact opposite of what she wanted. *Nice one, mate.*

'Come on up,' Ajay spoke into the intercom and swiped his Watch to let her in.

He probably had about a minute before she made it upstairs. Get ready in a minute. He was back at the dressing table. His hair was wild. He'd had more than two hours sleep last night and had clearly slept on it in a creative way. Pulling the comb through it, he soon managed to tame it. He stuck his fingers into his hair wax, its texture squishy and cold.

'Ajay?' Genni shouted through the apartment door. *You're joking? That wasn't a minute. The girl moves fast.*

Ajay looked at himself; all he needed was to button up his shirt and put a tie on. So he was practically ready. Though he was sweaty and felt like he needed another shower. He walked towards the door while simultaneously buttoning his shirt over the uneven patches of his chest hair.

He welcomed Genni, trying to make light of the obvious.

'Are you not ready?' Genni stepped into the apartment wearing a short teal dress with sequins around the halter neckline. Her hair was curled and fell beautifully just above her shoulders. Ajay paused. He'd have preferred the red dress she'd tried on the week before, but she still looked good enough to make him forget what he was doing. Tie. He needed a tie.

'You look stunning,' he said, running towards his wardrobe.

'Thanks,' he heard her say timidly.

'Just getting a tie,' he called out from behind his wardrobe door. He began hunting through his drawers and up on the hangers for his ties. Where were they? In frustration, he started throwing clothes out onto his bed. Genni came through from the kitchen.

'What are you doing?'

'I can't find my ties.'

'Ajay, stop it. You're making a mess and we're already late. Just ask your wardrobe and I'll put stuff back.'

He moved to his wardrobe mirror, Genni piling clothes back into the drawers behind him. Tapping at his screen, he was shown a clip of himself moving his ties from the wardrobe to his chest of drawers beside it. *Why did I do that?*

He'd been wasting too much time recently. Sleeping, reading irrelevant news updates, or eating. He blamed it on the phase of depression sparked by seeing Grandma, and almost getting caught. Her dying body kept appearing in his head, but he couldn't bring himself to ring the Side, just in case. His paranoia about Genni and Ace's suspicion had consumed him for the best part of a week. Every time they were together, he tried to think of ways he could prove to them that he really had gone there because of an educational movie. So, he kept dropping lines from a few to show it was a merit pastime he invested in. It was stupid. He knew he needn't do that. It'd blown over so quickly, even Ace had settled down in his jokes about Ajay being an Unworthy lover. While it was painfully close to the truth, Ajay had started to move on. Yet he was still being ridiculously inefficient, like with this tie thing – and he couldn't even think about the Prosper networking event from the day before. It was nothing short of a disaster. Ace, of course, had breezed through, lapping up merit through conversations like a drone delivering orders in a heaving restaurant. Ajay, on the other hand, was completely distracted and only educated one person with a feeble explanation of his meal planning. He did well to avoid any questions about how much merit he'd earned while Ace had boasted about his success. Hopefully, he could forget the whole thing.

Ajay wrapped a tie around his neck. *A red tie would be a better choice for the current season,* his wardrobe spoke. *For Tulo's sake.* He could feel Genni getting agitated behind him. She was doing that thing where she looked around the room as if she was being casually patient, but really, it was a stab at him to shift himself. He threw the blue tie on the floor and she picked it up again. Ajay quickly perfected the knot on his red one.

'OK, ready.'

'Your jacket?'

'Right. My jacket is ...' Ajay paused. *Where is my jacket?* 'Hanging up by the door.'

'Shoes?' Genni seemed to laugh sweetly, but he couldn't ignore the patronising tone she was carrying.

'Sorry,' Ajay sighed, and sat at the end of the bed, pulling his smartly polished shoes on.

'Why are you so late?' Genni asked.

'Just got caught up with work,' he responded quickly. That was a lie. Well, a half-lie, he justified himself. He was working until he got a communication piece through from volunteering. Mrs Laptoff had died. It was a peaceful moment. Ajay didn't feel the slightest bit of sadness, only relief. The only person in the City who clearly knew his secret was dead. Plus, he'd no longer have to feed pills to the demented crone. He'd congratulated himself for a great Liberation Day present and that's when he realised, he hadn't got Genni anything and did a panicky online search to find anything that would do. He'd settled for a silver bracelet with a charm in the shape of a paintbrush. She'd think it was thoughtful, but really it was a luck of the moment thing when a charm bracelet advert had appeared on his feed. A drone delivered it straight away. It was fine. It wasn't the present he wanted to give her. He wasn't too keen on encouraging the painting thing, despite how much social merit it'd got her since she came out as an artist. He'd told her that the *Personi* stuff was a bad idea, but she'd proved him wrong, which felt unnatural. They were together when she did it the first time.

'I just wonder whether the inspiration I feel when painting could be felt by others if they saw them,' Genni had said, grabbing a sandwich from the fridge and plonking it onto the counter.

'Hmm. It's just a big risk, Gen. Eyes are on you after what happened and I'm not sure if people would respond in the way you want them to.' Ajay had thought about how her work was beautiful as he had readied himself for a boost on the sofa. But he knew Tulo. It wasn't always kind towards openness. Genni had nodded, leaning on the breakfast bar. Ajay had watched her. She was clearly thinking it over. The right side of her lip curled in its characteristic way. Ajay had noticed that her freckles were particularly stark in the morning light. Her yellow skirt also clashed miserably with her pale-green blouse. He'd wondered whether he should advise her to check the wardrobe again. He didn't, distracted by Genni giving up on her sandwich and dashing to the apartment cupboard. Watching as she had pulled out her paintings' tubes, he felt nervous for her, knowing what she was doing.

He had stood from the sofa, ignoring the SkipSleep asking for his arm. 'Gen, are you sure?'

'Don't talk. You'll convince me not to do it.'

Flattening out her landscape of the waterfall across the black rug on Ajay's floor, she sat back for a moment to admire it. Flicking her fingers and angling her Watch, her camera took artistic, close-up shots of the painting. She started tapping at her wrist. Ajay had wondered what the caption would be. Would it be a heartfelt story about her journey as an artist? A twisted tale about it not being her work? He wasn't sure. This Genni was new to him. She wasn't usually this impulsive, this brave. Then, in a small whisper to herself as if Ajay wouldn't hear – although he did – she said, 'This is for me.'

He had been wrong about the caption. She'd gone much simpler, with Command-worthy prose. Something about finding a life more beautiful than the one you have, and reaching for something better. She may as well have written 'Progress is Strength'. To Ajay's surprise, the loves came flooding in. Genni had been erratic in excitement. Pearl rang within minutes. There were, of course, a few comments about her being a timewaster and a good-for-nothing, mostly by the Glorified, but she'd somehow managed to filter that out. Ajay was so impressed he wondered if it was only a show. *Could she really not be hurting from that?*

'Are you ready now?' Genni said as Ajay finished tying his small, thin laces and the memory faded.

'Yes, ma'am.' Ajay tried to stop the words he'd never once said slipping from his mouth. Genni bent her eyebrows.

'Are you alright? You seem jittery.'

'Yeah, just tired after yesterday. Too much talking.'

Genni let out a small grunt as the sun from the apartment window fell over her face and exaggerated her natural beauty, despite the heaviness of her make-up. Ajay's Watch vibrated. He drew his eyes away from Genni and looked down. He'd been awarded a Liberation Day Bonus. *Nice.* As soon as the thought passed his mind, a small speck of shame crept in and settled on his chest like an irritable itch. *Why do you feel guilty all of a sudden?* He'd been hacking his Watch on ad hoc occasions for years. He never felt like this. He'd normally feel a bit naughty, like when he stole his father's Watch as a kid, but never would he feel remorse. It was merely a nice coincidence that he'd boosted his score on a City holiday after wasting time looking for Genni's precious bracelet charm. His feelings were probably an aftermath of everything. Genni overdosing. His grandma. The paranoia. But he decided that from now on, he would be all good. Ajay discreetly put his sleeve over his wrist and walked towards Genni with an open arm. She was slow to embrace him as they left the apartment together.

Ajay stared vacantly at his fingers curled around the metal pole. He gripped it tightly as the sky train stopped at the next station and he almost kissed the pole thousands of others had touched. When it was this busy, he felt trapped, like he was never going to enjoy solitude again. Genni was leaning against the glass of the door beside him. He could feel the heat of her body against his, as well as the warmth of the sweaty crowds around them. Genni was right. He shouldn't have been late.

Even his people-watching habit was a no go; everyone was so squished up, it was hard to pick out a detail about them. He looked down and wondered if he could decide what people were like by their shoes. No luck. All the same. Smart, polished lace-ups like his own, or strappy sparkling heels like Genni's. The train stopped again. No one got off but there was a stream of people wanting to board, all standing eagerly on the platform. *You can't get on here.* But people did as Ajay heard the familiar shout of Ace's voice. He'd squeezed through the crowds and managed to get so close that Ajay could smell his fresh, minty breath.

'We're practically kissing, mate,' Ace said while puckering his lips.

'You'd be so lucky.'

'Fighting talk.' Ace smiled as his body tilted with the movement of the train.

Pearl was in front of Genni, her face bright with happiness and blended contour lines. Genni incessantly complained about how Pearl looked glamorous even in sweatpants and Ajay had often reminded Genni how beautiful *she* was. He didn't know how much she believed him and having the same conversation had become so laborious, Ajay couldn't remember if he even bothered responding anymore. Ajay gave Pearl a greeting nod, to which he only received a faint effort at a smile. Genni also mentioned Pearl's incredible ability to belittle people who didn't do what she wanted. She was clearly distant due to Ajay's avoidance of their social 'collaboration'. After one call, he'd basically refused. He did not want his face plastered all over the socials; what a way to fuel his paranoia, having the public interested in him and making enquiries about his past or his parents. The amount Genni knew about some influencers was frightening, like how they liked their meals prepared or their favourite brands of perfume. He was probably being overly pompous. The public surely wouldn't care about the intricate details of a Prosper engineer's life. That didn't mean he would take the risk, and he could handle Pearl's aloofness.

Ajay saw a large hand rise over Ace's head.

'Hi, Ajay,' said a voice from behind Ace. It was Jaxson. Ajay reached up and tapped his own hand to Jaxson's, scraping the side of Ace's face with his arm.

'Eh,' Ace shifted his head away. 'Can we save the meet and greet until after we're out of the sweat box?'

Ajay caught Jaxson's amused eye, as well as noticing he'd shaved his head. It wasn't a surprise. Jaxson always mirrored Ace in whatever trend he was following. Ajay considered this one a mistake; Jaxson's neck and shoulders appeared wider, which was incongruous with his slim chin.

The train stopped again and Ajay braced himself as everyone had to shift and change positions. He was pleased to find Mila next to him.

After complimenting each other on their outfits, Ajay congratulated her on getting a higher-merited job. Mila thanked him but her sparkling eyes turned dim. She immediately whispered into his ear, her breath warm on his skin.

'I just want to do patient care. Technology will only take us so far.'

Ajay didn't respond, not knowing what to say. There was little merit in the patient care jobs, as they were gradually becoming redundant. He suddenly connected her to Genni and her painting; stuck with a passion incompatible to a M-500 life. There was nowhere to go with that. Like there was nowhere to go with helping his grandma or maybe, even staying with Genni. Ajay was thankful when the train rolled into the Glorified Gate, whistles and shouts erupting as the entire population of the carriage fell out. Ajay could physically breathe again as he stepped out into the open air, but mentally, he still felt claustrophobic. The crowds ushered him down the platform. He tried to remind himself that this was Liberation Day; a day of celebration. But what was there to celebrate? His relationship could end and his grandma could be dead. Yet there he was, surrounded by varying colours of dress – sequins, glitter, frills and tassels all widely featured. Under all that, though, every woman's dress was the same: all long, tight and halter-necked. Should he ring? To know if she'd made it through the last few weeks? But he'd worked hard to distance himself, he couldn't get too emotionally attached or he would lose everything.

'How are you?' Blake appeared beside him. He wasn't as colourful as Ajay would have liked or expected. Despite their talk through the intercom when Ajay had Sam in his apartment, he never expected Blake to have dulled down his entire wardrobe. He looked like a stranger in his navy suit and tasteful plum bow tie.

Ajay asked how the apprenticeship was going as they came to a stop, the queue forming at the Gate.

'It's good. Working on a fun project,' Blake ruffled his hair. 'It's basically a new idea to ease the demand on the sky train. It'll be underground and the carriage will be private pods shot at speed through air-tight tubes.'

'How will that work? We're just walking on concrete above sand.'

'Yes. That's our first hurdle. The safety and stability issue.' Blake spoke professionally. 'But think how good it will be. Of course, the pods will be plush and glamourous – for the Glorified and friends.'

'That'll take years.' Ajay kept his eyes on the thousands of heads bouncing beneath the Glorified Gate. Part of him wanted to run away, another ready to go all in.

'Not as long as you might think. Command has put real resources behind it with the hope that the time saved will mean more of our generation will have children,' Blake said.

Ajay nodded, thinking it through; the population decrease had been a news headline for a long time. But he couldn't think any more about it as his depression invaded again like a grey mist. Closing his eyes, he told himself that he'd got the life he wanted, and he had to choose that, even if he lost people along the way. Despite the hole forming in his heart, he mustered up some enthusiasm to ask Blake if he'd be dancing.

Blake giggled joyfully in his usual way as they shuffled forwards. 'Yes, I'll be dancing. But maybe not any samba, something less flamboyant might be more acceptable.'

Ajay agreed despite some sadness. Blake was right to choose the job over the dancing, the merit over the passion. Just like he chose merit over a family he never asked to be born into. *That's right, isn't it?* Ajay wished he could shake his rising doubts, but they stayed like leeches on his skin. As they reached the front of the queue, Ajay took a deep breath and prepared himself for the entry scan. There'd be so many distractions beyond the walls and he was ready to fall headfirst into them.

CHAPTER
THIRTY-FIVE

Pulling his sleeve away from his wrist, Ajay admired Blake's new blue strap engraved stylishly with his initials. He glanced at his own Command-branded wrist before turning his attention to the words beneath the decadent archway.

Entry: M-300 and above. Internal venues: M-400 and above. Progress is Strength. Remember to still have a merit-making day.

He felt his heart beat faster as it did whenever he approached an identification scan. The system could have been updated and he'd missed something. He felt the tight grip of his shirt around his neck as he held his arm out to the scanner and Genni was being checked to the right of him. The drone began its scan. *Scanning*, it said. *Scanning*, it repeated. *Scanning*, it repeated again. Ajay avoided eye contact with any of the nearby officers, but looked beyond the drone to see that everyone else in the group was already through, and were looking back, waiting. *Scanning*, the drone said for the fourth time. Ajay closed his eyes, but they were soon forced open by the sound of a positive ping and the green light shining from the drone onto his wrist. *Entry accepted,* the drone murmured.

He was surprised that Genni opened an arm to him without any hesitation as he caught up with them. All for pretences, he supposed. They walked together down the main streets, whose planted trees and flamboyant flowers had been replaced with bunting, balloons and banners. The smell of freshly baked goods as usual accompanied the aroma of weak ethanol and cooked meat from the gourmet burger and healthy salad stands. Music played loudly from the drones hovering overhead.

'Hey, Gen, shall we make early use of your discount at the spa?' Pearl shouted across the crowds of happy and fully contented attendees.

'Sure. Probably best before the gig,' Genni said, after having taken her arm out from Ajay's.

'I'll come too.' Mila hooked her arm around Genni's, taking his place.

'Me too, I fancy a swim,' Blake said.

'See you in a bit, then, guys,' Genni said, her voice disappearing as the four of them scurried away towards the spa, leaving the remaining three men alone by a hot dog stand. Ajay didn't voice his annoyance that she'd not even asked what he, Ace and Jaxson wanted to do.

'So . . . dodgems?' Ace suggested.

Any thoughts of Genni suddenly faded as he remembered the hilarity of the dodgems from the year before. He and Ace had managed to get Pearl stuck in a corner and she couldn't figure out how to reverse so just sat in her cart whimpering. It would probably be considered bullying by some people, but Pearl held her own. She put salt in Ace's drinks for the rest of the night.

As the three of them got deeper into the Quarters, Ajay saw what Command had meant by 'bigger than ever'. The *Challenges* section was an absolute marvel. Ajay felt nauseous at the explosion of colour. There were red and yellow striped stands and others with exteriors of pink and purple polka dots. Multicoloured balloons were taking off through the blue sky and towards the white sun, shining over another endless day. Looking around, Ajay saw so much laughter, as well as some occasional aggression from those playing at one of the many competitive Virtual Reality stands: there was laser shooting, basketball, boxing, dancing and driving challenges.

'They've seriously gone for it,' Jaxson said, pointing towards one of the challenges. 'Ace, you should have a go at that.'

It was *Revolution Combat* and in front of the stand, a willing subject wore VR slimline glasses and was holding a computerised laser gun. The man was ducking, kicking, jumping and shooting as spectators watched on the observer screen within the stand. There were groups of armed men coming straight for him, all donning old city uniforms. Intense music and battle sounds accompanied the virtual construction.

'He's doing pretty good. Go on, mate, get em.' Ace roared as the three of them joined the group gathered around the agile player. The game was over quickly; a man could be seen on the screen charging towards the camera. He jumped with all his computerised weight, which physically threw the player backwards onto the ground; without time to get back up, he was shot by another computerised official. The small crowd sighed and cheered in sympathy.

Twelve minutes played. Credit of three earned, the stand's drone bleeped.

'Only three?' the player moaned as he pressed his Watch to the drone, gathered himself up, returned the VR glasses and headed back with his friends into the crowd in pursuit of their next game.

'You have a go then, Ace,' Jaxson loosened the collar of his high-quality shirt.

'I think I'm alright for now, mate. Maybe after the dodgems. You can, though?' Ace's tone was tentative, clearly unsure whether Jaxson would ever be bold enough.

'No. That's fine,' Jaxson shook his head. 'I'd just look stupid.' He gave both Ace and Ajay a self-deprecating smile as another willing subject had gone forward to don the slimline glasses, this time a lady in a see-through green dress.

Ace pushed them both towards the slickly designed hover carts with brightly patterned exteriors. The carts whizzed around in a metal cage with sparkling lights and flashing colour; the momentous noise of them banging and bashing into each other injected some violence into the otherwise dazzling scene.

'Guys, look,' Jaxson said as they joined the line. He was referring to two well-dressed, slightly older men who stood a few people back. 'They're from Command. Obviously come to give themselves a break too.' Jaxson looked at them adoringly.

'How do you know?' Ajay asked, as he saw no clear indication of their employment.

'The one on the right gave me my Watch.' Jaxson shook his wrist at Ajay, who responded with a nod. A mighty noise boomed as a digital countdown began at ten seconds in the centre of the cage.

'Poor sucker's got himself in knots there,' Ace said as he watched a group of women ramming repeatedly into a man's cart before the end of their session was announced.

'What are we saying, then? A point for every bash when it's your turn?' Jaxson asked the other two, who immediately agreed with his suggestion.

'So, you ready to be a sore loser?' Ace playfully punched Ajay on the arm, to which Ajay rolled up the sleeves of his jacket, squared his friend sternly in the eyes, and walked backwards slowly towards the cage gate.

'You just wait.' Ajay let the words fall gradually from his lips. Ace and Jaxson laughed as the three of them skipped up the small concrete steps to find their hover carts. It felt good to let his guard down, and it occurred to Ajay that he hadn't thought about things for at least twenty minutes. Progress.

Walking past the floating drone on his left, who was robotically calling out safety instructions, Ajay stepped into the cage and chose the number seven cart. It had a purple glitter exterior, slightly ruined by the layers of 'bumping' rubber that covered most of its bottom half.

These were an upgrade from last year. Much more advanced, and the paintwork had a better polish. The cart hovered slightly lower to the ground as Ajay gave it his weight. He sat uncomfortably in the plush seat and observed the dazzling mechanics of decorative lights that covered unusable buttons. He felt the warmth of the last driver as he gripped the steering wheel.

'Wouldn't mind one of these to get to work.' Ace tapped Ajay on his left shoulder from his blue cart.

'Not bad, are they?' Ajay strapped his waist belt.

'So, Jaxs, you wanna form an alliance?' Ajay heard Ace mumble to Jaxson on the other side of him in cart number five.

'I don't think so, mate. You'll just stab me in the back. You fight this fight alone.' Jaxson then slowly put on his reflective sunglasses and sat poised and ready in his cart.

'Yeah, we fight this fight alone.' Ajay raised his eyebrows playfully at Ace.

'So be it,' Ace said, just as the buzzer for the start of the ten-second countdown began.

Ajay looked to his right and spotted the two commanders in carts ten and eleven. He instantly felt threatened. *Stop it.* This was the first time he'd felt happy in weeks and he wouldn't let them ruin it. He'd come this far. People walked past him every day and never suspected anything. He was above the system. Invincible. He'd even got caught in the Side and got away with it. A quick round of hover dodgems with Command officers wasn't going to be his downfall.

Three, two, one.

The buzzer sounded and the carts all took off at once, except Ajay, who was caught internalising and ended up with a false start. He quickly repositioned his feet and floored the accelerator, sending him hovering rapidly into the mix of carts bouncing in every direction. Upon reaching the far edge of the cage, Ajay turned to his right, just missing a bash from one of the officers. As he scooped around the circumference of the cage, he spotted a person watching the mechanical chaos in a hooded green cloak that just covered their eyes.

'Ramming speed!' He heard Jaxson's usually timid voice explode as he plummeted into Ajay, sending his cart to the side of the cage. His cart vibrated and an LED display of electric sparks ran up and down the outside rubber. Jaxson rejoiced as he'd won his first point. He then scooted around to find Ace.

Ajay turned again into the centre of the cage, narrowly missing colliding with another driver. As his head went side to side and he felt a slight muggy breeze on his cheeks, he saw Jaxson coming for him again but amazingly, he just dodged him and Jaxson rocketed into another driver and into the right-hand wall. Ajay turned as he could hear Ace wildly laughing where he was driving. When Ajay looked to find him, he saw Ace look up at the clock, and his facial expression changed. It was Ace's turn.

Ace spotted him and gave him a predatory look. Continuing to drive and skilfully dodging others, Ace was coming for Ajay – fast. Ajay let out a girlish squeak and hovered quickly in the opposite direction. He put his foot down to gather more speed.

'Ha ha, better luck next time, Acey boy!' Ajay turned to see Ace cornering Jaxson and repeatedly ramming at his cart, its lights reflecting up the metal of the cage. Ajay smiled and looked at the clock. His turn. He took the corner at speed, causing his cart to hover at a perpendicular angle up the sidewall. Ace was still ramming Jaxson, clearly unaware of his impending fate, but Jaxson, the good guy that he was, indicated to Ace that he had a killer on his back.

Ace screamed with a certain hilarity as he left Jaxson beside himself in laughter. Ace and Ajay found themselves in a showdown where Ajay did not waver his focus from the back of Ace's blue cart; he was determined to win. He edged ever closer. Ace produced another whimsical cry of distress. Ajay then felt someone close to him; one of the officers was pursuing him. Ajay panicked: a bump from him would set him off course to catch Ace. The drama intensified when the ten-second countdown boomed from the central speakers of the cage. Ace was heading round the left edge of the cage and Ajay had about eight seconds to make his move. He swung his cart out wide from behind Ace and floored his accelerator so they were side-by-side. *Five . . .* boomed the speakers. Ajay then turned sharply, causing the front of his cart to spin rapidly, but he simultaneously floored it again, thrusting his spinning vehicle forward.

He bashed Ace at serious velocity, hurtling them both into the side of the metal cage. The merging lights of their rubber was almost blinding. Further vibrations rippled through Ajay's cart when his pursuer, the officer, consequently plummeted into his cart from behind, forcing him forwards just as the *game over* buzzer sounded.

Ace cried from his cart. 'You got me good, mate, but you get what you give. He just burned you.'

Ace threw a wink at the officer who responded with a faint-hearted laugh, driving his cart back to the starting line. Ajay didn't respond but only felt disgruntled that his victory had been downplayed.

As they walked away from the cage, Ajay noticed the strange character again. It was a man, or maybe even a woman – it was hard to tell. They were wearing a long, green cloak with their hood so low that Ajay couldn't see a face. Just a still, unmoving mouth. He'd seen them watching the dodgems; they'd been standing at the edge of the cage. Ajay felt anxious by their presence. They were standing still, facing his direction. Like they were there for him.

'Had a go at the dodgems, then?' Genni was back, flashing the golden sparkles of her newly manicured nails in his face. He gently grabbed her hands, looked at them and told her they were tasteful.

As she smiled incessantly over her hands, he looked back at the hooded stranger. They were gone. The space where they'd been standing now occupied by happier people. *Forget it. It's probably nothing.*

CHAPTER
THIRTY-SIX

'Anyone fancy a drink?' Blake straightened his new square spectacles as the group wandered aimlessly.

Pearl gasped and let her words fall slowly from her lips. 'Yes. Please.'

'Wait. Everyone stop.' Ace stretched his arms across the group. Ajay felt its force across his chest.

'What?' Genni said.

'Did Pearl just say please?' Ace laughed as Pearl smacked him playfully.

It was the consensus that the group would go and get a drink, and perhaps meet a few strangers to network and merit-make with, before heading over for The Tulip Twins concert. Ajay hated their music. It was just generic pop that carried no substance. No individuality or meaning. Just the same old drivel churned out in a slightly new way. He tolerated it, though, because it was popular, and he could sing along to the blandness of it along with everyone else.

He and Genni walked under an arc made from tree stumps and a wooden sign engraved with 'Drinks & Networking'. The area they entered was laid out in a square, formed from numerous wooden chalets that resembled architecture Ajay had seen in films set in much colder climates. They were serving weak ethanol spirits, soft drinks, iced water on tap and some slightly stronger stuff. He wondered whether Ace would indulge as much as last year. He'd got so blindingly drunk that he was deducted almost a whole merit point the next week. Ajay doubted that would ever happen again. Not when Ace was so close to being back in the Quarters. He watched as Ace scurried forward to save a plastic table that had just become available.

'What do you want, darlings?' Blake waved to them from the nearest chalet to the entrance.

'Hey, Jun,' Genni shouted towards the crowd of talking people. She ran away from Ajay, leaving his arm back by his side. He followed her and watched her embrace a man wearing an entirely white suit. The stubble on his face must have scratched the side of Genni's cheek; their faces were that close. It hurt and he couldn't stand there and watch, so he casually wandered over as if it didn't concern him that Genni was still holding onto this stranger. When he reached them, he deliberately slipped his arm back around her waist, the small gems on her dress scratching his skin.

'Jun, this is my boyfriend, Ajay.' Genni was smiling brightly and pressed her hand into Ajay's chest. 'Jun and I work together. He's the marketing lead for the project.'

'Ah, awesome. Great to meet you, Jun,' Ajay lied as he allowed Jun to shake his right hand.

'Hey, you're a rightie, too,' Jun said as he pointed to Ajay's Watch on his left wrist to which Ajay didn't bother responding.

'I'm going to sort our drinks. Why don't you two chat?' Genni said sweetly. She kissed Ajay on the cheek and ran over to Blake at the chalet bar. Ajay watched her go, her dress slightly rising as she moved. 'Well, I guess we're supposed to talk,' Jun said as he stroked his shaved head. Yet another one following the trend. 'So where do you work, Ajay?'

'Prosper,' Ajay said. 'I work in transactional technology.'

'No way. That's a great gig. How did you land that job?' Jun asked, before his cheeks turned red. 'Sorry, I didn't mean it like that. I just mean getting in at Prosper . . . it's big.' Ajay felt pleased with the way Jun was suddenly flapping around his words. The Prosper privilege; it demanded people's respect.

'I guess they saw something in me.' Ajay shrugged his shoulders. 'How is the project going? From what I've heard, it could be quite effective for people's well-being and merit scores.'

'Yeah, it should be good. Despite my reservations, you know, encouraging people to be thinner, its testing has had amazing results, and if people can be healthier because of it, everyone in society will be better off.' Jun took small delicate sips of his iced water. 'I've got a bold strategy, but I think our targeting is really refined due to more sophisticated online trackers that have been introduced this year. So, the likelihood is that we'll reach the right people, really fast.'

'I bet there's some social influencers that would be good ambassadors,' Ajay added.

'Oh, for sure. We're already pursuing some people, but that's a secret that'll die with me.' Jun tapped his nose twice and leaned closer towards Ajay. He expected Jun to smell overwhelmingly of mediocre aftershave, but there was no smell at all. 'So, what marketing happens at Prosper?' Jun paused. Ajay couldn't help himself. He screwed up his face. He had little interest in this conversation, as he knew exactly where Jun was trying to take it.

'Given the look on your face, it seems you need some education,' Jun laughed, waving his wrist. 'I can share some stuff, if you like?'

There it was. The merit-making grab. Ajay couldn't think of anything worse. Why should he bore himself to let this bald, girlfriend-hugging man get merit from it? He turned around to see Genni and Blake still giggling together at the bar. It was better to comply; if Genni found out he'd said no, she'd murder him for it and he may as well try not to do anything that could further strain their relationship.

'Yeah, why not!' Ajay gave a fake smile as Jun started tapping at his Watch to set up the interaction. But his fingers stopped. Like a switch had been flicked. And then, the atmosphere changed.

The air became irritable. The music of joyful chatter turned into something else. What was that? A scream? Gunfire?

As it happened, Ajay was watching Jun. Watching as his body turned stiff. Ajay heard the piercing scream of a woman from across the square. The ground rumbled beneath him. Jun's eyes widened, his pupils conveying a meshed story of fear and pain. Bright red blood trickled down his forehead and out from his nose, the blood seeping through the fabric of his pristine white shirt. Before Ajay could even think, Jun's body fell towards him so he took his weight, and they both plummeted fast to the ground.

CHAPTER
THIRTY-SEVEN

His back was on fire, having smacked the hard concrete. He scraped his fingers along the ground, feeling tiny specks of loose dirt lodge themselves beneath his fingernails. At first, for a moment, Ajay had forgotten what he'd just seen. When he opened his eyes, it was impossible to forget. It was staring straight at him. Jun's silent, static face layered with blood fresh enough that Ajay could smell its iron. Disorientated, Ajay didn't know how long he had been lying there, but the raw wet redness of Jun's skin confirmed it couldn't have been long. He turned his head in the hope to get away, but all he saw were blurred bodies falling to the floor and lasers tearing through the air, birthed from guns held by people in green-hooded cloaks, just like the illusive figure Ajay saw by the dodgems. He looked to the sky, almost frozen with fear but shielded by the dead.

The screams and the blasts were unbearable; Ajay had never experienced fear that sliced through every bone, nerve and muscle. Considering everything he'd gone through, he couldn't quite fathom that this would be how he would die: by the hand of some unknown lunatics probably not even Worthy enough for the Side.

Who were they? What did they want? Why were they doing this? Ajay felt as if he could weep, but as he caught the silence of Jun's wide, lifeless eyes, he thought back to Theo Badds who was silent and cold, but restful. This dead body was different. Horrific and premature. Ajay could feel Jun's escaping warmth against his skin; and his eyes yelled with the anguish of being cut down in your prime. Ajay knew he needed to stay, protected by Jun, so he wouldn't be handed the same fate.

Then Ajay's thoughts turned to her. Genni. Where was she? Was she dead? Did her eyes carry the same suffering as those that looked at him now? He couldn't be a coward for her; he needed to survive, find her and get them both out of this battleground. Struggling some more, he managed to lift his arms out from underneath Jun's torso. He wanted to lift Jun's body slowly out of respect, set him down and cover him over, but there wasn't time for that. The sounds of the nightmare continued. He steadied his hands against Jun's sides, feeling the squelch of his blood on the once-clean suit. He pushed and threw Jun's body off himself, grunting as he did so. Jun's landing gave a small thud as he hit the concrete beside them. Ajay jumped up; a relief that he could still walk passed quickly as he saw Jun's killer standing with his back to him, still shooting into the crowds. Ajay looked around frantically at bodies: the injured were crying out for help, some of them screaming in agony. Ajay fumbled over them, feeling inhumane and sick by leaving them all behind, but he had to find her and get out. He made his way over to the still-standing chalet where he'd last seen them. *Ace.* Where was Ace? Ajay moaned out loud, limping towards the chalet, his back and legs starting to feel bruised. Scanning the area, he could see smashed glass scattered like celebratory confetti, cursing the spot where they all once stood. They weren't on the ground, which Ajay took as a good thing, but as he moved closer, he saw him. Ace.

He didn't look like him. Ajay had never seen his face expressing such emotions. Distressed. Traumatised. His eyebrows were bent down at an unfamiliar angle; he'd squeezed himself in between the opening of one chalet and the next. He anchored his eyes on Ajay.

'Genni?' Ajay mouthed as he rushed towards him. Ace nodded, turned his head and mumbled something behind him. Due to the tight space, Genni obviously couldn't lift her head up, but he could see the golden shimmer of her fingernails as she slipped her hand underneath Ace's armpit and ushered Ajay to come to safety. Relief caught his breath. He picked up the pace and started to run towards the opening. Almost there, he staggered between the dead, trying to respectfully kick off the injured who grabbed at his legs when a hot, burning pain ricocheted across his right arm. He felt his body flop forward and settle into what he assumed were Ace's arms. He looked up and saw he was right: though obscured, he could see Ace's alarmed eyes over him. His right arm was on fire, as if boiling water was being poured right through his skin to the bone. He yelped out in pain and he heard Genni squeal with desperation.

He'd been shot. Ajay's breathing lost its balance. He'd been shot. Shot. With a gun. So he was going to die here? Looking down at his arm and breathing heavily, he saw the wound: sore, red and gushing fluid, but not that deep. Ajay settled his breath. This wasn't going to kill him, but something else might.

'Ajay! Ajay, you OK?' Ace's voice was like a high-pitched whistle, his words hard to distinguish.

Ajay managed to reassure him and then used his left arm to rip the right arm of his shirt and jacket to fully reveal the throbbing burn beneath. 'Just scratched me . . .' Ajay moaned, biting through his lip.

'Ajay!' Genni's voice rang wildly. Ajay could feel Ace's body being forced forwards by her efforts to get to him.

'I'm here. Don't move,' Ajay said slowly, wiping blood from his bottom lip. 'Where are the others?'

'We're all here, Ajay,' Blake called out from further down the side of the bar wall. He couldn't see, but he could imagine them all – Genni, Mila, Blake, Jaxson and Pearl – squished together, faces repulsed and fearful, yet painted with a hope that they might survive the horrors outside.

The sound came then; the sound of that hope. The sirens of the TPD were clear and Ajay felt his body relax despite still being an audience to ongoing destruction. Then he felt a twinge in his stomach.

'What is going on?' said Ace, repeatedly, his words mingling with expletives.

'We need to move,' Ajay said instinctively.

'Are you crazy?' Ace's voice cracked. 'Those madmen are still out there.'

'We can't stay here,' Ajay said. 'There's nowhere to run if we stay here.' Ajay tore his jacket arm further and proceeded to tie it around his burn tightly. His eyes watered before he exhaled. 'OK, everyone needs to follow my lead.' He steadied himself to stand, surprised at his sudden bravery. There was a whimper from behind.

'I can't go. We can't go . . . We'll die.' He'd never heard Pearl struggle so much to get her words out.

Ajay knew it in his gut. They needed to move.

'Pearl! If we don't go now, we could be stuck in a trap.' Ajay spoke loudly enough so Pearl could hear him from the back of their single line squash. 'Blake's with you. Hold his hand and be brave. We'll all be brave together. OK?'

Ajay heard nothing for a couple of seconds, but soon Blake responded, 'Let's go, Ajay,' indicating that Pearl had given a silent indication of her unwilling but essential bravery.

Ajay remained in a half-squatting position and started to creep slowly around the front of the chalet; the others followed. He felt slightly faint as his arm began to swell.

Fever and nausea were rising from the pain. He used his left arm to clutch his right, stopping it from moving. He reached the edge of the chalet and forced himself to filter out the tormenting screams, the continuing gunfire and the flurries of panicked people. Looking behind him, he could see them all: Genni and Pearl had blackened eyes, and the bright, glorifying sparkles of their dresses had been marred by dirt and blood. Then he noticed someone was missing.

'Where's Mila?' he screamed down the line.

Sirens muffled his words as TPD drones and planes flew overhead. The group were frozen as they watched the shooters change their target from people to drones. The laser beams caught a few, like shooting birds from the air, sending them plummeting to the ground – lethal fireballs dressed in deep black smoke. Ajay and the others covered their ears as the blasts penetrated the ground. The drone swarms were too big for the attackers to hold off; the group watched as the drones took control with their tasers and Ajay caught the sight of Jun's killer being held, body squirming in every direction until he stopped moving. The hood of his cloak flew off, revealing his deep olive skin, well-defined chin and neck.

Genni gasped. Ajay turned back to her; she had grabbed Ace's shoulder.

'I . . . It's him . . . I . . . feel . . .' Genni was breathing erratically, and Ace held her up for support. She began to heave and vomited violently onto the ground. Ajay moved behind Ace and grabbed her with his good arm. Breathing through his own pain, he wiped the tears and vomit from her cheek with the cuff of his shirt, his right arm beginning to lose all feeling.

'We've got to go now, Gen,' Ajay said compassionately, not quite sure what triggered the vomit, nor if he could hold down his own. He helped Genni stand, who was hysterical. With her persistent loud sobs in his ear, Ajay asked if the others were all ready to go, and with Genni on his arm, they ran in the direction of the Glorified Gate. Genni blubbered as they struggled. 'It's him.'

'It's who?' Ajay asked.

He didn't hear her response but only saw her lips move as he felt an almighty blast of hot air hit his body and he was thrown down to the ground again.

CHAPTER
THIRTY-EIGHT

Ajay squinted, his blurred vision slowly coming into focus as more screams were muffled by the temporary tinnitus. He could feel the hard concrete against his back again. It was like the ultimate déjà vu, except this time, he wasn't flattened by a body, and the sight of gunfire was replaced with towers of thick, black smoke sailing towards the white sun. They were borne by great flames resembling the fallen drones from moments ago. He sat up, his back feeling like a brick. Trying to make sense of his surroundings again, he looked down at his legs, his trousers completely tattered and his limbs boasting several superficial cuts. He could see that the flames were engulfing the chalets, their structures all but blown apart around him, the opening where they were hiding non-existent. It was a bomb; a second line of attack. *Whoever these people were, they hadn't thought this up this morning. This has been meticulously and carefully planned. But why?*

'Blake!' Pearl screamed, elongating Blake's name so it cut right to Ajay's core. He twisted his head to the left, his vision only just readjusting itself.

'Ajay, Ace, help him. Help him,' she bellowed again, this time with more despair as she crouched over Blake's body.

Everything inside him dropped like a rock to his stomach. Then Ajay heard Blake's wailing, and he experienced the relief he imagined new parents felt as a baby cried for the first time.

Blake was alive, but Ajay knew by the distress in the cry that there was potential he soon wouldn't be. He hobbled to his feet, feeling the weakness of his body and hissing at the forgotten discomfort in his arm. He looked at Pearl, who was crying wildly, make-up running down her face enough to mask her natural complexion. She had a significant gash on her upper lip that was dripping blood down her chin and onto her neckline.

'Jay, Gen . . .' It was comforting for Ajay to hear Ace's voice and feel his hand on his shoulder, and to then feel Genni's hand fall into his own. He looked up and saw her again, her eyes just as fearful and anguished as before. Her lips were quivering as she looked at Blake, struggling and thrashing beneath the great piece of concrete that was crushing his legs. Blood was running out from underneath the rock as they all hurried around him. Ajay looked around for Jaxson, whom he found standing still, with his olive skin turning almost white. He was staring at Blake, who was yelping in agony. Jaxson looked as Ajay felt: shocked, numb and disbelieving. Ajay wanted to concentrate on Blake, to try to find a way to help him. As he met his desperate eyes he started to think, perhaps selfishly, that he needed to survive. There could be a third line of attack. First the guns, then the bombs – what was coming next? They shouldn't stay to find out, even if it meant leaving Blake behind. The thought cut into Ajay painfully, as if it never should have existed in his head.

'Get . . . it . . . *off* . . . ' Blake squawked, his voice cracking harshly.

'But . . . but won't that make things worse?' Genni asked frantically, looking at Ajay with persistent, pleading eyes. Her hair was frizzing wildly off her head. She wanted him to decide? He had no clue what to do. Blake was losing blood by the second as half the concrete bar from the chalet was probably stealing his ability to ever walk again. Yet she expected him, a lad who sat behind a screen all day, to know whether moving it was the right thing to do? It wasn't just her, either; Pearl and Ace looked at him for answers too. He was useless and he didn't like the feeling. He'd gone from the saviour, leading them all out of that opening, to the let-down in a matter of minutes, unable to live up to the role that was apparently expected of him.

'Out of my way.'

Ajay felt his body being pushed back as Mila took his place beside Blake. She was welcome to it. Ajay stood behind her and examined her back; she was covered in blood, but Ajay was pretty sure it wasn't hers. There wasn't a scratch on her. Plus, with the way she had strategically ripped her dress that was once long and golden but now a short, dishevelled party dress with a torn rim, Ajay assumed she had been treating people, using her dress and what she could find to make emergency tourniquets. She was Blake's real saviour and thank goodness she was there. Ajay felt the pressure taken from him, yet the situation was still pressing hard on his mind.

'OK, everyone calm down,' Mila said as she looked around and retied her brown, tatty hair into a messy bun. She bent closer to Blake and Ajay heard her words of assurance. 'Blake, you're going to be fine. Just try to breathe. OK. Like this.' Mila demonstrated how she wanted him to breathe. Slow inhale, slow exhale. Blake began to copy.

'Now, can you feel your legs?' Mila asked.

'Yes I can . . . feel them.' Blake's words fell out quickly before he struggled to return to his breathing rhythm.

'That's good, Blake. That's a good sign.' Mila held his hand. 'OK, so we need to get this off you now. Everything will hurt, Blake. But we're all here with you.'

Ajay imagined the medical teams would get there soon, now that the shooters had been contained, but as he looked around, he saw how they would have their work cut out for them when they did get there. It was a sea of bodies, some moving like fish without water, and others just completely still. A massacre. *What would this mean for–*

'Ajay!' Mila's voice pierced through him. 'Come on. It has to be now.'

He refocused and saw that Genni, Pearl and Ace had steadied themselves around the slab of invading concrete, ready to lift. He took his place and looked at his arm, doubling in size from the swelling. He didn't know how he was going to be of any help.

'Shouldn't we wait until the medical team gets here?' Ajay asked, knowing he had little strength left for his friend.

'No,' Mila instructed. 'The longer it's on him, the more likely–' Mila couldn't finish her words, but Ajay understood.

He nodded, letting her know that he was willing to try. 'One . . . two . . . three . . .'

The group grunted and yelped as they mutually gave everything to lift the thing off. Ajay was panting, puffing through the weight of it and the anger of his burn. He couldn't cope. He was too weak. Pearl was also struggling to hold her side. It was lifting, but it wasn't stable. It felt as if it was tipping towards Blake's torso. Ace let out a frantic cry as he too realised the increasing potential of disaster. But then, in that moment, the concrete changed its momentum away from Blake as Jaxson had run in to assist. They all moaned and breathed heavily as they successfully lifted the piece away from its victim and down beside him. Ajay coughed violently with his head down towards the ground.

For those few seconds, as he stared down at his scuffed formal shoes, he knew he would never forget that day. The day he heard cries of distress and anguish vibrate constantly through his eardrums; the day a man he'd just met stared at him with lifeless eyes; the day he was shot and his friend's legs were crushed; the day he felt only a temporary relief when the medical trucks and planes arrived. Somehow, even through all of that, the most pressing thing on his mind was how this had happened, and what such a security breach would mean for him and his secret.

'Pearl, just calm down.' Ajay heard Genni plead with a distressed Pearl from behind the tall plastic cubicle dividers.

He winced as the android wiped a wet, antiseptic cloth over his burn site. A four-hour wait in the Treatment

Centre had driven him almost to insanity. The aching discomfort in his arm had been intensifying and he'd been sick at least five times. Only as he rested his head back on the bed did he feel connected to reality again. Even during his treatment, he hadn't had a clue what was going on. He remembered the stinging of the Stitch Bots burrowing their way into his skin to fashion the stitches, and he had a vague recollection of seeing them retreat into a machine like long, metal worms. Now, in aftercare, the android was taking its time to dress the wound to prevent infection.

As the robot was finishing up, Genni demanded the glass door to the cubicle to slide open. She was still in her dirty dress, but having managed to clean her face, Ajay was comforted by seeing it.

'Hey.' She kissed Ajay on the forehead, and then moved around the bed to have a look at the scar. 'Wow, it's like it barely happened.' Ajay was speechless. She was right. He looked down at his arm to see a wound that merely resembled a superficial knife scratch. He lifted his arm to touch Genni. Pain. Hot and fresh.

'Don't.' She helped him lower his arm before pulling its bandage back up. 'It may look good, but it'll still hurt like crazy. Come on, you have to help me. Pearl's driving me mad.'

'I can hear you, Genni!' Pearl screamed from the neighbouring cubicle.

Genni raised an eyebrow, to which Ajay smirked. He wasn't sure whether to feel confused or thankful that such trauma seemed to have diffused the tension in their relationship. It wasn't a question he was willing to consider so he shook it off, and shuffled down from the beige-coloured bed.

Please confirm this bed is finished with by pressing the 'Available' button at its end, the voice of technology demanded. Genni did so and a green light shone from the end of the bedframe. It wasn't even a minute before a Tuloian nurse rushed in and took the bed away.

With his arm bent across his torso, Ajay steadied himself to walk with Genni to the next cubicle. Only then did he realise how unbearably loud it was in there. There were beeps and bleeps of machines, shouts and screams, Tuloians running up and down the long corridor with beds, equipment and injured patients in their destroyed glad rags. The only ones who were calm were the androids, walking leisurely while observing patient stats on floating screens. Another hurried nurse collided with the machine.

'Seriously?' She looked up at the oblivious android who continued on its path. 'Stop hanging about. There are people dying here.' The nurse rushed off, ignoring the pleas of patients waiting for beds.

As the android passed him, Ajay saw Pearl on the bed, looking deeply into the mirror extension of her Watch and pulling the skin tissue around her lip. Ace was beside her on a leather armchair, absorbed in his own Watch, eyes dilated at whatever he was reading. Genni opened the door and Pearl whimpered as they entered.

'Ajay!' She stopped prodding at the scar on her lip and sat up in bed. 'Are you alright?' Ajay, slightly surprised by her concern, walked over to Ace and patted him on the shoulder. Ace drew one arm around Ajay's back and then returned to what Ajay could see was a news article on his screen. He sighed, looked at Pearl, whose red eyes had followed him around the bed, and responded, 'I'm OK.' He unwrapped the bandage on his arm. 'It's healed over pretty well.'

Pearl leaned forward to observe the slight scar on Ajay's arm and then let out a wail of frustration.

'They can do *that* when he gets shot?' Pearl's pupils dilated. 'I got a cut on my lip and I'm left with *this* on my face. Is this a sick joke?' She started to bellow into her hands. Genni rushed to her side and told her to calm down. Ajay might have let out a disbelieving laugh, if it wasn't completely inappropriate.

'She's been like this since we came in,' Ace said, looking up from his Watch. 'You'll get used to it.'

Ajay nodded and turned his head to the corridor, where he saw an android pushing a bed trolley slowly. Its occupant seemed to be lifeless. He then saw Mila sprint past the cubicle. She had abandoned her golden dress and donned some medical scrubs.

'This is carnage,' Ajay said.

Ace agreed. 'There's no way the hospital could have been prepared for a terror attack,' he said, shock clear in his voice.

'You don't understand, Gen,' Pearl was shouting louder. 'With this on my face,' she pointed violently to her scar, 'no one will give me loves. I'll have no job and no merit.'

She was silent then, and Ajay saw Genni take her hand. Pearl breathed heavily as tears oozed down her face. Genni took a tissue to wipe them away. After exhaling deeply, Pearl said, 'Now, all people will know of me is that I'm an Unworthy ex-socialite.' Genni gave her a sideways hug. Ajay could sense the sheer amounts of pain and disappointment that were bouncing off every corner of the building's walls. He thought of Blake, still in surgery, who may never be able to walk or dance again.

He turned to Ace. 'Is that what they're calling it? A terror attack?'

He felt Genni and Pearl's eyes lock on him.

'Well, yeah,' Ace said as he scrolled further down the article. 'What else do they call it? Here, listen.' He began to read:

'*Command Officials have confirmed that this was a savage attack believed to be executed by members of a group that call themselves "The Rogue". Drone patrols have been deployed across the Country, where it's believed they have congregated. Investigations are well underway to determine how they were granted access to the Quarters at today's Liberation Day celebrations. Security is due to increase to unprecedented levels. We will stop at nothing to ensure Tulo is safe again.*'

Ace fell silent as he closed his Watch.

'How do they know it was these Rogue people, though?' Pearl asked, folding over a tissue.

'I don't know. I guess it might be an educated assumption from what they could have already known,' Ace said.

'It was them,' Genni said, exhaling. The three of them looked startled and confused. Ajay ushered Genni to explain. How could she possibly know that?

'Ajay, just before the chalet blasts, you remember I said it was *him*?'

Ajay nodded. He remembered that he hadn't cared at the time, he was just trying to get her to run.

'The shooter who got you, who killed Jun . . .' She started to tear up. 'I was with him the night I hurt my shoulder.' The silence in the room felt like another bomb had dropped.

'What? Why were you with him, Gen?' Pearl asked, pinching the skin of her throat.

'He was Downtown, instead of the usual guy who'd give me the illegal *SkipSleep*.' Genni paused and then walked around the bed, towards Ajay on the other side of the cubicle. He felt the sincerity behind her voice and reached out for her. 'I remember him talking about it being nice in the Country, about how he had a group of people out there. And he was beautiful, you all saw him. The most striking features. He grabbed me. And that's when I ran, got hit by the car and someone helped . . .'

'He grabbed you? What do you mean, he grabbed you?' Ajay crossed his arms over his chest, feeling an angered tension trap his body. It wasn't only frustrated that another man had touched her, but that she had never bothered to tell him. How long ago had she remembered?

'He tried to hurt me, but I got out, and today, it was him, with the gun.' Genni put her head on Ajay's chest, crying lightly. Ajay looked down to see her usually delicately washed hair smothered in dried blood and sand. He wasn't sure whether he wanted to hug her. She kept keeping things from him. The *SkipSleep*, the painting and the details of her accident. But he was reminded that anything could have happened to her that night and today. He decided to hold her tightly, and if he was honest with himself, he never wanted to let her go.

CHAPTER
THIRTY-NINE

One month after the attack

Ajay's hands trembled as he tightened his grey tie. His mind was numb and he snarled at Genni's wardrobe when it told him he needed 'a spot of colour'. He smacked the mirror to turn the commentary off. Genni walked in from the shower room, having fallen into a black trousers and T-shirt combination. She had little make-up on, and her hair was tied back simply. Ajay knew she was watching as she pressed earrings into her lobes, but he dismissed it, leaning against the wardrobe and looking down at the wooden floorboards of the circular apartment.

'You ready for this?' she asked softly, but Ajay didn't respond. 'Ajay?' She walked closer.

'You'd think with all this technology, they could update the wardrobes so they know why I'm not wearing any colour.' Ajay didn't look at her as he walked to the large bay window to look out over the dark river and grey architecture of the now-empty shopping centre.

'You don't have to go today, you know. We can even stay here and tune in. Blake would understand.' Ajay felt her fingers gripping his shoulder.

'No, I'm going.'

Ajay stared out blankly. Genni's apartment sat above a line of empty buildings, once retail shops before drone deliveries and the shopping mall punched them out of business. She'd recently redecorated, on the advice of Pearl, as apparently refurbishments added up to a whacking amount of social merit if done right. That was before she came out as an artist. Still, she'd gone for a very on-trend historical look: the walls were burdened with a lining of fairy lights, and she proudly displayed her paintings. The waterfall hung above the sofa, the only piece of furniture not thrown together with oak wood and wicker. Ajay didn't mind it, but he much preferred being at home. This all felt too close and claustrophobic, like a dull haze hanging over him and he couldn't come out for air. He hated that he didn't have a choice; there was food here, and he couldn't risk buying any for himself anymore. He didn't know the level of Command's new security measures; every time he scanned his Watch, anywhere, that could be it. So he had to be selective.

'Shall we go?' Genni said as she wiped her fatigued eyes slowly, reddening their edges. His Watch vibrated. *Ace calling.*

Ajay said nothing as Ace's face sprang up on a floating screen.

'Hi. You heading over soon?'

'Yeah. Almost through the door.'

'Alright. See you soon, then.' Ace disappeared into the Watch. The lack of pep in Ace's demeanour fell over the room as Ajay and Genni stood on opposite sides of it.

Genni walked towards the door. 'OK. Let's go,' she said.

The sky train had reopened its route for the first time since the attack. As they approached the pallid platform, dense swarms of TPD drones covered the sky. It was becoming increasingly difficult to see the whiteness of the sun, its canvas even more littered with mechanical black dots. The streets had been sapped of their previous energy – mainly because the usual vibrancy of advertising had been muted black by anti-Rogue messaging. It hadn't stopped the City from working. Their days were still endless, but a darkness had emerged from the shadows that no amount of merit could fix. He and Genni found themselves drooping through the station's entrance. People were slow to get onto the platform. Ajay hadn't realised the reason before she said it.

'Oh, really? They're checking us here too?' Genni was rolling back the cuff of her black bomber jacket to get her Watch ready for authentication.

It had become as common as *SkipSleep* boosts. Ajay had hoped Command might let up once they were relaxed enough to reopen the sky train. That was naïve of him. Ajay could see there were at least six Command guards – actual humans dressed head to toe in dull purple military suits. Accompanying them were TPD drones in high numbers, ready to restrain anyone whom the turnstiles rejected.

Dropping Genni's hand and slowly shifting backwards, Ajay told himself to sound calm. He didn't want her to notice his anxiety.

'Hey, Gen. Do you fancy walking to Jaxson's?'

Genni stopped and others rudely murmured at the two of them for blocking the entrance. Ajay ignored them and led Genni back out into the anaemic streets. He felt her hand snap away from his.

'What do you mean? It'll take us at least ten minutes.'

Ajay grabbed Genni's hand again and calmly sauntered with her along the pavement. 'I didn't fancy going back into the crowds just yet,' he lied.

Genni sighed and stroked the inside of Ajay's right arm. 'We've got to at some point, Ajay. I can't live in fear forever.'

Ajay hurt inside. He always hurt. Any hope of keeping his secret was getting smaller with every rise and fall of the sun, as quickly as Tulo had transformed from a hard worker's paradise to an imprisoned nightmare. He hurt every time he used Genni to protect himself. Though, if she never found out, it wouldn't hurt her. Surely?

Ajay had always thought that Jaxson's place was like a blanket copy of Tulo Command. It had floor to ceiling glass windows that fell over the spectacular view of the City's Inner-Ring Park, where fox walkers and children looked like small pinpoints on a much bigger map. Industrial steel shimmered and sparkled on the worktops, and the ladder that led up to the second-floor platform was decorated with fake green vines. As they were welcomed in, Ajay could see that Jaxson's bed sat on the upper platform and the white bedding was pristine, folded neatly with light-blue pillows placed thoughtfully on top.

'Blake's been anxious to see you all,' Jaxson said, as he took them through to the living room.

Ajay hadn't managed to make it over yet. He had been so wrapped up in himself, a friend trapped within four walls seemed to fall to the wayside. Those walls were suffocating, too – bleached white and clinical. Ajay imagined Blake felt the absence of colour strongly. The white sofa had been shifted to the side to make way for the borrowed hospital bed that was floating inside the room. Ajay felt a heaviness when he saw Blake smile sweetly at him. He looked awful. The purple marks around his eyes tried to shine with a certain graciousness, but really, it was only pain. Mila and Pearl were already there, engaged in muffled conversation.

Ace nudged Ajay with his elbow. He was looking longingly at Mila.

'What d'ya think about Mila?' Ace asked, his voice lowered.

'What about her?' Ajay replied, drawing his eyes away from Blake.

'You know . . . What do you *think* about her?'

Is he joking? After all that's happened, he's still thinking about girls? Ajay couldn't figure out if Ace was ignorant over the severity of the situation or if he was trying to distract himself from it.

'She's great.'

Ajay meant it. He thought very highly of Mila; sometimes he thought that out of everyone, she would be the only one who would understand why he'd lied and tricked his way into the system. But that was probably only a pipe dream.

Ace agreed. 'She was saying how they've sent the androids back for development on her suggestion. The attack showed that they couldn't deal with crisis management and made things worse. She was so brilliant. I might ask her out. What do you think?'

'Pearl, pass me my glasses.' Blake's strained, spirited voice vibrated across the walls.

Pearl walked slowly over to the white cabinet opposite the bed and picked up Blake's square specs. Blake placed them slowly onto his face. He lifted his arms up as he said, 'Ace, Ajay. I can see you more clearly now. Get over here, you beauties.'

'I'm coming. I'm coming,' Ace insisted, and laughed.

Something compassionate came over Ajay. He just did it. He reached out and grabbed Ace's arms and spoke with authority.

'I think you can't force yourself to love someone just because their numbers work with yours.'

That was probably the most truthful thing he'd said for years. It was the most honest he'd ever been with Ace. It felt strangely nice to be authentic. Ace looked thoughtful and gave a small, resistant nod of the head. Ajay followed him to Blake's bedside.

'You're looking a bit worse for wear, my man,' Ace said, as he and Blake clapped hands.

'Oh, I'm not too bad.' Blake looked over as rustles came from the door. 'Ah, thanks, Jaxs, I was getting a little peckish.' Jaxson placed a few vegetable fried crisps in Blake's hand before placing the bowl on the side. Ajay watched Pearl throw her hand into the bowl immediately.

'So, do you like it here Blake?' Ace asked.

'It's OK,' Blake spoke through munching. 'Very comfortable and much better than the chaotic sick place I would have been left in if Jaxson hadn't offered to help me out.' Ajay, still standing away from the bed, wondered if Blake was stabbing at his inadequacy as a friend compared to Jaxson, who had given up everything to help him. Ajay hadn't even bothered to call. 'Anyway, Ajay, darling. Where have *you* been?' Blake peered over his glasses and Ajay caved into himself, his suspicions confirmed as he edged closer to the bed. 'Oh, I'm joking. Come here.'

Ajay felt the chill of Blake's skin as he grabbed his hand to pull him closer. Ajay looked over at Genni as she chatted to Pearl, and Jaxson ordered a large screen to spring to life. It spanned almost the entirety of the back wall. Blake's soft voice drew Ajay away.

'I want to thank you.' Blake stared deep into Ajay's eyes, who felt saddened by the severity of Blake's facial bruising.

'Thank me?' Ajay felt the room go silent.

'If you hadn't moved us from behind that chalet, we'd all be dead.' Blake was still, tears forming in his eyes. 'And I have to be thankful for that. You're a leader, Ajay.'

Ajay looked around. The girls were both crying, Ace stared down at the ground and Jaxson worked through the silence by crunching on crisps. Ajay didn't know what to say. This man, a lively and passionate friend, was *grateful* to *him* – a liar and a hypocrite. But he'd only been those things because he had to be. To be Worthy. To be their friend in the first place. That was right, wasn't it? He held Blake's hand tightly in gratification for his words.

'Here, Ajay. Have a seat,' Jaxson said, as the scraping of an armchair shook the tiles on the ground. 'Ale?'

Ajay refused, politely, as he took the chair and held Blake's hand again. 'So, what's next for you, Blake?'

'What do you mean, what's next?' Blake narrowed his eyebrows as he munched through more crisps. 'I'm back at work next week. I ain't gonna let having no legs slow me down.' His notorious laugh loudly intruded into the commentary of a news reporter onscreen, who was detailing yet more cancelled sporting and musical events.

Ajay stared forward, lifeless.

'Don't look so worried. I've got some merit compensation for the first few weeks, but it won't be enough,' Blake sighed. 'I can always get healthier but once you're Unworthy, that's what you are. It's too hard to get back, so I can't let it slip.'

Ajay found himself struggling to look Blake in the eyes. A strange sense of anger rushed through him, but on looking up and seeing Blake thanking Jaxson for the drink he had brought, laughing openly with him, Ajay convinced himself that maybe his friend would be OK. Maybe the trauma he'd been through would be exactly what he needed. But Ajay had the ability to give Blake points, even when he didn't deserve them. It made his treachery feel all the dirtier.

'Don't be scared for me, Ajay.' Blake turned back to him. 'I'll stay Worthy. Nothing a few boosts won't solve.'

Blake smiled once more, but he didn't manage to control a quiver in his lower lip. Ajay also worked hard to mask his distress and turned to the screen, where a news reporter stood in front of the Glorified Quarters.

He realised this would be the first time anyone would see into the Quarters since the attack. Well, other than those who lived or worked there. He'd been annoyed when the new barricades had meant even volunteering was a no go. Did the streets still glisten, or would they be forever marred by their troubled past? He assumed not when he finally saw the roof that they'd put over the Quarters' walls. They towered behind the news reporter, who was wearing a light-blue blouse. She was talking, but Ajay wasn't really listening. The walls didn't even look golden anymore; their magnificence was diminished by a domed, black roof. Ajay had read that only drones and authorised signals could travel through it. He didn't understand why Command thought they needed to protect the skies when the murderers had walked right through the front door. He felt pain ricochet through his gut at that thought. Command wasn't going to take any risks, and people like him wouldn't have anywhere to hide. Yet not everyone was like him, he convinced himself. He certainly wasn't like Genni's obnoxious mother, who complained about the sky going dark one afternoon, and then when the light was artificially restored, was distressed about ash and dust remaining on their balcony.

'They could have chosen a better colour,' Blake complained about the roof. Genni shifted uncomfortably; Pearl looked down at her wrist; Mila observed the sky above the park outside, and Ace and Jaxson kept their eyes focused on the scene as the news reporter announced the memorial service was about to begin.

The shot switched to a drone's camera inside the Quarters. Clearly, they wouldn't even let the press inside. Its main street was lined in its usual floral bloom, and not a concrete block or speck of blood remained. The drone camera spiralled to show a floating stage in front of the Command building and a petite woman standing on it. She was wearing the usual Command attire – a white suit with a white Command branded shirt with a white tie. Her brown hair was tied back in a slick bun.

Pursing her lips and looking up to her audience of millions, she held out her wrist and produced a screen from her Watch. Only when she was fully in focus did Ajay recognise her as Sandria, a presenter who led trivial debates on *YourVids* or the news.

'This is a different gig for her,' Ace said to the room. 'We're a long way from the fox and lynx debate now.'

Ajay smirked, but not deliberately. He agreed that all Sandria's work did seem to revolve around insignificant topics, such as the reasoning behind why merit deductions should be introduced for poorly manufactured pet foods. *A healthy pet is a healthy you.* That sort of joviality was gone; her tone and language were sombre as she started reading robotically from a script. Respectfully, Ajay noticed how they all stopped talking. He followed suit when they all looked to their wrists. He set his Watch to record. He may as well get the small merit for attendance.

'Progress is Strength. They will never be forgotten.' Ajay and the others had bowed their heads at the closing of Sandria's speech. 'And now we will have a two-minute silence.'

Ajay imagined what it was like outside as silence fell like a sheet over the entire City. The sky train, he assumed, had stopped moving and all drones and vehicles had been ordered to stop. As he thought about this, he also saw the faces of the 102 identified victims rolling one after the other on the screen. Jun's face appeared. The eyes that Ajay saw without any life shone with ambition next to an M-400 score. Ajay heard Genni's tears from across the room and watched as Mila held her hand. Then, as the scores got lower, the images got quicker. It was difficult to even see them as they soon flickered into nothing.

Ajay still saw him, though: the grey, messy beard and the bruised face.

Sam.

Ajay almost mouthed his name with his lips. He felt even more numb than he did before. Sam, the Glorified reject, died. Meritless and without love. Why was he even in the Quarters? Was he part of The Rogue? Trying to get in to sell or steal? As the commentary from the news reporter brought life back into the room, Ajay decided it didn't matter now, and he painfully detached himself from the Unworthy he once helped in his apartment.

Ajay was about to get some fresh air when Ace pointed to the screen, his eyes wide.

'Arneld Hevas? Are they joking?'

CHAPTER
FORTY

Heads snapped back to the screen to see him.

He was a man of small stature, wearing a Command white suit with its purple trim. His skin glowed with expensive product and his blond-tipped hair puffed above his short forehead. Looking into the camera, Arneld Hevas craned his neck, further highlighting the sharp definition of his cheekbones. As he stumbled over his opening words, he caught himself and found a rhythm while keeping his eyes fixed and strong.

'Our treasured citizens should be aware of the measures we're taking to make our City safe again.' A quick cough from Arneld gave Ajay enough space to shiver. 'It is at this time that we want you all to know who committed this attack against us. They call themselves The Rogue.' Ajay heard Blake's breathing quicken, and he swallowed. 'The majority of their following are individuals who were once accredited citizens, or in some cases, come from the Side. They live by a distorted ideology that requires them to destroy those who are Worthy.' Arneld's eyes were still keenly staring into the camera. 'This means they have a good knowledge of our streets and our systems. So, in addition to the security measures already in place, we are now introducing the following laws . . .'

Ajay's wrist beeped loudly as his heart rate shot up. His hands turned clammy, and he could feel his legs freezing; he shuffled in his seat. No one seemed to notice his Watch's interruption; all eyes and ears were transfixed on the speaker.

'Our officers now have the right to raid anyone's home who is considered suspicious. Arrests will be made, and trials conducted if evidence is unsatisfactory. Watch-tampering checks will be intensified: they are now in place for all shops, sky train stations and drone transactions. Additionally, anyone suspected of having helped or facilitated unauthorised access into the City will be arrested and tried. If found guilty, you will be stripped of your merit and privileges, and any resistance will be dealt with. It saddens us to introduce such serious precautions, but we hope it will not be forever. We appreciate your support and cooperation at this difficult time.' The vibrations of his final words barely reached the broadcast as he was cut off and the screen turned black. It was soon coloured with the news reporter returning, scrambling for what she should say next.

'Did they have to do that after the remembrance?' Mila said as she picked up the empty crisp bowl and moved quickly to the kitchen.

'Guess they knew people would be watching.' Ace walked behind Genni to stand by the window. He raised his chin, and Ajay watched the white sunlight fall over him. 'But Arneld Hevas? Nobody's seen him for about a year.' Ace crossed his arms and looked straight at Ajay. Ajay shrugged his shoulders. No words came to him. He was going to get caught. All of this would be gone. Ace – their friendship – gone. Genni – her trust – taken from him. His merit – and what it meant – stripped away. As the reality of it started to set in, his eyes fell on Genni. She didn't look OK.

Her gaze was fixed on the floor, but she was gripping the arms of her chair. He could tell she was controlling her breathing with the deep rising and falling of her shoulders. After instinctively moving towards her, Ajay stroked her arm as both he and Pearl looked at her, concerned.

'Gen, hun, what's the matter?' Pearl's ponytail flopped over her small shoulder.

'He's never going to go away, is he?' Genni said, continuing to seize her armrests. Pearl and Ajay both remained silent, swapping puzzled looks. 'Just when I think he's out of my head, out of my dreams, something comes up that gets him right back in there again. Today was meant to be about them, about Jun and all the others, but that ending announcement spat on them. It made everything about *him* and his dirty little friends.' Genni finally released her hands, throwing her head into them and groaning. Ajay said nothing, as he had for the last month. He hadn't wanted to talk about Genni's run-in with The Rogue the night of her accident. Not only was he grappling with her inability to tell him, but every time it was mentioned, he was hit with the vulnerability of his position.

'Look, Gen,' Pearl sighed, her lips tight. 'We've all been through trauma; it's how we deal with it and help others that matters.' She shook her head. 'At least you don't have a facial deformity that's costing you everything.'

Ajay observed the scar that ran from the right side of Pearl's lip to her inner cheek, impossible to completely mask with concealer.

'You're going to be fine, Pearl,' Genni said, sitting up again. Ajay managed to bring himself to hold her hand as they talked across him.

'Am I?' Pearl suddenly delivered tears. Ajay knew he needed to intervene before the two of them ended up at each other's throats about whose trauma was the most detrimental. He didn't; his thoughts turned frantically back to Arneld's announcement. How could he live without ever scanning his Watch? Maybe he'd get away with it. Maybe The Rogue tampered with their Watches differently and Command wouldn't be looking for what he'd done. Perhaps he was safe.

'If I can't figure out how to stop people judging me for this thing . . .' Pearl pointed to the scarred lump, 'which stops them from listening to or liking my content, my main merit-maker and contribution to society is gone. What do I do then? Get a new job?' Pearl stroked at the bunching skin around her eyes. 'You watch, people will see me Unworthy before the year is out. And I'll never be able to step foot into the Social Sphere again.'

Ajay managed to catch the crinkling of Genni's nose as she tried to hold her composure.

'You could still use your trauma, Pearl.' Blake joined the conversation from his bed. Whether he was merely trying to diffuse the tension, or he had something to add, Ajay didn't care. He stared forward blankly; their words were muffled around him.

'What do you mean?' Pearl pulled a tissue from the box beside her, and tapped lightly at her eyelids.

'I just wonder if you could use your experience to create a whole new area of content.' Blake went on to explain, 'You said it yourself. Why don't you use what you've been through to help others? Help them feel more positive about their own trauma because you, an influencer, have been through a similar thing and are stronger for it.'

Ajay tuned back in to see Genni smiling approvingly at Blake. Would she ever look at him like that again? Surely, not when she found out. It could happen in the next few hours, whenever Ajay tried to buy a drink or even get into his apartment. Would they initiate checks there too? They could even search his place. They'd find his equipment under his desk. Evidence, plain and simple.

'You mean, I should be honest?' Pearl grimaced.

'Well, yeah,' Blake said.

Ajay squinted at Pearl then. He had never decided what he felt towards her; she was a constant mood swing, compassionate one minute, a liar the next. She perked up and said, 'That could work. Blake, thank you.' She hopped up from her seat and slathered a kiss on Blake's cheek, pushing his glasses to a slant. 'I could talk about my scar and how that really hurts my image, and oh, I could talk about the nightmares.'

'You've been having nightmares too?' Genni said, a dazed stare on her face.

'No, but you have.' Pearl danced off the bed and returned to Genni. 'What are they about, Gen? So I can use it.'

Pearl's smile had no knowledge of Genni's revulsion.

'I think it's time for us to go,' she said, not once glancing at Pearl. She grabbed her bag, springing from her seat. Ajay felt her angered grip on his hand as she pulled him from the room.

The yellow moon shimmered in the dark sky as Ajay and Genni dropped each other's hands and walked down the Inner-Ring streets away from Jaxson's apartment.

'It's been nice to walk everywhere,' Genni said lightly. Ajay smiled, but his feelings inside were dark and sombre. He could feel himself on the edge of a panic attack. *We have the right to raid anyone's home.* Arneld Hevas was ringing in his ears. *Arrests will be made.* He was a train heading for a wall. *Watch-tampering checks will be intensified.* Soon he would be nothing but crumpled steel and fire. *You will be stripped of your merit and privileges.* There was nothing he could do. He would crash, hard and fast. But a niggling feeling kept him grounded. He'd *always* beat the system. Surely, he could do it again?

'What do you think about what Pearl asked me?' Genni's voice penetrated through the chasm of his thoughts. A delivery drone swooped low from above, causing Ajay to duck slightly to avoid its delivery box scraping his head. It was difficult to see them without the bright lights of many adverts, now darkened with anti-Rogue messages.

'What?' Ajay hadn't heard her.

'The nightmares.'

'Oh.' Ajay paused, forcing himself to streamline his thoughts. 'Were you surprised?' He jammed his hands in his pockets. 'She's always making stuff up for the channel.'

He spotted a billboard above: *Notice anyone suspicious? Report it on your Watch.* He hoped his face didn't look as ashen as he felt.

'I suppose.' Her voice got louder. 'I just don't want to talk about them.'

Ajay then caught the pained expression on her face – so beautiful, so innocent, so hurt. *Anyone suspected of having helped unauthorised access into the City.* He'd put her in danger too. And she would only hurt more, should everything come out. If he could only know more about Command's plans, maybe he could hack himself through.

'I agree the whole of Tulo shouldn't know about the root of your nightmares, but you can tell me,' Ajay said, the words falling quicker than his thoughts. But he realised, if her small interaction with The Rogue could give him any sort of head start, then he should know about it.

'What?' Genni stopped walking.

'I still don't know what really happened,' Ajay traced his way back to her. 'I know he tried to grab you. But what did you talk about? What did he want?'

'Ajay, I just . . . I can't.' Genni glanced around uneasily.

'Just try,' Ajay said, holding onto her shoulders softly. 'Try, for me.'

So I can stay here, Worthy, with you.

She looked back at him with love in her eyes, took a deep breath, but continued to walk.

'I don't remember everything, as I told you. But we were Downtown.' She kept her stare away from him, only taking her eyes from the street to the moon. 'And the memory is a little fuzzy, but he was talking about the Country. And asking about me.'

'What do you mean?' Ajay swallowed, taking quicker steps to keep up with her.

'Just stuff about me. Like my merit score and where I worked. He definitely asked me where I was born at one point but I don't remember much more, other than when he tried to hurt me.'

'He was asking about your identification?' Ajay's words blew out in a whisper.

'I suppose he was. He was certainly determined to find out everything about me.'

Ajay felt the physical drop of his heart within his chest. His worst fears confirmed. And what Genni said next would consolidate his theory.

'But Ajay, when he touched me and grabbed me . . .' Genni stopped again and struggled to speak as tears found themselves dropping off the edge of her chin. 'It wasn't a touch like he was going to rape me, or kiss me, or anything like that.' She took another breath. 'It was like he was going to *kill me.*'

Ajay pressed his fingers hard into his forehead. He felt them force themselves into his skin as if a hat were being fitted tighter and tighter around his scalp. He saw the moon across the vast horizon, speaking of the sheer extravagance of nature, and he felt the deep sorrow of his insignificance: everything he had built to be Worthy would soon be a mere news story or case file buried deep into the Command archive. He'd always known it. They'd done the same as him. The Rogue had chosen people to impersonate and presumably, based on what Genni had said, killed them to cover their tracks. Ajay had never asked who Ajay Ambers really was – whether the woman had made him up or he existed somewhere – but it had never mattered. Either way, Ajay was safe to assume that Command was looking for the same tampered code that sat on his own wrist. It was also fair to believe that if they found it, he would instantly be considered as a member of The Rogue.

'What's wrong?' Genni was tugging on his right arm. 'You look like a ghost.' She joined Ajay with a hard stare at the moon. 'Ajay?'

Ajay felt the tears fall down his dark skin, and he imagined they made his face shine in the moonlight.

Ajay was speechless, embarrassed to let her see him cry, but he had to say something. 'I'm sorry he made you feel like that.'

'Hey,' Genni turned his face towards hers, her own eyes turning glassy. 'It's OK. I'm OK.' Genni didn't hesitate to embrace him as he cried violently into her shoulder. 'You're so tired. When was the last time you had a boost?'

Ajay felt the tender stroke of her fingers across his neck. He didn't answer; he clearly couldn't admit that he hadn't had a boost in weeks. They were checking Watches there too. So, he was silent, she was quiet, and they stood – two crying lovers in the moonlight, soon to be broken apart.

CHAPTER
FORTY-ONE

A week had passed since that night and Ajay had spent the last seven days in a spiral of paranoia. He always held his breath when he had to scan into his apartment. Every intercom chime sent him running for a window; every noise in the corridor insisted he spied through the peephole; every TPD swarm drifting past, and there were more than ever, made him squirm. Sitting at his desk and working with his hacking equipment, he ranted at himself again. *Every time you do this, you're taking a huge risk*. But he had no choice. He had to maintain his merit.

After the announcement, and the increasing home raids and day-to-day arrests, he knew Command wouldn't stop there. *They'd stop at nothing to make Tulo safe again*. Something else was coming. He'd tried to find out what. Drilling down into news updates and networking with security geeks online had been a dead end. That wasn't the only thing sending him delusional, though – there was also the lack of food and *SkipSleep* boosts. He was managing to scrounge food by staying at Genni's or inviting himself to Ace's for dinner and getting him to do the order.

He pulled himself from his desk, having boosted his points, and made it to the fridge. Watching the door slide back, he couldn't believe he'd managed to keep Genni away from its lack of milk or leftovers. Retrieving his last bottle of water from the drawer, he yanked off its lid and thought about how long he could keep this up. *Find a solution.*

Ajay wandered sluggishly towards the sofa, the water refreshing his barren throat. He was sweating, yet he couldn't be bothered to change even though the hems of his joggers were dirt-ridden after dragging across the concrete floor. He needed to get back to recognised productivity soon. A sudden and unusual fall in merit would not be tolerated by anyone, especially not Mr Hollday.

Ajay flopped onto the sofa and placed his half-empty bottle down on the coffee table next to the dormant *SkipSleep* port, hovering his Watch far away from the activation pad. Not that he hadn't been tempted. The withdrawal had been very real; the sweating and fatigue, the irritability and the nausea, and the headaches, all of which didn't help his anxiety. He'd run scenarios in his head about how he would explain it to Ace, about how he would say goodbye to Genni, and how or where he would end up. He imagined himself in a Command detention cell made mainly of impenetrable glass. He was always on his knees and crying out in physical or mental agony, or both. The only light he ever saw was a small spotlight of the white sun that creeped its way through a slit in the cell roof.

Ajay always stopped thinking at that point. He usually diverted to searching on his Watch for Command updates, but there was never anything. Not a peep. Not since the remembrance. This led Ajay to believe he was safe, that maybe he could slip under the radar. Then, reality would hit him hard in the chest, he would grieve and start the entire thought cycle again. He'd be back in the Detention Centre.

But this time, on the sofa and alone in the apartment, the infinite motion of his uneasiness was interrupted by a call on his Watch.

Unknown calling. Ajay knew it was one of his parents. He'd tapped them in as *Unknown* years ago and they hardly ever rang, but since the attack, it had been relentless. Ajay never answered. Only now, in a sudden clearing of brain fog, did it occur to him that maybe they weren't trying to talk to him, but Grandma may have died.

He sat up, curse words on his tongue and swiped to accept the call.

His father's rounded face sprung up.

'Son . . . you're alive!' His eyes bulged from behind his glasses.

Ajay heard the screeches of his mother, who came running into the camera's view. Ajay almost didn't recognise her with her hair down; she looked younger as it grazed the thin shape of her chin and concealed her developing wrinkles.

'Karle . . . Ajay . . . You're OK?' his mother said, moving herself closer to the camera. Ajay could see her emotion.

'Yes,' Ajay breathed. 'Grandma is alright?' That was all the information he needed.

'Your grandma's doing OK, better actually,' his father said, the two of them nodding at each other.

'She was startled that day when she woke up and you were gone. She doesn't totally understand about the attack–' His mother was interrupted.

'Why have you been ringing me, then?'

He took little notice of his mother's wounded look.

'Well, it was an emergency. We didn't know if you were alive or dead. We knew you go to the celebrations,' she said.

'You've got news out there. I'm not on the list,' Ajay rubbed the back of his neck. They'd broken their agreement. Don't call unless it's an emergency, and to be honest, his grandma's welfare in harm's way was the only thing he'd consider urgent. So, why had they called? It was dangerous for him. He didn't know what calls could be intercepted. He was emotionally and physically exhausted; their stupidity was tipping him over the edge.

'There are still names missing, son. We needed to know you were OK.' His father returned Ajay's vexed look.

Ajay glanced through the window as he saw a drone carrying a box potentially double its weight, bobbing up and down slowly in the scorching heat. He reinstated eye contact with his parents.

'Karle.' His father paused. 'Ajay . . . Don't you think it's time to come home? Command is not going to let anyone slip through. You're in real danger.'

His father looked at his mother, who was wiping tears slowly away from the edge of her cheekbones. 'Just come home. Reverse whatever you did to your identity. Tell whoever helped you to keep quiet and no one will have to . . .'

Ajay thought of the mysterious woman from Downtown and the deal he'd made with her. He hadn't thought about her since that day in the Quarters when she'd slipped Ajay Ambers into his dirty trouser pocket. A collage of memories ran through his head: the small box room behind the pink curtain, the braid that fell over her right shoulder, her harsh voice, and the Fo Doktrin he collected for her. A plan weaved itself together in his mind.

'How?' He tuned back in. 'They've already cut off the line to the Side. And what would I do? I can't disappear. People will see me; they'll see me Unworthy.'

In that moment, Ajay felt a shot of that possibility drill itself deeply through his body, almost stinging in his gunshot wound for the first time since its healing. As he looked again at his parents, he remembered their sorrow when he left; the image of them standing in the kitchen alive in his mind. They hadn't moved from their spot as he'd opened the front door. His mother was being comforted by his grandma, and Ajay had never erased the memory of Tara with her arms wound tightly around their father's torso, dampening his T-shirt with her uncontrollable tears. In his despair, he no longer cared about distancing his emotions from the details of his family's lives. He briefly looked over to his desk and thought of the photo of Tara stuck to its underside, untouched for weeks.

He glared into his father's eyes, 'Where's Tara?'

His father sighed and his mother disappeared off the screen.

'Tara's been gone a while,' his father confirmed. 'But the most important thing for now is for you to get out of there. However you became someone else, switch it . . .' His father continued blabbering, but Ajay became distracted by the shuffles of movement from the corridor. He jumped up, recognising the lightness of the footstep. He hadn't anticipated Genni's arrival. In his fright, he hung up the Watch without any form of goodbye. Just as he did so, the door slid open, and Genni entered wearing a short blue T-shirt dress Ajay had never seen before. It was nice. She looked nice.

'Who were you talking to?' Genni put her purse on the counter.

'Just the office.' Ajay thought fast. 'I'm going in this afternoon.' He walked towards her and kissed her lightly on the cheek before walking to the bedroom.

'Oh, OK,' Genni said, sounding disappointed. 'Have you had a shower? You look a bit . . .' Genni paused. 'Never mind. I was going to ask if you wanted to go to the library. Don't worry, I'll see if Pearl can make it.' She leaned against the kitchen worktop and swiped at her Watch as Ajay disappeared into his bedroom, slightly paranoid she might look in the fridge.

He could hear Pearl's muffled voice through the door as he shut it. With his mind spiralling once more, he walked slowly towards the wardrobe and donned a discreet long-sleeved top. He wasn't going to the office. In the seconds between hanging up the Watch and arriving at his bedroom, he had decided to take action to protect his fate.

Against all odds, his father's words had shown him how – he needed to find the woman from behind the pink curtain.

The late afternoon sun was caught behind a small, whispering cloud, allowing for a dark shade to fall over the Outer-Ring. Ajay felt the air get cooler, refreshing on his perspiring body. His hair was laden with sweat, and he had patches on his armpits. He had never felt, or looked, so disgusting. He didn't care – he needed to find her, and he no longer had time to worry about appearances.

He approached the familiar market stalls as if he had been there yesterday, yet something was different. Everything was quiet. There were cardboard boxes upturned and remains of product packaging strewn across the pavement. A few TPD drones seemed to be patrolling the area. Ajay walked through and noticed that the once-flickering neon lanterns had been punched out, the glass of their bulbs on the ground. He looked around longingly while keeping himself away from the TPD.

'You ought to come back tonight, lad.'

Ajay twisted himself to see a middle-aged man squeezed into a small plastic chair. He stretched out his legs, smoking a cigarette while grabbing from an open packet of Tulo Choco Bites. As he chewed, his black eyes stared at Ajay beneath unkempt eyebrows.

'I don't want to trade,' Ajay said, not really looking at him but all around the abandoned market. He focused on the curtain, now tattered and torn, that led to the inner room. He remembered the table, the coffee machine and the hatch. It was all so vivid in his memory. Yet disappointment punched into his gut. She wasn't here.

The man's sinister laugh filled the air.

'You won't get much down that end, lad.' He drew another drag and his eyes turned alert before saying his next words. Once he was satisfied no one was listening, he continued. 'The lot of them were cleaned out.

Command finally got wind of what goes on. We are more discreet now.' He stood up and stubbed out his cigarette.

As he got closer, his sweaty stench became more pungent. He moved his mouth towards Ajay's ear. Ajay stood still, clenching his fists, but the man only spoke.

'You look tired and like you need the merit. I can give you a boost, off the record.' He looked into Ajay's eyes and raised his bushy eyebrows with invitation. Was this the guy, Ajay wondered, who Genni would come to? Who allowed her merit obsession to manifest in ways she never anticipated? Maybe he should get his fix, he thought. It had been so long. He was stronger than Genni, he could handle it. If he moderated it, he could feel alive again. Alive enough to get out of this mess. Soon enough the memory of the blue-green veins across Genni's face came back. *Who knows what this guy puts in the shot?* He had to think straight.

'No. I'm fine.'

Ajay's refusal led the man to shrug and walk back to his plastic chair.

'There was a woman . . .' Ajay shouted after him, before lowering his voice and stepping closer. 'There was a woman here. Years ago. She worked in security and . . .' Ajay nodded at him. 'I imagine she sold you Fo Doktrin for what you do.'

'I know her, yeah,' he said as he lit up another cigarette. 'But she ain't been around these parts for a long time. Like I say, those lot down there got kicked out right after the attack, but she stopped even before that.' He flung his arm up in the direction of the pink curtain.

'Do you know where I might find her?' Ajay asked flippantly.

'I dunno.' The man shrugged his shoulders. 'Don't suppose she would have given up that job at Command in a hurry. Unless she got caught, that is.' His deep laugh vibrated down the length of the stalls but soon transformed into a solid husky cough that sounded painful.

'Thank you,' Ajay said as he walked away, back towards the river and the bridge, not thinking about how he'd thanked a grimy drug dealer. His time was getting shorter. He marched determinedly away from Downtown to begin his long walk across the City, to the Glorified Quarters.

His feet began to burn with a ferocity that made walking difficult. It was a pain Ajay had never experienced before. He reached the outskirts of the Inner-Ring and people were, as usual, dashing from one place to another, and his hobbling wasn't inviting the nicest looks. He hated that. He got himself out from the crowd and perched against a wall. Ripping off his right trainer, he winced as his foot throbbed. He threw off his sock to reveal small, fluid-filled bumps colonising across the lining of his toes. Blisters?

It was often reported that Tulo Games athletes had blisters, but it wasn't a condition an everyday citizen suffered with.

Ajay knew he had to keep going. He saw an arguably clean tissue on the pavement, maybe dropped by someone rushing by. *Don't do it. Have you really come to this? Picking up litter to treat your wounds?* He swallowed his pride, grabbed it and folded it two ways. Then he lodged it between his foot and his sock. Starting to walk again, the pain didn't stop, but the padding seemed to alleviate it a little.

Ajay was forced still again.

It wasn't the pain that made him.

Hevas had said it would happen. There'd been a few reports. But Ajay, and apparently everyone else around him, didn't truly believe it. The entire activity of the street froze as a house raid unfolded into the darkening streets.

CHAPTER
FORTY-TWO

Ajay watched the sparks fly and fall beneath the drone as it lasered through the building's door. It was joined by men in their purple Command overalls, carrying guns and barging their way into the house. A man started screaming. A woman swearing. Ajay's mouth dropped open as smashes and bangs filled the street. He noticed that those around him had started to move again, but slowly. It was as if they were all trying to ignore it, but that was impossible. There was no way to avoid listening to the trauma as Command pulled the house apart. Ajay stepped forward discreetly. It was a good thing to walk slowly anyway, given the exploding blisters over his toes. He decided he would casually walk past the guard standing at the door, holding his gun as if it was as ordinary as a Watch. Ajay saw the growing black dots come from a distance. They grew into two more TPD drones that flew through the hole in the door. He acted aloof, and soon he was limping beyond the house and onwards through the Inner-Ring. As he was walking away, the man stopped screaming, alongside a gunshot and the woman's shout of anguish.

It had taken him hours to get there. He'd staggered through the streets, whimpering occasionally from the pain in his feet, and only stopping now and then to relieve it. It wouldn't have helped his pace hiding in alleys or doorways whenever he thought he saw a familiar face in the crowds. Explaining his limp, sweating brow and his refusal to use public transport would not have been easy. He didn't have the energy to lie. His body felt numb with exhaustion.

Finally, outside the Quarters, Ajay dropped himself against a wall a few metres from the Gate. His legs screamed and his head felt like a heavy-duty weight flopping on his neck. His breathing was laboured. He put his hand to his chest. Should his heart be beating so out of rhythm? It was embarrassing how breathless he was. It was as if he'd never walked before. He then reminded himself he hadn't. Not that far, not for a long time, and especially not in battered trainers; the left one's sole had ripped off so far it could flap up and down like a mouth. Ajay considered that if the shady woman couldn't help him, he couldn't even buy himself a new pair. He'd have to convince Genni to give them to him as a gift. That tactic wouldn't work forever, he knew that. Despite his breathing settling, his heartbeat remained fast and frantic.

This had to work. He had to find the woman. She had to walk out of those gates.

He looked towards the Quarters, which he barely recognised. Before, the golden walls would softly glimmer in the sunlight, and the Glorified Gate would stand strong with magnificence. Ajay couldn't even see the words 'Progress is Strength' on its archway anymore.

All its sparkle was masked by the deep dark covering above its walls. It looked grotesque. He watched as two stale-faced Command guards paced back and forth, cradling guns with a pet drone each. *Bet this wasn't what they signed up for.* Apparently, the security dome was only temporary, but Ajay still couldn't fathom how they thought a protective covering would stop a group seemingly as determined as The Rogue. There must be a more aesthetically pleasing way to create a false sense of security for the Worthies inside. Then again, he realised that he didn't know anything anymore.

Hearing that gunshot silence a man had sent cold shivers up his spine. Command was killing now? Maybe they weren't. They could have just knocked him out for being uncooperative. Ajay had battled with this for almost the entirety of the walk. As he leaned his head back against the wall, he mulled it over again. They were raiding the house, that woman was using every curse word in the book, and the man was screaming with a sort of anger rather than pain, and then, bang. He was quiet. Ajay stopped himself from denying it any longer. He was dead. Command killed him. For resisting? For suspicious behaviour? Did they find something that linked them to The Rogue? The answers didn't really matter. A small, light tear trickled down his left cheek. He noticed that his hands were shaking. He turned his head to see the guards continuing their patrol. If they were to question him right now, he didn't know if he could even speak. The fear was paralytic. When they found him, Command was going to kill him.

'Ajay?' The hard voice made Ajay jump and clench his fists.

A vehicle hovered by the roadside and green eyes glared at him above a fading black tinted window. He couldn't believe it. If ever he hadn't had the energy for Roderick Mansald, it was then. Suddenly the tear on Ajay's cheek, the sweat patches on his clothes and his shoes were the heaviest weights of all. Rod was an appearance man. It wouldn't go unnoticed. And running wouldn't do him any favours, either. He stood still, the broken soles of his shoes the only thing tethering him to ground.

'It's been a while.' Rod ushered Ajay to step closer to the car. Ajay took a deep breath and managed to walk normally despite the still pulsating pain of his feet. 'Is Genni alright? Haven't seen her at the parents' since just after the attack. She knows blood relatives over M-400 are allowed in, right?' Rod blew hot air onto his sunglasses, wiping them with a silk cloth.

'She does know,' Ajay said, casually swinging his right leg against the kerb. 'She's just up against it with work.' He was guessing, not having paid attention to the current ferocity of their family politics.

'Those are a bit scuffed.' Rod nodded down at Ajay's feet before quickly changing the subject, to Ajay's relief. 'What are you doing round here, anyway?'

Ajay swallowed. Perhaps he would have preferred further questioning about his trainers. *Just lie, like you've always done.*

'I was waiting to see if I could get the village manager. To get an update on when volunteering is back on. I walked because the sky train was rammed, and these shoes are quite old and . . .' Ajay stopped himself from rambling.

'OK.' Rod narrowed his eyes. 'But things are ticking along at Prosper?'

'Yeah,' Ajay said too quickly. 'Yes. I guessed some people have struggled since . . .'

'The weak ones, right?' Rod pulled his clean sunglasses closer to his face. 'If anyone should have struggled, it would be me. I had a big responsibility in organising that event. I could easily have got caught up with what people thought of me. But there's too much progress to be made for that. People don't blame me. I mean, they can't, can they?' He donned his sunglasses. 'I've got business Downtown, so maybe see you around if I ever get an invite to yours or Genni's for dinner.' Rod didn't laugh or smile but told the vehicle to drive. The window faded back to black, and it was gone before Ajay managed to conjure up the word 'goodbye'. He watched it float around the corner at speed and wondered what Rod could possibly have to do Downtown. Ajay had always thought there was something off about that guy, but he didn't care enough in that moment to waste any more brain cells on him. He turned back to the Gate, leaning back against the wall, waiting for *her* to appear. The belief she would be there was the only thing keeping him standing.

The dull illuminations of The Rogue report adverts and the floating streetlights were reflecting off the white surface of the pavement. Ajay was slumped on the ground like an Unworthy, after hours of watching people swipe out of the Gate, hopping in hover cars or running for the sky train. Finally, there she was. She came out in a wave of people. Ajay wasn't surprised that he'd managed to spot her. That notorious cream coat gave her nowhere to hide in among the greys and whites of others' Command attire. Only she seemed to break the dress code. Then again, Ajay remembered, she was hardly normal. She looked the same as she did back then. A cold, drawn face with her long brown plait flopping over her right shoulder. As she got closer, Ajay could make out the distinctive clopping of her knee-high boots that skimmed the edge of her coat. She walked past him, not noticing him, but Ajay slid discreetly from the wall and followed her. His excitement was mounting. He didn't really know why. She might not have a solution to his impending death or exile, yet it was hope.

As he limped a few paces behind her, he could see wisps of thread sprouting out from the stitches of her coat. She seemed to slow down and started to turn her head. Ajay acted on impulse. Even though he wanted to talk to her, instinct told him he shouldn't get caught. He jumped into the entrance of a resident building, guarded from the street by its protruding wall. After counting to twenty, Ajay set out again in hot pursuit. Yet a strong force grabbed at his chest and dragged him back into the entrance, whacking his head against the glass sliding door.

'What you want, kid?' His eyes were closed but he could smell her breath. Tulo Ale. Undeniable. Edging his eyes open, he saw how the developing wrinkles around her eyes made them look fiercer, and he could see that grey hair was developing within her plait. Her menacing pupils burrowed into him and caused an immediate headache. The grip she had on his T-shirt and his skin underneath it started to sting.

'I need to talk to you,' Ajay said as she let him go. He bent over to get his breath back.

'Alright, but not here. Come on.' She pulled on his right arm, causing him to hiss and pull away. She stepped back, her eyebrows drawn down.

'What's wrong with ya, kid?' She hesitantly supported Ajay's left side.

'Healing gunshot wound,' Ajay said, holding up a hand to keep her back. 'It's alright.'

'The attack?'

Ajay nodded and straightened up, still wincing. She sighed before slipping out from the entrance of the building. Ajay assumed the invitation to go with her was still valid. He staggered on behind her through the midnight sun of the billboards until she led him down a side alley. It was dark and narrow. Ajay felt aware of his vulnerability as he listened to the tapping of her heels echoing up the enclosing walls. He was reminded of how he imagined she might kill him when they were sitting in that Downtown room all those years ago. The pink curtain was his only way of escape. This time, it was the small entrance they'd come through, getting even further away. Like the small room, this alleyway was only lit by one small lantern. Maybe he'd predicted his brutal murder when he'd first met her, all of it running up to this moment. The claustrophobia started to grip at his breathing. But there was no reason to run and anyway, if Command were going to kill him without her help, why not let a nameless woman get there first?

The heels stopped as she loitered below the flickering light. Ajay's heart quickened. His knuckles tightened. But when an attack never came, he noticed they were standing next to a grey door indented into the wall. The banging of her fist upon it vibrated down the alleyway. It was uncomfortable. He'd committed his fair share of criminal actions, yet it had been a long time since he was so far out of his element. He looked cautiously up and down the alleyway, but there was nothing to see other than the movement of people walking on the faraway street. A faint grinding of metal seized his attention back to the opening door. Without hesitating or knowing whether it was brave or stupid, he followed her through it.

The two of them entered a small hallway lit by red neon lighting and dressed in white drapes along the walls. Ajay reached out to touch one. Moist. The floor was sticky beneath his feet and there was a stale smell. What was a place like this doing so near to the Quarters? He felt the need to hold on to something, but there he had nothing, so his own arms had to do. The door shut. His Watch vibrated and he flicked its mute control to avoid her hearing about his rising heart rate. She disappeared down some concrete steps towards an unknown destination. He stepped forward. The maroon lights made everything even more sinister, like she was leading him to some gruelling torture chamber where she'd pull out his fingernails one by one. As soon as his foot landed on the first step, he heard music, and something within him relaxed. Then the angered shouts came, and his whole body tensed once more.

'Come on, kid.' Her gruff voice travelled up the stairs.

He held his breath with anticipation. The mouldy smell got worse as he moved himself down the stairs and into what was, to his surprise, a bar full of people.

They were all squeezed around tables in front of a long bar, everyone looking towards the centralised attraction: a blue-roped boxing ring where two large men were jabbing at one another, grunting and sweating. Both were shirtless and Ajay noticed how one was wearing a golden hooped earring, adding to his hairy, wild appearance.

There were only spotlights and not one drone was serving drinks. It looked to have an old-fashioned 'order at the bar' set-up. Ajay had never done that before. Anyway, he wasn't thirsty, but the hard metal music was giving him a headache. He needed to get out of there as soon as he could, but he still hadn't got what he needed. Information about how to avoid Command.

'Can we talk, then?' he approached her as she snarled at the boxing ring. The brute with the earring floored the other man, cheers erupting around the tables.

'I'm gonna get myself a drink first,' she said over the music. 'Sit over there.'

She pointed a wrinkled finger at a booth on the other side of the boxing ring. As she marched off to the bar, Ajay tentatively headed for the table, but not without noticing the row of small locker-type cupboards that were built along the wall beside him. Above it floated a sign that read: *Watch Lockers*.

What was a Watch locker? Curiosity took hold of him. He peered into one of the glass-fronted lockers. A Watch floated on what looked like an activation pad. Startled by a loud dinging sound from behind, he turned to see two new men entering the ring, both bearded and much more muscular than the previous two. Looking towards the bar, he saw a man with purple hair staring at him while rubbing a tea towel around the inside of a glass. He wasn't welcome here. Without another glance at the lockers or at the bar tender, he soon found himself at the agreed seat and sat down, failing to avoid the sponge of the ripped upholstery.

'Saw you checking out the lockers over there.' She arrived, carrying two small glasses full of a clear liquid. Ajay smelled it instantly. Pure ethanol. She hissed as she took a sip.

'Why are people doing that?' Ajay nodded towards the lockers.

'Not everyone wants to be judged for every move they make,' she said. 'And before you say it . . . the privacy setting doesn't always cut it. People who come here have some . . . let's say . . . issues with the system.' Her focus darted everywhere but at Ajay.

'Like the Rogue?' Ajay swallowed.

She stayed silent, finally turning to look at him. Her eyes were stern even though she was smirking. It sent Ajay cold inside, yet he knew he had to fight any fear. For his life.

'Look, you know they claimed identities to get through the Gate. Just like you did with my Watch. Swapping Karle for Ajay,' he said, his hands gripping the edge of the dirty table.

She still said nothing and slurped another centimetre off her drink.

'I need to know if you can help me,' Ajay said, just about keeping a lid on his frustration. 'I can't function anymore. They're checking Watches everywhere. And it's obvious they're not going to stop with house raids. We're both in big trouble.' He pointed at her and back at himself. 'We're screwed if you don't do something.'

She sat back in an overly relaxed manner and began stroking the rim of her glass with her fingers; her many silver rings tinted in the maroon-red glow of the bar. She'd grown ugly in her old age. Exasperated by her demeanour, Ajay shuffled uncomfortably in his seat. He tried to ignore the music and the inconsistent shouts from the boxing crowd, but they continued to annoy him, like they existed only to press in on his irritability. She laughed. It cut through him, making him numb.

'What are you supposing I do, kid?' She leaned forward.

'Give me admin access.' Ajay tensed his shoulders. 'I can see what I can do in terms of covering our tracks—'

'That ain't gonna help you.'

Ajay sat back and threw his arms up, infuriated.

'Look, kid. *That* ain't gonna help you. I know it. And you have nothing to offer me now so I wouldn't give it to you anyway.'

Ajay felt something rising within him, but he didn't feel angry. Only desperate. Really desperate. He spoke, trying to ignore the trembling of his lips.

'If I go down, you go down.'

He moved closer, their faces almost touching. He could smell her ethanol-coated breath.

'I'm already going down. I was done with this years ago and I have no cell in my body that cares about you, either. There is no help for you now, kid. Just go quiet.' She patted his right cheek, her fingers clammy against his skin. 'The Side ain't gonna reject you.'

Ajay snapped his face away and went silent as he watched her finish her first drink. Despite her mocking, he couldn't shake something in the back of his mind. If admin access wasn't going to help him, what would?

What would she give him if he did have something to offer?

'Wait. Why are you going down? What do you know?' Ajay was so excited by the possibility of information that he forgot to control his tongue. She drunkenly twisted her lip.

'It don't matter what I know no more. I'm gonna be spending me last days with this.' She raised her second glass and drained it. Ungracefully slipping off her chair to head back to the bar, Ajay couldn't believe the ethanol had taken her ability to walk straight so quickly. Tempted to indulge as an act of dismissal over his situation, he stared at the empty glasses, but she was back, grabbing quickly at his right ear. He hissed, and as he felt the warmth of her breath on his earlobe, he wondered how he could ever have trusted such a psychopath. Because he was desperate. He'd always been desperate.

'Seriously, kid. Get out of the City. Or steal some fingers.'

What in Tulo does that mean? He cursed at her. Her laugh was deep, long and undeniably punctuated with evil. It vibrated through Ajay's eardrums and induced a strong nausea in the pit of his stomach. Then she let go, turned away and before Ajay could further contemplate the meaning of her words, she had finished her next drink and was gone. Ajay remained sitting there, staring into his hands, knowing there was little hope left.

CHAPTER
FORTY-THREE

Ace calling.

Pulling his tired, depressed eyes away from his apartment ceiling, Ajay limply swiped at his wrist and cleared his throat.

'Hello.'

'What's this about you being close to death?' Ace's chirpy voice boomed through his earphones. He drew a circle on his wrist to lower the volume.

'What?' Ajay spoke roughly. He wished that for once, Ace didn't sound so happy. His face was even worse – beaming, his perfectly straight white teeth filling the screen.

'I can't see you? Turn your video on.'

'No, thanks.'

'Is it because you look tired? Genni said you haven't had a boost in weeks.'

'Oh, I just . . .' Ajay paused. So Genni had noticed. 'Everything OK? I'm busy,' he said, looking around his apartment, littered in clothes and scraps of unappetising cupboard food.

'Alright, calm down. I've just been missing you in the office,' Ace said.

'I'm working from here,' Ajay lied.

'Why?'

'Just felt like it.'

'Then why is Hollday asking where you are?'

'He's probably forgotten. I did clear it with him last night.' Ajay tensed. Hollday never forgot things.

'Right . . .' Ajay watched Ace's face turn uneasy. He wasn't pulling this off. Ace, Genni, everyone knew something was up. 'Ajay, if you're struggling, there's people you can talk to . . .'

'I'm fine.'

'I haven't seen you in days, Genni said you've been avoiding her, and I've seen your merits dropping. I'm worried, mate.'

Ajay didn't say anything. *He's watching my merit. Of course he is. They all watch each other but they'd never normally admit it.*

'Well,' Ace sighed. 'You know where I am.'

His face disappeared into Ajay's wrist quickly, though his tone of disappointment still hung in the air. Ajay rubbed his head. Ace would have seen just how rapidly his score was falling. He had two days until the missed work penalty kicked in, and that would be it. The start of the end. He wondered what Hollday thought about him. The fact he was asking after him gave Ajay a strange feeling of pride; he'd obviously made enough of an impact for his boss to miss him, yet it also told him that he was running out of time to hide. He'd even contemplated the risk of scanning in from home, but he just couldn't do it. The less he scanned his Watch, the better. Leaning back on the sofa, he thought of the office and how he longed to be there. It would be less lonely, even though the flurries of people never actually spoke about anything but work. Since leaving that boxing ring bar two days ago, he hadn't seen another person. He felt too fragile. If he were to see Genni, for example, he knew he'd crumble into a pathetic, weeping heap. He'd completely lost the rhythm of life. He didn't even know what day it was. Was he just riding the storm until Command found him? Was he waiting to die?

Ajay looked around at the tatters of his life: clothes were strewn everywhere, dirty pots with the remains of his out-of-date cupboard food sat on the worktops and tables. As he waited for death, or his arrest, he'd become a wild boar. If anyone were to see this, it would be mortifying. Tears started again. That was another thing, he couldn't stop sobbing. Every time he thought about Genni, he cried. Every time he read about increasing house raids and arrests, he shook and wept. He was utterly hopeless. Even Ace was worried about him. Ace, who never seemed to care much about anyone or anything but girls, work or training. *Stop it. Get a grip.*

He picked himself up off the sofa and marched towards the bathroom. He ran his hands under the tap that glowed blue at his touch and splashed cold water across his face, disguising his tears. Ajay looked at his reflection and observed the plum rings around his eyes. The mirror confirmed his skin moisture was below 20 per cent of its optimal level and needed serious attention. His skin was tight across his cheekbones, dry and stretched, ready at any moment to crack. It was as if his body and mind had become a water balloon that had been growing for years – filling up with life and all its joy and aspiration, with dedication, pleasure and hard graft until it was too much. The pressure was mounting, and water was leaking as the balloon stretched and screamed for its skin to burst.

'The Side isn't an option. You must hold on,' Ajay demanded, looking sharply into his own eyes. 'She knows something you don't.'

For the last few days, he had wished he could have recorded their conversation under the maroon neon light. She'd said some stuff that Ajay couldn't let go. Firstly, she'd claimed she was already going down. Why? Was she involved? If Command already knew about her hand in identity theft, she'd already have been arrested. Yet she was going to work and then staggering around in underground bars. Then there was the other thing. That he needed to 'steal some fingers'. After some time with his thoughts, Ajay had realised she was talking about the fingerprint authentication on the Watches. Exactly like when he needed the finger of Theo Badds. But what did that have to do with anything? He couldn't make sense of it. Then again, his brain was mush. He missed his old self. Intelligent, quick and respected. Now who was he? A hermit hiding in an apartment he'd soon not be Worthy enough for.

As he dragged himself back to the sofa, feeling the sweat of his legs inside his joggers, he wondered how he might find her again. He'd already been through this. Several times. He could go back to the Quarters and find her like before. Plead with her for the information. As soon as he'd imagined himself falling at her feet with desperation, he'd been repulsed by the thought. He didn't know her well, but well enough to know she'd laugh or even spit in his quivering face. He'd also been through the kidnapping scenario. That maybe he could catch her off guard, drag her to his apartment, and pull out every one of her teeth until she spoke. Or rip her greying plaited hair from her head. The more he'd thought about it, the darker it had got. As he stretched himself out over the leather seat, Ajay landed back at the same conclusion as always. *You could never pull that off. You're not that person.*

So, he would stay in his apartment and agonise over her words until he figured it out himself. There must be something. There must be.

As he stared back up at the ceiling to think, his wrist vibrated. He lazily lifted his arm and squinted at the notification. He sat bolt upright and shook violently as he tapped at his Watch.

There she was. On the news. Her cream coat, the greying plait, her menacing eyes, and that sardonic smile. The word 'WANTED' ran beneath the picture. Ajay lost his breathing and panicked. She was on the run. He questioned whether he would soon be joining her.

Command have identified this woman as Lillie Trumin, a high-level Command security executive, proved to be a member of The Rogue and a key instigator in the Liberation Day attack. There is reason to believe she led multiple cases of identification theft that made the attack possible. If anyone has any information about her whereabouts, please contact Command Security. Merit and credit reward.

Ajay read the words over and over, trying to process it all detail by detail. Her name was Lillie? That couldn't be right. It was too pretty, too precious, too gentle. Nothing like the woman she was. She was from The Rogue? Of course, they had someone on the inside. That much had been obvious to him, and Command, he supposed, for a while. Yet he'd never suspected her. Why? All the signs were there. She had him supply Fo Doktrin so she could assist those who made anti-constitutional drugs, hung out in secret underground bars, and she happily helped a kid from the Side hack his way in. Lillie hated the system and hated Command. Ajay had just never seen it. He'd been too absorbed in what she could offer him.

He was damp with sweat, a puddle forming on the sofa. His hair felt wet as he tucked it behind his left ear. Another thought occurred to him, one that made him desperate for fresh air. If they had *reason to believe* she'd changed people's identity, could they trace her actions back to him? Of course they could. Ajay said it himself to her in the bar.

'If I go down, you go down,' he whispered to himself. Both their dirty deeds were interconnected. He was going down. It was over. All of it was over. He couldn't report her, not without exposing himself, and he doubted that Command would give him any grace. *She* still could have warned him. His body screamed inside, despite only a small grunt escaping from Ajay's mouth. He wiped the sweat from his brow, knowing he needed air.

Dashing over to the window, he threw it open, but the air was warm and muggy. He felt sick. Numb. Inconsolable with the pain of his Unworthiness.

Then, as he was about to hurl out his insides, his wrist vibrated again. He didn't even think but just looked down.

Unknown: *I can get you out. Meet me.*

Unknown: *Inner-Ring 0647*

Ajay swallowed his vomit. A tiny essence of hope sneaked back in.

CHAPTER
FORTY-FOUR

'Look mate, I can do you a deal . . .' the street seller said, opening his scab-covered hands.

'No, thank you,' Ajay said for the second time as he looked anxiously for any sign of Lillie. It was surely her who had sent the message. She had changed her mind and was going to help him after all, not that he understood why. He did know that this seller deserved a slap. He was relentless in throwing his airborne product screens in Ajay's face.

'I'll give it you for a third off, or even half price,' he said, tapping at one screen to expand the image of a subscription cleaning drone.

'I don't want it. Leave me alone,' Ajay raised his chin. The seller looked insulted. What did he expect? Ajay had been standing here, looking intently into the swarming ebb and flow of the crowds, and the seller had just bombarded him. Rude. He had much more pressing concerns than a robot cleaning his carpets. The seller stared at Ajay with stabbing eyes before he quickly switched his selling efforts to a woman in a lynx-skin T-shirt.

Where is she? Where is she? Ajay tapped his right foot on the concrete pavement and glanced at his wrist for the millionth time.

Inner-Ring 0647

This was the right place. It was a typical Inner-Ring street, lined with apartment buildings and adverts. Ajay gazed over the one calling for more house raid volunteers. *They're doing so many raids that they don't even have the resources. Surely drones could do that . . . Clearly not.* Ajay breathed and dug his nails into the palms of his hands, yearning to see her. And then, he did see her. Just not the *her* he was expecting.

She was standing across the street, her small head low beneath a wide yellow hat and straggly hair. Their eyes met. She nodded. It must be a coincidence. It couldn't have been *her* message. Why would she be involved now? It had to have been Lillie. He would wait here. A moment passed, and he glanced back to where she'd been standing. Gone.

Relieved, Ajay settled his shoulders and continued looking for Lillie.

'It's rude to ignore people, boy.'

Her voice and the heat of her body beside him made Ajay jump. He took two steps away, only for her to take four steps closer, the rough skin of her birthmark almost grazing his chin, unchanged on her face since the day he lost Callum.

'Why are you here?' Ajay said, swallowing.

'I can get you out,' she said in that deep, coarse voice. No, he thought. It *was* her. She was his only hope? A deranged woman he met as a teenager?

'Let's go,' she said as she moved quickly back into the street, disappearing into the sea of people.

'Are you following me?' Ajay demanded as he bounded after her, barging into the shoulders of a small girl. He didn't have time to apologise, as the woman he was following was moving fast. For a moment in the civilian chaos, he couldn't see her, until the hum of a hover taxi swayed to a stop in front of her outstretched hand.

'Get in, then,' she said, huffing through sharp deep breaths and opening the car door with a definitive flick of her wrist against its exterior. Ajay was obedient and slipped into the vehicle, which was completely leather upholstered inside with an activation pad on each of the two armrests. He kept his wrist away.

She joined him. Ajay stared at her. Just as he remembered, the birthmark covered the right side of her chin and neck. He couldn't recall if he'd seen it this close before. The few hard hairs that sprouted from it were repellent. Ajay assumed she still lived alone, and he looked away as the hover taxi set off towards whatever destination she had instructed.

'Hot today,' she said, and he glanced at her to see a hint of a smile. She lifted her hat off her head to reveal more of her unbrushed hair. Ajay narrowed his eyebrows at how nonchalant she was being. He was on the brink of losing everything, she'd sent him a mysterious message and she was talking about the weather. He'd forgotten how odd she was. He felt like he did before when she'd cooked him that burger in a graceful, compassionate way, yet acted like he was a sour taste in her mouth.

He wasn't going to be polite. She needed to give him answers.

'What do you want?'

She sighed and shrugged her shoulders. 'To make it clear, I've not been following you. I've been looking out for you. Ever since you left my house that afternoon, Karle.'

'Don't call me that. I'm Ajay now.'

'Right. Of course,' she grunted.

'How is it you think you can help me?'

'I can get you safe passage back to the Side.'

The car sprang into a tunnel. Ajay's eyes adjusted to the semi-darkness. He felt slightly nauseous as the small flickers of daylight through the tunnel's windows turned the car into a flashing disco. He breathed, disappointed. It was stupid of him. Despite the message saying it could get him out, he didn't want to leave, and was still holding on to the possibility of staying without getting arrested or killed.

'I don't think I want to get out,' Ajay said, quietly.

'I can't help you with that,' she said, her eyes firm on the road through the front window.

'Well, what good are you, then?' Ajay fell back into his seat.

'I was good that time I hid you from those drones, and that time I helped your girl.' The car spat out from the tunnel and as it was flooded with light, Ajay saw her right eyebrow rise suggestively.

'You?' Ajay felt the blood drain from his face. 'You carried Genni to my apartment? Why?'

'I'm a friend,' she said.

'I don't know you.'

Only the soft hum of the car filled the momentary silence as they stared at one another.

'Don't you think it's time you go home?' she finally said, playing with the rim of her hat on her lap.

Ajay laughed and shook his head. He stared out the window at the City. *This is my home. And who is she?* His thoughts turned dark again. There was no one else in this car. He could attack her right here in the back and no one would know. Maybe she'd stop toying with him then. He felt his fists clench.

'Your grandma said you'd be stubborn about it.'

Ajay relaxed his hands and whipped his head back towards her. She now had one leg crossed over the other beneath her dress while she looked at her jaggedly cut fingernails.

'You know . . .'

'Your family? Yes. Very well.'

'So *they* told you to help me?'

'Of course they did. They're worried for you – you'll be caught. Especially with what's coming.'

What's coming? Ajay couldn't allow himself to get angry at his grandma or his parents for employing someone to spy on him because *she* knew something. Something about Command's plans to protect the City. That's all that mattered to him. There must be a way he could get ahead of the game. Then again, how could he trust her? She was so perplexing. She worked in the Quarters, taught Glorified kids, yet lived further out in the Outer-Ring when she presumably had higher merit to live elsewhere. Ajay recalled her disorganised, repulsive home with a fox and children's drawings as wall art. But she was helping his grandma, and he did trust her. So it wasn't inconceivable that he could at least get something useful out of this interaction.

'Tell me.' He grabbed her arm and could feel her silky, excess skin between his fingers. 'It's about the fingerprints, right?'

'You're right. It is.' Her brown eyes stared into him. 'Let go of my arm, please.'

Ajay complied, but in his mind, he was still gripping on tightly, determined to know everything. The car stopped abruptly, sending both their bodies lurching forward. Before Ajay recovered from bracing himself, his accomplice had already gone through the open car door. He jumped out, taking a step back to avoid being windswept as the car departed.

She was standing on the pavement, waiting for him. Ajay saw the wrinkled texture of the skin on her pale legs, making him wonder how old she really was. Her eyes looked young, but her skin creases and that repulsive birthmark confused things. Ajay reminded himself that her age was of no importance.

She walked down a street Ajay didn't recognise. They must still be in the Inner-Ring, as the buildings looked clean and attractive with their walls painted in tasteful whites and creams. There were still people coming and going and they all looked high merit.

He shifted his long legs to catch her, almost grabbing her arm again but deciding not to. 'Where are we going?'

No answer. She kept walking forwards, as if she were trying to blend in and not bring attention to herself.

'Tell me what you know,' Ajay continued to squawk in her ear. 'What are Command going to do?'

No response. He felt like he was talking to the air. Anger and frustration started to spew up inside him as they walked alongside the Inner-Ring's river, its artificial blueness reflecting off the white buildings. Just as Ajay thought he might spit at her, or worse, hit her hard, they approached a small house on the river's edge.

'In here,' she said, holding the creaking door open for him and ushering him in quickly.

The small house was no bigger than an average-size bathroom. The walls were empty. Some were still bare brick. There was nothing in there at all. Ajay felt sweat instantly puddle across his back. It was painfully hot and enclosed, but she disappeared through a small door. Why was she doing this, leading him around on some strange treasure hunt? Was there some sort of test he was meant to pass and then she'll talk? Ajay considered walking away. He was bigger than her little games, but he had nowhere else to go. He followed her. She was bending down by a padlocked steel door that felt like it was leading straight to the river.

'What are we doing here?' Ajay said, spittle in-between his teeth.

Ajay noticed an outdated Watch scanner to the right of the door, covered with grime and cobwebs. Yet she battled with the key, totally inconvenient compared with a swipe. She heaved open the grey industrial door that crunched as its heaviness echoed down the dark steps that Ajay could see behind it.

'Almost there.' She laughed slightly. It threw Ajay over the edge.

'How dare you laugh right now,' he said, resisting the urge to hit the wall beside him. 'Just tell me what Command are doing!'

'I will. Down here,' she said, unfazed by his outburst. She simply turned her back and walked down the sloped steps.

Ajay breathed heavily. *If she doesn't tell me soon, I'll kill her.* It scared him how much he meant it.

He needed to find a way to keep it – the City, Genni, all of it. He fell silent as they descended further down the steps, barely lit by repetitive nightlights until they reached an old arch that read 'River House'.

Suddenly the space opened into a huge room alive with blue light. Ajay was both disturbed and awestruck. He held his breath. What was this? The creaking of the outside walls caused him to look up and find the river was moving above him. They were under it? He stared at the hard glass, the only thing stopping the violent water from flooding in. He looked around: solid steel walls, held together by strong yet rusty-looking steel bolts; four booths built into the far wall, each with blue, padded benches and a table nailed in its middle; and a small window with blue velvet curtains that looked out to the river. A bar? This thought was confirmed to him as he saw the long bar at the end of the room, covered in cardboard boxes. It must have been completely abandoned. He noticed that the walls were littered on every side with photos and wall art. When Ajay finally breathed, he coughed at the musty smell.

'What is this place?' he said, without knowing where she was standing. He turned and saw her by some sofas that surrounded a circular rug. She was looking longingly at some photos on the wall. Ajay stepped closer. All the photos were taken in this room. He briefly scanned the groups of people smiling, laughing, arms around one another.

'It was an underwater bar,' she said calmly, and removed her hat again. 'Before the accident – they went out of fashion after that.' Ajay had heard talk of a river accident from years ago, but had never paid much attention. 'We met here before the attack. We're being more careful now.'

Ajay narrowed his eyes. Her dress looked green under the blue-tinged light and her birthmark appeared less sore.

'Who's we?' he asked.

'Those in the City who follow The Guiding Light.'

Ajay didn't say anything. He had no thoughts for a moment, unable to process what she'd said. He must have misheard her.

'What did you say?'

'The Guiding Light. It's here in the City. Look.' She pointed behind him.

He turned around. Perhaps his subconscious had filtered it out at first, but behind the bar, tall shelves once filled with weak liquor were stocked with *them*. Rows and rows of the holographic device of his childhood.

Ajay didn't understand it. How had they kept them here? Completely out of sight. Hidden.

'How did . . .' He paused. *Stop it. This isn't the most important question. Think about Genni. City. Merit. Everything.*

He turned back to her. She was now sitting in a large brown armchair.

'Tell me what you know about Command.' Ajay towered over her and felt himself expand his chest.

'Sit down, boy.'

'No, I'm fine here . . . Tell me.'

'I really think it's better if you just go home.'

'I don't.'

'Yes, you've made that clear.' She raised an eyebrow before nodding to the seat opposite. 'Sit down, please.'

He forced himself into it, the large cushion taking his weight with ease.

'I suspect a new model of Watch,' she said.

Finally. This was it. An answer. A chance to stay Worthy. He listened to her voice in rhythm with the moving river above them.

'A model that considers the security oversight Command has missed for all these years. Our fingerprints won't just be for device operation but for device activation. The identification on the Watch and the fingerprint must match with their database so, for example, using Karle's fingerprints with Ajay's identity will be impossible.'

'Are you sure?' Ajay's dread gave him nothing else to say.

'I believe so, yes.'

'So they're going to call for upgrades? New initiations? What?'

'That, I don't know.'

'But what if . . .'

'You can't stop it. You can try, but the path of the City always leads to destruction . . .'

'Don't,' Ajay said, not wanting anything akin to those words to be part of the conversation. It only reminded him of the family he'd left – the grandma and sister he'd left. He had to be strong to protect Ajay Ambers. He was smart, charming, M-463 and loved by many. That was who he was. Not Karle Blythefen. Limited, weak, M-nothing and forgettable. Ajay stood up, his self-control dwindling with his merit. 'I went most of my life with that Guiding Light stuff going in one ear and out the other. It's not for me. It's not Worthy. So, if you're meant to protect me, how long until Command brings in the new models? How much time have I got?' Ajay was half-inclined to fall to his knees with every sincere cell in his body and plead with her until she gave him the answer. He didn't. He'd learned to ignore his Karle impulses.

'There's nothing more I can do for you,' she replied, calmly. She swirled her hat around in her dry-skinned hands and twisted it in one smooth motion to place it back on her quirky head.

Standing, she wandered over to one of the booths and handled a small silver tin. Opening it, she retrieved a biscuit and shoved it into her mouth.

'Want one?' she said, mouth full.

'No,' Ajay said. It was time to go. But go back to what? He thought deeply, managing to ignore the disgusting crunch of her biscuits and the squeaking of the pressurised walls. Then he landed on something.

He had a plan to buy him time. He would head home, break open his Watch and attempt to delete its existence. Command wouldn't send a new model or ask him to attend an initiation if they didn't know his device was there. It might not work. It wasn't a complete solution. But it was something.

Ajay ran without looking back. In all his distraction, he never even noticed his sister's matured face in some of the photos on the wall.

CHAPTER
FORTY-FIVE

Across the City, Genni found herself inside another dream. Not a nightmare or a paradise, but somewhere in-between. *She was floating inside a beautiful garden. Green vines ran down both sides; flowers burst with colour in pinks, yellows and reds. The sound of water trickled, and a slight breeze cooled her skin. Genni reached out to touch a rosebud. Before she felt the fragility of its petals, the pink bud plucked itself off its vine and sailed towards her hand, deciding to gracefully hover there. Genni brought it to her nose and smelled its fine fragrance. Strong yet delicate.*

She went to walk but as she looked down, she realised her feet weren't touching the ground. Floating along, rose in hand, she found a waterfall much like the one in her painting. The water descended a freestanding rock face. Droplets flicked from the fall and wet the surrounding vines and bushes. Genni felt water spray on her nose. She looked back to her hand. The rose was gone.

Glancing at its original bush, buds and petals were now strewn across the path and the bush had been ripped apart and had turned a solemn grey. The rest of the garden still bloomed with life. A bird tweeted. Trees swayed. All was peaceful and calm, until she felt a rush of movement behind her. She spun around. Nothing there, but another destroyed flowerbed, now also grey.

She turned back to the waterfall, where a sudden mesh of lights materialised from its stream. A dancing body of illumination. It was floating to the other side of the garden. Genni walked towards it, now mesmerised, and called by its light. It didn't come any closer, but Genni jumped back as a small fox appeared in front of her. A tiny, strawberry-red fox. It floated too, with a cunning look in its eyes. Dashing off, it moved in floating somersaults towards some green vines. It ripped them down ferociously and the green faded from their leaves too. Genni now saw what she had missed before. She stepped back, moving away from the body of light, watching as dozens of floating little foxes ran across the garden. Spoiling everything. Until it was all grey.

Genni opened her eyes. She sprung up in bed, never needing much time to ground herself back to reality. That was strange. Little foxes in a beautiful garden and a dancing body of lights? She rubbed her hair with a flat hand to straighten it down, and quickly moved from the bed to remaster her make-up in the mirror. The green lights on the mirror told her that her pores were healthy. As she finished, she realised it was the first time she'd dreamt, and *he* hadn't been there. Ever since the attack, the man she'd met from The Rogue had haunted her from beyond the grave. Well, she hoped it was beyond the grave and that Command had done their job right. Sometimes, the dreams had been a pretty accurate reliving of the attack but instead of him shooting Jun, it was Ajay. Other times, she'd dreamt that he was in her apartment, standing by her bed, his huge muscular frame standing over her in the nightlight. One time, she'd just been falling. Forever falling in some darkness where his face was all she could see.

This dream was different. He wasn't there. She wasn't terrified, and in some ways, she'd slept soundly. Whipping off her grey T-shirt that hung loosely over her knickers, she moved simultaneously to her wardrobe, her mind still fixed on dreams. Even though her sleeping sessions were only ever a maximum of two hours long, her brain still seemed to tell her so much. No one else had dreams. If they did, they never talked about them. There wasn't even much research about them in the library. She'd once mentioned it to Mila, who had never had one. Genni quickly threw on a mint-green flowy dress, which the wardrobe approved. Just about ready to go, she lobbed her handbag, full of make-up and other essentials, over her shoulder and marched to the kitchen to grab a glass of water; it was refreshing as it flowed down her throat. For a moment, she leaned against the kitchen worktop and looked over to the sofa and her waterfall painting that hung above it. That came from a dream. It was in *this* dream, too, in that delightful garden.

Genni stood up straight and checked her Watch.

A message from Ace. She looked at the clock first: 8.33 p.m. She had time. Going back to the office an hour later wouldn't matter, as she'd only slept for one. Excited, she dashed to her easel that stood empty by the window. She sat a blank canvas on it. Briefly looking out to the dark river running beside her apartment, the question of the office came back to her. Should she paint now? Work had been going well lately. Mafi had even started asking for Genni's opinion now. Though part of her no longer cared. Her previous frustrations about the impact she'd made towards the project or the credit and merit she earned, or how much she belonged in the beauty industry, no longer seemed to matter. They did matter, she reminded herself, but just not as much. Especially in that moment – she couldn't pull her thoughts away from the garden and the foxes. She had to paint it.

She wrapped an apron around herself to protect her dress and began sharpening her pencil, her thoughts turning to Ajay. The attack had affected him more than any of them. Of course, they all had their baggage, but he had become completely disjointed. The way he'd sobbed into her shoulder the night of the memorial was bizarre. Genni was pleased he could be so vulnerable with her, but she didn't know what to do with it. He was usually so emotionally closed. She leaned forward and softly began to sketch an outline of the first rose bush. As she drew, she thought again of how unfriendly Ajay had been recently, speaking to her as if she was Unworthy. He was clearly irritable, and presenting behaviours of *SkipSleep* withdrawal, so he probably didn't mean anything, but that didn't stop it hurting. Then, every time she was planning to call him out, he'd turn up at the door or pop up on her wrist, and they'd have dinner at her place. Serious mood swings. Though, it had been nice to spend more time here. With her paintings now all over the walls, she wondered whether Ajay liked seeing them. Soon, he would be distant again. He'd been off work for two days, too, which was out of character.

The message from Ace told her that Ajay sounded off on a call. What was wrong with him? Why wasn't he having boosts? She'd have to go round later if she had time. Genni yawned, stretched out her arms, and looked over the first sketch of the rose bush. It was pleasing. Re-sharpening her pencil, she turned her head towards the many bottles of paint on the table beside her. She would mix them to make a deep pink for the roses. Not a baby pink but a stark, breathtaking pink. The foxes too would carry their crisp, red colour. She got back to work on the canvas. Maybe Ajay was jealous about her recovery. She'd always wondered if he resented her for it. When she overdosed, he sacrificed a lot of merit-making time, and now she was the one doing better. Especially with the social merit. It was never very much, but she knew her paintings had an audience. This one would be popular with the fox-owners. Perhaps Ajay was distant because he was too arrogant to admit that he was wrong about that. Genni sighed; she had no idea. He'd be alright. Though, maybe she should call him. Before she could action the thought and as a vine was partially stretched, her wrist vibrated.

Mafi (Work): *Genni, are you coming in soon? Last-minute sales meeting. I need your thoughts and input. See you there.*

Her manager needed her opinion. Genni smiled. That was nice, though she was disappointed not to get very far with her painting. She could finish it later, not being at risk of forgetting the details. Setting down her pencil, she lightly stroked the canvas with her hand as if to tell it she'd be back later. Then, jumping up and swiftly grabbing her handbag, the canvas was left, soon to be home to those mischievous foxes and that dancing ball of light.

CHAPTER
FORTY-SIX

Ajay rushed into his apartment, almost colliding with the breakfast table as he lost his footing. Running over to his desk, he fumbled over clothes and packets and swung into his chair, tucking his fingers under his desk. Gathering the long, black cable out from its hiding spot, his nails fringed the photo of young Tara, still stuck down with tape. After fiddling to connect the cable to his Watch, he commanded his four screens to appear. Time to get . . .

The sound of the toilet flushing. Movement from the bathroom.

Who. Is. That?

For about half a millisecond, Ajay paused, confused with reality. Was there actually someone in his apartment, or was he hearing things?

'Ajay?'

Ace's deep voice travelled through the walls. Nope. It was real.

Ajay's hands moved like lightning and his heart rattled around inside him. Panting, he yanked the wire from his Watch and shoved it back beneath the table, but not without sending the Watch spiralling onto the floor. There wasn't time to close the screens, as Ace stood in front of him. *Don't close them straight away, do it casually during the conversation.* Despite trying to convince himself that he was in complete control, Ajay felt riddled with panic. Ace's face was only metres away from a command window that displayed the internal workings of his Watch. He'd get through it, though, if he just stayed calm. That's if Ace didn't pick up on the horrendous sweating and deep panting. That would be alright if he breathed deeply, and it was always hot, so the sweat shouldn't raise any alarms.

Everything was completely fine.

'Ace ...' Ajay smiled. 'What are you doing here?'

'I came to see if you were . . . alright.' Ace frowned. 'What are you doing?'

'Nothing, just work stuff.' Ajay cleared his throat.

'But you've just come in? Where have you been?' Ace said, as he started to walk around the desk towards Ajay and the open code on the screen. *Turn it off.* Ajay leaned forward in what he thought was a relaxed way. He lifted his arm fast, but Ace was quicker. The grasp of Ace's hand around Ajay's wrist was sharp and firm. The screens stayed where they were, and Ace had a full view.

Ajay's heart stopped and clunked down into his stomach like a heavy weight. As Ace spoke, his voice sat on Ajay's eardrums, sending pangs of uneasiness through his body. Ajay felt his heart beating fast to the rhythm of his disbelief that Ace was seeing this – that this was really happening.

'Ajay? What is this?'

Ajay didn't say anything. Everything became a glazed and misted vision he wanted to repress. He imagined he'd gone deadly pale with shock.

Then the adrenaline seemed to subside. He looked up at Ace's questioning eyes and observed him properly for the first time since he'd emerged from the bathroom. He was wearing his smart, khaki trousers that made him look suave.

'Here.' Ace calmly gave Ajay his Watch back, which he must have picked up off the floor. Ajay took it and rolled it in his hands while maintaining awkward eye contact. 'Why did you take it off so quickly?'

Ajay stayed quiet.

'Ajay? What's going on?' Ace clenched his jaw as he paced back beside the desk.

'I . . . erm . . .' Ajay ran a shaky hand through his hair. 'Work asked me to have a look at some . . . erm . . .' He couldn't think. There was no lie good enough. Ace could see it.

'Don't lie to me.' Ace pointed a hard finger. 'You've been off the radar for days. Missing work, merit falling, avoiding me and Genni. I was worried and now you show up acting all shady.' He peered closer at the screens. 'Wait . . .'

Ajay lost his breath, as he knew Ace would eventually recognise the code. It wasn't particularly difficult, Command's logo was right there, on the Watch's interface, crafted together in a green font.

Ace shook his head. 'This ain't to do with work, mate.' He held his arms out wide, shrugging his shoulders, pleading for the truth. Ajay began to lose control, he felt his breathing falter, his fingers tingle and dizziness set in. He began to wobble sideways, but Ace was there to catch him.

Ace cursed as Ajay felt the warmth of his arms support his back.

'Come on, mate. Sit down.' He guided him over to the sofa. 'I'll get you a drink.'

Ace walked towards the kitchen, but not without looking back at Ajay, whose muscles had turned rigid. By the time Ace returned, Ajay had regained the ability to think and could feel the saliva coming back into in his mouth. He took the water from Ace and gulped the pint down almost in one. He said thank you as he wiped his mouth. This was it. There was no going back.

As Ace sat next to him, Ajay took one of the biggest breaths he'd ever taken, hoping that he wasn't wrong about his friend – that he would have his back, Worthy or Unworthy.

'OK. The truth is I'm not Ajay Ambers. My real name's Karle Blythefen. And I was born on the Side.'

CHAPTER
FORTY-SEVEN

An hour or so passed as Ajay took Ace down the high street of his childhood, along the track of his adolescent rebellion, and across the white walkway of his fabricated life in the City. He included everything – his family, Callum, birthmark woman, Lillie, the Fo Doktrin, and where he and Genni fitted in within the timeline of his transformation. Until he came to an end.

'And now, I've got to figure out a way to bypass this new model. I don't know for sure that's Command's plan, but if my Watch doesn't exist on the database, it'll buy me time.'

Ajay was very aware that Ace hadn't spoken for the entirety of his storytelling. Nor had he looked at him. Not once. Ajay knew he'd been the perfect companion through this life: popular, funny and a master at appearing chilled out when he was always on top of his game. He was also remarkably resilient. As was Genni. Anything slightly difficult, they both bounced back stronger than before, ready to take on the world and all its merit-making joy and struggle. It was the Glorified upbringing. Ajay knew that. He'd had to train himself not to be vulnerable or show any weakness; Ace had been taught it straight out the womb. Ajay was reminded of when Ace had told him about his M-290 fling. How hard that was for Ace, and even after that day, they never spoke of it again. Perhaps he was embarrassed. It occurred to Ajay how stupid he was. Why would he bother telling Ace all this? He wasn't going to help him. He wouldn't even risk his status for the perfect girl, and he'd been through enough of them to know that she was hard to find. There was no way he'd help protect an Unworthy bypass Command. But Ajay wasn't Unworthy. Surely, he'd done enough to prove that.

And he was his best friend. That should count for something.

At last, Ace spoke in a surprisingly calm and controlled voice as he rubbed his large fingers over his high-arching forehead. 'This makes so much sense.'

Ace rose from the sofa and walked slowly across the rug, flicking some sand from his boots between its fibres.

'I mean, you've always been nervous about the TPD. I've never understood that. I thought you were just soft.' Ace looked around the apartment, chewing his tongue the way he always did when he was deep in thought. 'And you never have drones in here. Then, that time you went to the Side and said it was because of the fire? I knew that was off.' Ace sat back down on the sofa and stopped chewing.

'This is so crazy,' he said quietly. 'You haven't been eating, have you? You can't buy anything.'

Ajay nodded. 'I've got what I could through Genni.'

There was silence then. Ajay didn't know what Ace was thinking. He was unnerved about how calmly Ace had reacted. It was as if someone measured and rational had been transfigured into Ace's body, replacing his reactive and explosive personality. Ajay would do anything to get inside his head. Just to know his next move. Maybe he was conflicted between reporting him, helping him, or staying quiet and letting Ajay find a way out of this. Perhaps it wasn't the worst thing to tell him. To continue in the City, minus the slight complication of the new Watch model, with someone knowing the secret would be liberating.

But that hope was broken when a four-letter word exploded from Ace's lips. His skin was reddening, eyes building with fury as he jumped from the sofa. In front of Ajay now, he almost whispered through quivering lips. 'They're going to think we were involved.'

Ajay's entire body slumped with sadness. A sadness that was always there, because it was always going to be over, the moment he opened his mouth and told his story. Once someone knew the secret, there was no recovery. No forgiveness.

Ace stared right into Ajay's eyes. Ajay felt their power rip through him. Ace's voice grew louder.

'How could you do this to me? To Genni? We're now part of your game. You've put us in danger of fraternising with an illegal Unworthy,' Ace said, his voice rippling around the room.

'I know. I'm sorry.' Ajay stood slowly. 'I never expected to be in this deep.'

'What did you expect, Ajay?' Ace threw his arms up. 'That you'd just come here and be a loner, and not fall in love? Not have a best mate or a *life*? This was always going to get others involved.'

Ajay didn't know if Ace expected a comeback. He didn't have one. Ace huffed some more and paced furiously towards the window.

'Why didn't you just wait?'

'What?' Ajay lowered himself back to the sofa.

He watched Ace scratch at his eyes, but he couldn't confirm if he was crying or had an itch. Surely, Ace was too strong for tears.

'You could have waited. Served the Glorified and then applied for Purification? Would have been a lot simpler and you wouldn't have broken the law. You wouldn't have violated–'

'Would you have wanted to wait?' Ajay said as Ace retreated from the window. 'And anyway, it's not like Purification solves the problem, we all know it's nonsense. They're still hated.'

'That doesn't matter. That's how things are, but what you did was completely insane.'

'To be honest, if it was insane, it was surprisingly easy. It's no wonder what happened on Liberation Day happened.' Ajay stood again, gesturing. 'The measures they're putting in now should have been done from the start. It was as if they wanted people to invade. There's so much more going on than Command knows.'

'What does that mean?' Ace tilted his chin.

'Nothing,' Ajay said, dismissing the memory of the Guiding Lights under the river.

Ace held both hands on his hips, the concentration on his face growing stronger than ever. 'I've got to report you,' he said under his breath, but loud enough for Ajay to hear. Time seemed to freeze and blur as Ajay watched him move swiftly towards the apartment door. Then instinct kicked in and Ajay dashed from beside the sofa to catch Ace's arm.

'What?' He could feel his eyes bursting from his sockets over Ace's unwavering face. 'You'd do that to me?'

'You said it yourself, you're just like The Rogue. You did what they did. If they think I helped you, they'll strip me of my merit.' Ace tapped Ajay forcefully on the chest with his finger before turning back to the door. 'You've seen what's happening out there.'

Ajay grabbed him again. 'With the Watch. I'm like them with *the Watch*. I didn't go around killing people. I've contributed just as much to this society as any Glorified kid. My merit score shows it,' he said.

'Your merit score isn't even real,' Ace said in a cruel whisper.

The two men stood, looking each other in the eyes and witnessing each other's emotions – anger, pain and devastation – until Ace said, 'I've got to go. They must know I had no part in this.'

Ajay felt his lower lip tremble and part of him felt as if he could wail with desperation. 'Please, Ace, I just needed . . . I need . . . people to say I'm Worthy. I've worked for it. I deserve it. Please,' Ajay said as he lifted his hands up.

'Look, Ajay . . . Karle . . . urgh, whatever or whoever you are,' Ace pulled his wrist down from the door's activation pad, his jaw taut. 'The point is, you're not Worthy. You're a wannabe, a waste of space that two Light-believing lowlifes puked up on the Side. You don't belong here. You broke the law. I must report you; I can't lose the merit.' He lifted his wrist again without as much as a second glance, but Ajay, now on the surface feeling only anger, stopped him. He grabbed Ace around his middle and shoved him backwards into the apartment. Ace stumbled and was steadied by the rim of the breakfast bar. Ajay spread out his body across the doorway. 'I can't let you go. Please just listen, we can figure . . .'

'Ajay, get out of the way.' Ace stepped forward towards the door and gripped hard onto Ajay's wrists to force his arms back. Ajay squeezed and pushed with everything he had against the doorframe to keep his arms stable, but eventually Ace's strength caused them to buckle. As his arms fell, he swung his left fist to punch Ace hard in the stomach. Ace let out a yelp in pain and bent over. Ajay stepped back to shield the doorway again. Ace pulled himself up using a breakfast stool, his nostrils flaring.

Ajay held up his hands. 'Ace, just listen to me.'

His pleading was cut short – Ace moved too quickly and settled a solid punch across the top of Ajay's nose. A ringing began in his ears and a throbbing descended into his head, but his feet stood firm in front of the door. He could taste the iron in his blood as it ran from his nose into his mouth. Ace was pulling him up again; another punch settled across his face. Ajay yelled. He felt Ace get him up again, but this time he dodged the punch and threw one of his own, hitting Ace above his right eye. Ajay wrapped himself around Ace's waist and pushed hard towards the sofa, throwing them both onto it. Fists started to fly, and blood merged in splatters across the leather.

Ajay knew how ludicrous the situation was; he couldn't fight his fate. Ace was right to report him, but he needed to hang on – he needed him to listen. They could beat the system together.

As the combat continued, Ajay knew he needed Ace to be still. He flung his arms above him to block Ace's blows. Ace had clambered on top of him. Just as he threw another punch into Ajay's stomach, Ajay spotted the *SkipSleep* port sitting on the coffee table beside them. He had an idea. Ajay took a deep breath, used all his remaining strength and managed to pull Ace off him and grip his left arm. In a smooth, premeditated, almost impossible motion, he swiped the port with Ace's Watch. Still grabbing tightly onto Ace's arm, who was struggling and moaning for him to get off, the two of them saw the port come up from the table.

Ace was whining, and Ajay just managed to step on Ace's ankle to stop him moving. He pressed hard to push Ace's arm down into the port.

'Ajay, stop,' Ace moaned into the air as Ajay succeeded. Ace's arm was in place and the metal straps fastened it down. The moderation scan appeared on the port's small, transparent screen. It was soon completed, instructing the needle to spring to life and lower itself towards Ace's skin.

Ajay knew he had about two minutes to convince his friend to save his Worthiness, and he hadn't even considered the spike in energy that Ace would be gifted with after those two minutes were up. He needed to talk quickly and clearly.

'What are you doing?' Ace was screaming so hard that his voice cracked. The needle was in, and Ajay watched the progress bar creep up.

'Just listen!' Ajay held his hands out wide. 'We can find a way that you are protected, I promise I can find . . .' But Ace wouldn't listen. He began repeatedly shouting profanities, his screeches blocking out any of Ajay's pleas. The heat was bubbling faster and harder inside Ajay's volcanic body cells; he could feel his face reddening and his knuckles clenching. The balls of his feet were pressing so hard into the ground that his heels lifted a few inches. And he exploded.

'Listen!' Ajay pulled back his right arm and threw it forward. The noise of the hit to Ace's face resembled that of a hard clap that would leave hands stinging; Ajay felt the bones of his knuckles crack and disperse underneath his skin. The bruising and discomfort of his hand quickly became the least of his concerns. He'd hit Ace with such momentous force that his body moved violently. Ace crashed sideways beside the coffee table, pulling his arm and the needle in the same direction. It sliced the skin of Ace's wrist and ricocheted through both his radial and ulnar arteries. Blood squirted furiously and extravagantly across the coffee table, the sofa and onto Ajay's chest.

Ace squalled in pain as he tried to reach for his arm, still held under the straps. His eyes were wide, thunderstruck by the volumes of blood that were flowing from his body. Ace's expression mirrored Ajay's, who felt as if it were all happening in slow motion. Dizziness began to fall over him as if his own blood was loose to the atmosphere, but after only a few seconds, he flew into motion. He dashed to the kitchen and found an unused tea towel from the cupboard. Ajay sprinted back to Ace, who was screaming for help; he hit the cancel button and freed Ace's arm while ignoring the erratic beeping sounds coming from both their Watches, informing of dangerous heart rates, blood loss and blood pressure. The medical service would be informed about Ace, but there was no time to try to reverse that.

'It's alright, mate,' Ajay said in a feeble attempt to comfort Ace, whose body was beginning to flop. Ajay applied direct and hard pressure to the gash on Ace's arm and launched it into the air for elevation.

'Get ... off ... me,' Ace said, as his eyelids drooped.

Ajay was speechless, unable to contemplate what he'd done. He cried liberally through a gush of tears and shaking; he glanced down to see that stains of blood were stark against his pure white T-shirt, and the olive skin of his arms and hands was bright red. He watched his friend's eyes droop quicker and lower, and he begged for him to stay awake. Ajay wailed out into the apartment, still elevating Ace's arm, applying as much pressure as he was physically able. The moment lingered as Ajay pressed hard, but Ace's eyes closed.

CHAPTER
FORTY-EIGHT

Ajay couldn't feel. *This isn't real.* The words were pounding in his head. *This isn't real.*

This. Isn't. Real.

Ace's eyes were not motionless. His lips were not parted with his tongue rolling back into his throat. His shaven skull and face were not covered with blood like raindrops splattered over a window. Because none of it was real.

Any second Ace's eyes would blink into life, and he'd ridicule Ajay for a nasty coloured tie or his pathetic excuse for biceps. They would laugh until they thought they might vomit, or until others around them felt jealous. Because it was special. It was real, but what was happening wasn't.

Ajay's hands were not resembling red latex gloves. His arms and legs were not burdened with the weight of Ace's unmoving body. It wasn't real. Nothing about it felt real. He looked around his messy apartment and everything felt distorted. The coffee table and destroyed *SkipSleep* port looked smaller and far away, but he knew he and Ace were sitting right by them. His ears were blocked, and his eyes stared forward, but it was like he couldn't move them. Move anything. Like he couldn't even cry, speak, or scream. Everything he wanted to do. The shock of the moment had locked his body in a glass cage, and his brain was the only thing trying to get out. Everything else was numb. Because it was all real. He'd killed his best friend.

His best friend lay dead in his arms. Eyes staring up, lifeless, to the high-rise ceiling. Ajay felt himself breathe again, and control seemed to return to his arms. He took his left hand and stroked it slowly across Ace's cheek. A tear fell down his own face and dropped onto his friend's. What had he done? He wanted to wail out into the apartment but speaking still felt impossible. It meant that Ajay had seen three dead bodies: Theo, Jun and Ace. Theo had been peaceful, Jun had been scared, but Ace was unreadable. Ajay couldn't imagine from his eyes what Ace had been thinking in those last moments. Was it fear? Sadness? That this would get Ajay caught for sure? Ajay didn't even know why it mattered, other than he wanted to know how Ace had felt about him when he died. He stopped himself because he knew it wouldn't be the answer he wanted. Nothing about the last few hours would have convinced Ace to sing his praises.

Ajay looked again into Ace's eyes, their charming sparkle fading away. He considered his question. Why didn't he wait? Ajay knew he would have breezed through Purification in his sleep. But he did not want to wait. It didn't feel fair. Merit was as much his right as anyone's. That had always been his belief. The clarity of the situation blurred further with the tears in his eyes.

There must be a way to take it back. To rewind the time. To take back his punch.

Ajay felt toxic to himself, disgusted at the thought of what he'd done. Or was it at who he was? He didn't know, not understanding how he'd lost complete control. How was he ever going to explain this? Genni would leave. There was no going back to Grandma. Two people he'd perhaps never really appreciated like he should have. Ajay cast a brief look at his desk, musing over the picture of Tara beneath it. Its further reminder of his failures passed when he heard it. The sound that had been there all the time. A long, high-pitched beep from Ace's wrist, confirming his lack of heartbeat. It had been muted to Ajay before, but it became loud and clear. He thought about the coming knock or barge through the door by the medical service. They would find Ajay there, with the dead man in his arms, guilty as the sun was white. Should he escape? His arms felt limp, with no energy left to survive.

Ajay had not stopped looking at Ace, whose eyes were even darker now. He was gone. He had been for a while. Ajay was just holding on to that small speckle of life he thought he saw in his eyes. When that was gone, he fully gave in. Ajay fell forwards onto Ace's body, shaking uncontrollably, wailing out loud until his mouth couldn't make sounds anymore. His irregular jumps of breath felt like his heart might give out. The tears streamed, wetting Ace's T-shirt, merging with his blood.

'I'm sorry,' Ajay caught his breath and wiped his nose. 'Sorry.'

In his self-loathing, he held on to his friend and glanced at the Watch around Ace's wrist. Ajay's brilliant, technical mind gave him another problem to solve. Merit had been everything, but as the sky turned lilac with the arriving dusk, he questioned: was it ever worth it?

END OF BOOK ONE

The story continues in *Storm at Dusk*:
Book Two of the Merit-Hunters Series

Turn over to read the first chapter . . .

CHAPTER
ONE

It was disappointing, infuriating and confusing all at once.

Genni Mansald couldn't move; she stared at the icons swirling around the televised sphere in the distance, bright against the twilight view of the City. Her digital notes on the large, oval table flickered in the corner of her eye and a hypothetical glue stuck her dress to her chair. Mafi swiped the air and dismissed the hovering presentation, and didn't even look at Genni with her penetrating lynx-like eyes.

Her words from moments ago spun around Genni's head.

'Angi will be taking the lead on this now.'

She watched Angi as everyone left the conference room; she had that annoying, delighted look on her face, like her merit had been quadrupled. With the way she was tapping on her wrist, Genni had no doubt her *Personi* feed was pending a new, boastful update.

That wasn't a bad thing; it's only what Genni would have done, but it surely shouldn't be Angi doing it. Despite her welcome appearance and her 'I know everything' façade, Angi's attention to detail was shocking, she couldn't delegate and she got visibly stressed. Maybe Genni could outstage her and Mafi would see she was better for the role. Except, really, Genni knew she wasn't – Angi had a background in marketing and she didn't. Jun had only pulled her into the team because of her chemical knowledge of the product.

Still, Angi was younger than her. That felt wrong. How could she now be leading a team, along with the accompanying merit bonus, and Genni still only be a junior? Had the attack not happened, Jun would have praised her name to Mafi and she'd be getting the promotion or the extra merit that was well due. Had the attack not happened, everything would be different. For one thing, Jun would be alive. *How can you be so selfish? This doesn't even matter.*

She couldn't help herself, though. All she could think about was how she could do that job. She'd learned enough about the target personas, the content for each stage of the funnel and the various tactics for acquisition. She shared some of this in the meeting, adding the 'thoughts and input' Mafi had requested. It didn't even feel worth it now; she should have stayed at home and continued with her painting. Yet, she dragged herself in, quite passionately, actually, only to be sidelined.

Stop it. This is ridiculous.

She reminded herself she couldn't expect to be offered a leadership role, not even in her department. It also wasn't fair on Angi; they got on well, often spending their ten-minute lunch breaks together, chatting about work and, very occasionally, their limited lives outside of it.

She was torn, not wanting to care so much. With everything that had happened in the last year, she longed to break the grip that work and merit had on her. It had almost killed her once.

But seriously – Angi?

A strange look from Mafi pulled Genni from her chair, as if to look attentive.

It wasn't long until she arrived back at her desk, making sure to sit down gracefully while internally she was slumping into its swivel. The Beauty Dome was buzzing within its glittering, pink-frosted walls, faces and merit scores beaming from the staff board.

Maybe it was time for a new job. After all, she was a stronger person than she was twelve months ago. It was probably all holding her back, she considered, as she watched her colleague Hyi fill his glass from the water dispenser.

Maybe she should go for it; find a more accredited and merit-worthy job. That would solve a few problems in her life: her relationship with Ajay would be more stable as he was less likely to leave her for some gifted M-520; it would also elevate her in the eyes of her parents, not that she really knew why she cared. She hadn't even bothered going to see them, not fancying returning to the Glorified Quarters, even just for a drink served by an M-200 Unworthy from the Side.

Hyi turned from the dispenser, walking past her, cradling the cold glass in his right hand. Genni took a deep breath and opened her Watch mirror, examining the statistics around her face as they fluttered across the screen.

Your moisture levels are at their optimum, but there is significant swelling around your eyes. Here are some products to help with that.

Genni swiped mindlessly to scan the eye mask options and clicked on the top-rated option. The dreaded red message spanned across the product page.

Merit validation warning: M-490 and above. Only the most Worthy can have skin this smooth.

She sighed, flicking back to the list and buying one of the lower-tiered options, letting the voice of technology wash over her in a mist.

SkipSleep can also help alleviate the symptoms of fatigue.

The screen, as usual, pinpointed the location of Genni's nearest accessible port, just upstairs in the Dome. *Always use SkipSleep responsibly.* She closed it, tempted to go upstairs and have the boost, then work on her actions before morning; how else could she better Angi and show her leadership potential?

Staring lethargically through her screens, Genni calculated the exact details: she could not only get her reports in early, but also improve their quality; then research deeper into the desires of the market in this post-attack world and present an entire campaign fleshed out with product placements, marketing messages and campaign creatives. Her mind began to whirr.

What is it that people really want?

Before tapping at her desk to begin, a news alert flew into her left-hand screen, stopping her with the burden of a familiar heaviness. Was she really doing this? Planning deliberately to undermine someone she liked, just to better her own prospects? All for a stupid reason. She knew that even if she did the work, it was outside of her role description; she was a product analyst, not a marketer. Idiotic. Genni closed her tabs and didn't need to expand the news alert as the face of Arneld Hevas hovered centrally over the office floor, willing workers to lift their heads from their desks.

In the last week, we have seen a 40 per cent increase in the number of house arrests, detaining those suspected of Rogue activity. The majority of these arrests were conducted on the Outer-Rings and in the Side.

Genni scanned through the write-up of the new precautions on one of her screens. *When will this end?* Arnold Hevas had been like a glitching video, saying the same things over and over, the hopeful things only overcast by more difficulty and even more questions. Everyone, including Genni, seemed to be wondering how much Command was in control of this, and it was frightening. If they didn't know what the Rogue were doing, what hope did the rest of them have? She looked through more updates, seeing the face of Lillie Trumin from Command security who facilitated the Rogue's entry into the Quarters on Liberation Day last year.

Genni pondered over her picture, surprised at the large reward figures by her name, even though she'd caused so much drama. She was hard to look at. Harsh facial features, aged skin and greying hair that fell in a plait over her right shoulder. It was surprising that no suspicion was roused about her in the first place; she looked obviously criminal. If Genni were to paint a felonious character, the shadow under her stern eyes would be the exact shading she'd use.

A shiver fluttered down Genni's spine, giving her chills, so she turned back to her work and immediately put her earphones in, letting them crawl through her brown, mousy hair to secure themselves around her head. *Is there anything positive out there at all? Where are all those Purification success stories now?*

Still distracted, Genni flicked through some newly released products she would never want or need. She was disappointed at the lack of content, though she shouldn't have been surprised. Most commercial endeavours had been completely sidelined; the same anti-Rogue advert taking up all the space. *Surely, we have to keep living?* She hadn't had a Tulo Tia in weeks with the bars still being closed. Of course, she considered, she could make them at home; the tiny drop of ethanol in each glass wouldn't be an expensive investment, but it wasn't really the drink she liked. It was the fact it was made for her, and its association with socialising, that gave it its refreshing and relaxing power. She supposed that the news update was positive in that sense. A 40 per cent increase in arrests was a good dent and the sooner they squashed this Rogue problem, the sooner she'd have a Tulo Tia.

She continued scrolling through, trying to ignore the alerts interrupting the flow: news of arrests, tutorials for reporting activity; evidence to prove that drones weren't corrupt and the improving developments of interrogation androids. There were new models of *SkipSleep Pro* in situ and those more aesthetic solar panels were hitting the mass market, but that was it. Slouching back on her chair, Genni couldn't turn herself off from it. The Rogue was everywhere, on the news, in her Watch, in the workplace, in her head. She remembered the man who she met the night of her accident, a few months before the attack. She could still hear his voice, falling on her like an ominous blanket of darkness, and his harrowing face following her into her dreams. *He was going to kill me.*

Genni breathed, feeling the tingle in her fingers and the shake starting in her legs beneath her desk. No, no, no. She needed to get out. The office started to become like a blurry watercolour painting, out of focus and lifeless. So far, she had been able to prevent these things from triggering her memories and her fear of that man and their encounters – that night, at the attack and in her nightmares.

No. She had too much to lose to let it affect her so badly. She needed to relax.

There was her painting with the foxes, standing unfinished at home.

Jumping up and dismissing her screens, she pulled the back of her mint-green dress away from her sweating legs, and grabbed her handbag. She headed for the exit, trying not to bend her ankle to the will of her cream heels as she rushed.

'Genni, you're going home?' Angi invaded Genni's path; Genni noticed the upturned collar of her baby-pink blazer. She let the thought go, her anxiety to leave too strong.

'Yes. I'm going to turn in for the night.' What a stupid thing to say. It was only 10.46 p.m.

'Why don't you have a boost?' Genni admired the shine of Angi's neatly cut blonde hair grazing her shoulders, one side cutely tucked behind her left ear. Her wide blue eyes were captivating and almost convinced Genni to have the boost she suggested.

'Oh, I mean I'll do some work from home. I've obviously got my port there,' she lied, not having had a boost at home since her overdose, another reminder of that night. Looking at Angi again, she noticed she had no bags beneath her eyes. 'What do you use for puffy eyes?'

'Revive by Inspire.' Angi smiled. *Angi has an M-490 score?* Genni stopped herself from expressing her shock and jealousy that Angi could buy what she couldn't.

'Anyway, I've got to go.'

'Alright. Well, look out for my messages, I may need some tasks from you by tomorrow morning.' Angi's tone was authoritative and patronising, so Genni left with a feeling of resentment as she strode through the sliding doors, the air outside alleviating both her panic and her annoyance.

Ajay wasn't picking up his Watch, annoyingly; passing time on the sky train would have been much easier if she could rant about Angi and how her boss didn't appreciate her, and her dry eyes and that man who gave her the eye outside, and frankly, about her whole life being intolerable. *Would speaking to him really help, though?* She considered how miserable he'd been. Maybe he would tell her to get a grip in that sharp, brutish way he had been talking to her recently. Still, she wanted to hear his voice, even if it was the monotone version. He would pick himself back up soon and Genni couldn't blame him for being distant, what with everything around them right now. She glanced up at the carriage screen to see more depressing alerts and, looking down at her wrist, she decided to try Ajay again.

'Excuse me,' a voice croaked from behind her.

Genni flipped her body around to find an old lady, standing there in an extremely baggy, polka-dot dress. She was clutching onto a lit-up cane, trying to squeeze past, tapping it onto Genni's leg, whether intentionally or not, it wasn't clear.

'You're standing right in the carriage. Sit down, dear.'

It was intentional. Genni felt sad at the disingenuity of the 'dear' before realising that standing in the middle of the carriage was awkward, especially when empty seats were available. She slithered backwards into one and commanded her Watch to ring Ajay again.

It was odd that he wasn't picking up. The only time that had happened was when he took that wild trip to the Side. There was still something about that which made Genni feel nauseous. It didn't quite add up. Was he with another girl? Genni cursed herself, just like every time that thought came into her head. She knew it wasn't true. It couldn't be. Sometimes she hated the creative side of her brain, it always took her down imaginative routes, often unhelpful and intrusive. She swiped to check the Visual Positioning Guide.

Ajay was at home. Ace was there too.

She looked over their two faces pinned to the coordinate of Ajay's apartment and then flicked to call Ace.

As her Watch rang into her earphones, she glanced down the carriage to see if the old lady was still around. She was a few seats down, staring at Genni disapprovingly until she jerked her wrinkled face towards a young boy with a fringe covering his eyes. Still the ringing persisted. Ace wasn't answering either. *What could they possibly be doing? Oh no – they haven't started gaming again?* Ajay's merit was already falling with the missed work; surely Ace wouldn't let him. Would he?

She wouldn't cope if she had to reconsider their relationship because he was falling into a merit coma.

Was that fair? She had no idea; he wouldn't tell her anything to let her know if it was fair or not. So of course, her fluttering brain would have to make up its own mind. Though there might be a reasonable justification for his solemn behaviour. She should just ask him, but was she overthinking it? Glancing at the screen, she saw the train was one stop from Ajay's. After mulling it over, Genni decided she should at least check on him.

Mum calling.

Not now, Mother. In a fumble of fingers to hang up the call to Ace, Genni accidentally accepted her mother's. She wanted to whine but instead, greeted her mother with a smile.

'Genni, sweetheart. Would you believe it – you're actually alive! Boris, she's alive!'

Genni could hear her father's distant laughter above her mother's cackle. Given the circumstances, it was pretty insensitive to be laughing about her absence from their life as if she'd died. She stared at her mother on the camera and got irritated by her hair; why did she have to scrape it back so tightly? It gave the illusion that her blonde highlighted locks were stuck down with some sort of plastic film, though Genni often thought it was reflective of her uptight demeanour. Standing in their regally decorated bedroom, Genni could see her mother's golden dressing cabinet displaying some statistics behind her plump, moisturised face. She had never been overweight, but naturally on the weightier side, which was where Genni got her hips from, completing her hourglass figure – mostly a blessing, but definitely irritating when buying trousers, as most were too baggy for her scrawny waist, yet a real squeeze over her bum.

Though, of course, her mother never had that problem, revelling in the delight of the Glorified tailor-made clothing service.

'Yes. I'm sorry I haven't been around much,' she lied.

'Much? You've not been around at all.' Her mother's eyes flicked distractedly at whatever other content was active on her screen. 'Ah, that's the one. In white or grey?'

Genni found it strangely comforting that the whole City had changed yet her mother seemed exactly the same; self-involved, cocky and too busy with 'more important' matters to have time for her daughter. At least her father made the effort to walk out the Glorified Gate and have lunch with her from time to time. Though they hadn't done that for a while either, which was nice.

'Mum? Did you want something?' Genni moved her legs under her seat to save her feet from being run over by a man's self-rolling suitcase.

'Oh, yes . . .' Her mother looked down then, ruffling the collar on her silk blouse. 'We're moving house.'

'Again?'

'Well, yes, we had to. We're far too close to Command, so we're building a place further up the mountain.' Her mother's eyes ran across the camera again before she shouted, forcing Genni to remove one of her earphones. 'Boris, do we want the pool chairs in white or grey?'

'So, what is the house–'

'What?' Her mother roared, moving herself from the bedroom into the corridor where multiple pictures of Genni and her brother, Rod, hung decadently along the wall.

'Where are you?' Her mother made her way down the grand spiralled staircase, across the marble-floored entrance and out onto the front driveway. Genni got flashes of their multiple hover cars being cleaned by a young boy with red hair. He was new, so she wondered if they'd finally given 'Number Two' that reference for the completion of their Purification. So maybe he was the new 'Number Two'? It was always confusing growing up in the Quarters, when no one addressed their servants by their real names. It was never obvious whose Number One or Two people were talking about.

'White or grey?' her mother howled. The camera was now by her side, giving Genni a view of the ceiling.

'Mum, shall I call you back?'

'No, hold on.' Her mother's face was back and Genni could see her father, lounging out in the front garden space, scrolling on his Watch. She imagined he hadn't been sitting there for long and she could just spot his concentration face as he worked off his wrist. The freedom he'd earned, she supposed. 'Boris, white or grey?'

Her father responded, too mumbled for Genni to hear.

'Black? I don't think they have black.'

Pause.

'Black won't go.'

Another pause.

'What about white?'

Pause again.

'They won't get dirty. Number Three will clean them daily.'

Ah, so red-head must be Number Three. So there's still a Number Two? No citizenship for her, then?

Genni used to think it was funny, yet something inside her had shifted to sympathise. That poor woman. She'd come from the Side, served those tyrants for two years, only to be refused a reference. Doesn't she deserve it? Working that hard to be purified from The Guiding Light should mean she was a merit-worthy citizen now. *She was also unlucky to end up with you. You really can be monsters.* Before she went momentarily insane listening to them squabble over the colour of the pool chairs, Genni silenced her mother.

She'd ring back if she had anything else to brag about. Genni could hardly fathom how she was birthed from such narcissistic characters. Though, to be fair to them, they'd done well; a Glorified house up in the small mountains in their sparkling, luxurious bubble and two children earning merit, admittedly one better than the other. She stretched her neck, forgetting them and briefly looking over at the boy sitting opposite her. The laces of his boots were untied, stains crawling up the bottom of his trousers and he slouched torpidly, but he had nice eyes.

Remembering Ajay, Genni peered at the digital display and slumped her shoulders; she had completely missed Ajay's stop.

Pre-order *Storm at Dusk* now

www.malcolmdown.co.uk

ACKNOWLEDGEMENTS

There are many people in my life who have influenced the writing and publishing of the Merit-Hunters Series.

From the very beginning, I've had supportive friends who took the time to take me seriously: thank you to Ben, and a special thank you to Anika, who has dedicated many hours to encouraging and challenging me. Also, a shout out to Julian for his technical brain and to Malcolm Down and Sarah Grace for being fantastic publishers. To all my immediate family who have always been there; a special mention to Dad for encouraging me, and to Mum, whose memory keeps me writing and who I know would be cheering me on as I relaunch the series.

And to Stephen, my chilled-out, patient, loving and all-round brilliant husband. You have been the real pursuer of this series all along, and without you and God's guidance, I'm not sure I would have persevered. You inspire me every day.

Finally, and above all, thank you to God my Father. This book was never my idea.

The Merit-Hunters Series was born from my experience of redundancy within the first two years of my working life. Through praying over the stresses and pressures of 'success' in this modern world, I have learned a lot about what really matters. I have seen that we can be released from grappling with a working life ridden with overwhelming struggle into one full of fantastic challenge that brings us joy, peace and fulfilment. My faith in Jesus Christ has undeniably led me to realise that my worth is not defined by my wages, title, achievement, or success, but is rooted in an intimate relationship with God and others. With that assurance, working life becomes exhilarating as we pursue something beyond money or success – life itself.

I praise you, for I am fearfully and wonderfully made. Wonderful are your works; my soul knows it very well.

Psalm 139:14, ESV

I have been crucified with Christ. It is no longer I who live, but Christ who lives in me. And the life I now live in the flesh I live by faith in the Son of God, who loved me and gave himself for me.

Galatians 2:20, ESV

STAY UP TO DATE WITH ALL THINGS MERIT-HUNTERS

Be 'in the know' about Merit-Hunters releases and writing updates by joining my mailing list.

In addition, you'll get access to my newsletter – 'For the Love of Dystopian Fiction' – to enjoy dystopian book recommendations, giveaways, exclusive author interviews and more. If you love dystopian worlds and stories – it's not to be missed.

Join by visiting lgjenkins.com or scan the code.

Find me on TikTok and Instagram too –
@lgjenkinsauthor

And remember, have a happy merit-making day!

ABOUT THE AUTHOR

Lydia Jenkins is an author, booklover and coffee drinker. When she isn't immersed in writing dystopian worlds, you'll either find her reading in a coffee shop, playing netball or spending time with friends in 'sunny' England.

Sun of Endless Days is her debut novel and she hopes to encourage others in their purpose, worth and faith through writing for years to come. Follow Lydia on Instagram and TikTok to keep up with all her antics – @lgjenkinsauthor